DARKTIDE

A WITCHES OF CLEOPATRA HILL NOVEL

CHRISTINE POPE

DARK VALENTINE PRESS

DARKTIDE

ISBN: 978-1-946435-10-1

Copyright © 2018 by Christine Pope

Published by Dark Valentine Press

Cover design by Lou Harper

Print formatting by Indie Author Services

PROLOGUE

Miguel de la Paz

THE DE LA PAZ WARLOCK PARKED HIS CAR IN front of the rundown apartment building and glanced quickly from side to side. The precaution probably wasn't necessary, since he hadn't spotted any activity on the sidewalk in front of the building as he pulled up. That was partly the reason why he'd planned this trip for the middle of the afternoon—he had a much better chance of avoiding any of the building's residents at a time of day when most of them would be at work, or possibly school.

Still, being wary was second nature to him by now.

Nor did he think anyone would give him a

second glance, even if he did happen to encounter any civilians…nonmagical people…in the vicinity. What was there for them to look at? Fifty-odd years on this planet had granted him perspective if nothing else, and he knew he was less than remarkable—short, balding, carrying about thirty more pounds than he should. But hey, "less than remarkable" was a valuable trait for a private detective to have. He always wondered how his cousin Jack Sandoval had ever managed to pull off any kind of undercover operation when the guy walked around looking like a goddamn movie star all the time.

Not that it mattered now, since Jack had retired permanently from his position at the Scottsdale P.D. And all because of a woman…and a civilian woman at that. Yes, Kate Campbell was a stunner, but Jack had been a damn good detective and had loved his job. It must have been hard for him to give up, even for someone like Kate. As far as Miguel was concerned, it was never a good thing for a witch clan like the de la Paz family to lose an insider with one of the local police departments. No matter what was going on, it always helped to have some eyes and ears on the inside.

But then, that was where Miguel came in. He could move around the fringes if necessary, operate in a gray area where a regular cop might not have the same freedom to do what needed to be done. Which was the reason why he was here, in front of the shithole that Matías Escobar and his cousins had used as a base of operations down here in Tucson—and where one of the McAllister clan's young witches had met a sudden, violent end.

The apartment had been empty for more than a year after Roslyn McAllister's death. Miguel knew this because he'd thought it a good idea to keep tabs on the place, just in case. Eventually, the two-bedroom unit was rented out again—housing tended to be tight in this university town, especially places college students could afford—but those first occupants had stayed only a few months, saying that the place creeped them out and that they kept hearing strange noises, had personal items moved around without anyone touching them. The apartment was rented again not too long after they picked up and left, but again, none of the residents who came after them seemed to stay longer than six months.

The latest occupants, Tara Elizabeth Montoya and Lisbeth O'Neil, both students at the University of Arizona, had fled the scene the night before, screaming that someone—or something—was in the apartment and trying to get them. Who that person was supposed to be, no one could tell, because the Tucson P.D. had sent out a patrol car, and two officers had searched the apartment and found nothing. Nevertheless, the girls made the officers remain on the scene while they packed their bags with as much as they could carry before they took off in Tara's RAV-4, saying they were going to crash at a friend's house and didn't think they'd ever be coming back.

Miguel knew all this because he had a police scanner, and he'd listened to the back and forth between dispatch and the officers on-scene at the apartment. He'd trained himself to keep a weather ear out for anything remotely connected to his clan, or to anything supernatural...just in case. And as soon as he heard the address, he knew some kind of serious shit must be going down, something much more sinister than a few strange noises or a misplaced cell phone.

Of course, when viewed in the glaring light of a late May afternoon, the desert sun already brutally hot even though it technically wasn't summer yet, the apartment building didn't look all that threatening. The brown stucco was patched and faded to a sort of watery tan color, and the palm trees planted out front looked depressed, too, as though they'd once had dreams of waving in the breeze at a tropical resort rather than being stuck here in a crappy-ass part of Tucson, Arizona.

After double-checking the pistol in the shoulder harness he wore—a gun wouldn't do much against a supernatural opponent, but it sure could help in case he ran into any drug dealers who'd decided to squat in the now-vacant apartment—he got out of his car, a silver Honda Accord chosen mostly for its complete anonymity, and began to walk toward the building. It was two stories, a hollow rectangle built around a courtyard area with more palm trees and a dingy swimming pool that looked about as inviting as the rest of the structure.

The unit in question was on the second floor, located toward the back of the complex. A woman in her forties, with sun-fried blonde hair and tanned skin as wrinkled as a cheap linen suit, came down the stairs toward him. Miguel caught the way her gaze—partially blocked by a pair of tortoiseshell Ray-Ban knockoffs—slid in his direction for a second or two before she continued on her way. Clearly, she didn't consider his presence worthy of note. He wasn't worried about the shoulder holster, because a while back Luz, his clan's *prima,* had cast a minor spell of illusion on it so it would blend in with whatever he was wearing.

He was glad the blonde woman hadn't paid any particular attention to him. Even the Hawaiian shirts he favored weren't enough to make him noteworthy, precisely because that kind of attire was the sort of thing you might expect to see men of his age and build to be wearing, especially in this climate.

He headed toward the apartment where Roslyn McAllister had been murdered. Unlike some in his clan, Miguel couldn't really sense dark energy, didn't have the talent for detecting where forbidden magic had been used—unlike his cousin Luz Trujillo, head of their family. Even so, he couldn't quite help shuddering as his fingers touched the doorknob. He might not be able to actually feel the bad juju, but he knew it was here, and that was enough.

Because he was a warlock, the knob turned under his fingers, even though the place had been securely locked up. No police tape on the door barring entry, probably because no crime had been committed here. Not last night, anyway.

The interior was decorated in a hodgepodge of what Miguel tended to think of as "early garage sale." Several textbooks sat on the scratched glass coffee table, and underneath it was a pair of abandoned flip-flops, bright pink with rhinestones on the straps.

Something about seeing those flip-flops made him want to shake his head as a wave of sadness washed over him. Foolish; he knew the girl who owned that footwear was just fine, since she'd had the good sense to get the hell out of the place when her hinky-meter went off the charts.

There was nothing here to indicate anything out of the ordinary had ever occurred on the premises. Just the expected college-girl clutter, stylized posters of Che Guevara and Frida Kahlo competing for wall space with posters of bands Miguel had never even heard of, which meant they must be just obscure enough to be considered cool. Did college kids even say "cool" anymore? He didn't know. Unlike most witches and warlocks, he'd stayed blissfully single, never had any children of his own. It was a lot easier to be the fun cousin—or uncle, he supposed, since his own brothers and sisters had definitely done their best to be fruitful and multiply.

Despite the apartment's mundane appearance, the hair on the back of his neck prickled. Power of suggestion, stemming from what he'd heard on the police scanner the night before, what he knew had gone down in this place now more than three years ago? Maybe, but he'd never been one to spook easily. Besides, Matías Escobar was now dead, and his partners in crime, the cousins Jorge and Tomas Aguirre, were still locked up in separate maximum-security facilities. Yes, it seemed that Matías' father Joaquin was just as bad as his son—or even worse—but he was off in California, apparently occupied with consolidating his power there. The portal that had been opened to allow demons into this world to wreak their particular havoc was now closed, so Miguel wasn't too worried about an otherworldly attack, either.

Mostly, he just wanted to know exactly what the hell *had* gone on here last night.

He moved from the living room and peeked into the tiny kitchen, but there wasn't much to see, just some dirty dishes piled on the counter, and a plate with a piece of pepperoni pizza sitting on it next to the microwave, as if one of the girls had just finished heating up her food when whatever it was that scared the crap out of her had occurred.

Two small bedrooms, and a shared bathroom across the hall. One of the rooms was definitely neater than the other, the bed made, and only a folded pair of jeans sitting on top of the shabby dresser, while the other was a disaster area, clothes piled on the unmade bed, some on the floor, mingling with a dizzying assortment of shoes. Miguel wondered who of the roommates was the neatnik, and who was the slob…not that it really mattered at this point.

Even so, in a way it was good to see the ordinary clutter, just because he could look at it and do his best to ignore how two girls had been sexually abused in those rooms, and one of them tortured to death.

The thought of what Roslyn McAllister and Danica Wilcox had suffered in this place made him clench his fists. At least Danica apparently was happy and settled now, but there would be no happy endings for Roslyn.

A rustle from the hallway made Miguel turn at once to see what had made the sound. Eyes narrowing, he headed back toward the main section of the apartment, the one that comprised the kitchen, living room, and dining area. A quick scan of his surroundings told him that he was alone. And yet....

Another of those odd rustling sounds. It almost sounded like a taffeta dress his mother had once owned...or maybe like dead, dry leaves blowing down an empty street.

Mouth tightening, he reached back and pulled his Ruger from its shoulder holster. He was a warlock, and so he knew that just because he couldn't see something didn't mean it wasn't there. The skin at the back of his neck prickled, and for the first time, he wondered if he should have had someone come along with him. His own gift of knowing whenever someone was speaking the truth came in very handy in his chosen vocation, but it didn't help much when it came to self-defense, magical or otherwise. Miguel's cousin

Alex Trujillo, with his talent of generating a sort of force field that protected anyone inside it, would have been a good person to invite along on this expedition. But Alex was at work at his job with one of the local television stations, and couldn't drop everything to come running out on what Miguel had thought would probably be a wild goose chase.

All right, the smart thing to do would be to leave and come back with some magical reinforcements. Just because he hadn't actually seen anything yet didn't mean that something wasn't here. Something decidedly not friendly, judging by the way his skin was crawling. He could call Jack. The former detective's talent was defensive magic, and he certainly didn't have a job to worry about anymore. He'd probably jump at the chance to come here and poke around a bit.

That seemed to settle it. Miguel returned his gun to its holster, just because going down the stairs with a 9mm in hand would probably be enough to attract attention, even in this neighborhood. He began to head toward the door...

...only to have what felt like a net made of a thousand needles descend on him, biting into his flesh. Repressing a cry of agony, he clawed at his face and throat, thinking that if he could just tear it away from his eyes and mouth, he might stand a chance. But then the needles sank into his fingers as well, and he couldn't seem to move them, couldn't seem to....

Can't breathe. Can't....

The world went red, then black.

And then it was gone altogether.

1

Angela McAllister-Wilcox

I STOOD AT THE LIVING ROOM WINDOW OF Connor's and my house in Jerome, watching Levi and Hayley head down the front path before they turned onto the sidewalk and continued toward Main Street. They held hands, and Hayley's bright blonde hair rippled in the sunlight as they walked.

Connor's arm tightened around my waist. "You okay?"

"Define 'okay.'" I tried to laugh, but it just came out as a hoarse chuckle that wouldn't have convinced anyone, let alone my husband. "I suppose I have to be. It's not as if I have much choice."

"I thought you'd be happy to hear that there haven't been any further incursions. Levi said that he hasn't seen evidence of any demons for the past two weeks."

"I know. It's just...." I let the words trail off there. Problem was, I didn't even know how to articulate the creeping dread which seemed to have overtaken me, that made me wake up in the middle of the night and stare at the ceiling for what felt like hours as Connor peacefully slept beside me. Levi had done the McAllisters—and all the Arizona witch clans—an enormous favor by closing the portal that connected the demons' world to this one. Ever since then, things had been quiet enough. But I couldn't shake the feeling that this was only the calm before the storm. "Maybe it's just watching the two of them. I can tell how happy they are, but is this really the time to start a relationship?"

Connor's hand, which had been resting on my hip, moved gently to my stomach, which was still completely flat. "Is this really the time to start anything?" Before I could speak, he went on, "We can't all put our lives on hold because of what's been happening."

"I know that." I placed my hand on top of his, taking some comfort in the quiet strength I could sense emanating from his very fingertips.

There wasn't much use in pointing out that, when I'd conceived, this latest mess with the Escobars hadn't yet begun. Connor and I had quietly decided it was time to try for another baby, now that Ian and Emily would be starting school in the fall and I didn't feel as if I'd have to run after the two of them every hour of every day. I'd just passed my twelfth week, and it was certainly safe to make the announcement to the McAllister and Wilcox clans...but did I really want to add another complication to everything else that was going on? I might be the *prima,* but I knew everyone would turn all protective and try to keep me out of harm's way the second they learned I was pregnant. Of course I would *prefer* to stay out of harm's way, but I also knew I couldn't ignore the needs of the clan just to protect the fragile life I now carried within me. It was a frightening balancing act, yet another responsibility connected with being the head witch of my clan.

"Then just be happy for them." Connor withdrew his hand, but only so he could push away the heavy hair from the back of my neck and place a gentle kiss on the skin there. A pleasant tingle moved through me before he went on, "Anyway, Levi and Hayley make a pretty potent combination. I don't think you need to worry about them."

No, I probably didn't. They were most likely in a better position to take care of themselves than anyone else I knew. And, although I'd been preoccupied lately, I wasn't so distracted that I hadn't noticed another possible romance budding, this one between Hayley's brother Brandon and Lucinda Santiago, whom Levi and Hayley and Brandon had rescued from the Escobars only a few weeks earlier. It wasn't that Brandon and Lucinda had moved in together the way Levi and Hayley had—in fact, Lucinda was back staying with my Aunt Rachel, in the room that had once been mine—but I'd seen the two of them walking around Jerome together, or in our little town's tasting rooms and restaurants. You certainly didn't need to be psychic to see what was going on there. I was happy for Lucinda because she'd suffered enough and deserved a little happiness, and it was nice to finally see someone distract Brandon from his car obsession and the long hours he worked at a custom car and motorcycle shop down in Cottonwood. I'd seriously started to think he was asexual or something…until Lucinda came along.

If only all I had to worry about was the various love lives of my fellow clan members. Unfortunately, even if he'd been quiet for the past few weeks, I knew that Joaquin Escobar was still lurking out in California, probably plotting his revenge. Levi had been the one responsible for Matías' death, after all, which meant there was a greater chance of being struck by lightning than of having Joaquin give up his plans for vengeance.

Problem was, I just didn't know what form that vengeance would take.

My cell phone, which I'd left sitting on the kitchen counter, began to ring. Unwilling as I was to leave the comfort of Connor's arms, I knew I'd better answer the phone. I slipped away from him, murmuring an apology, and hurried to the kitchen. As I picked up my cell, I saw that the number on the home screen was Luz Trujillo's.

That couldn't be good. We didn't speak all that often, unless we had to deal with an unpleasant bit of clan business.

Luckily, I was able to answer before the call went to voicemail. "Luz? What's up?"

Her voice was steady enough, but by now I knew her pretty well. I could detect a certain tightness behind her tone, a tension that told me this definitely wasn't a social call, and my stomach clenched in anticipation of what she might have to tell me. "Bad news."

Is there any other kind? I thought wearily. However, all I said was, "What's happened?"

"It's—it's my cousin Miguel. The private detective. Remember?"

I wasn't sure if I did—it was hard enough to keep track of all the Wilcoxes and McAllisters without trying to remember all the de la Paz witches and warlocks as well. Still, I did my best to wrack my brains and pull up some recollection about Miguel from the memory banks. "Um…he helped Alex and Caitlin capture Matías, right?"

"Right, with Jack Sandoval's assistance." A pause, as though Luz had stopped to gather her breath. "The Tucson P.D. just found his body."

My reply was instant, and instinctual. "Oh, I'm so sorry."

"It's more than that." This time her sound of her expelling a breath was clearly audible. "They found him at the apartment where—where Roslyn and Danica were held three years ago."

What on earth had Miguel been doing there, of all places? From what I'd heard, the place was being used as a rental again, although I had to admit that I hadn't been paying a lot of attention to the situation. I couldn't change the past, so there didn't seem to be much point in dwelling on it, no matter how tragic it had been. "Do you know why he was there?"

"It seems there was a disturbance the night before. I guess the girls who were living there ran away, saying something was in the apartment with them."

Tiny fingers of dread began to trail their way down my spine, and I shivered. Connor, who'd arrived in the kitchen a minute after I had, stared at me, concern plain on his features. The Goddess only knows what he saw in my expression. "Did they say what it was?"

"No. My cousin Oscar is with the Tucson P.D., so he was able to access the police report, but they didn't reveal much. It seems that the place has a bad record of retaining tenants—a lot of people didn't seem to stay for more than a few months at a time."

I hoped the property management company that handled the apartment only offered month-to-month rentals; that was an awful lot of broken leases otherwise. However, I knew that Luz probably didn't much care about such a minor concern right now. "Did any of them say why they left?"

"Not formally, no. But Oscar talked to some of the other tenants. The general consensus seems to be that the apartment is haunted, although no one could give any real proof of that. It just seems to be the reputation it has."

No big surprise there. It wasn't as though spirits always remained at the scene of their deaths —and, because Roslyn had in fact briefly communicated with her sister Jenny before passing beyond the veil, I knew that the apartment couldn't be haunted. Not by Roslyn's ghost, anyway.

"Did Oscar pick up anything?"

A small sigh, and then Luz replied, "No, but that wasn't his talent. We're going to have one of our mediums go and look things over once the scene has been cleared. That shouldn't take too long, because there wasn't any sign of foul play."

I hated to ask for details, but this wasn't just about sharing Luz's grief with her—this was a conversation between two *primas,* both of whom knew all too well that we were dealing with a cunning and vicious enemy. Almost subconsciously, my hand went to touch my belly, an instinctual gesture to protect the child I carried. "Do you know how Miguel died?"

"Valentina—she's the clan's healer down in Tucson—says it seems he had a heart attack." Another sigh, and I got the distinct impression Luz had shaken her head, even though of course I couldn't see her. "And who's to say that isn't what happened? I love my cousin Miguel, but he was fifty-six years old, about forty pounds overweight, and seemed to live on coffee, Coke, and burgers and tamales."

The rueful note in her voice made me think that Luz had probably gotten on her cousin's case more than once about his physical fitness, to no avail. Well, people were going to do what they were going to do. "Do you think it was just a heart attack?"

Her response was immediate. "No. It would be easier if it had been. As it is, Oscar is trying to cover things up as best he can. The story he's giving is that Miguel was hired by the girls to come look at the apartment, and that he suffered a cardiac arrest while inspecting the place. Since there's no sign of supernatural activity or any kind of foul play, there's no reason for anyone to think differently."

"But...."

"I know in my heart that something killed him. Something evil."

Another shiver worked its way down my spine. I looked over at Connor, who was still watching me, his expression solemn. I hated to ask the next question, but it seemed unavoidable. "Do you want us to come down there?"

"Could you?" Luz asked, the relief in her voice so palpable, I could practically reach out and touch it. "We're going to have our own medium visit the apartment, but your talent is speaking with the dead, and also, you've had recent experience with—well, with demonic presences."

In point of fact, I really hadn't. It was Levi and Hayley who'd had to face down the demons Joaquin Escobar sent against us. Still, because I was *prima,* and therefore could sense when the town's hidden barriers had been breached, I knew a little of what it was like to have the stink of demons around a place. Actually, that was almost exactly what it was—a lingering trace of sulfur, of spent gunpowder, although their residue was psychic, and not something you could actually smell.

"Yes, we'll come," I said, trying not to betray my reluctance. Not that I had anything against Tucson, but the weather was already heating up in Jerome, which meant it must be downright brutal in the southern part of the state. However, I knew I couldn't use such a flimsy excuse to stay away. Luz needed me, and that was that. We all had to stick together, to present a unified front to our common enemy. "Is tomorrow all right?"

"It should be. Oscar said the apartment should be accessible by the end of the day."

"Good." I hesitated, and wondered whether I should even mention the strange niggling fear that had begun to pluck at the back of my mind, like an itch I couldn't quite scratch. "But Luz—"

"Yes?"

"Have your medium wait until Connor and I get there. I think it's better if we all go in together."

A long pause, and then she said, "Of course. Do you need the address?"

"Yes. I had it once, but I didn't think I'd ever need it again. You can text it to me."

"I will. And—thank you, Angela."

You can thank me when this is over, I thought, but I only replied, "It's no problem.

You'd do the same for us. I'll call you when we're in Tucson."

"I'll wait to hear from you."

I ended the call and set my phone down on the granite kitchen counter. Connor was still watching me, those cloudy green eyes I loved so well now narrowed slightly in concern.

"It must be bad if we're going to Tucson."

About all I could do was shrug. "I'm not completely sure yet. Luz's cousin was found dead in the apartment where Roslyn and Danica were held, but it sounds like he had a heart attack. No rampaging demons or anything like that."

Connor's expression didn't change. "That you know of."

"True. But Luz seems to think we can help."

"Can we?" He reached up to pass a hand through his hair, which he'd cut back to shoulder-length this past winter. I was still getting used to the change—he'd let his hair grow to almost the center of his back before he cut it—but he still looked as handsome as ever, just…different. Without waiting for me to reply, he said, "Do you think we should bring Hayley and Levi along, just in case?"

"No." The word escaped my lips before I had time to even think about Connor's question. Just an instinctual, gut reaction…and I'd learned to trust those. "It's bad enough that we're having to leave Jerome without their *prima* and *primus*. I'll feel much better knowing that those two are here to help the elders if—well, if anything strange happens."

"And Ian and Emily?"

Usually I'd simply ask Victoria Lynch, who lived on our street, to watch the twins. Her two children were grown and married but hadn't started families yet, and so Victoria got a chance to get her grandma wiggles out by playing with Ian and Emily. Now, though, something was telling me it might be better if the kids were safely out of Jerome altogether.

"Let's see if Lucas and Margot can take them for a few days. Lord knows they've got enough space in their house, and the twins love playing with Mia."

This suggestion earned me a lifted eyebrow, as if Connor had guessed I wasn't proposing this plan entirely for the twins' sake. No, it was mainly because—so far, anyway—all the "action" involving Joaquin Escobar and his associates had taken place either down in the Phoenix area or up here in Jerome. Flagstaff just seemed safer, far away from the fray.

However, Connor didn't make any arguments, but only fished his iPhone out of his jeans pocket. "I'll call them."

"And I'll start getting the twins' things together." I knew the call was only a formality, that Lucas and Margot would agree to watch Ian and Emily for as long as was necessary. At least it was still early enough in the afternoon that we could get them up to Flagstaff and safely settled before night fell.

For some reason, I didn't much relish the thought of driving Arizona's highways after dark.

Despite my misgivings, we made it down to Tucson the next day without incident. I wished I could pretend that Connor and I were just taking a road trip for old times' sake—getting away alone with him reminded me of the drive we'd taken to Southern California all those years ago, although even then our trip had its own dark and compelling purpose—but I knew this was no joyride, that I couldn't be certain of what I might find at the end of this journey.

Well, except I'd known we'd end up here, at the rundown apartment building that Matías Escobar had once used as his hideout and private supernatural torture chamber. I'd been here once, right after Roslyn's murder, and at the time had prayed I'd never see the place again.

The heat hit me like a wall as soon as I opened the door of our Toyota SUV. I blinked, glad that my eyes were protected from the scorching sun by the Ray-Bans Connor had bought me for Christmas. And I'd thought ahead, had put on a sleeveless top and a knee-length skirt and sandals. Even so, I felt like I was suffocating.

"You okay?" Connor asked as he met me on the sidewalk. About all he'd done to prepare for the trip was put on a T-shirt instead of the long-sleeved henleys he tended to live in most of the time, but he still looked cool and collected enough.

"Fine," I replied.

A shiny silver Lexus pulled up and parked behind our Toyota FJ, and Luz Trujillo got out. A moment later, the passenger door opened, and man about her age—in his early fifties—emerged. His black hair gleamed in the sun, and he wore immaculately pressed chinos and a loose white cotton shirt. Looking at him, I could only hope he wouldn't be able to tell that everything I was wearing was at least three years old.

"Connor, Angela," Luz said as she approached us, the crisply dressed man just a pace behind her, "this is my cousin, Domingo Velasquez. Domingo, this is Connor Wilcox and Angela McAllister."

I'd been using a hyphenate for my last name ever since Connor and I got married, but I didn't bother to point that out. Instead, I summoned my best smile and extended a hand. "It's very nice to meet you, Domingo."

"It is unfortunate that we had to meet under these circumstances," he replied. "But I am happy to meet the *prima* of the McAllisters...and the *primus* of the Wilcox clan."

"You're the medium?" Connor asked.

I wanted to shoot him a sideways glance at his abrupt tone but decided it was better to refrain. From the way his mouth had tightened briefly as I shook hands with Domingo, I got the feeling my husband wasn't exactly thrilled that the de la Paz clan's medium had turned out to be so, well, suave. True, he was nearly old enough to be my father, but....

"Yes," Domingo replied, looking completely unruffled. "I am hopeful that with all of us working together, we will be able to solve this mystery so my cousin's soul may be at peace."

I hoped so, too. I'd only met Miguel very briefly, when he and Jack Sandoval had delivered Matías and his partners-in-crime to Connor and me so we might strip their powers from them, but even so, I'd never encountered the ghost of someone I'd known as a living person, and I really didn't want to start now. What could I possibly say to Miguel if his ghost really was haunting this place?

"Let's go up and see what we can find," Luz

said. Her expression appeared calm enough, and as usual she looked as though she should be off to the country club, in an immaculate linen dress in sherbet green and nude sling-back sandals. However, I thought I detected some carefully applied concealer around her eyes, as if she'd spent at least part of the previous night crying and was now doing her best to hide the evidence of her grief.

"Sounds like a plan," Connor replied. "I assume the coast is clear?"

"Yes, the police released the site yesterday afternoon, and Oscar made it known that some relatives might be coming by to check on the things the girls left behind. No one should pay any attention to us."

That sounded like a plausible enough cover story. However, I figured it was better to keep quiet until we were safely inside the apartment, just in case anyone was around to overhear our conversation. Good thing, too, because we did pass a man in his late thirties who was coming down the stairs with a basket of dirty clothes and an annoyed expression on his thin features. Well, I supposed I'd be annoyed, too, if I had to maneuver around a bunch of strangers while on my way downstairs to do my laundry.

Luckily, though, he seemed to be the only person around, and we made it inside the apartment without being seen by anyone else. The place was full of typical college-girl clutter and looked very different from the one and only time I'd been here, when I'd attempted to see if Roslyn's spirit lingered anywhere on the premises. Back then, the walls had been bare, the furniture even more mismatched and far shabbier, and there had been a suspicious stain in the middle of the beige shag carpet, a stain that I hadn't wanted to look at too closely. The carpet had been replaced by more beige, but at least now it was a halfway decent-looking berber.

However, I knew I shouldn't be paying attention to the decor, but the feel of the place. Privately, I thought that most of the claims about the apartment being haunted had been based mostly on reputation and nothing else. After all, I'd once stood just about where I was standing now and had done more or less the same thing— that is, reaching out with the best of my innate abilities to see if any presence lingered here.

And right now I was having about the same result. I couldn't feel a damn thing. Not sure whether I should be relieved or annoyed, I lifted my shoulders and looked over at Domingo. "I'm not getting anything. Are you having better luck?"

The de la Paz medium's expression was almost preternaturally calm. "Not yet. But then, sometimes it takes me a while to settle into the energy of a place. Perhaps if I sat down."

He went over to the couch, which was dark brown chenille with a few worn spots, and passed a hand over one of the cushions, as if making sure to dispose of any crumbs or other dirt before he placed his immaculate trousers on the upholstery. Behind me, I felt rather than saw Connor's mouth twitch, and told myself not to get distracted. Who cared if Domingo was overly fastidious, as long as he was talented enough to detect whether anything was truly wrong here?

Luz appeared used to this behavior, because she didn't seem to be paying much attention to her cousin, was instead surveying the apartment, arms crossed and mouth tight. While I knew she had sensitivities of her own, they were skewed more toward detecting if and when magic spells had been cast, and I wasn't sure whether that was what we were dealing with here.

"Do *you* feel anything?" I murmured to her, and she shook her head.

"No. That is," she added, "only sadness at all the death this place has seen. It is too bad it's an apartment and not a house, because otherwise, I'd say the best thing to do with it would be to raze it to the ground and start over. But I suppose that's not really feasible here."

She had a point. Sometimes a place just

couldn't be salvaged. I was glad that Connor's brother Damon's house had been sold to civilians —at least they would probably be oblivious to any bad energies that might be lingering in a place where two people had died violent deaths. That is, I had to hope so. The house had been far too valuable not to sell; demolishing it really hadn't been an option. And it seemed, at least according to reports from some of Connor's cousins, that nothing untoward had happened to its current residents, so whatever negative energy that might have once existed there was now long gone.

"Demolishing the building would displace a lot of people," I agreed. "And really, if none of us are sensing anything here, there wouldn't be much point. What would we be protecting these civilians from, if the place is clean?"

Luz nodded and opened her mouth, as though she intended to reply. She didn't get the chance, though, because Domingo abruptly stood up, hands clenched into fists at his sides, dark eyes staring out at something apparently only he could see.

"Oh, it's there," he said, his voice not much more than a hushed murmur.

"What's there?" Connor asked, brows drawing together. His gaze moved around the room, but as far as I could tell, we were alone here.

"Dark energy," Domingo replied. "Perhaps

once it was human, but no more. Now it only watches and waits."

"Waits for what?" Those creepy crawlies were back, whispering up and down my spine.

"For whatever it can feed on. Fear. Despair."

I took a step back, felt Connor's fingers wrap around mine. The warmth of his touch didn't completely dispel that shivery sensation on my back, but it helped a little.

"Can you communicate with it?" Luz inquired. She looked as though she would have been glad of a little comfort, too, but of course her husband hadn't accompanied her on this mission. To tell the truth, I couldn't even remember what his magical talent was.

Domingo shook his head. That blank expression remained on his aristocratic features, but now it wasn't so much calm I saw, but an attempt to keep his mind clear of any emotions that might attract the entity...or whatever it was.

"Can...can you see it?" The words were barely a whisper as they left my mouth. I supposed I should be glad that whatever was here in the apartment, it certainly wasn't a good old-fashioned ghost, which meant I couldn't see it. On the other hand, even if turned out to be terrifying to look at, maybe it would be better if I could detect some kind of physical presence. That way, it would have far less of a chance of sneaking up on us.

"No. It's just a sensation." Domingo paused. "With an entity such as this, there's nothing to see."

Luz's mouth tightened, compressing her normally full lips. "Is it what killed Miguel?"

"Difficult to say." The medium reached up to rub his temple with his fore- and middle fingers, as though his head had begun to ache. "I—" His words faltered then, and he put both hands to his head, eyes widening abruptly, so that I could see a ring of white all around the dark irises. "Oh, God, it hurts."

"Domingo!" Luz hurried to her cousin's side —and not a moment too soon, because he abruptly slumped as though his legs could no longer hold him up. She grabbed his arm but still staggered under his weight.

At once Connor let go of my hand and went to help, slipping an arm around the faltering de la Paz warlock. "We need to get him out of here."

No arguments from me. I still hadn't felt anything, but Domingo's reaction was enough to convince me that it was time to go. Connor and Luz began hauling the medium toward the door, and I followed, lagging behind by a pace or two.

And then it was as if a cold hand had descended on the nape of my neck, and the chill from those unseen fingers began to flood through my entire body. I gasped, and staggered, and then forced myself to turn around so I could confront my unseen assailant.

"Get away from me!" I cried out, summoning the *prima* energy from deep within to send a wall of shimmering power outward and away from where I stood.

Dimly, I heard Connor call out my name, but I didn't turn. No, I knew I had to stand my ground, couldn't give this thing the opportunity to come after me from behind again.

And, for the briefest moment, I saw it. As Domingo had said, it was shapeless, an amorphous being of pure malevolence, floating in the air of the dingy living room like a blob of shivering, evil smoke. For a second, it almost looked as though it was trying to extrude arms that reached out for me—until the wave of *prima* energy, bright and golden white, crashed into it. A tinny, far-off cry scraped at my eardrums, and then it was gone.

Dead silence. Domingo began to stir, and pushed himself away from Luz and Connor's support, as though his strength had returned to him now that the entity was gone. Luz's dark eyes were wide, staring, while Connor appeared to be focused only on me.

"What," he said, "the fuck was *that?*"

2

Angela

Domingo's house was much the same as the man himself—impossibly neat, decorated in impeccable taste. The Spanish villa–style home was perched in the hills above Tucson, but even though the sun was beginning to set, casting a shimmering golden light over the sharp-edged mountains that surrounded the desert town, I couldn't allow myself to enjoy the view.

Actually, I couldn't stop shivering, even though Domingo had made a pot of hot tea for those who wanted some. It was ninety-five degrees outside, my fingers were wrapped around the mug he had given me, and yet I still felt as though I might never get warm again.

"More of Joaquin Escobar's dark magic?" Luz

asked. We sat in the living room, a large space with white plaster walls and a white plaster ceiling ornamented by thick dark wood beams. On the walls hung an impressive display of abstract art, all of it original. I didn't know enough about art to judge the technique, but under normal circumstances, I would have at least enjoyed looking at the range of colors, blue and green and coral and ochre. Now, though, I kept wishing there was some brandy or whiskey to pour into the tea I was drinking, something to lend me a little courage. But I couldn't drink, because of the baby, so instead I shut my eyes briefly and prayed that exposure to the dark spirit hadn't caused any harm to the child I carried. It wasn't exactly sort of thing that was covered in *What to Expect When You're Expecting.*

"It didn't feel quite like that," Domingo said, and I had to nod. Whatever that thing had been, it had been alive. Or rather, it had possessed some kind of intelligence and free will. It wasn't only a force sent here by the Escobar warlock to cause more havoc.

"Then what?" Connor asked. He'd turned down the hot tea but had accepted a tall glass of iced tea. After sipping from the glass, he added, "I didn't really feel whatever it was that you two experienced, so you're going to have to be as specific as possible."

"I think," Domingo began, then paused, as though gathering his thoughts. "I think whatever it was, it knew how to focus on my weakness. I am prone to migraine headaches—a byproduct of my talent, I've always believed. So it focused on causing excruciating pain in my head. I assume you felt nothing like this, Angela?"

"No," I replied. "It hadn't really started to attack me before I went ahead and attacked it. Maybe it was too occupied with you to stop me."

"Possibly." The medium glanced over at his *prima,* who had also accepted a mug of hot tea, although she didn't seem too inclined to drink it, since she hadn't touched it yet. "It would definitely be easier to deal with if it's only capable of focusing on one person at a time."

Luz didn't seem too heartened by this possibility. Her fingers clenched on the pale yellow stoneware mug in front of her, and she paused a long time before making a reply. "Maybe that's how it got Miguel. It somehow knew his heart was weak, and so that was where it concentrated its energies. No wonder there was no sign of foul play. The creature gave him a heart attack."

A frown pulled at Domingo's straight black brows. "And no doubt, if we'd allowed it to continue, it might have given me an aneurysm."

We were all silent for a moment, digesting that lovely little piece of information. I wondered what the entity would have tried if it had had the chance to truly go after me. It would have had a harder time of finding anything to focus its energies on—except for some mild seasonal allergies, I was as healthy as a horse.

But then I thought of the life just stirring inside me, the secret that no one besides Connor and I—well, and my OB-GYN—knew. If this creature or being or whatever it was had been able to figure out I was pregnant, that was one vulnerability I had no doubt it would try to exploit.

Although so far my pregnancy had been a placid one, with no sign of morning sickness or any real symptoms to speak of, right then my stomach twisted with a sudden bout of nausea. I grabbed the mug in front of me and took a large swallow of tea, hoping that might help to settle things a bit. At least the drink had been sitting in front of me long enough that it wasn't terribly hot anymore, or I might have scalded my tongue.

Next to me, Connor shifted on the leather sofa. "You okay, Angela?"

I nodded. "Just a little jumpy."

"That can be excused, I think," Domingo said, his eyes meeting mine and holding. Was he able to guess that I carried a tiny life within me? No, I didn't think that was possible; he was a medium, someone who communicated with spirits that had moved on to the afterlife. His talent for dealing with those who had gone before, not those who had yet to live their lives.

"None of this answers the central question," Luz put in, "which is, what on earth is this thing? It's not a ghost, not the soul of someone departed."

"Not a demon, either," I said. "I mean, I'm not intimately acquainted with demons the way that Levi is, but I know enough to be able to recognize when one has been around."

"And that puts us back at square one." Connor ran a hand through his hair, pushing it back off his brow, since it had begun to slide forward in that way which always annoyed him. Of course, if he'd kept it longer, he would have been able to pull it back in a ponytail, but he'd said it had started to get too heavy and hot. "If it's not a ghost or a spirit or a demon, then what is it?"

"Nothing I've ever come across," Domingo said. "My gift came to me in my tenth year, so I have been communicating with the dead for more than four decades now. I've dealt with many spirits, some sad, some angry, but nothing like this. It felt like a being of pure malevolence, whose sole purpose here was to cause harm and destruction."

Yes, that was similar to what I had felt, too, right down to that one particular word. *Malevolent.* Even Damon Wilcox at the height of his destructiveness had never felt anything like that.

Not even Matías Escobar, who was usually my go-to when it came to compiling a list of truly horrible people. They were still people, though, despite all the terrible things they'd done. This thing…it definitely wasn't a person.

"It's too bad it's not a demon," Luz remarked, and I raised an eyebrow at her. "Well," she went on, sounding somewhat defensive, "Levi has shown that he doesn't have too much trouble getting rid of demons. At least if it was something like that, we'd have a built-in solution. As it is…."

As it was, we were basically all spinning our wheels here. Although I'd made the decision to have Levi stay in Jerome, I wondered now whether it might not be better to have him come down here and poke around, see if his otherworldly sensibilities could pick up on something the rest of us simply weren't equipped to detect. Not until Connor and I were back home, of course. Now more than ever, I knew it was vital to keep as many people with useful powers in Jerome, so they might safeguard those who couldn't protect themselves.

I hated to divide the clan into those with "useful" powers and those without, because really, all powers had their uses. Instead, I really just needed to think in terms of defensive or offensive powers, rather than the more subtle talents that might help in maintaining our quality of life, but which couldn't do much to protect us from Joaquin Escobar and the Santiagos who now did his bidding, or from the dark powers of the spirit which seemed to be inhabiting that awful little apartment in south Tucson.

"Why don't we ask Levi to come down here and take a look around?" I asked. "He might be able to provide some insights."

"That sounds like a great idea," Connor said, not bothering to hide his relief at the suggestion. I could tell he wanted to get back to Jerome as soon as possible. Maybe it was simply that he didn't like being so far away from the twins, even though Ian and Emily were perfectly safe at Lucas and Margot's place—possibly even safer than they would be in Jerome.

Luz tilted her head to one side, as if considering the possibility, then nodded. "Yes, he might be able to offer some different perspectives. But he should probably be the only other person to go to the apartment. Oscar tells me that the girls have no plans to return here to live, are going to have some college friends come over the weekend and help them move their things out, but still, it's probably better if we don't have too much coming and going over there."

"Will they be safe—those friends who're helping with the move?" Connor asked.

Although he'd directed the question at Luz, it

was Domingo who responded. "I believe so. The girls lived there for several months and came to no harm. This entity...it seems to be attracted to witch-kind—or at least, it appears much more inclined to make us its prey. Perhaps it has a way of feeding on our powers." His shoulders lifted, a fatalistic sort of gesture, as though he knew some dark magic was at work here, even if we were powerless at the moment to do anything about it.

"Well, that's a lovely thought," I remarked. "Also, horrible as this thing is, we're overlooking something here. My *prima* powers were enough to drive it off. I didn't even have to link up with Connor to get rid of it, and usually, if I'm trying anything big, I need the extra boost."

"Yes, that's something," Luz said. "However, even if Connor and I are also able to do the same thing, there are only three of us. We can't be everywhere at once."

"True, but at least it's a start. It means we aren't completely helpless."

Domingo laced his fingers together and frowned slightly, not in disapproval, but more as if he was concentrating on something. "Also, the attacks only occurred at the apartment. Does that mean the entity is locked to a particular location, possibly because of the deaths that have already occurred there, the dark spells that were worked in that place?"

Well, it would make all our lives easier if that turned out to be the case. I experienced a pang of guilt at thinking of some innocent civilian moving into the apartment once the current hubbub had died down, but I tried to reassure myself that the most any nonmagical people had suffered while living in the apartment were some serious attacks of the heebie-jeebies.

Then I realized we had a very simple solution to the entire problem. "We should rent the apartment."

Luz blinked. "Excuse me?"

A slow smile spread over Connor's face. "I get it. If the entity really is confined to the apartment, then all we have to do to make sure no one else comes to any harm there is to rent it ourselves. Or at least, to someone from one of our clans. It would probably make more sense if it was one of the de la Pazes, though, just because you're local."

"Of course," Domingo said. "Rent it, and keep it vacant. If nothing else, that should tell us whether the entity is fixed in that one place, or whether we've made a false assumption simply because the attacks occurred there."

"And if that turns out to be the case?" Luz asked.

"Then we'll have wasted a little money," he replied. "It's not as if the clan can't afford it."

Her gaze slid away from his, and I knew she

wouldn't bother to contradict him. Even the McAllisters could afford such a minor expense, and we were nowhere near as wealthy and settled as the de la Paz clan.

"Very well," she said after a pause. "I'll have someone talk to the management company about renting the apartment. We might as well wait to have that settled before you send Levi down here —once the unit is rented to one of us, then there'll be less chance of anyone asking questions."

"I don't think we should wait too long, though," Connor told her. "We still don't know what we're dealing with here."

"I should think we can have it settled by next Monday. That's only four days from now."

I had no doubt Luz would have everything managed by then. She might not be quite the same force of nature that her mother had been, but she was still an eminently capable woman.

"And we'll talk to Levi," Connor went on. "I'll let him know that he can expect to come down here on Monday, unless you tell us otherwise."

"That should work. We will keep in touch."

There didn't seem to be much more to discuss after that. Connor and I thanked Domingo for the tea, and we headed out soon afterward, the setting sun in our eyes and unanswered questions filling our thoughts.

Would those questions ever be answered? Right then I didn't have a clue.

~

It was too late by the time we got back to Jerome to think of continuing to Flagstaff and picking up the twins—they were probably already in bed, or would be soon.

"Besides," Connor pointed out as he parked the SUV by Bordello's, where we'd decided to grab a late dinner. "I'm starting to think it might be better if we just leave Emily and Ian with Lucas and Margot."

"Forever?" I asked, my mouth quirking despite the seriousness of the situation. To tell the truth, there had been a few times during the twins' toddler stage when I would have happily dumped the kids on Margot and Lucas until they reached the age of reason...say, when they were old enough to vote. We were mostly past the tantrums by now, and every day I was surprised and moved by the changes I saw in my children, their rapidly developing personalities—Ian's stubbornness and questing spirit, Emily's little flashes of insight, the way she'd taught herself to read with very little help from me.

"For an undefined period of time," Connor replied. He turned off the engine but made no move to open the door; although of course the staff at Bordello's knew who—and, more importantly, *what*—we were, there were still some topics it was probably better not to discuss in front of civilians. "We haven't made any announcements yet, but everyone's taken it as a given that Emily is going to be the McAllister *prima*-in-waiting, just as the Wilcoxes expect Ian to be my heir. Isn't it better to make sure they're someplace safe?"

I wanted to be angry at Connor for bringing up that particular topic, because I really hadn't wanted to start thinking about it. The twins were only five and a half, and we shouldn't have been forced to begin considering their futures as possible leaders of the clan for a long while yet.

However, Emily was already starting to show little signs of her abilities flaring up, even though most witches and warlocks didn't really start to come into their powers until they were ten or eleven years old. The thing was, we were all in sort of uncharted territory here, because as far as we knew, Connor and I were the first *prima* and *primus* couple, and certainly the first to have children, which meant no one really had any idea what kind of powers our offspring would have, or how strong they would be.

So yes, everyone did think that Emily would be my *prima*-in-waiting, and although the Wilcoxes didn't have anything like a "*primus*-in-waiting," the same principle held; the eldest son from Jeremiah's line would be the next to lead the clan. I didn't know whether Ian would be a powerful warlock like Connor, or his late uncle, because, unlike his sister, he hadn't yet begun to reveal any sign of the abilities he'd inherited. Truthfully, though, Connor hadn't really been thought of as a strong warlock until his brother Damon died and the mantle of leading the clan fell on him. His gift for illusion was a subtle one, and he'd never been able to bend magic to his will the way Damon once had.

And thank the Goddess for that, I thought. *No one should have that kind of power.*

Unfortunately for all of us, it seemed that Joaquin Escobar did. Or, at the very least, he possessed a singular combination of talents, something that made him very difficult to fight. We did have Levi on our side, which meant we had a better chance of defending ourselves than otherwise, but even so….

I pushed those thoughts away and focused on the question Connor had just asked me. "Are you sure that they'll really be safe in Flagstaff? I mean, for a night or even two, it's probably okay, because we didn't tell anyone where they'd be staying. Still, if Escobar really comes gunning for us, then you can know for damn sure that he's going to exploit every weakness. Ours is our children. Do you know without a shadow of a doubt that the Wilcoxes can protect the twins?"

"No," Connor replied without hesitation. His gaze was straight, forthright, and I was comforted by the firm set of his chin, the resolve in it. "But," he continued, not giving me a chance to reply, "I don't know they'd be safe here, either. And unfortunately, with the way the witch clans tend to stay isolated from those in other states, it's not like we can send them off to Nantucket or Hawaii for the summer until we get all this settled. So I suppose I'm just basing my feelings on the simple fact that Flagstaff is farther away from Pasadena than either Jerome or Phoenix, and also that—so far, at least —Escobar hasn't made any attacks there."

As much as I wanted to argue these points, deep down I knew that Connor was right. However, I wasn't sure I wanted to admit defeat, either. The reality of having to go days and days— or possibly even weeks and weeks—without seeing my children was not one I was prepared to face right then. Even a weekend away was enough for me to start craving their presence, the sound of their voices. "I'll think about it," I said at last. "But we'd better go in. Bordello's closes in half an hour, and I'm starving."

"Sure," Connor said, and appeared to let it go, opening the car door so he could get out.

And that was just one of the many reasons

why I loved him. He knew me well enough to understand when I needed time to wrestle with a problem, to give myself a chance to work my way to a conclusion…even if it was one I didn't like very much.

I feared that was exactly where I would end up with this one. Because as much as I hated the idea of sending my children away, I also knew that I couldn't count on Joaquin Escobar not to bring the battle right to my front doorstep.

After all, he'd already done so only a few weeks before.

Arrangements were made. The awful part was, I couldn't even take my children their extra clothes and the toys and games they'd need to keep them occupied during the time they'd be spending with Lucas and Margot. If Joaquin Escobar had somehow managed to get his spies anywhere close, it would be too obvious if Connor and I took another trip up to Flagstaff so soon after the last one.

That was why my cousin Ali, who was eighteen and who would be starting at Northern Pines University in Flagstaff in the fall, took the trunk full of Ian and Emily's belongings to them. "I've been going back and forth anyway," she told me, "getting paperwork handled, looking for an apartment. It's not going to look suspicious if I run back up there for an afternoon. I can drop everything off for you, and no one will be able to tell I was doing anything out of the ordinary. I'll even go to this one apartment complex I was considering first, and head over to Lucas and Margot's house after that. It'll be fine."

I had to hope she was right. My *prima* powers could come in pretty handy, but they didn't seem to include being able to detect whether someone was being followed, or even if I was under surveillance. Yes, I'd know right away if Joaquin Escobar or any of the Santiagos under his control passed the wards that protected Jerome. However, those spies didn't need to infiltrate my town. They could simply hang out in Cottonwood and watch all our comings and goings. Unless you were going overland in a seriously sturdy 4x4, you had to take Highway 89A to get out of Jerome, which meant you either came down through Cottonwood or Clarkdale, or out in Prescott Valley on the other side of Mingus Mountain. The topography of the area made surveillance pretty damn easy.

If we were even being watched. All these precautions could simply stem from my own paranoia, in which case Connor and I were depriving ourselves of our children's company during these last few precious months before they started kindergarten, for no reason at all.

Somehow, though, I didn't think that was the case. We'd had peace and calm for the last few weeks, but that didn't mean much. Escobar was probably biding his time, plotting. He wasn't the sort of man who would allow the death of his son to pass by without him attempting some sort of revenge. And then there had been the incident in the apartment in Tucson. Whether that entity— or whatever it was—had any connection to the dark warlock in California, I honestly didn't know. About all I could do was hope and pray that Levi would be able to dig up something when he headed down there two days from now.

In the meantime, I had to pretend everything was fine when I knew good and well it wasn't. Connor and I told the elders where we'd sent the children, and why, and we also had to let Levi in on the secret, just because he was one of our last lines of defense if things really did go sideways. We also briefed him on what we'd experienced in Tucson, and how we wanted him to do his own investigation.

"Of course," he said in that gravely charming way of his. Connor and I had asked him to come to the house alone, without Hayley, a request that clearly puzzled him but which he didn't protest. Now, though, as he sat on the couch across from the one Connor and I occupied, he frowned slightly, blue eyes troubled, and said, "I would like to bring Hayley with me, though."

"I'm not so sure that's a good idea," I replied.

"Why not?"

Connor went ahead and answered the question, since we'd already discussed this possibility, and what we should do if it came up. "Because even though Hayley's gift has helped you in the past, we don't think it will make much of a difference in this case. This isn't a demon you need to dispel. It's something we want you to investigate. You're the logical choice because you have experience with forces and beings that didn't originate on this plane."

"It's not a ghost," I said. "Or at least, if it is, it's not like any ghost I've ever encountered…and I've dealt with a fair few."

"And, as far as we can tell, it's not a demon, either. It's not something you'll be fighting," Connor pointed out. "If you're just there to observe, Hayley may be more of a distraction than anything else. Also, this thing seems to seek out people's weaknesses. Your connection to Hayley could make her a target, since it might attack her to get at you. On the other hand, there's nothing you've gone up against that you weren't able to handle. That's why we think it's better if you make this trip alone."

Levi was quiet for a moment, appearing to ponder what we'd just told him. "You may have a point," he said. "I'm still not sure that I agree, but if that's your wish, I'll abide by it, since you are the *prima* and *primus*."

"This isn't a dictatorship," I protested. "If you have a really good argument for taking Hayley with you, then we'll listen to it. But…."

"No, I understand," Levi said. "My only argument would be that I love her and feel more comfortable with her at my side. But that's not enough of a reason. Actually, based on what you've told me about this entity, I might be putting her in danger by taking her with me. I will go alone. After all, I won't even be gone overnight."

"True," Connor agreed. "That's a lot of driving for one day, but it's doable. And probably a lot better than spending the night away from Hayley."

"That much is true."

Levi smiled slightly, his expression faraway. It was kind of cute to see how besotted he was with Hayley, especially when he'd lived here for so long without making any kind of a real connection. But that was how it tended to be with witch-kind —when we found the right person, we fell hard, and we fell fast. It had been like that with Connor, even though I'd tried to fight the connection with every cell in my body, had tried to tell myself that a son of the Wilcox clan couldn't possibly be my soul mate, the man who woke the *prima* powers within me.

But the universe has its own plans, and all we mere mortals could ever do was try to make peace with that idea.

Right now, though, I was just a little worried as to what the universe intended for all of us....

3

Levi McAllister

HE'D NEVER DRIVEN THIS FAR ON HIS OWN
before. Up to Flagstaff, yes, and on the dirt back
roads that connected Jerome to Williams, off
Interstate 40. But he'd never come back to the
Phoenix area after Zoe Sandoval rebuffed him and
instead chose Evan McAllister for her consort, and
he'd certainly never passed through the city's
urban sprawl and headed out into the open desert
once more, driving south to Tucson.

More than once he'd glanced over at the
empty passenger seat of his hand-me-down truck,
thinking to share a comment on the terrain with
Hayley. But she wasn't there, had remained behind
in Jerome because both Connor and Angela
thought she wouldn't be needed on this trip, that

it would be better if she stayed in Jerome. Perhaps they were right.

Levi supposed he'd find out in a few hours.

Hayley had not liked the idea of remaining behind. No, not at all. Even when he explained that this wasn't his idea, that the command had come down from the *prima* and *primus,* her blue eyes had glinted mutinously, and she muttered something about them not being her parents, that they couldn't boss her around. Perhaps that was true; Levi had never really seen anyone openly defy the head of a clan, so he wasn't sure what the consequences of such an action might be.

In the end, though, Hayley had calmed down somewhat, mostly because he kept reassuring her that this would be a quick day trip, and that he had no plans to remain in the Tucson area overnight. She still wasn't pleased by the idea— and Levi guessed she'd be even less pleased if she knew the entire truth about what might be awaiting him in the apartment in Tucson—but she'd abandoned the arguments, had given him a quick, fierce hug, and said she expected him to be home by dinner. He'd said he would try, which was about the most he could offer. The round-trip drive alone would take more than six hours, and he didn't know how much time he would have to spend in the apartment. Yes, he'd left at a little after nine in the morning, and so would show up in Tucson around lunchtime, but....

At least the details with the apartment itself had already been handled. A de la Paz cousin had taken care of renting the place, and had even moved in a few sticks of furniture to make it look as if someone would be living there. No worries about leaving a key under the mat, though; although Levi wasn't precisely a warlock, as his origins were not human, he still possessed the magical ability to open door locks with the touch of a finger. Getting in wouldn't be a problem.

What might happen after he went inside the apartment—that was the real question.

Traffic in Tucson was thicker than what he'd imagined. Was everyone out and about on their lunch hour? Maybe. Still, he was able to maneuver through the congestion and get off I-10 at 22nd Street, then weave eastward through shabby neighborhoods of modest homes that had seen better days, until at last he came to the Tucson Tropics apartment complex.

It was definitely not the sort of place that inspired confidence, with its patched and faded stucco, and the drooping palm trees that clustered out front. A chill went over Levi as he looked at the building, although he tried to tell himself that he was only projecting, that he hadn't actually experienced anything negative here.

Yet.

He managed to squeeze the truck in between a Chrysler Sebring convertible with oxidizing red paint and a Nissan Altima that was missing all its wheel covers. Both vehicles had the same aura of forlorn neglect as the apartment complex itself, and Levi had no doubt that the cars' owners must live somewhere within.

After taking a quick look around and determining no one appeared to be present, he got out of the truck and headed for the exterior stairs that led to the second level of the complex. Angela and Connor had told him the apartment was located toward the back of the building, so he went in that direction, praying under his breath the whole time that no one would emerge from their apartments and get a good look at him. Yes, he could erase their memories if he had to, but this whole expedition would be a lot less complicated if he could simply avoid any encounters with the residents here.

His luck appeared to be holding, because he was able to make his way to the designated unit without bumping into anyone. Levi supposed it was possible that someone might be inside their apartment, watching from behind the blinds, but he somehow doubted it. If people were home right now, they were probably trying to grab a quick lunch before they headed back to work.

As he approached the apartment, a sensation of cold began to overtake all his limbs, a cold so intense that he could feel his teeth start to chatter before he clamped down on them and forced them to stop. And yet it was very hot here, so hot that even the T-shirt he was wearing felt as heavy as a wool sweater. If it was this warm toward the end of May, he didn't want to think what it might be like here in the depths of summer.

The weather, however, was not his immediate concern. Along with the cold came a sensation of pressure, as if whatever inhabited the apartment was exerting all its will to prevent him from getting any closer. Gritting his teeth, Levi made himself push against that pressure, telling himself that it wasn't real, that it couldn't prevail against him.

Somehow he managed to get to the front door, touch his fingers to the doorknob. It was like dipping his hand in liquid nitrogen, but he forced himself to focus his own will against it, to make the knob turn and the door open.

Which it did, opening inward with a faint squeak.

All at once, the cold and the pressure dissipated. However, Levi refused to take their absence as a good sign. He had the distinct impression that the entity which dwelt here wanted him to drop his guard.

Well, that wasn't about to happen.

He stepped inside, body braced for whatever assault might come next. Nothing...at least for now.

A quick glance around told him that the apartment had been stripped of the previous inhabitants' belongings. The walls were bare, and the only furniture was a green fabric couch, a glass-topped coffee table, and a low entertainment unit with a flat-screen television sitting on top of it. The little alcove that was probably intended as a dining area was empty. Perhaps there was some more furniture in the bedrooms, to keep up the façade that someone actually was living here. At the moment, Levi didn't feel terribly inclined to go take a look.

He stood in the middle of the living room and breathed in. For some reason, the air tasted acrid on his tongue and made him cough as it went down his windpipe. Even with the cold and the pressure gone, he knew he was not alone here.

Time to reach out with his mind, to try to take the measure of the entity that had apparently made its home in this place. Even though he hated the thought of having to pull in another breath of tainted air, he forced himself to inhale deeply, knowing he needed to center and strengthen himself to face the being who now inhabited this apartment.

A swirl of hate, of a cold, gnawing hunger so intense, Levi knotted his hands into fists and forced himself to remember that this was not his hatred, nor his hunger. He stood still as a statue, and let the energy flow around him. It could not hurt him, as long as he did not allow it to enter his soul.

The force—or being, or whatever it was—had a strange resonance unlike anything Levi had ever encountered. It possessed a strange echoing thrum, almost as if there were two entities here, so tightly joined together that they at first felt like one.

Not demons. While he certainly would not say that he cared for their company, at least they were recognizable creatures, beings who had their own lives and personalities and quirks. In a way, one could almost pity them for the unfortunate trait which allowed them to be bound and exploited by mortals, if the correct rituals were followed.

At any rate, Levi knew at once he was not dealing with demons here. Of course there were other beings that dwelt in the spaces between worlds, or the planes that were separated from this one by strings of atoms thinner than the finest hair, but none of those entities had ever shown any interest in the corporeal world. There was certainly no reason for them to inhabit this shabby apartment, to tie themselves to a place that had no meaning to them.

So did this thing—or these things—come from this world? They were not ghosts, that was for certain. Levi could almost fancy he felt them brushing against him, faint little ghost-whispers of touch, like the cool, deathly glide of a jellyfish as it brushes against one's leg in open water.

"Who are you?" he asked out loud.

He hadn't really been expecting an answer, and he didn't get one. However, he had the sense that the silence was now a listening one, that whatever was here now knew he had detected it, even if it wasn't inclined to respond.

Still, he had no choice but to persist. Sometimes asking a question wasn't enough. It also had to be the right question. "What ties you to this place?"

The temperature in the room dropped at once, as though someone had just switched on an industrial air conditioning unit. In fact, the apartment's A/C had been left on, but at a very modest level, so that it was still warm in here, even if not as scorching as the temperatures outside.

This time he distinctly felt something brush against his hair and he tensed, wondering if he should raise the same invisible shield he'd used to protect himself from the demons when he was visiting their plane…and wondering if that shield would even be of any use here. However, he didn't detect anything overtly hostile about that unseen touch. Rather, it was almost as if the entity—or entities—had reached out in such a way to reaffirm their contact.

Then came a wave of sadness, of regret, so strong that tears began to sting at Levi's eyes, even though he knew this wasn't his sorrow, his remorse. Could something inhuman even experience those emotions? Possibly; after all, his own body was human, while his soul was not, and yet he knew he could love, could feel frustration and rage and despair.

"Is it what happened here?"

Again that brush against his hair, along with what felt like cold fingers clasping around his forearm. Just for the briefest of seconds, so quick Levi wasn't sure he hadn't imagined that touch, but it was enough to convince him that, despite what he might have thought previously, the thing living here must have once been human. Why it hadn't revealed itself to Angela, whose talent was speaking with ghosts, he didn't know for sure. But perhaps this wasn't a true ghost, but only a tiny fragment of the person it had once been, a sliver of a soul and nothing more.

When he spoke, he knew his voice sounded tentative, as if he'd already figured out that he was making a wrong guess. "Roslyn?"

The wind whipped around him, icy, so cold it felt as though it would freeze him in that spot. He clenched his fingers with an effort, made himself visualize the shield of protection he'd conjured on the plane of the demons.

However, he got no further than that, because the door burst open, and a group of men and one woman entered. Ordinary-looking enough, most of them Hispanic in appearance, wearing jeans and T-shirts, or a sleeveless blouse in the woman's case.

They weren't ordinary, though. Levi was able to tell at once that they were all witches and warlocks—and although he hadn't met that many of the de la Paz clan, he knew them well enough to tell when magical folk were from that family, and these people weren't from Luz's group. Another of his gifts, he supposed, to be able to detect the signature scent of a particular witch clan. The Wilcoxes were dark and woodsy, like the pine forests that surrounded Flagstaff, while the McAllisters always seemed clean and aromatic, like freshly cut rosemary.

These were not de la Paz witches and warlocks. Which had to mean….

Instincts went into overdrive. No need to say the words of a spell when you yourself were magic.

But the shield didn't appear. Blood running

cold, Levi realized that somehow even his own powerful magic had been blocked, could not function the way it was supposed to.

There was only one person in the world who could prevent him from using his magic.

One of the warlocks stepped forward. He was probably in his late forties, not overly tall, but with a commanding presence, and handsome, aristocratic features.

"Hello, Levi," said Joaquin Escobar. "How do you like our trap?"

4

Angela

I KEPT EXPECTING A PHONE CALL. LEVI HAD
said he would call as soon as he had any information. But my cell phone had remained frustrat-
ingly silent all afternoon, although Margot sent
me a text a little past four, a text that was really
just a picture of the three children playing
together, Ian and Emily building what looked like
the beginnings of a log fort in the expansive backyard of Lucas and Margot's property, while
Margot's daughter Mia looked on, apparently
supervising.

Despite everything, I had to chuckle. Mia was
that rare child who always managed to make
things work so she never got dirty. Sometimes I
wished my own daughter was even half as neat—it

would have made my life a lot easier, especially when laundry day rolled around—but then, she wouldn't be Emily if she had Mia's fastidious habits.

Six o'clock. I picked up my phone for what had to be the thirtieth or fortieth time, and still nothing. My stomach, which had been giving me grief all afternoon, felt even more acid. The sad thing was, I didn't know whether to blame my queasiness on the early stages of pregnancy, or simply extreme nerves. If anything had happened to Levi....

Connor came into the kitchen through the back door and paused at the sink to wash his hands. He wasn't any happier than I about Levi's continuing radio silence, but he'd decided to burn off his nervous energy by decluttering the garage. It was kind of amazing, the mountains of crap that could pile up in a place after you'd lived there for five years, especially when you put a couple of kids and their cast-off toys into the equation.

"Still nothing?" Connor asked after taking one look at my expression.

"Nothing at all," I replied. Somehow I resisted the urge to pick up the phone and check it once again, just in case. I'd avoided calling to check in with Levi, because the last thing I wanted was to interrupt him while he was communing with the spirits, or whatever. "This just isn't like Levi. He's very conscientious."

"He's probably fine." After wiping his hands on the kitchen towel that hung on the oven door rack, Connor came over and started rubbing my shoulders, kneading the knotted-up muscles there. "Maybe he forgot to charge his cell phone before he headed out. Remember, that old truck of his doesn't have built-in USB ports and all that other fun stuff like our cars do."

"Maybe," I said, my tone dubious. What Connor had just said was true enough, but it seemed out of character for Levi to take off on a mission like this without making sure his phone was charged. Anyway, even if that turned out to be the case, he was in friendly territory. He knew where Alex Trujillo and my cousin Caitlin lived, could have driven to their house to use the phone once he was done at the apartment. Alex probably would still be at work, but Caitlin worked from home and could have helped him out.

Connor's fingers dug into my tense muscles, comforting, reassuring. I loved how he knew exactly the right thing to do to help assuage my anxiety. Problem was, it was going to take more than a neck massage to make me feel better about the situation. "If he didn't get much of anything, he might have just turned around and come home, in which case he should be back any time now."

"No," I said. "If that's really what happened, then he should have been back hours ago."

"Not if he hit traffic. Phoenix can be pretty dicey. Remember that one time someone had an accident on the connector road to the 202, and we sat on the damn freeway for almost a half hour before the state troopers got it all cleared away?"

Unfortunately, I did remember. What a nightmare that had been, made all the more frustrating by the twins getting progressively more fidgety and restless the longer we sat there without moving. Maybe people in places like L.A. and New York and Chicago were used to craptastic traffic like that, but in my part of the world, we just didn't have those sorts of problems.

Anyway, I supposed it was remotely possible that Levi might have encountered a traffic jam along those lines. And I supposed it was also possible that, because he got stuck someplace with a bad cell signal, his phone could've drained faster than he'd expected it to.

All the same, I couldn't get rid of the queasy sensation in my stomach. It would have been nice to be able to pour a glass of wine, sit down in the living room, and let Connor try to soothe me with more plausible explanations. Unfortunately, wine was out of the picture, and I somehow doubted a cup of hot tea would provide the effect I was looking for.

The doorbell rang. Connor and I looked at each other, both of us with lifted eyebrows. In general, we really didn't get that many visitors, since it was the elders who handled the day-to-day issues of the clan. We were only called in when a problem arose that they couldn't solve.

"It's probably Levi," Connor said, letting go of my shoulders. "His phone died, but he came here straight away to give a report."

I hoped that was true. "Only one way to find out."

We both headed out of the kitchen and went to the front door. When Connor opened it, however, that wasn't Levi standing on the front porch. No, it was his girlfriend Hayley, her arms crossed and her blue eyes shooting fire.

"Have you heard from him?" she demanded, clearly too upset to worry about being polite and offering any sort of greeting.

"Come in," I said. I figured it was probably better to have this discussion behind closed doors.

From the way Hayley's chin tilted up at me, I could tell she noticed my lack of an actual answer to her question right away, and wasn't very happy about it. Without answering, she stepped into the foyer, and Connor shut the door behind her.

"Let's go into the living room," he suggested. "Can I get you a glass of water or something?"

"No, I'm fine."

There didn't seem to be anything to do except head into the living room and have all of us to take our seats there, Connor and I next to each other on one of the couches, Hayley sitting on the other, facing us across the coffee table of carved juniper that separated the two sofas.

"So you haven't heard anything," she said, her arms crossed, her slender form rigid with anger and worry. She was one of the fairer McAllisters, with her bright golden hair and clear blue eyes.

"No," I replied. There wasn't much point in dancing around the issue. "But Connor and I were just talking about that. There are a lot of reasons why he might not have been in contact. His cell phone could have died—"

"No," she cut in. "He left it charging all last night, and he has one of those cigarette lighter USB adapter thingies in his truck. There's no reason why he couldn't have called."

Unless something terrible had happened. I cast a helpless look at Connor, hoping he would step in.

Which, being Connor, of course he did. "It's still the most plausible explanation. Cell reception for a good chunk of that drive is pretty crappy. He might've tried to call and couldn't get through."

Hayley tapped her fingers on the knees of her jeans. Her fingernails were painted a bright coral pink, and looked freshly done. Well, of course she could keep up a manicure—she didn't have to worry about chasing after a couple of five-year-olds. I pushed the petty thought aside. I wouldn't trade Ian and Emily for all the painted fingernails in the world, and I knew it.

"Even if he didn't have a cell signal for part of the drive, he could've called when he got to Phoenix. I kind of doubt they have cell issues in a city that big." She didn't bother to hide the skepticism in her voice, and I couldn't blame her for it. What she'd said was only the truth.

"We can call Luz and have her people follow up," Connor suggested. "I'm sure someone will be willing to drive over to the apartment and check things out."

"Would you call?" Hayley asked. All her boldness of a moment before seemed to evaporate, and I saw the very real fear in her eyes. She might not have been with Levi for very long, but I could tell she loved him with all her heart.

"Of course," I said. "Let me go get my phone."

I got up from the couch, went back to the kitchen, and retrieved my cell phone. Still no missed calls or text messages. I expelled a worried little breath and typed in my security code, then navigated to the contacts list and located Luz's entry. A push of the button had me connected to her, and her phone ringing. She picked up almost at once.

"Angela?"

Caller I.D. made it so easy to dismiss all the time-consuming preambles. "Hi, Luz. Levi went down to check the apartment today, but we still haven't heard from him. Has he been in contact with any of the de la Paz clan down in Tucson?"

I could almost see her frown. "No, I haven't heard anything."

"Is there someone you can call to go over and take a look?"

"I'll have Alex do it."

Yes, he would be home from work by now. However, a little pang of worry went through me. I hated to put Alex in harm's way if something bad had actually happened to Levi.

But then I realized Alex had means of protecting himself that most other warlocks and witches didn't, thanks to his inborn ability to cast a bubble around him that was impervious to magic and just about anything else. Also, Alex was right there in Tucson and could probably get over to the apartment in fifteen or twenty minutes at the most. "If it's not too much trouble—"

"It's no trouble at all. You sent Levi down here. It's the least we can do, to make sure he hasn't come to any harm. And Alex knows how to handle himself."

I supposed he did. After all, if it weren't for Alex Trujillo, Matías Escobar might never have been caught in the first place. "Thanks, Luz. Caitlin has my number, so they can call me directly whenever they have something to report."

"I'll let them know." A pause, and Luz added, "Do you really think something has happened to Levi? I thought he was so powerful."

"He is," I said firmly, refusing to use the past tense. "I'm sure it's nothing—a dead cell phone, or something like that. But I figured it's better if we make sure."

"Of course. I'll call Alex and have him head out at once. You shouldn't have to wait for than a half hour or so to get some answers."

"Thanks, Luz. I appreciate it."

"It's nothing. We all have to work together now, more than ever. You take care."

She ended the call there, and I stood in the kitchen for a moment, staring down at the phone in my hand. Yes, it was true. We did all have to work together, no matter what our differences might have been in the past. Our very survival depended on that cooperation.

I went back into the living room. Hayley and Connor looked up at me expectantly; I could tell they hadn't spoken in my absence, had only sat there and waited for me to return with my news. "Luz is going to have Alex head over to the apartment and take a look. She figures he's probably the best equipped of the clan members in the area to investigate what's going on."

"He's Luz's son, right?" Hayley asked.

I supposed I shouldn't be surprised by the question. After all, Hayley had grown up in Payson, not in the thick of things here in Jerome. While she probably got some news and gossip through the clan grapevine, it wasn't exactly the same as living here and learning this stuff firsthand.

"Yes," I said. "His gift offers him some protections that a lot of other people don't have, so we're hoping he'll be able to handle whatever he might encounter at the apartment."

"If there's even anything to encounter," Connor put in quickly. "We still don't know that anything's wrong."

"*I* know," Hayley said. She put one hand on the center of her chest, about where you'd place it if you were reciting the Pledge of Allegiance. "Something has felt off all afternoon. I can tell he's in trouble."

Connor and I exchanged a glance, one of his dark eyebrows lifting ever so slightly. He gave the most infinitesimal of shrugs, as though he wanted to make sure Hayley couldn't see anything of his doubt. That was kind of him, but I was feeling the same way. I knew Hayley's gift was a prodigious one, but she wasn't psychic. She wasn't Caitlin, who could see both the present and the future. No, what Hayley was feeling right now was probably worry more than anything else, most likely mixed in with a good helping of resentment toward Connor and me for sending Levi down to Tucson alone in the first place.

Well, I couldn't really blame her for that, since I was already beginning to experience a healthy chunk of guilt for doing exactly that same thing. One could argue that Hayley probably couldn't have done much to help him if he really did come up against some kind of strange supernatural being, one determined to haunt the apartment. Unfortunately, I didn't know that for sure, one way or another.

No one did.

"We'll just have to sit tight and wait to hear what Alex finds out," I said. "And you're welcome to stay here with us, Hayley. We were thinking about ordering a pizza."

"No, thanks," she replied at once. "I don't think I could eat anything right now. Not until— not until we hear something about what's going on. I'll just head back down to our apartment. Maybe Lucinda can come over—Brandon had to work late tonight."

From Hayley's tone, I could tell she wasn't too thrilled about that development. Of all times, this was when she needed her brother close by. But if she could at least hang out with Lucinda until we got some news, I'd feel better about the situation. For some reason, I didn't think it was a good idea for Hayley to be alone in the apartment she shared with Levi.

"Okay," I said. "But I'll call you as soon as I hear something. And if you start feeling hinky again, you come on by."

"Thanks." She got up from the couch, and Connor and I rose from where we'd been sitting as well.

There didn't seem to be much to do except walk with her over to the door, then offer a few more comforting words. They didn't appear to have much effect; she only nodded in a distracted way, as though her attention was already fixed on something far from Jerome. We waved goodbye as she went down the stairs, and then Connor closed the door and turned to face me.

"Well, I don't know about you, but I feel like utter shit."

"I know," I said. "I'm starting to think we screwed up big-time."

He nodded. Then, after giving me a searching look from under his lashes, he asked, "Did you really want pizza?"

Fifteen minutes earlier, I'd been seriously contemplating the notion. Now, though, I was starting to understand exactly how Hayley felt. Just the thought of eating solid food made my stomach turn over.

"No. Maybe later. Or maybe I'll make myself a grilled cheese sandwich at some point. But if you want to order pizza for yourself, go ahead."

"No, I'm good." Connor gave me a rueful smile and added, "Well, all right, maybe 'good' isn't the right word. But I'm not hungry, either. How about we get some ice water and sit on the porch and watch the sunset?"

That sounded like it could work. I could lean my head on his shoulder, try to take what comfort I could from his presence. In Jerome about all we really got was reverse sunsets, where we watched the colors change on the landscape to the east because of the high, jagged mountain immediately to the west, but it was still pretty.

Maybe if I distracted myself with watching the sunset, I could pretend that I hadn't royally screwed up.

5

Alex Trujillo

HE HADN'T PLANNED TO TAKE CAITLIN WITH him on this little expedition, but as he shoved his phone in his pocket and headed toward the bar in the kitchen where he'd left his car keys, she emerged from her office and sent him an inquiring look.

"You're going out?"

With someone else, he might have asked how she could have known that, since he was still a few feet away from the breakfast bar and the basket that held his keys. However, Caitlin seemed to know things, even when she wasn't having an actual vision.

"My mother called. She needs me to check on something for her." Better to be vague, he thought. That way, there was a chance Caitlin would let it go.

He should have known better. "Check on what?"

"The apartment. Levi went down there today to take a look around, and he hasn't called or gotten in contact with anyone."

Caitlin's dark russet brows drew together. Alex hadn't bothered to tell her which apartment, because she'd already heard from him that some new disruptions had been occurring there. That information had upset her, because, even with all the time that had passed, the loss of Roslyn still hurt more than she wanted to admit. It was easier to keep an old wound from throbbing when something else didn't come along to tear off the scab.

"I'm coming with you," she said.

Alex knew he should have expected such a request. Actually, it wasn't even a request, just a statement of intent. Was it worth arguing over? Probably not, since he knew she'd get her way eventually.

Still, he thought he should at least make a token protest. "I thought you were writing."

"I finished the chapter I was working on. I'm ahead of schedule."

Of course she was. From almost the first moment he'd met her, he'd admired her grit, her determination. She'd made this writing thing work, was now much more than the modest success she tended to describe herself as whenever someone asked her how her books were doing. Actually, she now earned more than he did, and his salary as an advertising director at the local Spanish-language television station wasn't exactly peanuts.

"Okay," he said. "But I don't know for sure what we're walking into, so you need to stick close."

In reply, she gave him a brilliant smile and came close, slipped her arm through his. Her shimmering red hair brushed against his bicep, and he wished they weren't heading out on a possibly dangerous errand, but instead planning for a cozy night in—maybe a sunset dip in the pool, followed by dinner on the patio and love-making in the big bed they shared. It was because of evenings like the one he was visualizing that he didn't mind too much that they'd put off starting a family. Plenty of time for that later. Right now was all about enjoying one another.

And helping out the family when necessary. Everyone was on edge because of that mess with the Santiagos in California, although Alex had to think things would be better now that Matías Escobar was no longer around. True, it sounded like his father was a nasty customer, but....

"I hate the idea of going to that place, but I hate even more the idea of you going there alone, so yes, I will stick close, Alex. We'd better get going."

True. The sooner they got this done with, the sooner he and Caitlin could get back here, could possibly salvage the evening. He really didn't expect to find anything, but he knew he needed to stay on his guard. His mother had sounded almost rattled when she called him, and that was very unlike her.

Caitlin trailing along behind him, Alex headed to the garage and got into the BMW SUV they'd bought only a few months earlier. A splurge, but they could afford it. After all, what did they have to spend their money on? The house was paid for, and they'd already upgraded Caitlin's old Toyota to a Mini Cooper a year ago.

The sun was dipping to the west, but they still had a good hour or so of daylight remaining. That meant there should be plenty of bright sunshine left to run this errand, since the apartment was only about fifteen minutes away from the house in the hills that the two of them shared.

Lots of traffic, though, on this Monday afternoon. Alex wasn't exactly thrilled to be going back out into it after he'd only gotten home an hour earlier, but this was part of being a member of a witch clan—you never really knew when you might be called on to perform some kind of service for the family. And that just went double when your mother happened to be the *prima*.

He glanced over at Caitlin, whose expression was brooding as she looked out the window at the cars that surrounded them on every side. "You getting anything?"

"No. Well, nothing more than the creepy crawlies I've had ever since we found out about the Santiagos and the Escobars. But those aren't visions, just...." She trailed off there, as if she wasn't quite sure how to explain herself.

"Just feelings of impending doom?" he teased, hoping to coax a smile out of her. He did love her smiles.

But she remained sober-faced, her fingers playing with the strap of the purse where it rested in her lap. "Yes, basically. Like there's this big thunderhead just sitting out on the horizon, and you can feel the air getting charged and smell ozone, and you know it's going to be bad, but there's absolutely nothing you can do about it."

"I don't know about 'nothing,'" he countered. "I mean, Levi did us all a huge favor by getting rid of Matías Escobar. That had to have messed up his father big-time."

Now she did look away from the car window so she could meet his gaze, but the glance she sent him wasn't exactly reassuring. In her blue eyes he saw a haunted echo of the grief she'd experienced over her cousin Roslyn's death, a worry that their troubles were far from over. "I'm not sure that's necessarily a good thing. Yes, the world's a better place with Matías gone, but you can't tell me that Joaquin Escobar isn't plotting something to get back at us."

"It's been two weeks since Matías was killed," Alex said, slightly annoyed that Caitlin had pointed out that troublesome fact. He really didn't want to admit to himself that part of the reason for his annoyance was that he'd thought almost the same thing, even if he hadn't said it out loud. But now he'd taken up a position, he figured he might as well continue to defend it. "You'd think he would have done something by now."

"Maybe. Or maybe not. For all we know, he's backed off because he wants to lull us into a false sense of security."

"Well, if that's his plan, it's not working. My mother has everyone on high alert, and it sounds like it's the same for the McAllisters and the Wilcoxes."

Her fingers tightened on her purse. "Yes, but how long can everyone stay like that? People start to get tired, start to make mistakes. Maybe that's what Joaquin Escobar is waiting for."

Alex didn't much like the sound of her comment, mostly because it made too much sense. Still, what else were they supposed to do? Everyone was keeping an eye out for any strange witches or warlocks who might cross their paths, anything that seemed out of the ordinary. This sort of informal system wasn't exactly infallible, but it was better than nothing. So far, he hadn't heard of anything particularly unusual, except the phenomena that had occurred at the very apartment where they were headed. He had to believe in that, because his mother had been there, along with Connor and Angela and Domingo, the de la Paz clan's medium. None of them would have any reason to lie.

He got off the freeway at 22nd Street and headed east. The businesses here were fairly shabby; he even spotted some places with boarded-up windows. The residential neighborhoods weren't in much better shape, although it seemed like the people who lived here tried their best to keep their yards tended, even if those yards were mostly cactus and decorative rocks.

Then they turned down the street where the apartment building was located. In the seat next to him, Caitlin sat up a little straighter, her fingers still clenched on her purse. She'd never come back here after Roslyn's death. Why should she? Unlike Angela, Caitlin didn't possess the ability to speak with the dead, and because of her visions, she'd probably seen enough of the apartment Matías had used as his safe house to last her the rest of her life.

Since it was now almost six-thirty, and most people were home from work, the street in front of the apartment complex was choked with cars. They had to park a block away and walk.

Not that Alex minded. The short walk gave him time to clear his head, to mentally prepare himself for…well, whatever they might find. Even if it turned out to be nothing.

As they began to climb the steps that led to the second level of the apartment building, Caitlin's left hand stole its way into his right, holding on to him tightly. He knew how difficult this must be for her, to come to the place where her cousin had died.

Had been murdered, not to put too fine a point on it. He did his best to avoid using the word whenever the subject came up, just because being brutally blunt seemed as though it would just make the situation even worse. Actually, Caitlin rarely talked about Roslyn anymore, seemed determined to put the ugly episode behind her. And why shouldn't she? Both Angela and Roslyn's older sister Jenny had confirmed that Roslyn had moved on to the next world. She was at peace, despite the horror of her passing.

Alex put his free hand on the doorknob. To his surprise, it wasn't locked.

That couldn't be good.

A quick glance around told him the walkway outside the second-floor apartments was empty. He pulled in a breath and summoned his power, bringing to life the shimmering bubble that would protect him and anyone inside it from all kinds of physical harm, whether attack by magic or more conventional weapons.

Moving as one, he and Caitlin went inside the apartment. It was nearly empty, with only a few pieces of furniture placed there to make it look as if the place was inhabited. As far as he could tell, everything was in order. No signs of a struggle—in fact, no sign at all that anyone had been here this afternoon.

"Are you getting anything?" he asked Caitlin, and she shook her head.

"No. It just feels like an empty apartment."

Alex had gotten much the same impression, but he figured he should try something. "Hey!" he called out. "Anyone here?"

Only silence. He glanced down at Caitlin. Her big blue eyes were perplexed, but also worried. "Maybe we should look in the bedroom?" she suggested.

"Sure."

Still holding hands, still with that shimmering bubble surrounding them, they moved through the living room and down the short hallway that opened off it. Here were a pair of bedrooms, one of them slightly larger than the other, and one bathroom. The tile and fixtures were at least twenty years out of date—Alex was able to make even that much of an approximation because he had some relatives whose houses were basically time capsules of bad design choices—but it was scrupulously clean. In fact, it was obvious that the bathroom had been scrubbed down recently because the air still held a faint, lingering scent of bleach, harsh and acrid, making him want to cough.

One bedroom had a queen-size bed and a nightstand. That was it. The other was even more bare, and contained only a desk and matching office chair. No sign at all that anything had been touched after this furniture—props, really—had been set in place.

"Well, this is a big nothing," Alex said. "It's kind of weird that the door's unlocked, but maybe Levi forgot to lock it when he left. It's not like there's anything much to steal here."

"That's true," Caitlin agreed. She glanced around again, as though hoping that a helpful detail might reveal itself after she took a second look at her surroundings. Unfortunately, there really wasn't anything to see.

Alex pulled his phone out of his pocket and shot a couple of quick photos. The shimmer from the protective bubble would distort the images a little bit, but not so much that anyone looking at the pictures wouldn't be able to see the same thing he and Caitlin were seeing now—rooms that didn't look as if anyone had entered them at all today. Of course, just because they appeared that way didn't mean Levi hadn't been here earlier. Alex hadn't met the "man" his cousin Zoe had summoned from another dimension, but by all accounts, he had turned out to be one of the good guys. He certainly wouldn't have done anything to make a mess here in the apartment.

"Well, we've done our due diligence," Alex said. "Since we're out already, we might as well go out for dinner. It's not too far to El Charro. Sound like a plan?"

"Sure," Caitlin replied. Once again she glanced around the living room, obviously trying to spot that one detail, that one anomaly, which would tell them something had gone wrong here. However, it seemed as though she couldn't find anything, because she gave a small hitch of her shoulders and shook her head slightly. She began to walk toward the front door…

…and then stopped dead, so abruptly that it looked to Alex as if someone had put out an invisible hand and planted it in the middle of her chest. She pulled in a gasp of a breath and reached up to touch her temples. "Oh, no…."

Although he'd witnessed episodes similar to this one over the years they'd been together, Alex wasn't sure if he would ever get completely used to it. There was something eerie about watching Caitlin have a vision, as though some part of her was being taken away and dragged unwillingly to someplace else, someplace *other*. "What are you seeing?" he asked, and reached out to put a comforting hand on her shoulder.

She was shaking. A pause as she gulped in a breath, and then she stared up at him with wide, frightened eyes. "*He* was here."

"He who? Levi?"

A shake of the head, and then she stopped herself. "No. I mean, yes, he was here, too, but that's not who I'm talking about. It was *him*. Joaquin Escobar."

Although the apartment was stuffy, Alex went cold all over. Escobar, here? How the hell could that happen, especially with every de la Paz witch and warlock on the lookout for any strangers in their territory?

He didn't question Caitlin's vision, though. She'd never been wrong before this—and she'd seen Joaquin in another vision only a month earlier, so it wasn't as though she could have mistaken him for someone else. Trying to quell the sick feeling rising in his stomach, Alex said, "Was he alone?"

"No. He had four other people with him. Three men, one woman." Caitlin shut her eyes for a moment, obviously trying to recall every detail of what she had seen. "I think they must have been Santiagos, although of course I've never seen any of them before. And I'm not sure why Escobar would have bothered to bring them along—I thought his power blocked the talents of anyone with magical ability."

"Well, that's our best guess, but we really don't know that much about how his power operates. It's likely that he can control it just like the rest of us can control our gifts—"

"Speak for yourself," Caitlin broke in, her expression annoyed.

Oops. The way her visions descended, uninvited and unannounced, had always been a sore point with his wife, and Alex couldn't really say that he blamed her. They'd learned to work with it, and everyone in the de la Paz clan knew she could have a vision at any time, but it still made outings in civilian territory a bit problematic, depending on the intensity of the vision she was suffering. Not that she'd had as many of those lately, probably because the witch world had been quiet enough…until the Escobars resurfaced. "Okay, the way *most* of us can control our gifts. But I'm pretty sure Escobar can turn it on and off at will." He paused, not wanting to ask the question but knowing he had to. "Did they get Levi?"

Caitlin's lips pressed together, and she nodded. "Yes, they surrounded him and dragged him out the front door. I didn't really see what happened after that." She hesitated, then went on, "I thought Levi was super-powerful. How could they just grab him?"

"Obviously, it doesn't matter how powerful you are if there's a null around. I guess Escobar's talent overrides everything else. He wouldn't care if he knocked out the abilities of the people with him, because that many people could overpower Levi physically, even if none of them were able to use their magical gifts."

Frowning, she went to the window and peeked out between the blinds. The sun was starting to set, but it was still plenty light out. "Wouldn't anyone have noticed a bunch of people dragging a guy out of this apartment and down the stairs?"

"Maybe." Alex hurried over to stand next to her, a little irritated that she'd been so cavalier about stepping outside the shield he'd cast. Then again, Caitlin saw things that no one else could. She probably understood the threat was long gone. "*If* there was anyone around to see it. This all probably happened a few hours ago, before a lot of people would have gotten home from work.

And also, it sounds as though Joaquin Escobar has the same power of persuasion that his son did. If there were any witnesses, he could have made them think whatever he wanted."

That sank in as Caitlin gave a reluctant nod. "I suppose you're right. So now what?"

Well, hell. Good question. Alex ran a hand through his hair, wishing that just for once, he'd have some good news to deliver. "I'll call my mother. She'll have to let Angela know what happened to Levi. And I suppose we'll also need to get the word out that Escobar is in our territory, although if he has a couple hours' head start on us, he could be getting across the California border pretty soon."

"If they drove. Maybe one of the Santiagos has the power to send them from place to place, like that great-great-great-whatever uncle of Danica's that she told me about once."

If that was the case, then they would be well and truly screwed. Alex knew there was no one in the de la Paz clan with that particular talent—and no one in the Wilcoxes or the McAllisters, unless they were all hiding something. "Well, let's hope not. I think it's more likely that they're somehow able to mask their witch-kind identities. Wasn't Damon Wilcox able to do something like that?"

"I think so. Since it seems as if Joaquin Escobar has managed to bundle together every talent that helps him and hurts everyone else, I wouldn't be surprised."

Usually, Caitlin didn't sound quite so thoroughly depressed. However, this latest development was the last thing any of them needed to deal with. What was Escobar's end game, anyway? He couldn't expect Levi to throw his lot in with the Santiagos, could he?

Maybe…after a little bit of "persuasion" from Joaquin. Alex just didn't know enough about Levi to even guess whether the adopted McAllister warlock had the kind of strength required to withstand an Escobar warlock's mental manipulations.

He pulled Caitlin close and hugged her gently, as much to reassure himself that she was still with him, and safe, as to let her know that he was here for her. Without speaking, they left the apartment, Alex pausing to lock the door behind them.

What good that would do, he had no idea.

The damage had already been done.

6

Angela

My phone rang just as Connor and I were sitting down to eat the pizza we'd ended up ordering from Grapes. I didn't hesitate, however, but grabbed the phone, scanned the home screen for a second, then pushed the green button with its phone icon to accept the call.

I'd noted that it was Luz calling me, not Caitlin. I didn't know whether that was a good or a bad thing.

"Hi, it's Angela."

"Angela." Luz hesitated, and that small pause was enough to send icy tendrils of worry running down my spine. "I just heard from Alex."

"And?" I had to ask the question, even though I already knew the news probably wasn't good.

"Caitlin had a vision at the apartment. She saw Joaquin Escobar seizing Levi and taking him away. The vision ended after that, so I'm not sure where they were going, but—"

"I'm sure he was taking him back to California," I said. Was that my voice, so calm, so cold? I might as well have been speaking of a stranger, rather than someone who'd become part of my clan over the past eighteen months. But I knew I was forcing myself to a calm I didn't feel, because otherwise I ran the risk of losing it altogether.

"But why?"

"Levi's gifts are very valuable. Joaquin wants Levi working for him, not against him." Across the table, Connor was watching me, his narrowed eyes telling me he'd been able to guess at the parts of the conversation he couldn't hear. I cleared my throat. "Luz, is it okay if I put you on speaker?"

"Of course."

My husband shot me a grateful look. Leaning close to the phone, he asked, "Caitlin is absolutely sure it was Escobar?"

"Yes. She recognized him immediately."

"So Joaquin Escobar's null talent is able to override Levi's gifts."

"It looks that way."

Silence as Connor and I stared at each other across our neglected pizza. All sorts of terrible thoughts were running through my head, but the one that rose to the surface was, *What in the world am I going to tell Hayley?*

The truth, of course. Terrible as this was, we couldn't keep the news from her.

"You said 'they' earlier," Connor put in. "So Escobar wasn't acting alone?"

"No. He had a group of one witch and several warlocks with him. Alex says he assumes that was so they would still be able to physically control Levi even if Joaquin's null talent was blocking everyone's powers."

Which made sense. I didn't bother to ask how this gang of warlocks and one witch had managed to drag Levi out of the apartment with no one apparently noticing what was going on. Joaquin Escobar had already proved that he was able to manipulate a situation to his own satisfaction.

But…. "And none of the de la Pazes in Tucson were able to detect this incursion into their territory?"

Luz didn't answer right away. When she spoke, it was with a hint of defensiveness in her voice, although at least she did reply rather than trying to avoid the question. "No, apparently not. I didn't feel anything. I could try to explain this away by saying that I was in Scottsdale at the time, and therefore miles from the scene of the crime, but the truth of it is, I don't think I would have felt their presence even if I'd still been down in Tucson. Another of Joaquin Escobar's tricks, I am certain."

Although Connor was being the supportive husband and only had water set out on the table by his place setting, right then he looked like he could use a drink. I couldn't blame him—I felt the same way. When this was all over, I'd tell him to have a drink for the both of us, since I wouldn't be able to indulge for at least another six months.

"Did they leave any trace of their activities in the apartment?" Connor asked.

"Not that Alex and Caitlin were able to find. Everything looked completely undisturbed. Alex took some pictures, just to be safe, but I don't think a close inspection of them is going to reveal anything."

Like me, Luz was doing her best to be calm, but the brittle quality of her tone told me how on edge she really was. I couldn't blame her—after all, she'd just sent her son to investigate a place that Joaquin Escobar had invaded only a few hours earlier. What if Alex and Caitlin had gone there while Escobar and his gang were still present? They would have been captured, too. Both of them had talents that could be useful. Did the Santiagos have a seer? I couldn't remember, but I knew I could ask Lucinda and find out for sure.

First things first, though. We had to let Hayley know what had happened to Levi.

"Okay," I said. "I doubt that Escobar hung around—he'd want to get back to California with his prize. So I don't think there's any point in trying to find him, or catch up with him. We just need to figure out how to get Levi back."

"Yes," Luz replied, although her tone sounded skeptical.

I wasn't feeling very hopeful myself. Yes, we'd been able to mount a rescue right from the house where Joaquin Escobar was living, but only because we'd had Levi's assistance. I didn't think there was any way to do such a thing without his help, but we'd have to try.

"We'll think of something," I said, my tone firm. "In the meantime, I guess...stay vigilant, and let us know if you see or hear anything."

"Because vigilance served us so well in this instance." A pause, and Luz went on, "But yes, I don't see what else we can do. Take care, Angela, Connor."

"You, too," Connor and I said together, and I pushed the button to end the call. For a moment, the two of us just sat there and stared at each other, neither one of us sure what we should say or do next.

At last he reached over and closed the pizza box, then laid his hand on top of mine. "We need to go talk to Hayley. We can heat this up when we get back."

"Like I'll feel like eating anything after giving her this news."

"I know, but you need to eat. You need to keep your strength up." His fingers brushed against my skin, gentle, reassuring. Somehow with Connor there, I felt as if we could find a way to work this out, even though I couldn't think of one right at the moment.

"I love you," I said simply, and he smiled, green eyes shining into mine.

"I love you, too." He lifted my hand to his lips and kissed it gently. "Now let's go and talk to Hayley."

Yes, this conversation wasn't something that could be avoided. At least I knew Hayley would be at the apartment she shared with Levi, and that she would have Lucinda with her. Good. She wouldn't be receiving this news alone. Also, since Lucinda would be there, I could ask her some questions about the Santiago clan, could try to get as much information to help our cause as possible.

I really didn't know what else to do.

The sun had gone down behind the mountain, but the air was still pleasantly warm. It must have been baking down in Tucson today. I wondered how Levi had dealt with the heat, since he'd never been back to the southern part of the state after he'd come here to live. Had it weakened him somehow, made it more difficult for him to fight back?

No, the heat couldn't have had anything to do with it. Joaquin was just too strong for him.

That thought scared me more than anything else, because Levi's powers were really kind of staggering, when you stopped to think about it. He wasn't limited to the one or two magical gifts that most witches and warlocks possessed. As far as I could tell, he was able to do just about anything, whether he was dispelling demons or soothing a fever.

But Joaquin's null power was like a black hole, extinguishing anything that came near, even something as bright and as beautiful as Levi.

No, he wasn't extinguished. Escobar would want him alive. Levi might not be able to fight for himself right now, but he wasn't dead.

Connor's hand sought mine as we walked down the hill, and I wrapped my fingers around his, needing to feel him there, to know he was with me in this. We'd been in tight spots before and had always prevailed. This felt worse, but I knew we would find a way out.

I had to believe that.

Even so, my heart began to beat a little faster as we approached the building where Levi's flat was located. As *prima,* I knew that part of the job was delivering bad news...but this news was so *very* bad.

Nevertheless, I didn't allow my footsteps to falter as Connor and I climbed the two flights of stairs that led us to the building's third floor, where Levi's and Brandon's flats faced one another across a small landing outlined by a wrought-iron railing. And I made myself let go of Connor's hand so I could reach up and knock on the door.

Only a moment later, it opened, and Hayley looked out at us. As soon as she saw who was standing there, her face fell. "What's happened?"

"Can we come in?" Connor asked.

"Oh, sure." She stepped out of the way so Connor and I could enter the apartment. As we came inside, Lucinda picked up the remote for the TV and shut off the show the two of them had been watching. I didn't watch much television, so I couldn't identify what it was. Not that it really mattered. "It's bad, right?"

"Yes," I said, knowing that I couldn't dance around the issue, or delay in telling her the terrible news. "We just had a call from Luz. My cousin Caitlin—Luz's daughter-in-law—had a vision in the apartment. She saw Joaquin Escobar and some of the Santiagos taking Levi away."

Hayley's eyes widened, and she put her hand to her mouth, as if she needed that physical barrier to prevent a gasp—or a scream—from coming out. A long pause while she stared at us, and then she lowered her hand and said, "You're sure? I mean, it was just a vision—"

"Caitlin's visions are never wrong," Connor broke in gently. "They don't always come when you need them, but when they do, what she sees is always accurate."

I hadn't been sure exactly how Hayley would react to the news, but I was heartened by what I saw next. She went very still for a long moment, her jaw set. The glitter I saw in her eyes wasn't tears, but anger. Pure, unbridled rage.

Good. We were going to need that rage to get us through this ordeal. Anger could be a very powerful motivator.

"So what do we do?" she asked after a long pause, during which I could almost see her gather herself, bank that anger down to a point where she could manage it, draw on it when necessary.

"We're not sure yet," I said. "We just got the news a few minutes ago." I glanced over at Lucinda, who rose from the couch and faced me, her entire body practically radiating tension. However, her eyes met mine without flinching.

"What can I do?"

A rush of relief went over me. It wasn't that I'd expected her to outright refuse to help, but, despite the events of the past few weeks, the Santiagos were still her clan. I wouldn't have been surprised to find she was reluctant to provide any details that might have been too damning.

"Some information would help," I told her. "We really don't know that much about the Santiagos. I mean, I know your clan is a big one, but what exactly are we facing here? Whose talents is Joaquin Escobar most likely to exploit?"

Hayley glanced at Lucinda, whose mouth pursed, then tightened. It was obvious that she didn't like to think of her fellow clan members as only tools of Escobar's, but unfortunately, that was how we had to look at them. Any witch or warlock in the Santiago family was now nothing more than a resource to him, something that could be useful…or not.

"Well," she said at last, "one strike against them is that they're in the same boat as the McAllisters—they don't have a healer anymore, with Matías' mother dead these past few years. I've heard of a girl down in the San Diego branch of the family who's starting to show signs of possessing the gift, but her talent won't really manifest for a few more years. Anyway, without a healer, if they get hurt, they stay hurt."

Her voice was cool, calm, and I wondered how much of an effort it was taking for her to speak so dispassionately of fellow clan members. I knew better than to comment on that, however, and only said, "Well, that's something,

I guess, although there are always civilian doctors."

"True," Connor commented, "but if too many members of the same family start showing up in hospital emergency rooms, people might start asking questions. And even Joaquin Escobar probably doesn't want the civilian authorities looking at his activities too closely."

No, probably not. Even that arch-villain most likely didn't want the Pasadena P.D. snooping around his property. I nodded, then said, "What else?"

"My cousins Arturo and Elena—they're twins. Fraternal, but they still both possess the same talent. They're pretty powerful telekinetics."

Great. I had a sudden mental image of a brother and sister picking up identical cars and throwing them at some hapless de la Paz or McAllister witch. "How powerful?"

"Well, I don't know if they've ever really tested the limits of their strength, but one time at a clan picnic we held in a park, they picked up my cousin Sam's SUV and set it on the roof of the building where the restrooms were located."

So my fears about them hurling Volkswagens weren't entirely misplaced. "I'm surprised they'd do something like that in public."

Lucinda shrugged. "We were the only ones in the park. We'd made sure we'd have it to ourselves.

There wasn't much risk involved. Of course, that didn't stop my father from giving them hell about the episode."

"Okay, so we have Arturo and Elena to worry about," Connor said. "Who else?"

"I have another cousin, Amelia, who can control fire. And I mean *really* control it—summon it to her, throw fireballs, create walls of flame…that kind of thing. I'm sure Escobar could figure out a few uses for her. We don't have any seers, so we don't have to worry about having someone like Caitlin around to tell him what's currently happening with the McAllisters, or about to happen." Lucinda fiddled with one of the long, near-black strands of hair that fell over her shoulders. "We have weather-workers and mediums, people who can make nearly anything grow, but obviously their gifts aren't going to be of much use to Joaquin Escobar—except maybe my Uncle César. Technically, he's a weather-worker, but what he's really good at is calling down lightning. Of course, he tends to practice that gift out in the desert where it can't hurt anyone, and also because lightning storms aren't something you see much of in the L.A. basin."

People who could hurl balls of fire, or call the lightning. Or throw cars, or lord knows what else. And yet Joaquin Escobar hadn't been satisfied with all that, and wanted to make sure to get his hands on Levi so he could exploit his talents. Just what the hell *did* Escobar want with him?

"Do you think he'll try to come after me again?" Hayley asked then. "I mean, now that Levi isn't here to protect me." Her voice broke slightly as she spoke her lover's name, but she made herself continue the sentence. "Not that I really care," she added, "it's just that I could see why Escobar might want me to help amplify some of the people's powers that Lucinda just mentioned."

A legitimate concern, and something we'd have to make sure never happened. Connor clearly agreed with that sentiment, because he said, expression grim, "He'll have to get through us first. And we have you with the two of us. When Angela and I work together, we can achieve some pretty amazing things. I think even Joaquin Escobar would have second thoughts about trying to take us on if we have your gift amplifying our *prima* and *primus* powers."

Hayley looked almost relieved by that statement, although the worry never completely left her eyes. "You're right—I hadn't really thought about it that way. *Do* you even know the extent of your combined gifts?"

"Not really," I said. "We were able to strip Matías of his powers, and that's something I'm pretty sure no one else would have been able to do."

"Not even Levi?" Lucinda asked. "I mean, it sounds as though he has access to almost every witchy powers that's ever manifested."

Connor and I looked at each other. Good question, but…. "Levi's still just one person," I told her. "Neither Connor nor I on our own could have taken away Matías' powers, or the powers of Jorge and Tomas. Also, it's kind of hard to describe, but a *prima's* gifts—or a *primus'* gifts—aren't quite the same as those of an ordinary witch or warlock. It's more like they're overlaid on the talents we already have. I'm pretty sure Levi isn't able to use those sorts of powers."

"Even if that's true, he can still do a lot of damage," Hayley said. Now her arms were crossed, as if she was trying to hold on to herself so she wouldn't lose the control she was so desperately attempting to maintain. "I mean, he wouldn't do it willingly, but…." Her big blue eyes sought mine, imploring, wanting me to tell her something that would put her mind at ease. Unfortunately, I didn't have those sorts of answers.

Voice as gentle as I could make it, I said, "According to what Caitlin saw in her vision, it seemed pretty clear that Escobar's null powers were enough to negate Levi's gifts. If that's the case, then it's not too big a leap to believe that

Escobar can also use his talent for persuasion to keep Levi in line, to make him do his bidding."

"We don't know for sure, of course," Connor added, clearly wanting to do something to change the stricken expression that crossed over Hayley's features as I made my remark. "But I think it's better to assume the worst. The good news is that, once we have Levi back, we shouldn't have to worry about 'deprogramming' him or anything. As soon as Joaquin Escobar's influence is cut off, then Levi should return to himself."

"And how are we going to get him back?" Lucinda asked. "He was able to teleport into my house to get me out, but I assume that if he was the one taking on that job the last time, then you don't have anyone in your clan who can do something similar."

Both Connor and I shook our heads. "Not in the McAllisters, or the Wilcoxes, although I've heard it was once a Wilcox gift," I replied. "Maybe in the de la Paz clan, although I kind of doubt it. I'll check with Luz, though."

"In the meantime," Connor said, his tone deliberately soothing, "we all have to keep calm. Escobar's all about disruption, about making us feel off-kilter. He's not going to hurt Levi—he's way too valuable. It's pretty obvious that he went out of his way to capture him."

"Was it a trap?" Hayley asked then.

The thought hadn't even occurred to me before she said those words, but then I realized it must have been. How Escobar had done it, I didn't know, but it now seemed kind of obvious that he must have set up something he knew would lure Levi in.

Or rather, Joaquin Escobar had guessed that if he gave us a sufficiently difficult puzzle, we'd send in Levi to check it out. After all, he was sort of our ace in the hole, our *deus ex machina*.

And now he was gone.

"It might have been a trap," I said slowly. "But if that's the case, then we'll just have to figure out how Escobar managed to do such a thing…and make sure he never does it again."

7

Jack Sandoval

HIS PHONE WAS VIBRATING AS JACK CAME into the house, pleasantly warm and just slightly buzzed from sitting on the patio and sharing a pitcher of margaritas with his girlfriend Kate. Maybe now wasn't the best time to be tying one on, after everything that had been happening lately, but no one had reached out to him for help, and they'd both felt like having a little something to help them relax.

Jack's first instinct was to ignore the phone. After all, it was pretty clear that Luz and the other members of the clan were doing their best to give him and Kate a little space as they grew into their new relationship, and he doubted the call could be all that important. From what he'd been able to tell, things had pretty much quieted down right after Levi killed off Matías Escobar. Jack doubted the situation would stay this way forever, but he might as well enjoy the calm while he could.

In the end, though, years of training won out, and he picked up his iPhone from the spot where he'd left it charging on the kitchen counter. A frown pulled at his brows as he saw the number. Not Luz, nor anyone in the de la Paz clan.

No, it was his former supervisor, Larry Jansen, of the Scottsdale P.D.

Well, this should be interesting.

Jack pressed his finger against the phone's screen to accept the call. "Hey, Larry."

"Hey, Jack. How's retirement treating you?"

At that moment, Kate came into the kitchen from the patio, their empty margarita glasses in her hands. The early afternoon sunlight flooding through the French doors touched her warmly tanned shoulders, bare under the strappy sundress she wore.

"Retirement is good." *Very good,* Jack thought. Or at least it would be, if it weren't for the prick of unease that was already starting somewhere around the nape of his neck. It wasn't even precisely a warlock thing, just the instincts gained from fifteen years on the force. "What's up? You miss me already?"

"Hardly. It's been all peace and quiet, smooth sailing ever since you left."

Jack highly doubted that. Scottsdale definitely wasn't anything close to the crime capital of the country, but in any big city, you always had your share of petty larceny, home break-ins, domestic assaults, and too many other transgressions to list...including murders, although they weren't nearly as numerous as the residential crimes. Comments like the one Larry had just made were his way of trying to get under Jack's skin.

"So what is it, then?"

"Well, you know how you told me to let you know if I heard of any developments regarding the Aguirre cousins?"

The prickly sensation Jack had begun to experience a moment earlier just increased tenfold. Had Joaquin Escobar broken them out? It had seemed as though the dark warlock was content to let them sit in jail and rot, since apparently they were of no further use, but maybe he'd changed his mind and decided he needed as many lackeys as possible now that his son was gone. "Yeah," Jack replied, doing his best to keep his tone carefully neutral. "What about them?"

"They're dead."

Suddenly, sounding neutral didn't seem like an option. "What?"

"You sound surprised."

"Well, yeah. Last I heard, they were being model citizens, maybe hoping for time off for good behavior. Now you're saying they're dead?"

"Yeah." A pause, followed by a clicking sound, probably Larry pulling up some information on his computer. "It looks like they both died five days ago."

Five days? "Thanks for letting me know so quickly."

"Hey," Larry replied, sounding wounded, "this just crossed my desk today. It's not like it was marked as top priority or anything. I just let some people know—who let other people know—that I was kind of keeping track of those two. Things have to go through channels, you know."

Yes, Jack did know. He didn't miss the petty intricacies of the judicial system's bureaucracy, that was for sure. And as he watched Kate go over to the sink and rinse out their margarita glasses, then give him an inquiring glance, one eyebrow lifted, he was gladder than ever that he'd walked away from it all. He'd thought he might go stir crazy, being isolated out here in their desert hideaway, but the truth of it was, they had plenty to keep them busy, just doing things around the property, taking day trips to local wineries if the mood struck them.

Enjoying life. What a concept.

After tilting his head at Kate, indicating that

he'd fill her in after he was done with his phone call, Jack cleared his throat. "It's fine. So what did you hear?"

"Both of them were found in their cells—hundreds of miles apart—with no physical signs of trauma. The coroners in both cases did a full autopsy, because that's what you have to do when you have two healthy males in their twenties drop dead for no reason."

"They find anything?" Even as he asked the question, he somehow knew what Larry's answer would be.

"Nope. Nothing. No drugs, no foreign substances of any kind. No marks on their bodies. It's like their hearts just stopped."

Great. While Jack didn't know of any spell off the top of his head that would kill so quietly, so efficiently, that didn't mean much. His gift was defending against dark magic, not using it. No one in his clan practiced those kinds of black enchantments.

But Joaquin Escobar sure as hell did.

Larry went on, "You know what the real kicker is?"

"No."

"They both died at almost exactly the same time—somewhere around 3:00 in the morning. Of course it's impossible to pinpoint the exact minute, but they definitely died within an hour or so of each other."

Jesus. That sounded like the darkest of magic —not only to kill two people so silently, but to choose that hour of the morning? It was fairly well known that practitioners of the black path liked to do things in threes, in a mockery of the Holy Trinity, which was why so much dark magic was cast around three in the morning. Or rather, Jack knew that fun fact because he'd had to read up on such things when working to strengthen his defense spells.

Escobar had to have done it. But why? Had he decided that the Aguirres were a liability, that even though their powers had been stripped from them, they might at some point say the wrong thing to the wrong person?

Jack couldn't think of another reason for their deaths. His time working in the homicide division had helped him get inside the criminal mind a bit more than your regular person on the street, but Joaquin Escobar wasn't exactly your run-of-the-mill criminal. Truth be told, Jack didn't *want* to get inside that guy's mind—it was probably an abattoir of filth and blood and deep, dark hatreds.

"That is pretty messed up," he said, knowing that Larry was waiting for some kind of a response.

"Yeah." A pause, and then Larry added, "You have any idea what could have happened?"

"Not a clue," Jack said at once. "If they'd had some trace of drugs or poison in their systems, I would have said they must have managed to make some kind of long-distance suicide pact, but if toxicology came back clean—"

"It did. They could've gotten their hands on some drugs if they wanted to, I suppose—our prison system is like a sieve when it comes to that kind of thing—but they were both clean as a whistle."

"Maybe they willed themselves to die."

Larry made a disgusted sound. "You're kidding, right?"

"Not necessarily. There are documented cases of that sort of thing. You got a better explanation?"

"No." Through the speaker came a sound that might have been a sigh, although Larry had never been the sighing type. "Anyway, I just thought you should know."

It was a gruesome question to ask, but Jack knew he couldn't avoid making the inquiry. "What happened to the bodies?"

"No family came to claim them. Safford doesn't have a cemetery, so they were buried side by side in the prison graveyard in Florence."

A better fate than they probably deserved. At least the cousins were reunited in death.

"Makes sense. Well, thanks for the update."

"No problem." A hesitation, as if Larry could sense that he was leaving about a hundred unasked questions on the table. However, Jack knew his former supervisor was not the type to delve too deeply into the unknown. He could be dogged on a case, but he didn't like anything that had even a whiff of the weird about it. He wanted everything cut and dried. Because of that, he wasn't going to pursue this. He'd called Jack and provided the information, just as he'd promised he would, but at this point, he just wanted to be able to say he'd done his duty and then walk away.

Which was for the best. Jack still didn't know exactly what was going on here, but it sure as hell wasn't anything good. At this point, the best thing to do was end the call, get off the phone. "Actually, Kate and I were just on our way out when you called—"

"Oh, sure. Enjoy your day. 'Bye."

Larry hung up then. Had there been the faintest hint of accusation in his voice during that last remark, as though he was slightly jealous that Jack would be able to go on and enjoy his day, now that he didn't have to come into work anymore?

Possibly. But that was Larry's problem, not

his. Actually, Larry could take early retirement if he wanted to, but Jack knew his former supervisor was probably going to hang on until he was forcibly thrown out. It wasn't so much that he loved the job, more that he wouldn't know what to do with himself once he didn't have a reason to go to work every morning.

Jack set down his phone. Kate was still waiting by the sink, although now she leaned against the counter. "What was all that about?" she asked.

"More Escobar-related weirdness," he replied. "Tomas and Jorge Aguirre—the two cousins who helped Matías kidnap Roslyn McAllister and Danica Wilcox—were both found dead in their prison cells. No verifiable cause of death. They both died at approximately the same time, as far as the coroner was able to determine."

Kate's hazel-green eyes widened. She was tanned now from her time in the sun, and the contrast between her eyes and her skin was striking. "Um, that's pretty strange, isn't it?"

Beyond strange, really. Even so, Jack lifted his shoulders as he said, "Yeah, it is. I have to think that Joaquin Escobar had something to do with what happened to them, but what, exactly? I can't begin to guess what purpose their deaths might have served, except to make sure their mouths were permanently kept shut."

A frown, and Kate tilted her head to give him

a quizzical glance. "Do you really think they would have told anyone about who they were?"

"No. They'd already been in prison for a couple of years. If they were going to spill the beans, they probably would have done so already." Jack shrugged, then went over to where Kate stood. At once she put her arms around his waist and pulled him close. She wasn't wearing a bra under that sundress, and just the sensation of her full breasts pressing against him was enough to make him harden slightly. Unfortunately, he knew he couldn't allow himself to get distracted. Something very strange was going on.

He needed to call Luz.

Because he didn't want Kate to think he was rejecting her, he bent and kissed her, tasted the sweet-sour tang of the margaritas they'd drunk earlier on her full lips. God, he really wished he could take her into the bedroom.

Those sorts of diversions would have to wait, though.

Reluctantly, he pulled away, but he did reach up to touch her hair, to feel its softness under his fingertips. "I have to make a phone call."

She didn't look disappointed. More... resigned. "Luz?"

"Yes. I've been kind of out of contact the past few days anyway, so this new information just gives me another reason to check in."

"Okay. I need to go take a look at the shade cloth in the garden anyway, make sure those winds we had last night didn't loosen anything."

Jack sent her a grateful smile and watched as she let herself back out onto the patio before she disappeared around a corner of the house. The garden had been her idea; he hadn't really thought they'd be able to do much out here on this stretch of dry desert land, but she'd had him help her set up the shade cloth to protect their little garden patch, had bought plants from a Home Depot in Tucson because it was already too late in the growing season to get started with seeds. So far the garden of tomatoes and squash and peppers was doing pretty well, as was the little box of herbs that sat on the kitchen windowsill. Whether they'd actually be able to make their own salsa, the way she'd promised…well, he supposed he'd find out in a month or two.

For now, though, he needed to ignore such pleasant endeavors. Expression turning grim, he picked up his phone again, found Luz in his contacts list, and then pressed the phone icon to connect the call.

She answered almost right away. "What is it, Jack?"

Her voice was tense, almost clipped. Clearly, she hadn't been spending the same kind of relaxing day that he had, and he wondered what had been going on in the wider world while he was playing at domestic tranquility with Kate. "I just talked to my former boss. He wanted to let me know that the Aguirre cousins are dead."

"*What?*"

Basically my same reaction, he thought with a flash of grim humor. However, judging by the way she sounded, Jack guessed that Luz wouldn't find anything particularly funny about the situation. "They died five days ago, in their prison cells. The coroner wasn't able to find a cause of death."

A long pause. Then she said, "It was Joaquin Escobar."

"You sound pretty certain."

"Who else could have done such a thing? Also, there have been developments, Jack. I didn't call you because I wasn't sure how much help you could provide, but now…."

"What's happened?" he asked, already imagining the worst.

"Escobar came into our territory and kidnapped Levi McAllister while he was down here in Tucson, investigating the apartment where Roslyn was killed."

Holy shit. Jack scrubbed his free hand over his face, wishing right then he had another margarita sitting on the counter there next to him. No, scratch that. A margarita was too wimpy. A shot of Scotch.

"Why the apartment? Why now?"

"There was a…disturbance with the civilians who were living in the unit. I went there first, with Angela and Connor and Domingo. Domingo felt it first, but Angela sensed its presence as well."

"What was it?"

"We don't know." The edge to Luz's voice sharpened. "It was some kind of entity, but not a ghost, not a demon. Something…other. We left before it could do us any harm."

"You thought it would hurt you?"

"We knew it. The thing attacked Domingo first, probably because he was the most sensitive to otherworldly entities. Angela drove it off, and we hurried away. Afterward, she suggested that Levi should go and see if he could discover anything about the entity in the apartment. Because he is not from here, and because he's already shown himself to be successful at driving off demons, we thought it was a good idea."

"Apparently not," Jack said dryly. He really didn't want to think of what might happen with Levi McAllister—and all his attendant powers—in Joaquin Escobar's hands. And the problem was, Jack couldn't quite figure out how to get from point A to point B. How could Escobar have even known that Levi would come to visit the apartment? Was there a spy in either of their clans? No, that didn't make any sense, especially when you considered it had only been Angela, Connor, Luz, and Domingo present during the first foray into the place where Roslyn McAllister had died. Jack couldn't believe that any of them was a spy. No, it had to be something else…more like an elaborate trap of some sort.

A trap. Of course.

"Holy shit." This time he said the words aloud, instead of thinking them, and at once Luz responded.

"What is it? Did you think of something?"

It was crazy…but then, Joaquin Escobar was crazy. No, scratch that. The guy wasn't a maniac, just a cold, calculating killer. There was nothing he would stop at, if he thought it would further his cause.

Taking a breath, Jack said, "I think I know why the Aguirres were killed."

8

Angela

I WAS GETTING SICK OF MY PHONE, PROBABLY because every time it rang, it seemed as if it was someone calling with even worse news. The night before had been rough, with both Connor and me tossing and turning for what seemed like half the evening. No one actually called, so that wasn't the reason. No, it was more that my brain kept coming up with worse and worse fates for Levi to be suffering, even though I tried to tell myself that Joaquin wouldn't hurt him, that he was worth far too much.

If only I really believed that. Joaquin Escobar had already proved himself to be ruthless and unpredictable, which meant I really didn't know what the hell was going to happen next.

The morning passed with agonizing slowness. I called Margot to check on the twins, was able to FaceTime with Emily and Ian for a few minutes, where they told me, "Lucas and Margot took us to the movies!" and "We went on a hike and saw some deer!" in a cheery babble of voices before they decided that talking to Mommy wasn't nearly as interesting as the fort they'd been building in a corner of Lucas and Margot's backyard. But at least I was able to see that they were happy and healthy, and definitely not suffering from separation anxiety.

That was something, I supposed.

But after Connor and I shared a lunch of the pizza we hadn't eaten the night before, my cell phone rang. My whole body tensed.

Connor must have noticed, because he reached over to stroke my hand before he picked up the phone and handed it to me. I looked down at the display, saw that it was Luz calling.

Well, with Levi already captured, how bad could the news be?

It could be plenty bad, I thought. *Maybe Caitlin has had another vision, this time of Levi being tortured or something.*

I told myself to chill out, then touched the screen to accept the call and immediately put it on speaker so Connor could listen in. "Hi, Luz."

"Hello, Angela. I have some information that

may shed some light on what might be in the apartment."

"You didn't go back there, did you?" I asked, my voice sharp with worry. The last thing I needed was Luz taking unnecessary risks.

"No, I did not. But my cousin Jack just called to let me know that the Aguirre cousins are dead."

I wasn't sure how to feel about that particular piece of news. Yes, they were scum, nearly as bad as Matías himself, although they'd both protested that he had them under his control as well, that they shouldn't be held accountable for their actions. Maybe that was partially true, but it didn't excuse what they'd done. "And?"

"Their deaths were…suspicious. Jack has a theory about that. He thinks that Joaquin Escobar killed them precisely so he could trap their unquiet spirits here on this plane, in the very apartment where they helped to torture and murder your cousin Roslyn. That is what we all felt."

"Those weren't ghosts," I said, my voice flat. There were a lot of things I didn't know about this world—or the next—but I could tell when something was a ghost and when it wasn't.

"Not how you perceive them, no. But whatever dark spell Escobar used to kill them, it altered their spirits, changed them into the entity we all felt. That is why we couldn't identify it, and why we ended up sending Levi to investigate."

Again a wash of guilt went over me. Still, I wasn't so bent on self-recrimination that I couldn't recognize the truth in Luz's story. Besides, I'd had my own suspicions that the whole thing might have been a trap; I just hadn't known how the dark warlock might have accomplished such a thing. "You're saying Joaquin Escobar did all this just so he could trap Levi?"

"That's what Jack thinks. I can't come up with another reason for how Escobar knew exactly to be in the right place at the right time. He has many talents, but he is not a seer."

And, according to Lucinda, the Santiagos didn't have one. Joaquin Escobar would have to operate using his own instincts—which, I had to admit, seemed to have served him pretty well so far. He'd know that we'd turn to Levi, since Levi had already helped the McAllister clan defend itself against the demons he'd sent to attack us. How Escobar and his team of Santiago witches and warlocks had managed to infiltrate de la Paz territory, I wasn't sure, but if Damon Wilcox could come up with a spell to mask Connor's warlock nature so he could safely meet me and convince me he was a civilian, then I guessed Escobar could do the same thing. He'd already shown that he had access to a wide arsenal of magical weapons.

I had an uneasy feeling that we were going to see a lot more of those dark talents in the near future if we didn't start to get our act together.

"Well, the trap definitely worked," Connor said. He glanced over at me, expression grim. "I guess our next question is, what is Escobar doing to do with his prize?"

"I'm not sure," Luz replied. "Any number of things, I would think. I suppose much will depend on Levi's ability to resist him."

Having known and worked with Levi for more than a year, I'd learned a lot about his inner strength, about the goodness that fairly pulsed from him. He might have come from a different plane of existence, but he was no demon. More like the opposite.

No, he wasn't an angel. I still couldn't say exactly what he was, only that I—and pretty much everyone in the McAllister clan—were very glad that he'd come to join our little family here in Jerome. And while he still had a lot to learn about this world, he would know how much was at stake. He'd suffer a good deal to make sure we were kept safe, especially with the woman he loved living amongst us.

That thought sent a sudden chill down my spine. Would Joaquin Escobar try to come after

Hayley now that he had her lover in his possession? Without Levi here to help, it could be a lot more difficult to keep her safe.

"I think Levi would rather die than let harm come to the McAllisters, or anyone from the Arizona witch clans." I hated that I'd even had to utter those words, but I forced myself to press on. "Which wouldn't suit Escobar's purposes at all. So I guess we have to hope that Levi will be okay for now, at least until we can break him out."

Even as I spoke, Connor raised an eyebrow. I couldn't fault him for his skepticism, because prying Levi away from his captor wasn't going to be easy, especially in Santiago territory. However, we'd have to try. Leaving him in Escobar's hands was not an option.

Clearly, Luz shared Connor's view of the situation. "I admire you for wanting to rescue Levi, Angela, but how exactly do you propose to do such a thing?"

"You have any teleporters amongst your clan?" I asked. I had a feeling what the answer was going to be, but I needed to know.

"No," Luz replied at once. "That is, my cousin Marisela can move objects from one place to another with her mind, but only small things. She certainly doesn't have the strength to move a person from place to place."

Even though the talent seemed trivial for now,

I still filed it away for future reference. You never knew when you might be able to use even the smallest of magical tricks. "Invisibility?"

The de la Paz *prima* laughed. "No. I fear you have an inflated idea of what our clan is capable of. We may be numerous, but in general, our skills aren't terribly unusual. There is Alex, of course, but his gift is something of an outlier."

"Yes, but it will still be helpful if we need to make a frontal assault."

Although I couldn't see her, I got the impression that Luz frowned. I doubted she liked the idea of us sending Alex in alone to rescue Levi, of him charging into the Santiago house solo, like some modern-day equivalent of Audie Murphy charging an enemy line in one of those old black and white movies that used to be shown on the local station when I was a kid.

"It wouldn't work," Connor said gently, cutting in before Luz could reply. "As soon as Alex got close enough, Escobar's null talent would nuke Alex's dome of protection, and he'd be basically helpless."

Basically helpless. That was how I felt right then. It seemed no matter what idea or plan we came up with, it came crashing into that horrible "gift" of Joaquin Escobar's, the one that ensured no other witch or warlock had a chance against him.

"There has to be something we can do," I protested.

"Maybe there is," Connor said. "But it might not involve magic at all."

"What do you mean?" Luz asked.

"I mean that none of our gifts can stand up to Escobar's ability to render them useless as soon as we come in range."

"Do we know that for a fact about Angela's and my *prima* talents, your *primus* powers?"

For a second, I thought she had a point, and hope flared within me. Then I remembered how Joaquin Escobar had overpowered the Santiago clan's new *prima,* used his mind-control tricks to bend her to him. Yes, I supposed you could argue that poor Marisol had been reeling from the knowledge of her mother's death, hadn't had even a half hour to learn how to use the new powers that had come flooding into her. Even so, Caitlin's visions had shown someone who should have been a powerful witch being completely overwhelmed by the dark warlock.

"Remember what happened to Marisol," I said, and an uncomfortable silence descended.

Connor was the first one to speak. "Yes, Escobar got the drop on her, but she was only one person. We don't know what would happen if the two of us used our combined gifts against him."

"Or all three of us," Luz offered.

"Is there a way to do that?" I'd never heard of such a thing, but then, both Connor and I had experienced a lot of firsts in our time together. We'd learned how to join our powers, which made sense, since we were bonded as consorts in addition to being the *prima* and *primus* of our clans. But was there some means to bring Luz into that bond, to make it so all three of us were able to wield our combined powers as one?

"Not that I know of," she replied. "But it's something that might bear looking into. Escobar is powerful, but I can't see how he would be able to fight all three of us at once."

Connor looked over at me. His expression was grim enough, but I saw a certain speculative gleam in his eyes, one that meant he was beginning to think over the possibilities of such a collaboration. "We'll start doing some research here," he said. "Angela and I will talk to our elders, and I should probably pick Marie's brain, too. She's about the closest the Wilcox clan has to an elder, and I know she's been gathering information on our family history and a bunch of other stuff for years."

"That sounds like a good idea," Luz said. "I'll do what I can on my end. We also have a clan historian, and she might be able to dig up some information for me."

"All right, sounds like it's homework assignments all around," I put in. While I hated the thought of delaying our attempt to rescue Levi, I also knew that rushing in half-cocked wouldn't do him any good, either. We had to make sure that our effort was successful, because I didn't know if we'd be allowed a second chance. "We'll be in touch as soon as we have some information to share."

"And so will I." A pause, and then Luz added, "But if we learn nothing?"

That worry had already begun to tickle at the back of my mind, that the situation was so unprecedented, there literally wasn't information available to help us. And although I had weathered storms nearly as bad as this when I was pregnant with the twins, I couldn't help but worry that all this stress might be bad for the child I carried now. However, I did my best to push those nagging concerns away. Admitting defeat before we even got started wouldn't help anyone.

"Then we regroup and think of something else," I said firmly. "Even if it's hiring a bunch of mercenaries to storm the house and yank Levi out of there. Joaquin Escobar's null powers wouldn't be much use against a bunch of civilians."

"No, but he has other talents, and if he is not using his null powers, then the witches and warlocks who surround him will be free to use their own gifts," Luz said. She let out a sigh, then added, "But I take your point."

Connor was frowning. He said, "We'll have to hope it doesn't come to that. On the other hand, using civilians might not be a bad plan if all other routes fail."

"But let's focus on what we can do with our own powers for now," I said. "I only mentioned mercenaries because it never hurts to have a backup plan."

"All right. I'll be in touch."

Luz ended the call there, and I straightened up and looked over at Connor. That same pucker continued to pull at his brows, which meant he was still processing, still mentally weighing all the possible options that lay before us. However, he wasn't distracted enough to forget to reach over and take my hand. "You okay?"

Of course I really wasn't. The harder I tried not to think about what might be happening to Levi, the more gruesome possibilities flashed through my mind. Was Escobar torturing him to earn his cooperation, tormenting him with the specter of horrible futures for his adopted clan, the woman he loved?

At least now we had a course of action. The worst part was always sitting around and not knowing what to do next.

"I'm fine," I said. "But we need to contact the elders, have them come over now. There's just so much I don't know about when it comes to my family's history."

"I know the feeling." He reached for my phone and picked it up, then went to the messaging app and sent out a quick text. I knew he was probably contacting Trish, since she was the most tech-savvy of the three elders. A text to her meant she'd call the other two, thus saving Connor and me time and effort. "Well, that's done," he said. "I asked them to be here as soon as they could. Should we call Hayley?"

The thought had crossed my mind, but something made me shake my head. "No. I mean, we've already told her that we're going to do everything we can to get Levi back. Giving her details isn't going to change anything. Besides...." I stopped there, not sure whether I wanted to state aloud the worry that had been niggling at the back of my brain.

"'Besides'?" Connor prompted me gently.

I might as well say it. We'd long ago promised that we wouldn't keep secrets from one another. "Besides, if Joaquin Escobar does try to take Hayley again—and, Goddess forbid, succeeds— then it's better if she doesn't know very much. Safer for everyone, right?"

His lips pressed together, but he nodded and didn't try to contradict me. "Right. And that's what we always have to keep in mind—the safety of our clans. Lord knows I hate to even entertain the thought, but we can't let the safety of one person outweigh the needs of so many others."

I hated the thought, too, but I knew what he meant. As the heads of our clans, we had to make sure we protected all of the people in our care. We couldn't put the needs of one person ahead of all others, just because their magical talent might be greater, or because we personally liked them better.

It was an uncomfortable feeling, and one I'd never experienced before. And the Goddess help me if those noble sentiments were ever put to the test.

9

Levi

HIS HEAD WAS ACHING. WHEN LEVI REACHED up to attempt to determine the source of the pain, he found a large, tender bump on the back of his skull. At once he winced and removed his fingers, knowing that continuing to touch the sore spot wouldn't do him any good.

With the pain, memory came flooding back. How he'd been marched out the front door of the apartment and down the stairs, all his much-vaunted magical gifts of no use, thanks to Joaquin Escobar's null powers. When they reached the parking lot and approached a dark gray van with California plates, Levi had begun to struggle in earnest, knocking two of the warlocks who held him to the pavement. He'd seized that opening, had begun to run—only to have the third warlock, a big burly man who looked as if he once played that violent sport known as football, come up from behind and tackle him. Something rammed into the back of his skull, and the world had gone black.

Looking around, he saw that he was in a fairly large, well-appointed bedroom. Now that he'd located the source of his pain—and realized there wasn't much he could do about it—he pushed himself to an upright position so he could take a more thorough inventory of his surroundings. Besides the queen-size bed where he now sat, the room had a tall dresser and two bedside tables, and another low table sitting next to the armchair placed in a little alcove off to one side. Not too far from that alcove was a door; it stood open, so he could see into the bathroom beyond, cheery with yellow and blue Mexican tile.

Not precisely a prison cell, and he thought he could guess why. This room was clearly located in the house of the Santiagos' former *prima* and her consort. Joaquin Escobar might live here now, but it didn't look as if he had done anything to change the decor. And why should he? Evil the man might be, but changing the place over to look like the lair of a villain from a superhero film didn't make much sense.

Holding back a groan, Levi got up from the

bed and went across the room to a second door, this one closed. He laid a hand on the knob and attempted to turn it, but nothing happened. He supposed he shouldn't be too surprised; Escobar must have his null powers at full blast in order to make sure that his captive wouldn't have any opportunity to escape.

Despite the ache in his head, he knew he needed to perform another test, to be absolutely certain that his powers were as depleted here as they had been back in the apartment where he'd been captured. He stretched out a hand and tried to bring forth a floating ball of light, a will o' the wisp, something simple that required very little energy.

Nothing happened.

He hadn't expected much of anything to happen, but even so, he couldn't quite prevent himself from letting out a sigh of disappointment. The experiment appeared to confirm that Escobar's null powers were definitely strong enough to reach into this bedroom. How far did they extend outward from the dark warlock? Could he expand and contract them at will, depending on need? While Levi knew he must despise the man and all his acts, he still couldn't help but be curious about the limits of the dark warlock's powers, how they worked.

No doubt you will soon learn more than you

ever wished to, he thought, turning away from the door so he might go to the window. It, too, was locked, but the glass hadn't been covered up in any way, so he could see outside easily enough.

What he observed was a neighborhood of large, expensive homes, all sitting on fairly large lots, although closer together than many of the houses he'd seen in Cottonwood or Sedona. The sky overhead was blue, the sun shining brightly. Flowers bloomed in many of the yards. An expensive car of German make—Mercedes? BMW? he'd never paid much attention to that sort of thing—cruised slowly down the street before disappearing around a corner.

In all, it was the sort of view that most people would consider completely ordinary. Certainly no one would ever think that a dark warlock was holed up inside a house in a neighborhood such as this. While Escobar's powers were vast, Levi had a feeling that the man was doing everything he could to avoid rousing suspicion. He had to, surrounded by civilians as he was.

The door slowly opened, and Levi turned from the window, his heartbeat speeding up, adrenaline spiking in his blood. All those necessary flight-or fight reactions, completely useless to him here.

However, it wasn't Joaquin Escobar who entered, but a black-haired woman in her middle or late thirties, a tray of food in her hands. She looked familiar, and Levi guessed she must be the witch who'd accompanied Escobar to Arizona as part of the kidnapping crew. No real surprise; the warlock probably made sure to surround himself with those he trusted most.

The woman's dark eyes wouldn't quite meet Levi's. She crossed over to the chair in the alcove and set the tray she carried on the small table there. "We figured you would be hungry."

Now that some of the pain and shock had begun to recede, he realized he was. He'd been captured in the late afternoon, but the sun here was bright and high in the sky, which meant he must have been knocked out for all of the night before and most of this morning. A long time to go without food, and yet….

"Can I trust it?" he inquired, and the woman blinked at him. He supposed many might consider her attractive, with her big dark eyes and full mouth, but there was a certain hardness to her features that made her appear more intimidating than most of the women he'd met in Jerome.

However, she seemed surprised now, as though she hadn't expected him to be so forthright in his questioning. But then she shook her head and replied, "You think *he* is going to poison you, after all the trouble he went to get you?"

Levi supposed she had a point. "Possibly not, but it never hurts to be cautious."

The woman actually chuckled. "He wants you happy and healthy, Levi McAllister. After you've eaten and have recovered some of your strength, he'd like to talk to you."

"'He,'" Levi repeated. "I notice you don't say Escobar's name. Why not?"

That seemed to be the wrong question to ask, because the slight smile she'd been wearing abruptly disappeared. "Because it's not my place to do so."

"'Place'? But wasn't this your *prima*'s house? Isn't this your own clan's territory? I'm surprised you'd allow someone to tell you what to do here."

A frown touched her dark, arched brows, revealing a previously hidden line in the smooth brown skin between them. "You need to eat. He'll want to speak with you soon."

Before Levi could respond, she'd let herself back out and closed the door behind her. It seemed futile to test the lock again, but he did so anyway, just in case. Of course it didn't budge, and so he headed over to the table where she'd left the tray of food. On a bright yellow plate were a pair of tamales, with generous helpings of rice and black beans next to them.

Having lived in Arizona for the past year and a half, Levi was familiar enough with this sort of food. It certainly looked good, and smelled even better. His stomach growled.

Either you eat, or you don't, he told himself. *But being hungry and weak will most likely not serve you well in the long run. And, as your visitor just pointed out, why would Escobar poison you now? If he wanted you dead, he could have killed you back at the apartment.*

These arguments all seemed plausible enough. Levi picked up the fork with its heavy handle of twisted steel and scooped up some of the rice. It was very good, well-seasoned and cooked perfectly. The beans were likewise extremely tasty, rich and with an underlying spice, and the tamales tasted as though they'd been made by someone who'd been doing this for a very long time. One was filled with cheese and green chiles, the other with spicy shredded pork.

Well, at least they don't plan to starve you, Levi thought as he sat down in the armchair and placed the tray in his lap. Along with the food, a glass of water sat on the tray, and once he'd had a few more bites of tamale, he lifted the glass and took a long swallow. It was also good, sweet and cold, definitely not out of a tap.

However, if they were trying to offer him friendly hospitality in an effort to disarm him, Levi thought that Escobar and his Santiago minions were going to be sorely disappointed. He knew he could not let down his guard, not for a moment. Accepting the food was wise, because he needed to keep his strength up. That didn't mean he wouldn't do whatever he must to get himself away from here.

He very much feared what Joaquin Escobar might force him to do.

Still, that fear didn't prevent Levi from finishing all the food on his plate, or draining the glass of water. After he was done, he set the tray back down on the table, then got up from the chair where he sat and went into the bathroom. His reflection didn't do much to reassure him—he looked pale, with bruise-colored shadows under his eyes. Not so surprising, after being given a mild concussion and then shoved in the back of a van for a seven-hour drive to California, but Levi still would rather have been presented with a more reassuring reflection. Although he knew this body was human, he didn't like being presented with concrete proof of its inherent frailties.

He bent his head over the sink and splashed cold water on his face, then used the remaining water on the palms of his hands to smooth his hair back. That was a little better, although he knew that Joaquin Escobar would take one look at him and realize how taxing the journey here had been, would only see more weakness to exploit.

No, Levi knew he couldn't allow such

thoughts to enter his mind. He needed to appear strong, unruffled by his current situation. Perhaps Escobar would see through such subterfuge, but better that than present himself as someone who already knew he was beaten.

The view of the neighborhood outside had been somewhat reassuring, so Levi returned to the window and looked out again. Nothing much had changed, except that a woman in slim-fitting exercise pants and a tank top was jogging leisurely down the street. Her long, blonde-streaked ponytail bobbed up and down as she went, and a pair of white earbuds were barely visible in her ears. No doubt she had no idea that one of the houses on this affluent street was now occupied by a dark warlock, or that someone was being held captive within.

Although the woman didn't look much like her, Levi couldn't help thinking of Hayley then. Did she know he'd been taken by Joaquin Escobar, or would it seem to her and everyone else in the clan that he'd disappeared into thin air? Levi wasn't sure which alternative was worse, although surely it was better to know the truth, no matter how bad it might be. Hayley was strong; she was not someone to fall apart simply because she received some bad news.

Actually, the thing he feared the most was that she might take it into her head to attempt to rescue him. That would be a terrible idea. Levi in Escobar's hands was bad enough, but if Hayley— and her extremely rare power—should also become his captive?

He tried to push the thought aside. Unfortunately, the more he tried to ignore that terrible notion, the more it seemed to take on a life of its own. What if he himself was the trap this time? What if he was only being held captive so he might lure Hayley into a futile rescue attempt?

Levi tried to reassure himself that such a thing would never happen. Both Angela and Connor knew it was vitally important for Hayley to be kept as far away from Joaquin Escobar as possible. No, it seemed more likely that the *prima* and *primus* would mount their own rescue attempt. Together, they were very powerful.

But would they be powerful enough?

The door opened, and Levi immediately turned away from the window. At the door stood the same woman who had brought him his lunch, although she didn't seem terribly inclined to come inside and retrieve the serving tray and its accompanying dirty dishes. "He'll see you now," she said. "Come."

For a moment, Levi wondered what she would do if he refused. After all, with Joaquin Escobar's null powers voiding the magical gifts of everyone within its field of effect, the witch who stood at the door now wouldn't have much recourse if Levi attempted to overpower her physically.

But he disliked the idea of attacking a woman, even if she happened to be under Escobar's control. Besides, Levi didn't know for sure whether he would be able to escape the house before the dark warlock realized his prize had gotten away. If he tried and failed, the consequences could be dire.

And he did have to admit to a certain curiosity about what Escobar intended to say to him.

He went to the door and on into the hallway outside. There were several doors on either side of the corridor, all of them shut. More bedrooms? Probably. He'd already seen that he was being held on the second floor of the house, which presumably was where most of the bedrooms were located.

In between those doors were a series of paintings, all of them apparently original. Levi hadn't made much of a study of the art in this world— he'd had other, more practical subjects to take up his time—but he thought he recognized the styles of several of the pieces, even if he couldn't identify the artists. It seemed that Joaquin Escobar had also gotten an art gallery of sorts when he took this house for his own.

The witch—whose name Levi still didn't know

—led him down a curved staircase with a wrought-iron balustrade and shining oak handrail, down into a foyer with a gleaming tile floor and several flower arrangements sitting on occasional tables to either side. A large arched opening appeared to lead into the living room; it was here that the witch brought him, to a space with more rare art, and orchids on carved stands in the corners.

Standing in front of one of the tall windows that looked out onto the street was a man with his back to the center of the room. As soon as Levi entered, however, he turned around and fixed his visitor with a pair of piercing black eyes.

"Thank you, Esmeralda," the man said, and she inclined her head, then left without saying anything.

"Joaquin Escobar?" Levi asked, thinking he might as well get the preliminaries over with.

"Yes," the man replied. He was several inches shorter than Levi, and yet the difference in height didn't seem to matter much. Somehow he seemed to exude an aura of power, of being completely in control.

Well, of course he did, because he *was* in control here. Levi had always taken his powers, if not for granted, then as something as much a part of him as the color of his eyes. Now that they had been taken away, it was as if he'd had a limb amputated. He could function, but nothing felt quite right.

"But I am being a poor host," Escobar went on. "Please, sit down."

The words might have been framed as a request, but Levi knew it was better if he did not refuse. At any rate, getting into a power struggle this early in the conversation certainly would be a miscalculation. With any luck, the dark warlock might turn out to be like one of those villains Levi had seen in movies or in television shows, the ones who were so proud of their nefarious schemes that they inevitably ended up giving them away to anyone who would listen.

He went to one of the leather sofas and sat down. Escobar remained standing; another power ploy, Levi thought. Perhaps the other man did not like being reminded that he was not quite as tall as his captive?

"Are you my host?" he inquired. "Because I believe most would say you are much more my captor."

Escobar smiled. "You are quite forthright, aren't you, Levi McAllister?"

"I don't see any reason for subterfuge. We both know which sides we're on, don't we?"

The smile didn't waver, although Escobar moved away from the window to stand next to the mantel, above which hung another painting. Levi thought this one might be a Picasso—the style was quite distinctive—although he couldn't be sure. There was something vaguely theatrical about Escobar's movements, as if he wanted to stand next to the painting to show that he was also in control of all these priceless works of art, that he had claimed them just as he had claimed everything else in the Santiago clan he wanted.

"Are you so sure about that, Levi? After all, you were not born into your clan. You have a unique opportunity to choose that which is right for you, rather than being trapped by your blood into a family affiliation you might not want."

These words made Levi frown slightly. Never in all his dealings with the witches and warlocks of the various clans had he ever encountered anyone who expressed a dissatisfaction with the family that was theirs. They all seemed content enough, especially now that the lines between the various clans were being blurred, and the feud between the Wilcoxes and the McAllisters now several years dead and buried.

"I know I'm in the right place," he said, making sure his voice was clear, distinct. "Jerome is my home, and the McAllisters are my clan."

"'The McAllisters'!" Escobar repeated, not bothering to hide the contempt in his tone. "A piddly bunch with nothing much to recommend them. At least if Zoe Sandoval had seen fit to keep you, you would have ended up in a stronger clan."

Because Levi was secure in his love for Hayley —and hers for him—Joaquin Escobar's words evoked no sting. Zoe's rejection might have taken place a lifetime ago. Indeed, to Levi, it had, since his entire life encompassed only those scant eighteen months since he'd been brought to this plane to live.

Instead of taking offense, he tilted his head to one side and said, "Which clan are you running from, Mr. Escobar? It seems to me that you've taken over the Santiagos because the clan you should be with no longer wants you. Or am I misreading the situation?"

The dark warlock didn't even blink. "If you are trying to get me to reveal something of my past, Levi, you might as well stop there. I am here because of what was done to my son. Whatever I might have left behind is of no concern to you. I am only saying that you might want to consider the benefits of being part of the Santiago clan."

"Or…?"

"'Or' indicates that I might be threatening you. I am doing no such thing. I am only… making an offer."

One that I can't refuse? Levi thought, recalling a bit of movie pop culture he'd once overheard.

"An offer I think I must decline. I am happy where I am."

"Ah, yes." Escobar didn't blink. In fact, Levi was of the impression that the man didn't blink nearly as often as most people. A subtle show of strength? "With the lovely Hayley. The two of you can both come here, you know. Again, I think you might have a much more promising future than you would in Jerome."

"What kind of future is that? One where all witches and warlocks are under your control? It doesn't sound very promising to me."

The pleasant expression Joaquin Escobar had been wearing during this entire exchange didn't precisely alter, but something in his features shifted, made the faint smile he'd been wearing look more like the grimace of a shark. At the same time, Levi felt a strange pressure on his temples, almost a headache, but not exactly the same. Through his mind drifted a thought that felt alien, as though it had come from someplace outside his head.

You want to give in. You should. You can bring Hayley here to California, get a big house at the beach, leave that shabby shithole you're living in far behind....

Levi blinked. Never once had he ever thought of Jerome as a "shithole" or anything close to it. He loved the quirky little mountain town. Likewise, while he'd entertained thoughts from time to time of possibly seeing the ocean one day, never had he ever considered living there. How could he? Northern Arizona was his home now.

Then he realized that these thoughts weren't his. They had come from Joaquin Escobar. Levi had experienced something similar when he battled Escobar's son on the demons' plane, but Matías' attempted mental infiltration hadn't been quite so subtle. No wonder the dark warlock had been able to subjugate this entire clan—he promised all of them something they'd never thought they wanted, but now believed they couldn't live without.

In that moment, Levi could only pity them. None of this was their fault. But seeing Escobar's talent first hand only made Levi's resolve strengthen that much more. They must all prevail against him, no matter what the cost.

"Sorry, but I'm not much of one for the ocean," Levi said, making sure he smiled as well. "Or mind games. They might work on these poor people you've subjugated, but my brain isn't set up quite like theirs."

The dark warlock's deep-set eyes narrowed briefly. Then he lifted his shoulders. "Apparently not. Too bad for you."

And he raised his hand. An invisible fist smashed into the center of Levi's chest, knocking him to the ground. That same fist caught him on the temple as he tried to push himself to his feet. Balance lost, he slammed his temple against the coffee table on his way back down, sending shooting pains all through his head.

Mercifully, the world went black.

10

Lucinda Santiago

IT WAS PROBABLY WRONG TO GO OUT WITH Brandon and leave Hayley alone at the flat she'd been sharing with Levi. But Hayley insisted she was all right, and that she'd really rather be by herself right now. Brandon had also seemed dubious about leaving—despite his sometimes off-hand manner, he really did care about his sister—and in the end Hayley had to all but push the two of them down the stairs to get rid of them.

Now they were headed toward Sedona in Brandon's sleek restored Camaro, and Lucinda wasn't quite sure what to say. She and Brandon had planned this date when everything seemed about as calm and quiet as it could be, as though they'd all hoped that maybe Matías' death had driven his father into a brooding mourning which didn't allow room for anything else.

They should have known better.

Lucinda smoothed her skirt over her knees, feeling the faint roughness of the sequins stitched into the fabric against the palms of her hands. Angela had been nice enough to give her some of her clothes, the items she claimed she'd never worn all that much. It was true—this skirt didn't seem as if it had ever been worn, or the dark purple short-sleeved shirt that went with it. And Connor had told her to get whatever else she needed from the local shops in Jerome and Cottonwood, giving her one of those prepaid Visa cards with a thousand dollars loaded on it.

They'd all been so welcoming, these McAllisters. Lucinda wasn't sure whether she deserved all this largesse, but she had to admit that it felt good to be someplace where people were kind to her just because that was how they were, and not because they wanted something from her parents. And no more of those sideways, halfway pitying stares, the ones that made people look abruptly away if they guessed she'd noticed what they were doing.

She could almost have relaxed and enjoyed herself, forgotten what Matías had done to her, if it weren't for the knowledge that Joaquin Escobar had killed her parents, had taken over her clan by treachery.

"You okay over there?" Brandon asked, sending her a sidelong glance before he returned his attention to the road.

"As okay as I can be, I suppose." She shifted on the black leather seat, looked over at him. What a nice profile he had, forehead, nose, and chin all equally balanced. Once upon a time, she would have said that she preferred darker guys, but she had to admit there was something enticing about the cool blue-gray of Brandon's eyes, the way the sunlight caught whispers of gold within his light brown hair. "I just feel weird leaving Hayley there, no matter what she said."

"I know. But she's got Rachel next door, and the rest of the town to come running if she needs anything. This thing about Levi is awful, but...." He stopped himself there, as if he wasn't sure whether he should really continue.

"But what?" Lucinda asked, genuinely curious. Although Brandon had seemed mostly resigned to his sister's relationship with the man who was a little bit more than human, every once in a while his worry about the situation slipped out. She hated to even think it, but maybe he wasn't quite as upset about Levi being kidnapped as he wanted everyone else to believe.

"But it happened in Tucson, not here. It's

like...." Another pause while Brandon appeared to organize his thoughts. "It's like Escobar knew he couldn't pull that kind of crap here in Jerome, so he had to set his trap in de la Paz territory."

That made some sense. Lucinda had never heard of a *prima* bonded with a *primus* before. Actually, to tell the truth, she hadn't even known that *primuses* were a thing until she heard about the leader of the McAllister clan joining with the new head of the Wilcox family. Because the extent of their combined powers was still an unknown, it made sense that Joaquin Escobar would do his best to steer clear of them. "I thought the de la Pazes were pretty powerful."

"As a clan, sure," Brandon responded. The car's pace slowed; they were entering the edges of Sedona, which meant the speed limit had just dropped from fifty-five to forty-five. "I don't claim to be at the center of clan politics—"

"You?" Lucinda broke in with a grin. She might have been in Jerome for only a few weeks now, but it was impossible to ignore Brandon's need to fly low and avoid the radar. "And here I thought you were such a mover and shaker."

He shook his head, but she also noted that she'd made him smile. Just a quick flash of those white teeth, and an even briefer appearance of the lopsided dimple in one cheek, but it was enough.

She needed to see smiles like that after everything she'd been through.

"Oh, yeah, Mr. Go-getter, that's me," he said. "Anyway, I'm not exactly at the heart of things, but even I've gotten the impression that Luz isn't nearly as strong a *prima* as her mother Maya. During peacetime that might not be as big a deal, but…."

"But right now it could be a real problem." Lucinda went silent for a moment, watching the red rocks of Sedona appear, seeming to dwarf the buildings of the town built beneath them. She'd seen pictures, but they couldn't possibly replace the real thing, all those different shades in the formations, all the various shapes and the shadows they cast. It really was a spectacular place.

However, after the way demons had attacked Levi and Hayley at Red Rock Crossing, there wouldn't be any wandering around in state parks, far away from any help. Lucinda supposed you could argue it was safe now, since Levi had shut down the demons' portal to this world, but there was no way Connor and Angela would allow her to take that chance. No, Brandon was going to show her some of the local sights, and they'd drive up Oak Creek Canyon, but only to the Indian Gardens Market and not any further. The little café was enough of a tourist destination that there would be plenty of people around.

Safety in numbers....

"Do you think Joaquin will attack the de la Pazes?" she asked. Even inquiring about the dark warlock made her want to shiver, but she told herself she was safe here. Escobar was powerful, but he wasn't about to create an incident in front of a bunch of tourists. Besides, she doubted he could care less what happened to her now. It was Matías who'd made it his goal in life to torment her. His father had barely acknowledged her existence, once he realized she had no magical talents he could exploit.

"I have no idea." The traffic around them was getting thicker, and Brandon slowed down even further. Lucinda didn't mind, because their slow pace made it easier for her to look around. This part of town seemed a little shabby, with off-road rental places interspersed with New Age-y crystal stores and real estate offices and banks, but maybe it got nicer the farther in you went. He went on, "I'm not even going to try to guess what Joaquin Escobar might attempt next. I mean, it's pretty obvious that he took Levi because he wants to use his powers somehow, but I think he's going to find out that's harder than it seems."

She hoped so. She wanted Escobar's irresistible force to finally hit an immovable object. The bastard deserved no less. On the other hand, the last thing she wanted was for anything to happen to Levi. Hayley was crazy about him, and he seemed to be crazy about her. They deserved to have their happily-ever-after.

And I, she thought as Brandon looped them through a traffic circle, something she'd never seen before in her life, *I suppose I should just be happy that I'm here. Away from California, away from all those people who judged me. Matías is dead, and I might have actually found someone who doesn't care about my past.*

Problem was, she found it awfully hard to be happy with Levi in Joaquin Escobar's hands, with the uncertainty of what might happen next hanging over all of them.

They inched forward, crawling through traffic as bad as anything she'd seen in Southern California. Now they were in the part of Sedona called uptown, with shops and restaurants crowded together on both sides. The sidewalks were swarming with tourists.

"Is it always this busy?" Lucinda asked.

Brandon cast a quick glance out the window. "I guess so. I don't really come here very much. Super touristy."

That was obvious. Lucinda lifted her gaze from the shops up to the hills, to those fantastical formations of rosy-hued stone. No wonder people traveled here from all over the world to see the red rocks. Even so, she couldn't help but think that the crowds and the souvenir shops somewhat detracted from the natural beauty of the place.

But then they were away from uptown, following the narrow highway as it wound its way up through Oak Creek Canyon and echoed the twists and turns of Oak Creek itself. Trees began to crowd the roadside, freshly and brilliantly green.

"It's really beautiful," she said.

"It is," he agreed. "I think Connor used to come here a lot to paint, but I don't know if he still does that."

"I didn't know he was an artist."

Brandon shrugged. "I don't know how much time he has for it anymore. But I think some of the paintings in their house are his."

Lucinda had only visited the big Victorian that Angela and Connor shared a few times, but she recalled some of the gorgeous landscapes she'd seen in their living room. Plein air style, reminiscent of some of the California impressionists, such as Guy Rose. She knew that, because her father collected art and had several of Rose's paintings. Would he have ever purchased any of Connor's works?

Probably not. She doubted that Simón

Santiago would have ever wanted to admit that someone in a different clan had that kind of talent.

A pang went through her, and she pulled in a breath, glad that Brandon's attention was focused on the road so he couldn't see her face. Ever since Joaquin Escobar had invaded their house and murdered her parents, Lucinda had done what she could to avoid thinking about them, avoid letting herself feel pain over their deaths. If she let that pain in, she didn't know if she'd ever be free of it.

And the terrible thing about it was, mixed in with the pain was a healthy measure of guilt. She hated that she'd disappointed her father, that her talent wasn't a strong one…that she hadn't been strong enough to withstand Matías' mind-manipulations. Worse, she knew that deep down she'd always resented her mother, had hated the way she was forever wan and weak, deferring to her husband even though she was the *prima* and should have been the strong one. One could argue that Beatriz Santiago had been managing her own pain ever since the accident that confined her to a wheelchair and had little energy left for anything else, but Lucinda wasn't sure if she agreed with that particular point of view. After all, she'd seen people on TV participating in the Paralympics, performing incredible athletic feats even though they were amputees, or had lost the use of their limbs due to accident. Not everyone could be a Paralympian, true, but she found herself wondering whether her mother had possessed some kind of fatal flaw, something that had cracked within her the day she fell and which could never be repaired.

Lucinda knew she shouldn't be thinking such things. One didn't think ill of the dead—especially those who had expired in such horrible circumstances. It wasn't right.

Maybe if she and Brandon were closer, she could confess these things to him. Of course, then he might decide she was a horrible person and that he didn't want to have anything to do with her. God knows she'd thought the same thing about herself on more than one occasion.

The silence in the car was uncomfortable, she knew, but Lucinda wasn't sure what to say. She'd never been good at small talk, had always been quiet. Of course, her reticence could have had something to do with the way her father always seemed to dominate every situation he was in. It was easier to shrink into the background than try to compete, especially since she couldn't help wondering what people might be thinking about her, whether they were secretly finding fault because she would never be the next *prima*. It happened, of course, wasn't even that unusual for the heir apparent to be a niece or cousin, but all the same, Lucinda had always known that her father had taken the situation as a personal affront.

Right now she was damn glad she wasn't the *prima*-in-waiting. Otherwise, she would have suffered her cousin Marisol's fate, would be a mindless vessel in Joaquin Escobar's quest to replace the son he'd lost.

"We're here," Brandon said, somewhat unnecessarily, since he'd just pulled off the highway and into a gravel parking lot in front of a long, low wooden building.

Lucinda supposed he'd spoken up because the silence had become too uncomfortable even for him. "Oh, good," she responded. "I was starting to get hungry."

She really wasn't all that hungry, but she figured that was a safe reply, and would also help justify the drive out here. It was late for lunch, but they'd planned it that way, to hopefully avoid some of the crowds. Even so, the parking lot was almost full; Brandon had to squeeze his Camaro into the last spot at the far end of the lot, near the enclosure for the cafe's dumpster. Lucinda hoped no one would need to come out and empty the trash while they were here, because she'd hate to see someone accidentally bump into the vintage car and scratch its perfect black paint.

Brandon smiled, looking somewhat relieved. "They have great food here. And after we eat, we can go down and look at the creek."

Right—Oak Creek was just on the other side of the narrow two-lane highway. She could hear it now, chattering away as it flowed over its rocky bed. It would be nice to walk along its bank, watch the water flash in the sunlight. She certainly hadn't had much opportunity to do that sort of thing back in suburban Southern California, where fresh-flowing streams tended to be in short supply.

Lucinda followed Brandon into the cafe/market and went with him up to the counter; apparently you ordered your food cafeteria-style here. The menu wasn't big, but the brie and bacon sandwich sounded awesome, so she ordered that and a glass of rosé, hoping that the wine might help her to relax a little. Brandon asked for a Reuben and a local craft beer. She looked around as best she could, eyeing the assortment of local wine and beer for sale in the market section of the building, the homemade desserts and artisanal vinegars, the books on local cuisine. No wonder it was so crowded—not everyone was ordering food, but instead purchasing the components for their meals to take back to their cabins or campsites.

After the two of them were done with ordering their food, they headed out back, to a secluded little eating area surrounded by trees and flowers. Lucinda thought she might have liked to poke around inside a bit more, maybe get a few things to bring back with her to Jerome. However, she had to admit that it was beautiful out here on the patio, with the highway noise hushed to a low murmur and the call of birds all around them. Flowers bloomed in pots and beds, and there was even a little area off to one side where it looked as if the café grew some of its own herbs.

"Here's to getting away," Brandon said, raising his glass of beer.

Lucinda lifted her wine glass and clinked it against his. "To getting away."

Although their surroundings were soothing, and exactly what she would have said she needed, she still couldn't help feeling guilty for being here at all, for pretending as if everything was normal when it was basically the opposite. Never mind that Hayley had urged her to go out, or that, when it came right down to it, there wasn't a whole hell of a lot either Lucinda or Brandon could have done to help the situation with Levi. This still felt…wrong.

Brandon glanced around, as if taking the measure of the other people on the patio. There was a family at one of the larger tables off to one side, a couple of kids who looked around nine or ten squabbling over who would get to play with an iPad. Farther away was a man sitting by himself with a laptop, attention so focused on the screen that Lucinda wondered if he had any notion of the beauty surrounding him. Other than that, the patio was empty, the other diners apparently preferring to eat inside.

She knew exactly what Brandon was doing—checking to see how preoccupied the people who surrounded them were, trying to gauge what was safe to discuss and what wasn't. It was the sort of calculation that every witch or warlock had to perform when eating in public, since of course it was vitally important to make sure that no compromising information could be overheard.

"You really don't need to keep beating yourself up," Brandon said, his tone quiet. "It's okay to take a break every once in a while."

It was on the tip of her tongue to protest that she wasn't, but she knew it would be a lie. "You're right," she admitted. "I just can't seem to let go, though."

"I know what you mean. I hate feeling like I can't do anything. It's like—" He broke off there, clearly trying to work his way through the thought. "It's like, I have this talent for fixing things. I could probably put together a jet engine if you gave me the parts in a box. But this—this is something I can't fix. All I can do is stand by and hope other people can get it sorted out…and hope that Hayley doesn't get her heart broken."

For Brandon to come out and say something like that meant he really was deeply worried. A chill went through her as Lucinda wrapped her fingers around the stem of her wine glass, but she didn't take a sip. Not yet. "That's exactly it," she said quietly. "I feel like I should be doing something, too—to get justice for my parents, if nothing else. But instead I just have to wait, and hope."

He reached across the table and touched her free hand. Briefly, barely more than a brush of his fingertip over her knuckles, but still that touch awoke a warmth in her that she wasn't sure what to do with. Was that desire, or just a wash of reassurance? "I can't even imagine what you must have gone through," he said quietly.

She didn't need to imagine it, because she'd lived through it. However, the last thing she wanted right then was to revisit any of those terrible memories. This time, she did lift her glass and take a swallow, probably bigger than she should have. Unfortunately, one swallow of wine, no matter how large it might be, wasn't enough to erase what the Escobars had done to her, to her family.

"It's over," she said, her voice flat. "I mean, it's

over for me personally. You and Levi and Hayley came and saved me. I'm the lucky one—I got away. But my cousin Marisol is still trapped there, and Joaquin is using the rest of my family like his personal army...or servants, I guess. Whichever suits him best at any particular moment, probably."

"That's going to change." Brandon, who usually seemed sort of off-hand and casual, now looked grimly determined, his mouth set, brows drawn slightly together. The sun glinted in his blue-gray eyes, now flinty and hard. "I know that Angela and Connor are going to come up with some plan to fix things."

Lucinda wanted to believe what Brandon was saying. Unfortunately, she wasn't sure how much faith she could put in the *prima* and *primus*. Yes, they seemed to be pretty good at running their clans, but just because you were good with people didn't mean you also had the skills required to face off against a villain like Joaquin Escobar. Then again, they had managed to strip Matías' powers. Only temporarily, thanks to the dark magic raised by Escobar's daughter, but still, Lucinda had never heard of anyone else being able to do something like that. She wondered how Joaquin would feel if they did the same thing to him, reduced him to a mere civilian.

Yes, that would be sweet revenge.

"I hope so," she said, then stopped before she said anything more, because one of the girls who had been working behind the counter inside the café was now approaching them, a plate of food in each hand. She set down their sandwiches and asked,

"Do you need anything else?"

"We're fine," Brandon said. "I mean, I am. You okay, Lucinda?"

"Yes, great," she replied, an automatic response. It probably wouldn't be too long before she wanted another glass of wine, but that could wait.

The waitress smiled. "Okay, just let us know."

Then she disappeared back inside, leaving Brandon and Lucinda with their food. She had to admit that it did look and smell good, awakening a hunger she hadn't even been aware of until then.

They both went silent then as they started in on their sandwiches. Brandon seemed to realize that she wanted to be quiet for a while, because he didn't attempt to say anything else until he saw that she'd eaten almost half of hers.

"Did I tell you that the episode of *Dream Machines* they filmed at the shop will be airing next week?"

A blatant attempt to change the subject of their earlier conversation, but Lucinda didn't mind. She wanted a chance to talk about something normal, something that didn't involve her clan being taken over by a dark warlock apparently intent on world domination, or her brooding worry that poor Levi was going to suffer her parents' fate.

"No, you didn't," she said. "That's awesome. So you're going to be a TV star?"

A self-deprecating grin. "I doubt it. Mostly you'll see me in the background, because it was George, the shop owner, who ended up doing most of the talking. Still, it's great publicity, and should get us a lot of new business."

"Do you need that much more?" Lucinda inquired. "I mean, it seems like you're pretty busy most of the time." So busy, in fact, that she'd been surprised he'd taken the day off to be with her. Even with everything that had been going on, he'd still kept going into work each day—not staying as late as Hayley said he used to, but it wasn't as though he'd taken an indefinite leave of absence until this Escobar mess was cleaned up.

"Well, we've had a lot of work lately, but it can be feast or famine in this business. It never hurts to get a healthy waiting list going. Also, there's a sort of cachet to saying your car was restored by a shop that was on TV. People will wait for that kind of chance, instead of just moving on to the next place if the first one on their list is too busy."

She supposed that made sense. Since she'd

never worked a day in her life, she didn't know very much about the ins and outs of running a business. Well, some might say that looking after her invalid mother and keeping up with the demands of her autocratic father was a job in itself, but Lucinda wasn't so sure about that. She'd just done what she had to. Back in the day, she'd gotten a healthy allowance from her parents, money that allowed her to indulge her whims when it came to jewelry or shoes or books, even though a lot of the time she felt as though she hadn't done much to earn it.

That allowance had been cut off abruptly once her father discovered her affair with Matías, though. And even after Matías was banished from Santiago territory, Lucinda had never gotten her stipend back. Just another form of punishment, another way of showing who was really in charge in their household.

As if I ever was allowed to forget it, she thought then, her mouth twisting.

Across the table from her, Brandon frowned slightly, as though he'd guessed that her thoughts had taken a dark turn. However, since she didn't feel inclined to comment right then, he shrugged and went on, "George is also waiting to see how much extra demand we get. If there's enough, then he'll probably end up hiring a couple more people. It's not like I'm going to end up having to work until midnight all the time."

"Well, that's good," Lucinda replied. And she realized it was. She wanted Brandon around... wanted to spend those hours with him, even if all they were doing was sitting on his couch and binge-watching Netflix. Something completely, relentlessly normal.

He seemed to pick up something of her thoughts, because a slow, warm smile spread over his lips. That smile made her feel warm, too. Or maybe it was just the bright May sun shining down on them, but somehow she didn't think so.

They finished the rest of their sandwiches, then left a tip for the counter girl/waitress. After waiting for an opening in traffic, they darted across the highway and followed the path that led down to the water's edge.

The creek was much louder here, rushing over smooth, dark stones. Farther down the bank was a group that looked like the same family who'd been eating lunch on the patio earlier, but enough distance separated them from her and Brandon that Lucinda wasn't too worried about being overheard.

"I wasn't really expecting creeks in Arizona," she said as they paused at the water's edge. It was about five yards wide here, the water moving quickly. "What feeds it?"

"We actually have a lot of creeks and streams," Brandon told her. "And rivers, although in some spots the Verde River over near Cottonwood isn't much wider than this. Oak Creek gets fed by springs up in the mountains, and also by snow melt from the San Francisco Peaks in Flagstaff. It flows all year long, never dries up."

"Does it freeze?" Of course she knew that Flagstaff got a lot of snow, and Rachel had made an off-hand comment about it snowing in Jerome sometimes, too, although it didn't sound as if it stuck around for very long.

"I don't know. Maybe farther up the creek. I'm pretty sure it doesn't down in Sedona. They get snow in the winter, but it's not much. Definitely not cold enough for a creek to freeze over." He shrugged, turning so he faced northward, as if he could tell just by looking in that direction whether the water might freeze over when closer to its icy source.

For some reason, his reply reassured her. So much about this place still felt alien, even though she'd been living in Jerome for a few weeks now and had begun to get used to its rhythms. But at least it wasn't so alien that the rivers and creeks turned to ice in the winter. A little bit of snow— Lucinda thought she could handle that. It might even be fun.

Then she realized she was thinking ahead to

months and months from now. Anything could happen. What if Angela and Connor did manage to defeat Joaquin Escobar? Lucinda knew everyone would expect her to go home, to return to the clan that had been stolen from her.

Only….

She really didn't want that. She wanted to be here, in a place of red rocks and blue skies, of free-flowing creeks and majestic cottonwood trees. A place where you could take a breath all the way down to the bottom of your lungs because there wasn't any smog, weren't millions of cars choking the streets and freeways.

Most of all, she realized she wanted to be with the man who stood quietly a few paces away from her, his gaze now fixed on her, rather than the water rushing only a foot from where they stood.

She didn't know which of them took the first step toward one another. It probably didn't really matter. What mattered was that their fingers entwined, and they moved even closer, and then he was bending down to kiss her—tentatively, as if he wasn't entirely sure of how she would respond. They'd spent time together, had held hands a couple of times as they walked the streets of Jerome, but she'd kept telling herself she wasn't ready, that she needed time to recover from the shock of her parents' deaths, her renewed enslavement by Matías Escobar.

Well, it looked as if enough time had passed.

She opened her mouth to his, letting him know that she wanted this, that it was all right. His arms went around her, and he pulled her close, his body strong and lean against hers. He smelled good, something light and clean. Soap? Probably; Brandon didn't really strike her as an aftershave sort of guy.

This felt right. He was only the second person she'd ever kissed, and she couldn't really count Matías, not when everything about their supposed relationship had been a sham and a lie. But this— this was what it felt like to be held by someone who truly cared about you. Brandon felt steady and strong, everything Matías hadn't been.

In that moment, she understood how much she cared, how she'd tried so hard not to. Her heart had a mind of its own, though. Their world might be falling apart, but Lucinda somehow knew that Brandon would stand beside her and keep her safe.

He let go of her after a moment, but kept one hand in hers. Preventing her from fleeing? Maybe. Part of her did want to run away, didn't want to acknowledge what she was feeling now. But the other part—oh, it knew that it needed to stay here. Needed to look up into Brandon's eyes, that clear, forthright blue-gray, and let him see everything she'd been holding in her heart.

A smile touched his lips. "Yes," was all he said, but it was enough. She went into his arms again, felt his strength, and somehow knew it would be all right.

It had to be.

11

Angela

"WELL, HOW DID YOU THINK THEY WERE going to respond?" Connor asked, his tone all reasonableness. He probably knew he needed to stay calm, because right then I felt like punching a wall.

"I don't know!" I flared, twitching the living room draperies shut so I wouldn't have to see the retreating forms of the McAllister clan's three elders disappearing down the sidewalk. "I guess I thought they'd see reason."

After stepping over to a light switch and flicking it so the fixture overhead came to life, he said, "I'm pretty sure they think they are being reasonable."

"No, they're being hidebound and over-cautious."

He reached out a hand. For a second I hesitated, since I knew that he probably planned to sit me on the couch and get me calmed down. Right then, I didn't feel much like being calm.

However, I also knew that being this agitated probably wasn't good for the baby. So I let him take me by the hand and lead me over to the couch, then sat down as he seated himself next to me. Before he could speak, however, I said, "Desperate times call for desperate measures."

"I know that," he said, voice still calm. "And you know that. But you have to look at it from their perspective. Levi is a valuable part of this clan, but the elders have to balance his rescue against the cost of losing the two of us. What would happen if Escobar managed to beat us? The clan would be left almost undefended…and our children would be orphans."

A pang of guilt went through me. As much as I wanted to argue with Connor, I knew I really couldn't. The elders were strong, but they couldn't prevail against Joaquin Escobar's magic, not when he could nullify their gifts as soon as he got within twenty feet of them—or however close he had to be for his dubious power to operate effectively. Worse, although the clan basically already viewed Ian and Emily as the heirs apparent, we hadn't yet made any formal announcement as to who our *prima-* and *primus*-in-waiting would be. The twins were too young for their powers to even have begun to manifest, the little flickers I caught from Emily notwithstanding.

The McAllisters had been in much the same predicament when my mother died. Everyone guessed that I would be the *prima*-in-waiting, even though I was only a baby, but they didn't know for sure, not until I was ten years old and started talking to people who weren't there, who turned out to be ghosts. At least then they'd had Great-Aunt Ruby to hold the family together until it was clear who her heir would be. But if something happened to me, or to Connor…or both of us…then the McAllisters and Wilcoxes would be in a world of hurt. I had a sort of unspoken agreement with Margot that it would fall to her to lead if something terrible happened to me; she might have married a Wilcox and renounced her position as elder, but she was still the clan's most powerful witch after me. I could trust Margot to keep a cool head in a crisis.

Problem was, I knew deep down that even Margot's level head and her amazing abilities with illusions wouldn't be enough to keep this clan safe.

I twisted the turquoise ring I wore on my right hand, a nervous gesture that I knew Connor would immediately recognize for what it was.

Being him, though, he didn't attempt to stop my fidgeting, or try to say anything else on the subject. He'd made his argument, and so was waiting for me to respond.

Which I did, albeit with more questions. "And what happens if we let Escobar keep Levi? What if his powers end up being used against us? There are crappy outcomes on both sides, Connor."

"I know." He moved closer and I snuggled up against him, glad of the chance to lean my head on his shoulder. When I did that, it felt as if he was taking half my worry away from me. All right, not really, but I could pretend. "And it ultimately comes down to what you and I choose, and not what the elders say. All they can do is advise us."

"Better not let Boyd hear you say that," I remarked, grinning despite myself. My cousin Boyd did cherish his position as elder, and the clout it gave him. When I'd suggested to him a while back that maybe we should have the elders only serve for five years or so, and then switch out so no one found the duty too onerous, you would have thought I'd said I thought it would be a good idea to take out a full-page ad in the *New York Times* announcing that witches and magic were real. I doubted he could have been any more horrified.

"Oh, I know." With his free hand, Connor pushed his hair away from his face, tucking it back behind one ear. "I'm sure I'd get read the riot act. Even after all these years, I suspect that he still doesn't entirely trust me."

Probably not. Boyd had spent most of his life thinking that the only good Wilcox was a dead Wilcox, and so it had been quite an adjustment for him to accept Connor's place in my life. However, I didn't bother to point out the obvious, and instead returned to the matter at hand. "I guess it comes down to how much of a risk we're willing to take for Levi's sake."

"I think we both already know the answer to that."

Yes, we did. Levi had rescued Lucinda, had saved our town from demon attack, had made sure Hayley stayed out of Joaquin Escobar's clutches. We couldn't abandon him, no matter the risk. It simply wasn't the McAllister way.

No, it wasn't *my* way. Back in that tense meeting with the elders, Boyd had argued that I was a mother, and so I shouldn't be taking any chances. But I had taken a chance before, going into the spirit world to attempt to break the curse that had loomed over the Wilcox clan for more than a century, so I could ensure some kind of a future for the children I carried. I'd taken that risk because I knew otherwise I was dooming the twins to a life where the curse still reigned, where neither of them would have a happy future.

And that was why I knew I had to do the same thing now, and defy my clan's elders. It wasn't a curse I faced, but a dark warlock whose powers still hadn't been fully measured. However, I faced much the same outcome now—if we couldn't figure out a way to defeat Joaquin Escobar, then the twins and the child I carried and everyone in all the Arizona witch clans would be facing a very uncertain future. True, he'd only come here to kidnap Levi and had then retreated to his safe space in Southern California, but how long would it take before he decided that the territory he'd stolen wasn't enough, that he wanted to control the entire southwestern part of the country?

I couldn't take that risk. As much as it would have been nice to use my pregnancy as an excuse to hide myself away and let others do the fighting for me, I didn't have that luxury. On my own, I was pretty strong, thanks to the *prima* power that had passed to me when Great-Aunt Ruby died. Joined with Connor, though…then I was something the world hadn't yet seen.

"All right," I said. "We know what we need to do…but how do we do it?"

"I'm not sure yet." Connor pushed a lock of hair back over my shoulder, as if he knew I needed him to give me some kind of reassurance, even if it was something as simple as that brief touch.

"Without Levi, we'll have to revise our strategy, since we can't just pop in there and pop back out."

"Are you sure we can't?" I asked, suddenly sitting up straighter. My head was no longer pillowed on Connor's shoulder, but I didn't worry about that. I knew I needed to focus. "I mean, we'd never tried taking anyone's powers away, either, but we managed it with Matías and Jorge and Tomas."

"That's not quite the same thing," Connor replied. His eyes narrowed slightly, though, which told me he wasn't simply discounting my suggestion, but was thinking it over.

"I know it isn't, but the only reason we even thought of doling out that kind of punishment was because Marie told us about something similar that happened back before the witch clans even came here to America. We knew it was possible, and so we did it. We know being able to teleport in and out of a place is possible because we've seen Levi do it. So we need to try." I rubbed my hands on the thighs of my jeans, then got up from the couch. "Come on, Connor. The worst that'll happen is that we'll just stay here in the living room. We don't even have to tell anyone about the stupid thing we tried. Okay?"

A pause, and then he nodded and stood as well. "What should we do?"

"Well...." I hesitated as well. Obviously, it

wouldn't make much sense to simply teleport ourselves to some random place. And Levi had said it worked better if he was sending himself to someplace he knew, a location he could visualize in his mind's eye. "Let's go to the Flagstaff house. Since we're here, it's empty, and if something strange happens and we're not able to send ourselves back here to Jerome, we can always call Margot and Lucas to give us a ride home. Besides, it would give us a chance to stop in and see the twins."

Connor seemed to consider this suggestions, one hand rubbing at the stubble on his chin. Despite all the worries weighing on my mind, I couldn't help but notice how adorably scruffy he looked just then. "That makes sense. This place feels empty without them."

"I know, but—"

He held up a hand. "It's okay, Angela. They're safer with Lucas and Margot. I get it. But it still hurts to have them away from us."

How could I argue, when I woke up to that same feeling every day, of our house echoing and lonely because our children weren't here? But Jerome was much more of a target than Flagstaff, and until this situation was resolved, I wouldn't feel safe having the twins here. Without responding directly to his remark, I said, "We should probably hold hands. And…let's try to send ourselves to the kitchen of the Flagstaff house. Sound okay?"

"Sure." Connor reached out and took my hands in his, held them firmly. Once again I found comfort in the warmth and strength of his fingers, although there wasn't anything remotely comforting about what we planned to do next.

"Close your eyes," I said. "Imagine the kitchen. Imagine standing there with me."

"All right."

I shut my eyes and pictured the big kitchen of our second home, with its long, gleaming granite counters, the stainless appliances, the tall wine refrigerator...the big window over the sink that looked out onto a stand of pine, even the bird feeder we'd placed outside that window so we could watch the finches and the chickadees and the nuthatches quarrel over who got the choicest seeds.

A strange warmth filled my body, accompanied by a flare of light behind my closed eyelids. While I still could feel Connor's fingers pressing against mine, it was almost as if that was the only thing in the world, as if the very floor beneath my feet had somehow disappeared. The sensation lasted for less than a second, though, and in the next instant, I found myself standing on solid ground.

Cautiously, I opened my eyes. I was standing

in front of a large double stainless sink. Above that sink was a big picture window crowded with pine trees. And sitting on top of a shepherd's hook that held a box of bird seed—replenished every other day by a Wilcox cousin who was paid fifty dollars a week to make sure the birds didn't go hungry—was a plump little chickadee, its pert black and white head tilted at an angle as it appeared to be staring right back at me.

Dear Goddess, I thought, feeling a little limp in the knees. *We did it.*

Connor's fingers were still entwined with mine. He, too, had opened his eyes, was staring around at the kitchen of our Flagstaff house as if he'd never seen it before. "Holy shit," he murmured.

"I know," I said. "It worked."

He gently let go of me and went to the counter, ran a hand over the granite surface as if he wasn't quite sure that it was real. "I can't...." He stopped there, then shook his head. "This is crazy, Angela."

Was it, though? Connor and I had never done much to push the boundaries of the bond we shared, mostly because we really hadn't had much need to, except for dealing with Matías Escobar and his crew. Our quiet lives in Jerome didn't require vast exertions of our shared powers. Now, though....

As I'd said to Connor earlier, desperate times called for desperate measures. And I couldn't think of a situation more desperate than this one.

"And this was, what, about fifty-five miles?" I asked. "That's farther than Levi was able to travel."

"Yes." He was quiet for a moment, still looking around, almost as if he wasn't sure that the house wouldn't dissolve into mist around us. But there it was, solid and secure, spotlessly clean, since no one had been in here recently except our cleaning people. "He got close, with Hayley helping him. Still...."

"I guess we should see if we can get back as easily." I almost hated to use that word, because I felt as if I was jinxing the two of us before we even tried, but it was true—the whole thing had felt easy. Effortless. And pleasant. Just warmth, and golden light, and Connor's hands on mine. A blink, and we'd traveled miles and miles.

"Yes, we'd better. To the kitchen, or the living room?"

"Kitchen. I'm starting to get hungry."

A chuckle, and he came to me and took me by the hands once again. This time, we knew what to do—we both closed our eyes and imagined the kitchen of the house in Jerome, not as spacious as this one, but just as up to date, since I'd had the whole thing remodeled at around the same time we bought the home in Flagstaff.

There we were, with the creamy antique white-washed cabinets and the nickel-finished light fixture overhead, the garden with its rose-bushes and irises just visible through the window in the side door. I let out a breath. "Well, that answers that question."

"I guess it does."

My stomach rumbled. Maybe this kind of effort took a lot of extra calories. Then again, it was nearly one, and we hadn't eaten yet because of our midday meeting with the elders. I went to the refrigerator and got out the pizza box from Grapes, which still held a few slices. "Pizza?" I asked, opening the box toward Connor.

"Yes, thanks." He snagged a slice, and I got a piece for myself as well before returning the box to the fridge.

We both ate in silence for a moment. I think we each needed to process what we'd just done, that we now knew we could use the same teleportation talent that Levi possessed.

Which opened up a whole world of possibilities, not all of them pleasant. Now we really didn't have a reason for not going after Levi—we could be in and out before Joaquin Escobar even knew we were there.

Well, except for the part where we didn't know exactly in which room Levi was being kept. If he was even in the Santiago house at all. It was possible that Escobar might have moved him, but I kind of doubted that. Had our positions been reversed, I knew I would have wanted to keep my captive close.

"So…." Connor said after he went to retrieve a few glasses from the cupboard and get us some water. "How much do you want to test this?"

I cocked my head at him. "What do you mean?"

"Well, we can do the same thing that Levi did when he rescued Lucinda—drive within range, then teleport the rest of the way. But we don't really know how far we can go. Maybe we can go all the way on our own."

I knew what he was suggesting. Some part of me wanted to protest, just because the thought of being able to send ourselves such a huge distance seemed impossible. With magic, though, it seemed that all things might be possible for us…if we were willing to give it a try.

"Okay," I said slowly. "But where? It's not like we know Southern California very well."

"True," he replied. "There's always the beach, though. You know."

I did. I thought of the blue-gray house that backed right up to the sands in Newport Beach, the house where my mother had lived for a while with my father, Andre Begonie…formerly Wilcox. Of course, she hadn't known that he was a

Wilcox. And when she found out the truth, she left, taking her infant daughter.

The past that Connor and I had traveled to California to find. Now we knew the truth of my origins, but Newport could still prove useful. If we could send ourselves all the way there, then we absolutely could blink ourselves right into the house Joaquin Escobar had stolen from the Santiagos.

"It's a pretty public place," I said, knowing even as I spoke that the protest was a feeble one.

"We can come in by that little alley, the one that runs behind the house. Yeah, there's a chance someone might be driving by at exactly the wrong moment, but I'm willing to take that chance."

I knew the place. It was secluded, quiet, shielded from the beach and the people who were probably crowding it even now, although the true summer season wouldn't start for a few more weeks. "Okay," I said. "Let's give it a try."

He put down his water glass and came over to me, grasped my hands once again. "Ready?"

"Ready," I responded, although I really didn't know if I was ready. Flashing ourselves up to Flagstaff was one thing. But Newport Beach was five hundred miles away. Even if we managed to get ourselves there, what if we couldn't make it back? We'd be stuck in basically enemy territory, with no car, no luggage, no nothing.

But Connor had his wallet, which meant he had his bank card with him. That would be enough to get us airline tickets...or would it? Maybe I should go get my I.D. out of my purse, just in case.

However, I didn't have time to suggest that I should take that precaution, because Connor's fingers tightened on mine, and I immediately shut my eyes, visualizing the little alleyway with the expensive houses crowding in on both sides, the cool, damp air with its scent of salt, so different from anything I'd experienced growing up in Arizona.

Then from overhead came the sharp, keening cry of seagulls, and a wild salty breeze caught at my loose hair. I opened my eyes to hazy blue-gray skies, saw the house I recognized immediately, even though it had been almost five years since I was last here.

Connor was still holding on to me, but his eyes were open as well, taking in our vastly changed surroundings. When he spoke, his voice was full of wonder. "This is...unbelievable."

"Well, believe it, because it sure looks like we're in Newport Beach." I tugged at his hand. "We've come this far—let's go see the ocean."

He didn't protest, but let me lead him along a path that took us to the sand. We both paused to take off our shoes and socks, and then we walked toward the water, the sand cool and fine beneath our feet.

The beach was fairly crowded, but nothing like it would be in a week, when people would swarm here for Memorial Day weekend. Even though Connor and I weren't really dressed for beach-going—he had on jeans and a T-shirt, while I wore jeans as well, only with a peasant top—no one seemed to pay much attention to us. I supposed it wasn't that strange to take it in your head that you wanted a walk on the beach, even in street clothes.

This felt good, though. We went all the way to the water's edge, stopped there to let the waves come in and just barely kiss our toes before receding. Right then, I realized how much I'd needed some time with Connor, away from all our worries, from the weight of the clan's belief that we would keep them safe. We couldn't stay here for very long, but I was going to relish this moment while I could.

"Did it tire you out?"

I didn't bother to ask Connor what he meant. "No. It really didn't feel any different from—from our first trip." A woman about my age, holding her toddler's hand, passed by us as we spoke, which was why I figured I'd better be circumspect. She didn't do anything except flash us a quick smile as she went, but still....

"Same here. Which I suppose means our return trip shouldn't be too difficult."

"Hopefully not." I lifted my head into the breeze, looked out across the choppy, dark blue water. Far off in the distance, I saw a vague shadow on the horizon. A cloud, or an island? I wasn't sure, since I didn't really know all that much about Southern California's geography. "I suppose we need to find out."

"As much as I'd like to stay here on the beach with you, yeah." His voice lowered, and I had to move closer to make sure I didn't miss a word over the sound of the waves. "This is technically Santiago territory, although I didn't detect anyone of witch-kind the last time we were here. Still, it's probably better not to take too many chances."

Any more than the ones we'd already taken, of course. I nodded, and by unspoken agreement we turned away from the ocean and its misty horizon, started walking back toward the alley where we'd first materialized. The whole way, I kept looking from side to side, wondering if any of the people we passed or who we approached might be witches or warlocks, but I didn't get that little twinge that told me we were around others of our kind.

Maybe the Santiagos can't afford beachfront property, I thought, even though I knew their clan was an old and wealthy one, with far more resources than my own. Or maybe it was simply that in these tightly clustered beachside communities, where land was so precious and lots for houses tiny, they didn't think they could risk the loss of privacy. Or maybe all the Santiagos in this part of the world hung out in Corona del Mar rather than Newport.

Whatever the reason, Connor and I made it safely to the alley without encountering anyone who might challenge our presence there. We locked hands, and shut our eyes.

And there was the kitchen in Jerome again, just as we'd left it, with our water glasses sitting on the little table by the window and the sun shining in, clear and hard and bright, very different from the hazy day we'd left behind in Newport Beach.

"So…." Connor said, letting the word trail off, and I nodded.

"Now we know we can do it. We just have to decide when to go."

12

Angela

OUR LITTLE THOUSAND-MILE JAUNT HAD
made both Connor and me so hungry that slices
of cold leftover pizza just weren't going to cut it.
We headed down to the Haunted Hamburger and
took advantage of it being a little after the tradi-
tional lunch hour to snag some prime spots on the
patio, where we could look down on the entire
Verde Valley and feel the warm wind ruffle
our hair.

Luckily, because it was a weekday and nearly
two o'clock, we didn't have anyone sitting near us,
which meant we could talk freely without having
to worry about any sensitive information being
overheard. Jackie, one of the waitresses there,

came by and took our food and drink orders, and then headed back in to fetch our iced teas.

"I've been thinking about getting into the Santiago house," I said. "We have the photo Lucinda gave Caitlin, the one of Lucinda's old bedroom, but I'm not sure that's going to help us much. I suppose there's a possibility Levi is being held there, although I think it's much more likely that he's being kept in another room somewhere in the house."

"Probably," Connor agreed. He paused as Jackie returned with our drinks, offering her a smile and a thank-you as she set them down on the table in front of us. "I can see Escobar keeping Lucinda's room open because he thinks he's still going to get her back."

Yes, the dark warlock would be arrogant enough to believe that. Not because he had any personal interest in Lucinda—he'd clearly claimed Marisol for his own—but because it had to look bad for him to not have the former *prima's* only child firmly under his thumb.

I wonder how he explained that one away, I thought as I took a sip of my iced tea. *Assuming that anyone even asked. It's so hard to know how much control he has over the individual clan members' minds.*

But that was a question I'd have to put aside for now. "I thought maybe we could get Lucinda to describe some of the rooms in the house, give us detailed information on the furniture placement, that kind of thing. It should be enough to give us the destination we need."

"I suppose so. It's too bad none of us are mind readers. That would be the easiest way to be sure."

Connor's words made me pause as I was lifting my glass of iced tea to take another sip. Our adventures in teleporting had proved a very important point—if we imagined a power, visualized ourselves using it, then there didn't seem to be any magical gift that was out of our reach. We hadn't wanted to address the issue before this, because the power we'd summoned to destroy Matías Escobar's magic—and the magic of the Aguirre cousins—has frightened both Connor and me. We'd wanted to leave it alone. Now, though, with Joaquin Escobar forcing our hand, we didn't have much of a choice. "But we *are* mind readers, Connor. Just like we're teleporters."

He stared at me for a second, and then comprehension flared in those cloudy green eyes I loved so much. "Of course. Which means there's no reason why we can't get all the information we need from Lucinda."

"If she's willing," I said. "It can't be fun to have someone walking around in your brain."

"I don't think it would be like that," Connor said. He spoke slowly, as though formulating his thoughts right before uttering them. "At least, not the sort of thing we were talking about. We'd just ask her to visualize a room, and then we'd be able to see it, too. It would be more like... looking at a series of images on someone's phone."

That concept did sound infinitely better than trying to sift through all the memories and images stored in Lucinda's mind, some of which I would much rather not have to see. And it would make the process easier for her, since all we'd be requiring was a very particular data set.

"Okay," I said. "We'll talk to her after we eat. Hopefully, she'll understand that this isn't something we're doing lightly."

"It seems like she's gotten pretty close with Hayley," Connor replied. "I think she would do a lot to help rescue Levi."

True. I just had to hope that my hypothesis was correct, and that we'd be able to see into her mind as easily as we'd been able to send ourselves to Southern California.

In the meantime, though, there was a late lunch to be eaten. Jackie emerged from the restaurant with our burgers and set them down in front of us. "Anything else?"

"No," I said with a smile. "I think we're good."

"Enjoy."

She went back inside, and I picked up a

french fry from my plate. "Do you think any of them guess?"

Connor didn't have to ask what I meant—Jackie was a civilian, but she knew about us McAllisters. Even so, there was a lot that Jerome's civilian population didn't know anything about. "I don't know," he said. "Everyone's on edge, and so she and the rest of our civilians have to know something's up." He paused, fingers tapping against the edge of his plate. "Maybe we should have that town meeting after all. It's not really fair to keep so many people in the dark. If they're going to be caught in the middle of a magical war, then they should be given the chance to get out if they want to."

This was another topic we'd gone back and forth on with the elders. They didn't think it was a good idea to be too specific about what was going on with Joaquin Escobar, just because they worried that a mass exodus from Jerome might raise even more questions. On the other hand, letting the town's civilian population go along blithely, thinking that everything was okay, didn't sound like a very good option, either.

"Maybe," I allowed, then picked up my burger, although I didn't bite into it. "Do you think that many of them would leave?"

"I'm not sure. We're really careful about who we let live here, and so I want to say that they probably would stay, just because they feel a special bond to this place. But I can't really say for sure."

I took a bite of my burger, allowed myself to savor the taste of the meat and cheese, the fresh tomatoes and Thousand Island dressing. Nothing fancy, just an amazing cheeseburger. I could almost feel the nutrients flooding into my blood-stream, nourishing me and the child I carried. "I think we should let it go for now. If we can rescue Levi, then we'll have regained some ground, let Joaquin Escobar know that we're not people to be trifled with. Maybe he'll back off."

Connor lifted an eyebrow at me. "You really think that?"

More like I wished for it to happen. Right then, despite our success in our teleportation experiment, I was feeling more tired than anything else. If Escobar would leave us alone, I was willing to leave him alone. I would be the first to admit that such a sentiment wasn't exactly brave, but then, I wasn't Joan of Arc, just someone trying to guide her clan as best she could. Was it really my job to police the entire witch world? The other clans had to know something of what was going on in Southern California, even though we did tend to keep separate from one another. At the very least, I was fairly sure that the Ludlows must have some intel on the change in power in the

Santiago clan. Even if they decided to stay out of it, they were probably watching Joaquin Escobar with wary eyes, just in case he tried to mount any kind of an attack on them.

"I don't know," I said wearily. "Probably not. He hasn't exactly shown himself to be hands-off. But maybe once he knows that we can go in there and take back anyone he tries to steal from us, anyone he tries to hurt, he'll at least think twice before giving the McAllisters crap. A girl can hope, anyway."

"That would be something," Connor replied, although I noticed that his tone was noncommittal. I couldn't really blame him; he'd grown up with a driven and megalomaniacal older brother, someone who had no qualms about delving into old, forbidden magic if it suited his purposes.

It had taken death to stop Damon Wilcox. I had a feeling that Joaquin Escobar was no different.

"Anyway," I went on, after I'd consumed a few more bites of my burger. Damned if I was going to let the thing get cold while my husband and I tried to solve the world's problems. "If Lucinda can help us, then we need to act soon. The Goddess only knows what they're doing to Levi right now."

Connor's mouth tightened. Neither one of us wanted to think about that; we could reassure ourselves all we wanted that Escobar wouldn't do anything to hurt Levi, that he was far too valuable, but the problem was, you could do a lot to inflict physical pain without causing permanent damage. And that didn't even take into account the dark warlock's mind-control abilities.

"I know," Connor said. "Why don't you try texting Lucinda, make sure she's around?"

I didn't see why she wouldn't be, but I didn't argue, only fished my phone out of my purse and sent off a quick text to Lucinda, asking if Connor and I could see her sometime this afternoon. Just the week before, Hayley had taken her down to Cottonwood and gotten her a phone, so I knew she was connected, had made sure to enter her information on my contacts list.

The reply came back just a short time later. *Sure,* it said, *Brandon and I are on our way back from Sedona now. We should be in Jerome in about twenty minutes.*

No problem, I responded. *Connor and I are having a late lunch, so we'll meet you at Hayley's place when we're done.*

I set down my phone. "I didn't know Lucinda and Brandon were going to Sedona."

Now Connor looked almost amused. "I didn't know they had to file a flight plan." Then, apparently taking pity on me, he added, "Brandon told me about their little expedition. I didn't think it was that big a deal, so I didn't bother you with it."

Maybe it wasn't, but I still would have liked to have known that they were heading into neutral territory. After all, when Hayley and Levi ventured there, Joaquin Escobar had sent a pair of demons to attack them. Not that Brandon was of much use to Escobar, and going after Lucinda wasn't probably high on his list of priorities, either.

I didn't feel like arguing, though, and so I returned to my neglected burger. Good thing the sun was still shining down warmly on us, or the food would have started to get cold.

Connor tilted his head to one side and gave me a considering look. "I thought you were glad that they were spending time together."

"I was," I said. "I mean, I am. That's not it. Right now, I just feel like keeping everyone here in Jerome and putting bubble wrap around the whole damn place until this is over."

"It would be nice if it were that easy." He couldn't reach out and take my hand, since both of them were still wrapped around my burger, but he did pat my thigh under the table before going back to his own plate of food. "But they're both adults and probably thought it was safe enough, as long as they didn't go venturing out into the wilderness like Hayley and Levi did."

I wanted to argue that Red Rock Crossing wasn't exactly the wilderness, but I knew he was right. There were still very secluded spots in the state park, even as popular as it was. Whereas wandering around in Uptown Sedona, which was generally stampeded by tourists about 365 days a year, basically guaranteed your safety.

"You're right," I said. "And they're on their way back here, which is the important thing."

"Exactly."

Somehow knowing that Lucinda and Brandon would return before we were done with our meal lent a certain urgency to finishing the rest of the food on our plates. We were quiet after that, eating what remained of our burgers and fries. Connor didn't even wait for Jackie to come back out with the check, but instead put a couple of twenties down on the tabletop, knowing that would be sufficient to cover our bill and leave a very generous tip.

It did feel good to walk down the hill after that, to hold hands as we made our way to the building where Brandon's flat was located. All around us were visitors to our town, people who had no idea that the couple walking hand-in-hand past them were a witch and a warlock, or that this quaint little place had been under attack by demons only a few weeks earlier. I envied those tourists' ignorance, even as I halfway resented the way we had to hide our true natures from them. It was just the way things were, I knew, but even so, always pretending, always hiding, got to be tiring after a while.

We went up two flights of stairs to reach the third floor. I'd asked Lucinda to wait for us at Brandon's place because she was already with him, and also because we'd have a heck of a lot more privacy there than we would in my old room at Rachel's apartment. I loved Rachel—in a lot of ways, she was the mother I'd never had—but that didn't mean I wanted her involved in everything I did. For one thing, if she knew even half of what Connor and I were planning, she'd do everything in her power to stop us. Yes, she cared about Levi, but I was her niece, the girl she'd raised from an infant. I didn't think even my biological mother would have been as fiercely protective.

Brandon came to the door almost as soon as Connor knocked, which meant he must have been hovering there, waiting for us to arrive. "Come on in," he said.

Although he sounded casual enough, I couldn't help noticing the way he wouldn't quite look me in the eye. It wasn't very typical behavior, although I had to admit I didn't know him all that well. When my gaze moved from him to Lucinda, I noticed that she appeared a little diffident, too, as if she wasn't sure how she should react to Connor's and my presence.

When I came closer, I noticed the slightly swollen look to her mouth, and what appeared to be a faint reddish mark on the side of her neck. Well, that explained a few things. I didn't know what else the two of them had done on their trip to Sedona, but it sure looked as if they'd gotten in a fairly heavy necking session.

Again, none of my business, although I was happy for Lucinda—and happy for Brandon, too, since he'd been living as solitary an existence as it was possible to in Jerome...until Lucinda showed up, that is. Sometimes you just had to go with what the universe was telling you, even if the timing wasn't always perfect.

Now, though, it was telling me that we needed to rescue Levi. Soon.

Connor and I exchanged a glance, and then he nodded slightly, as if letting me know that I should go ahead and do the explaining. Although this had all sounded logical enough to me when the two of us were hashing it out, now I had to figure out the best way to tell Lucinda and Brandon that Connor and I had tapped into a whole new set of powers, and now we really needed to see into her mind so we could figure out where Levi was being held in the house that was once hers.

"Um," I began, as Brandon took a seat next to Lucinda on the couch. He didn't offer us a place to sit, although I thought that was more oversight than rudeness. Besides, right then I was so full of nervous energy, I didn't know whether I'd be able to sit down anyway. "Lucinda, we need your help. Connor and I think we can get into your parents' house, but unless we know exactly where Levi's being held, there's too much risk of appearing in the wrong place and alerting Joaquin Escobar that we're there."

For a second she didn't reply, only looked from one of us to the other, as if she wasn't entirely sure of what I was trying to say. Then comprehension seemed to dawn, and her dark eyes widened. "You mean you can get into the house the same way Levi did?"

"Yes," Connor replied, a small smile playing around his mouth. "A newfound skill. But it won't help if we don't have our destination securely fixed. That's where you come in."

"Right," I said. I inched closer to my husband, laced my fingers through his. Yes, I needed the reassurance—and also, we had to be touching for any of this to work, for our *prima* and *primus* powers to join and make this craziness possible. "Where do you think the most likely place is for Levi to be held captive?"

"The guest suite," she replied promptly. "The

house has five bedrooms—the master suite, my room, one bedroom that my father used as an office, and then two more. One of them is small, though, and has to share the upstairs bathroom with the office. The guest suite has its own bath, just like my bedroom did. I'm pretty sure that's where Escobar would have put Levi."

"We need you to visualize it," I told her, and her dark, arched eyebrows lifted.

"'Visualize it'?" she repeated, clearly baffled by the request. "How is that going to help?"

"Because we're going to look into your mind and capture the image. That way we'll know exactly where we need to go."

This explanation didn't seem to reassure her. Still with lifted brows, but an element of worry entering her eyes, she asked, "You're mind readers now?"

"Not exactly," Connor said. "That is, we haven't tried yet. But we do need to try, because otherwise we're going to have a hell of a time getting Levi out of that house."

Lucinda's mouth pursed. Brandon reached over and took her hand; a quiet gesture, but one I didn't miss. She didn't attempt to take it away, either, which meant there had obviously been some significant advances in their relationship. "I don't know—"

"Please, Lucinda," I said. "We just want to see

an image of the room. We won't—we won't be poking around at anything else."

"Imagine it," Connor put in. "Hold the image in your mind. Only that image, and nothing else."

Silence. Her free hand plucked at the sequined cotton of her skirt—my skirt, really, or at least, one I'd given her. I had to admit it suited her dark, exotic beauty better than it did me. "All right," she said at last. Her eyes shut, her dark lashes lush against her cheeks, so thick I wondered if they were even real.

Connor's fingers tightened on mine. I closed my eyes as well, wondering just how the hell I was supposed to do this.

Then I felt a surge of power from my husband…my consort, and so much more. In the darkness behind my eyelids, a warm light took over, showing me a room I knew I had never seen before.

It was large, but not overly decorated, with a queen-size bed, two bedside tables, and a wing chair and matching table off in an alcove to one side. The furniture was all dark wood, simple and heavy, similar to the hacienda-style pieces I'd seen in high-end stores in Sedona. Filmy curtains moved at the window, which looked out on a residential street lined with big two-story houses in a variety of styles—Spanish, Tudor, American Colonial. Through an open door opposite the alcove I caught a glimpse of what had to be the bathroom, cheerful with hand-painted Mexican tile in shades of blue and yellow. A flat-weave rug in blue and yellow and beige covered the wood floor, and a wrought-iron chandelier hung from the ceiling.

All this I caught in one brief glimpse, but it was enough to sear the room's details into my brain, enough so I knew I would never forget it, knew I would always be able to close my eyes and immediately take myself there. Connor squeezed my fingers briefly and I blinked, returning to this plain and small living room here in Jerome.

"Did you see it?" he asked.

I nodded. "Clear as day. You?"

"The same."

Lucinda was staring at us, her left hand still tightly held in Brandon's right. "You really did? You saw the room?"

"You didn't feel us?" I hadn't felt as if we were being intrusive, but then, we'd hardly known what we were doing.

"No. Except—suddenly I was warm, just for a second, so quickly, I hardly noticed it. But maybe that was your minds touching mine."

I thought that was probably a good guess, since I'd noticed the same sensation of warmth whenever Connor and I joined our powers. However, I was glad to know that the experience hadn't been a negative one for Lucinda. I hoped we wouldn't need to do this again, but you never knew.

"Probably," I said. "But we saw it all—the tile in the bathroom, the curtains at the window. We can get there."

Brandon shot me a quizzical glance. "*All* the way there? Even Levi couldn't manage that."

"I know," Connor said, the small quirk at one side of his mouth seeming to indicate that he was still a little surprised by the whole situation. "But we've figured it out. We just got back from a short hop to Newport Beach. That was why we went for a late lunch at the Haunted Hamburger afterward. That kind of effort requires a lot of fuel, apparently."

The two of them were staring at us like we'd just sprouted horns. Considering our newfound powers, I supposed we could sprout horns if we wanted to, although what would be the point?

"Anyway," I went on, "now that we know where to go, we can drop in there and grab Levi and go. We know it will work, because Levi was able to rescue you without any trouble, which means that Escobar's null effect doesn't seem to reach the second floor of the house."

"That's not exactly the case," Lucinda said. "I mean, he can shrink and expand the area of effect...up to a point. And yes, if he pushes it too far, then it starts to get weaker. It's still strong enough to fill the whole house, though. The only reason Escobar wasn't using it when Levi came to rescue me was that he knew I was no threat, that I was back under Matías' control. There's a good chance he'll be using it to keep Levi subdued, though."

Well, that little piece of information definitely threw a monkey wrench in things. Then again, Connor and I had already proved we were capable of feats even Levi couldn't manage. Which meant...what? That Joaquin Escobar's null powers wouldn't be strong enough to overcome our combined *primus* and *prima* gifts?

Maybe. That was an awfully big maybe, though.

From the way Connor's jaw hardened, it seemed he was still willing to give it a try...and his next words only proved me right. "Even Escobar must have his limits. Keeping Levi's powers in check isn't exactly like going up against your ordinary witch or warlock. It's got to be tiring. And when you add Angela and me into the mix—"

"The whole thing will collapse," Brandon said, then added, "Maybe."

Well, "maybe" was still better than a definite no. "It's also possible that Escobar's null field will prevent us from even appearing in the house at all.

If that happens, then we'll know we have to try something else."

Connor seemed to agree with this notion, because he said, "I hadn't even thought of it that way, but you're right. What would happen, though—would we get stopped short of our actual destination, or would we not even be able to teleport at all?"

"I have no idea," I replied. "We're in completely uncharted territory here. My intuition tells me that we'd be able to teleport, only we would get stopped outside in the front yard or whatever, wherever the null field ends."

"That sounds awfully dangerous," Lucinda said. Whatever afterglow she might have had from her afternoon spent with Brandon, it appeared to be gone now. Her face was strained, her big dark eyes haunted. "What happens if you can't course-correct in time?"

"That won't happen," I told her, hoping I sounded a lot more confident than I felt. "It literally takes Connor and me the blink of an eye to travel in this way. If we did come up against the null field and got dropped in the yard somewhere, we'd immediately send ourselves back home. Escobar's powerful, but I really don't think he'd be able to react quickly enough to do anything about it."

This response appeared to mollify her a bit, since she didn't reply. However, from the way her mouth seemed to tighten for a second or two, I could tell she still wasn't entirely convinced.

My phone rang from within the pocket of my jeans, where I'd hurriedly stuffed it before I left the house. Luz's number was on the display. I made a somewhat apologetic gesture toward Lucinda and Connor and Brandon, indicating that I needed to take the call.

"Hi, Luz," I said, after I'd dragged the phone from my jeans pocket. "What's up?"

Her voice, usually so calm and cool, practically quivered with excitement. "I think I've found a way for all three of us to meld our powers."

13

Levi

THIS TIME WHEN HE AWAKENED FROM HIS faint, or whatever it had been, Levi realized he wasn't alone. Once again, he was lying on the bed in the comfortable room that was now his prison, but now the wing chair from the alcove had been pulled up next to him, and a young woman sat there, watching him with a quizzical air, as if she wasn't quite sure what to make of what she was seeing.

Holding back a groan, he forced himself to a sitting position. His head throbbed, and the edges of his vision seemed fuzzy. That had been quite the blow. The thing was, he hadn't even seen Joaquin Escobar hit him. Perhaps he hadn't...not physically, anyway. Levi recalled that Matías had done much the same thing on the demons' plane, and was slightly annoyed with himself for falling prey to the same ploy.

But he needed to push that question aside for now. He knew he had better focus on the young woman sitting in the wing chair. Even as he moved, she'd remained quite still, regarding him rather like someone might watch a wild beast in an enclosure at the zoo. While his powers had been taken away, thanks to Escobar's null gifts, he was still able to sense that she was of witch-kind. However, she did not appear to be a Santiago, was nearly as fair as the McAllisters, with her pale fawn-brown hair and big blue eyes. Probably a few years younger than Hayley, although Levi knew he wasn't always accurate when it came to calculating human ages.

"So you're the famous Levi," the young woman said, her head tilting to one side. A long lock of hair slid over her shoulder, partially obscuring the embroidered white blouse she wore. At her throat dangled a silver pentacle studded with blue and purple gemstones.

He was a little surprised by the symbol; most of the witches and warlocks he knew among the McAllisters were more circumspect about advertising their pagan leanings. "And you are?" he asked politely. Since she was here in his room, he assumed she must be present thanks to Joaquin

Escobar's participation, but that didn't mean he had to be rude.

"I'm Brooklyn Ludlow," the young woman—barely more than a girl, really—replied.

Ludlow. Levi knew they were the other California witch clan, with the family centered around the Bay Area, although they'd spread out to occupy most of the northern half of the state. He did his best to keep his expression noncommittal, but he couldn't help but be surprised…and concerned. If this Brooklyn really was a Ludlow, then that meant some cooperation must exist between her clan and Joaquin Escobar.

That couldn't be a good thing.

"And may I ask what you're doing in my room, Brooklyn?"

She smiled. Her teeth were pretty and white, her rosebud of a mouth brushed with pink gloss. "Oh, Joaquin said I could wait here until you woke up."

On a first-name basis? That also wasn't a good sign. "You're acquainted with Mr. Escobar?"

"Well, it's not like we're BFFs or anything," Brooklyn said. "My parents know him, though. He introduced himself after he took over the Santiagos."

"And your clan is all right with that?" The girl spoke so casually, Levi was having a hard time reconciling her comments with all the villainous acts he knew Joaquin Escobar had committed.

She shrugged. "It's not our place to comment on what happens in other clans. I mean, yeah, Joaquin seems a little old to be the new *prima*'s consort, but that's not our business, you know? Anyway, when Joaquin reached out to my mother—"

Levi's head was spinning, and he didn't think it was only because of the blow he had suffered. Something seemed very off about this conversation. "And your mother is…?"

"The *prima* of the Ludlows. Carolyn Ludlow."

"Ah." Levi didn't want to interrupt any further, because he could tell from the way Brooklyn's brows had begun to pull together that she hadn't appreciated being stopped in the middle of her narrative. Still, his mind was racing. This girl's mother was the *prima* of the northern California witch clan. Was Brooklyn the *prima*-in-waiting? She hadn't yet said so, but possibly she was holding back that information for a time when she could deliver it with the most impact.

A sigh, followed by, "Anyway, when Joaquin contacted my mother, he just wanted to let her know that he was the consort of the Santiagos' new *prima*, and that because Marisol was still mourning her parents, he was going to be running things for a while. It seemed natural enough to us."

"Did he tell you how the *prima* and her consort passed away?"

"I guess it was a car accident?" Brooklyn shrugged, as if she considered that minor detail inconsequential at best. Then she frowned slightly. "Although it does seem as if you guys have a lot of car accidents down here. Joaquin said the same thing happened to you."

"I was in a car accident?"

"You don't remember?" A tilt of the head as she gave him a considering look. "Joaquin said you might have a mild concussion, but that doesn't usually make you lose your memory, does it?"

Right then Levi felt as if he was in a world where everything had suddenly been turned upside down. Clearly, Escobar had not been at all forthright with this young woman, or her family. That particular insight didn't precisely make Levi feel any better, although he supposed it was somewhat better to be a dupe rather than a willing accomplice. "I'm not sure," he said carefully. "But perhaps you could explain what you're doing here."

"Oh." For the first time, Brooklyn appeared almost uncomfortable. Her gaze slid away from his, and she seemed preoccupied with playing with the silver bangle bracelets she wore on her right arm. "Well, I'm the *prima*-in-waiting of the Ludlows."

He'd guessed as much, but it was good to hear her confirm that fact. "I see."

A low chuckle emerged from those pink-glossed lips. "I have a feeling you don't. See, I'm twenty-one. My birthday's in two months. You know what that means, right?"

Unfortunately, he did. It meant that Brooklyn was searching for her consort, just as Zoe had been when she'd been driven to summon him here, certain that she'd never find her ideal man, so she'd have to create him. True, Brooklyn still had some time, wasn't looking at a deadline only a week or two away. But....

"Should I assume that you haven't found your consort yet?"

"Bingo." She gave him a humorless smile, an expression strangely at odds with her "girl at the mall" appearance. "So far I haven't had much luck —and it wasn't for lack of trying."

"It can be difficult," Levi said carefully. "But you mustn't give up hope. I know someone who was in your very same situation, and she found her perfect soul mate when she was least expecting to."

"That's what everyone's been trying to tell me. Easy for them to say, when they're not the ones having to kiss a bunch of distant cousins you wouldn't even want to be seen in public with, let alone married to."

About all Levi could do was make a sympathetic noise. He very much doubted that Joaquin had sent Brooklyn in here merely to keep him company. But surely the dark warlock couldn't think that his captive would turn out to be the Ludlow *prima*-in-waiting's consort? The odds against such a thing were astronomical.

Not that it mattered. His heart was already given to Hayley. Even if, by some bizarre chance, he was able to have anything close to a consort bond with Brooklyn, Levi knew he would never follow through. He loved someone else. Simple as that.

"But then Joaquin told us about you. How you'd been summoned here from another world, how you really didn't owe allegiance to any particular clan."

"That is not true," Levi protested. "I am a part of the McAllisters now. They are my clan, just as much as if I had been born to them."

Brooklyn's blue eyes narrowed slightly. They weren't Hayley's clear turquoise, but more blue-gray, shifting, mercurial. Objectively, Levi could say the Ludlow *prima*-in-waiting was a lovely young woman, with her heart-shaped face and full little mouth, but she wasn't Hayley. "You can say that, but it's not the same. You don't have their blood, and you know how important that is in witch clans. It's just chance that you ended up with the McAllisters anyway. You could just as easily have come to be part of the Ludlow clan."

That wasn't precisely true, for of course he'd been brought to this world in Arizona, and so it was only natural that he would go to live with an Arizona witch family. The Ludlows had nothing to do with any of it. He could see what Brooklyn was doing, though. She was trying to make his connection to the McAllisters seem as tenuous as possible.

"But that's not what happened," he said. "At any rate, I don't see what this has to do with you."

"Well, it's simple enough," she replied. "I'm not having any luck finding a consort, and though it's always better to be bonded with a true soul mate, you don't *have* to be. I mean, because you're so powerful, it would be almost as though I had a bonded consort, if I were with you. That's what I want, Levi. I want you to be my consort."

The whole thing was so absurd, he wanted to laugh aloud. However, he knew he would probably pay the price for such misplaced humor. Trying to remain calm—and answer her respectfully, so as not to anger her—he said, "Joaquin Escobar suggested this?"

"Yes," Brooklyn said. "He said we could work

out an arrangement that would be beneficial to all of us."

"I see." Levi hesitated, knowing that the last thing he wanted to do was upset her, but also realizing that he needed to tell her the truth. "And did Mr. Escobar inform you that I was already involved with someone else, was living with her?"

That reply only elicited a lift of Brooklyn's shoulders. "Are you married to her?"

"Well, no, but—"

"Then it doesn't really matter. Joaquin did tell me that you had someone, but you'd only been together for a few weeks. That's not much of a roadblock, as far as I'm concerned." She gave him an arch look and toyed with the pentacle at her throat. "What, don't you think I'm pretty?"

Levi cleared his throat. "You are a lovely young woman, Brooklyn." *And I think you're already very aware of that fact.* "That is not what's at issue here. I am settled in another clan, and in love with a young woman from that clan. Nothing you say or do is going to change any of that."

To his surprise, she didn't frown, or appear angry. No, instead a small smile played on her glossy pink lips, as if she'd been expecting this sort of response. "I kind of thought you'd say something like that. To be honest, I'm not super thrilled about having to get tied down with a consort at all, but you know…tradition, blah,

blah. And if I have to go through all that, then I want my consort to be the baddest-ass consort around. It seems like you fit the bill, Levi, so why not go with the flow?"

He clenched his fingers in the quilt that lay on top of the bed. "I'm not much of one for 'going with the flow.' And, as I told you, I'm with someone else."

"I don't care."

Right then, he thought it was a good thing that he didn't have much of a temper. Otherwise, he would have been sorely tempted to lose it, to lash out even though he knew in the end that doing so would certainly not help his cause, or allow him to escape. Even so, he thought perhaps Brooklyn needed to hear a few home truths about the man her family was dealing with. "And what was Joaquin Escobar's explanation for my presence here? Did he tell you that he kidnapped me? There was no car accident, either—I was unconscious because he struck me with his magic."

This time, she did laugh outright, as though these revelations were a source of amusement to her, rather than the consternation he'd expected. Then she reached over and laid a hand on his arm. As much as Levi wanted to pull away, he didn't, mostly because he didn't want to get into a tussle with her. "Of course I knew all that. I was just trying to play along, in case you didn't remember what had happened to you. Anyway, Joaquin wanted to be honest with us, said that you would never have come here willingly. But my parents were willing to overlook that little detail, because they wanted to make sure I got the consort I deserved. And as soon as I heard about you, all your powers, I knew I needed you to be mine."

He couldn't help it. This time, he did yank his arm from her grasp, and also pushed himself off the edge of the bed so he could stand upright. The room spun around him, just a little, but he made himself take a deep breath and do his best to focus on the young woman who stood on the other side of the bed, an angry little frown beginning to dig itself into her forehead. "And what does Escobar get out of all this?"

Crossing her arms, Brooklyn replied, "An alliance with the Ludlows. He makes me happy, makes my parents happy, and we unite the two California clans. Seems like it's necessary, what with all the trouble you Arizona witches and warlocks have been causing lately."

More lies that Escobar had fed her, no doubt. However, Levi doubted he would get very far if he tried to explain the truth of the situation, since it was clear she preferred to subscribe to the dark warlock's version of reality. "And what makes you think I will go along with any of this?"

An unpleasant smile. "Oh, it's simple enough,

Levi. You come with me and be my consort—and we'll leave your precious McAllisters alone. Otherwise…."

Her words trailed off there, but their meaning was obvious enough. Either he cooperated, or Escobar would retaliate against the McAllisters. Against Hayley, and everyone else he loved.

How on earth could he ever make that choice?

14

Angela

My fingers clamped down tightly on my phone, even as Connor gave me an expectant look. "What did you find, Luz?"

"Well, I had an idea to look through my cousin Consuelo's papers and notes. She was the clan's expert in dark magic, but also arcane magic, the sorts of spells that have fallen out of use over the years." A pause, and then Luz added, "She's the one Escobar's daughter murdered."

"I'm so sorry," I said, but it appeared that Luz didn't want my condolences, because she continued without missing a beat.

"Everything is still something of a mess, but a few of the cousins had started to organize her work as best they could, had at least begun to separate her books and notes into categories. Among all that I found an account from before our clan even settled here in Arizona, back when they were still living in Sonora, down in Mexico."

"Go on," I told her, going over to one of the armchairs that faced the couch where Brandon and Lucinda sat so I could take a seat. This sounded as if it might take a while.

"It seems that the *prima* of the de la Pazes was being hounded by a *brujo*—that's a warlock, but a dark one."

"You mean like Joaquin Escobar?" I asked dryly, and Luz gave a faint chuckle.

"Yes, this man sounded as if he was cut from the same cloth. Because he was calling up dark spirits and invoking the very blackest of spells, the *prima* was having a difficult time keeping her people safe. She reached out to the *prima* of a clan in a neighboring province, and asked if there was anything she knew of that might help. Well, it turns out that the other *prima* and her clan were also being tormented by this same *brujo,* so they decided the best thing for them to do was to join forces."

"And how did they manage to do that?"

Connor hadn't sat down, and instead was leaning up against the wall a few feet from me. His eyebrows were getting a definite workout, but it wasn't like I could interrupt my conversation with Luz to give him a blow-by-blow. That discussion would have to wait until after I was done with the call. Lucinda and Brandon also looked intrigued, but they seemed content to remain silent while I was talking.

"They reached deep into their souls and tapped into their *prima* powers, then brought them forth. Those powers were described as being visible, like a glowing halo that surrounded the two of them. And they made those powers join. When the *brujo* came against them, he was utterly destroyed."

"Destroyed how?" Not that this particular fate didn't sound like something Joaquin Escobar richly deserved, but I wanted a little more detail.

"According to the account I read, when he tried to use his dark powers to fight against their light, his own black spells rebounded on him, and he burned to dust where he stood."

That was something I'd like to see…especially if it was happening to Mr. Escobar. A fiery death would suit him, although even a painful demise via immolation wouldn't be enough to atone for all the human misery he'd caused. "Well, that seems promising," I said, trying not to sound too hopeful. After all, I didn't know anything about those two long-ago *primas*, how powerful they'd been. While all of the women who led their clans were by necessity the strongest and the most suited to that role, it still didn't mean they were all equal. I was fairly strong, but what made me really strong was my bond with Connor. On my own, I was pretty sure Luz's mother Maya could have easily beaten me.

Or Great-Aunt Ruby, come to think of it. That woman had been a powerhouse.

"I think it's more than 'promising,'" Luz told me. Her tone wasn't exactly waspish, but I could tell that she'd been expecting a bit more enthusiasm. "Also, that was only two *primas* working together. With you and Connor and me joined, I think we'd be able to defeat Joaquin Escobar, even as powerful as he is."

"You might be right. But I need to talk it over with him."

"Of course. I wouldn't delay too long, though. We still don't know what's happening to Levi."

No, we didn't. He might as well be on another planet for all the information we had. Right then I could've used another of Caitlin's visions, but unfortunately, those came as the universe willed, and not when I really needed them. "I'll get back to you within the hour," I promised.

"I'll be waiting for your call."

She ended the call then, and I pulled the phone away from my ear and looked over at Connor. "We need to talk."

"I kind of got that impression," he said, and

moved away from the wall where he'd been leaning.

"Sorry," I told Brandon and Lucinda. "This is *prima* and *primus* stuff. Connor and I need to get going."

"It's fine," Lucinda said. "I hope it works— whatever you come up with, that is."

"Me too," I replied.

We made our goodbyes, and then Connor and I headed back up the hill to our house. I supposed we could have just teleported ourselves from the landing, since no one was around to see what we were doing, but it felt good to walk, felt good to have the reassuring warmth of the sun surrounding us as we made our way along Jerome's steep streets. Once we were back inside the house, I said, "Luz thinks she has a way for us to fight Escobar."

"So I figured. What is it?"

I related the story she'd told me. Connor listened intently, a faint frown puckering his eyebrows. When I was done, he said, "And you really think that's going to work?"

"Luz seems to think so. It worked in the past."

He didn't reply right away, which made me think he was trying come up with a tactful way to tell me that second- or third-hand accounts of something that had to have happened a couple of hundred years ago might not be the most reliable things to be basing our strategy on. While I couldn't disagree with that opinion, I also knew we didn't have a lot of options. I certainly hadn't come up with anything better.

"We can do a test run," I said. "That is, let's go to Luz's house, see if we can even make this combining powers thing work. We don't need to attack anyone with it, but we have to at least see if the three of us can get our powers to mesh. Her story was about two *primas* working together, so I don't know what's going to happen when we add you to the mix."

"You make me sound like an ingredient," Connor remarked, but I could tell from the way a corner of his mouth twitched that he was only teasing me.

"We're all ingredients in a super-powerful mix," I replied. "We just have to make sure it's a mix that works."

"You're right. Go ahead and call Luz, let her know we'll be right down."

I honestly hadn't been expecting too much of an argument with him, but I was still relieved to know he was willing to get started right away. But then, what choice did we have? The clock was ticking for Levi.

After extracting my phone from my pocket, I pulled up my list of recent calls and pushed the phone icon next to Luz's number. Her phone barely rang once before she answered.

"Angela?"

"We want to try this. We'll come down to your place and do a test run, see if we really can get all our powers to combine."

"Oh, good," she said, the relief in her voice obvious. "I'll see you in a couple of hours, then."

"No," I replied with a grin, even though I knew she couldn't see it. "We'll be there in a minute."

"What—"

"I'll explain when we get there. Expect us in your living room."

I ended the call there, even as Connor shook his head. "You do like to mess with people, don't you?"

"I'm not 'messing,'" I protested. "I just figured it would be easier to explain once we were there."

"If you say so."

"Whatever."

We didn't bother with the bickering after that, however. Moving as one, we stepped toward each other, then reached out to join hands. Luckily, we'd spent enough time in Luz's living room that we knew it well enough, which made it an ideal destination. I'd barely closed my eyes before the warm glow surrounded us and I heard Luz's shocked exclamation.

"*¡Madre de díos!*"

Very rarely did I hear her speak any Spanish, so I knew we must have really startled her. I opened my eyes to see her standing next to the coffee table, a tray with a pitcher of iced tea and three glasses waiting on the table. I had the impression that if we'd arrived just a second or two earlier, she would have dropped the whole thing.

"I told you we'd be right over."

Connor gave me a reproving look, even as he summoned one of his most charming smiles and said, "We didn't mean to startle you, Luz. Angela and I have figured out a way to exploit a whole bunch of new magical talents, among them tele-portation."

"Like Levi," I said. "Well, except better, because we can go a lot farther than he could. We figured it would be better to travel here this way, since it would save us a few hours."

"I—I suppose you're right." She put one hand up to her forehead, although she tried to disguise the movement by pretending to brush at a nonex-istent stray strand of hair. Then she straightened, and nodded slightly. "But this is good. If you've already begun exploring how to expand your powers and strengthen them, then I'm sure we will be able to do this."

"I hope so," Connor said. He looked through

the double doors that opened into a wide hallway, but there wasn't anything much to see. "Are we alone?"

"Yes," she replied. "David's at work, and of course Alicia is down in Tucson at school." A slight frown creased her forehead. "What does it matter?"

"It probably doesn't," Connor said. "But just in case any of this backfires, it will probably help that no one else is around."

I hadn't even thought of that. Probably I should have, since we were all working with forces we still didn't entirely understand. If our powers got out of control somehow, of course it would be better for there not to be any innocent bystanders.

Luz didn't appear entirely reassured, but I noticed that she didn't try to argue with him. Instead, she stepped closer to the two of us. "Then I suppose we might as well give this a try."

"What do we have to do?" I asked.

"From what I read, it seems that we each need to visualize our power as a separate force, something we can call forth from within ourselves. I suppose in a way that's true, because I know I felt the *prima* power come to me when my mother passed, felt a different kind of energy than the talents I'd possessed before then. Was it the same for you, Angela?"

I nodded. "Yes. It felt almost…alive…for lack

of a better term." A quick glance up at Connor told me that he didn't much like this topic of conversation. Of course I knew why—he and I had both been instrumental in his brother's death. Not that we'd had a choice, since Damon had invoked the dark magic of the skinwalker, his soul lost and hungry, seeking more and more victims, but Connor and I had purposely avoided the subject since then. Why bring up old wounds?

However, I had to ask. "What about you, Connor?"

"Maybe not exactly the same," he replied, reluctance clear in his voice. "But yeah, I could feel it come to me. I didn't much like the feeling, but I've learned to work with it since then."

His response made me think there had to be something fundamentally different about *primus* energy, although I didn't know how to ask without making him even more uncomfortable. Anyway, I'd never felt anything hostile or strange about his talent during those times when we'd joined, so I had to assume it would be safe enough for Luz to also combine her powers with ours.

"Okay," I said, hoping I sounded confident and in command, and not worried that we were a bunch of kids playing with dynamite, "then I guess we all need to try summoning our energy now."

Luz nodded, then closed her eyes and pulled

in a breath. Still looking like he'd rather be almost anywhere else, Connor did the same. And it was time for me to breathe in as well, to reach within and ask the energy that had been part of me ever since my Great-Aunt Ruby's death to come forth and show itself.

It wasn't exactly that I couldn't feel it anymore. The power was there, ready for me to use it as necessary. However, when I opened my eyes, I saw it floating before me, a softly glowing orb of golden-white light. And there was Luz's as well, hers tinged more bluish than gold. Connor's orb was closer to my color, although I noticed flickers of red pulsing through it from time to time.

I had no idea what the color variations meant —if they meant anything at all. Possibly they were a reflection of our individual auras, although since I couldn't see people's auras, that didn't help much. A question to be left aside for a different day. We had more pressing matters to attend to.

"Good," Luz said, her voice a low murmur, as if she was worried that speaking too loudly would somehow make the orbs disappear. "Now we have to see if they will meld."

"Okay," I replied, also keeping my voice down. Since I wasn't sure how else to do it, I made myself think of the orb, of my precious *prima* power, and silently told it to move toward the others so they might become one.

It shifted slightly, then went toward Connor's orb. Not so strange, I supposed, since we'd already combined our energies on more than one occasion. The two orbs blended, growing larger and brighter as they did so. At the same time, I thought I could feel the touch of Connor's mind on mine, although I couldn't make out any individual thoughts. Just a sense of his presence, familiar and reassuring, even though the current situation was anything but.

Then Luz's orb came toward the one made up of Connor's and my energies, and was somehow swallowed by it. I could feel her as well, although not as distinct as my husband, just enough to sense something of her worry, her fear.

"That's good," I said, still speaking softly. "Now we need to see if we can do something with it."

"What about Alex's field of protection?" Luz asked. "That's something I can't manage on my own, but it would be helpful."

That sounded like a good idea. I cast a quick glance at Connor to see if he agreed with her suggestion, and he nodded.

"Then let's imagine it," I said. "Surrounding all of us, protecting everything within."

Which I did, thinking of that miraculous shimmering bubble Luz's son was able to cast, and how it would keep us all safe. She and Connor obviously did the same thing, because at once the field leapt into life all around us, slightly distorting our view of the room, but still clear enough that we could see everything—the dark leather couches, the Saltillo tile on the floor, the worn Persian rug.

This bubble seemed bigger than the ones Alex could cast, taking up nearly the entire space. I also got the impression that absolutely nothing could get through it, a thought that reassured me...until I realized none of us were sure we'd even be able to retain our powers around Joaquin Escobar's null field.

As soon as that notion popped into my head, the bubble disappeared, and immediately afterward, my little glowing orb basically popped back inside me. I pushed out a breath, then shook my head. "Sorry about that," I said. "I let my concentration slip."

"It's all right," Connor said. As he spoke, both his and Luz's orbs also retreated, disappearing within their bodies. "The important thing is that we were able to make it work."

Luz's dark eyes were wide. She put one hand to her chest, as though attempting to feel the power that had returned within her. "It was extraordinary. Even after reading the account I found, I still wasn't sure it was possible to join power in such a way. And to evoke a gift that none of us had before this—well, I think we have a very good chance to take on Joaquin Escobar. The only real question is how."

"I've been thinking about that," I said. Connor shot me an inquiring look, and I continued, "I don't think it's a good idea to go in magical guns blazing, so to speak. A frontal assault isn't necessarily going to take him out. What I was thinking was that we should hit him where it hurts—by taking away his powers."

"Good one, Angela," Connor said. Although he didn't move any closer to me, I could still sense the warmth of his approval from where I stood. "It makes sense. Once you remove Escobar's power, then Levi is free to jump in and help us out —and I have to think that any Santiagos around who were under his control would also come to our aid. Even if he tried to fight back physically, he'd be way outnumbered."

"And of course this is a thing you've done before." Luz nodded, eyes narrowing slightly as she seemed to think it through. "Because you know what it is to take someone's powers from them, there won't be any need to guess, to feel your way through it. You can act decisively."

"Well, that's the theory," I remarked, glad that they both seemed to be in agreement with my plan and didn't want to discuss throwing fire bolts or something. "I mean, based on what Lucinda told me, there's a very good chance that Escobar's null field will knock us all out."

"You don't know that for sure," Connor said. "This thing we just did, combining all our powers —that's something different. We've never faced off directly against him. There's just as good a chance that null energy can't overcome *prima* energy."

"It did with Beatriz Santiago," I pointed out. I hated to be a buzzkill, but I knew we needed to go into this with our eyes open.

"Whose powers were weak, who'd spent the greater part of twenty years in a wheelchair," Luz said. "I don't believe she had the ability to fight back like we do. And although Simón Santiago was a powerful warlock, he was not a *primus*. We all know that our energy is different from that of the other witches and warlocks in our clans. And believe me, I've also combed through Consuelo's papers to see if I could find anything about a null being able to overpower a *prima*. While I found accounts of those with null powers, there was not a single story about them trying to take over a clan, which one would think was something a null might do, if he or she wielded that much power. So I have a feeling that a null's talent isn't enough to neutralize a *prima*, or a *primus*."

A feeling. I knew I should be somewhat relieved that she'd found at least a little anecdotal evidence to suggest that Joaquin Escobar's talent wasn't enough to take us out. Still, I would have felt better if I'd been able to know for sure that he couldn't touch us.

In the end, though, this was about taking a leap of faith. We could stand here and talk about it all day, go back and forth on our strategies, but in the end we simply didn't know. So much of witch lore was never written down, was only passed down from generation to generation. Problem was, if a gift disappeared and wasn't seen in a clan for decades—or not at all—then all memory of it could be lost. I'd certainly never heard of a null, and neither had Connor. Probably the only reason that Luz had was that her clan had a better track record for writing these things down. The Wilcoxes had Marie, who functioned as their unofficial historian, and the McAllisters had my cousin Melanie—except that all Melanie really did was keep track of our various family connections on a database on her computer. She certainly didn't have any kind of a history written down. Everything I knew about the McAllisters had come to me from things my Aunt Rachel had said, or that the elders had told me.

If we managed to survive all this, we really needed to remedy that situation. Too much valuable information was being lost.

I looked over at Connor. He was rubbing his chin, which meant he was thinking. Good. When

I got too close to a problem, I tended to have a hard time picking my way through it. Connor tended to be more analytical. I valued that quality in him, because I thought I sadly lacked it sometimes.

"If there's no historical precedent, it means we probably have a good chance," he said at last. "Not a hundred-percent-guaranteed chance, but I think the odds are good. And, in the end, we have to make a decision. It's fine to get theoretical, but in the meantime, Levi's still Joaquin Escobar's prisoner. We're running out of time."

I'd thought basically the same thing, but it was good to hear Connor say it. "So…what's our plan?"

"We'll go to the room where Levi is being held. Best case, we grab him and go, and leave Joaquin Escobar for later."

"We shouldn't strike while we're there?" Luz asked. "I thought we were going to attempt to take away his powers."

"If the opportunity presents itself," I said. "There's a good chance that Escobar will be in an entirely different part of the house, and so not close enough for us to attack him. Remember, when Connor and I took away Matías' powers and the powers of the Aguirre cousins, we were standing in the same room. It took an enormous amount of energy, and I don't know whether even the three of us working together would be able to cast that spell at a distance. Chasing after Escobar when we have a clear shot at getting in, rescuing Levi, and getting out doesn't make much sense, especially if it turns out that Levi isn't alone and we have to confront one or more Santiagos at the same time."

"I suppose not," she responded, although I could tell she wasn't happy about the direction this was going.

I understood her disappointment—I would have been more than happy to make sure Escobar's powers were stripped from him, and that he was forced to face civilian authorities for the murders of Simón and Beatriz Santiago, not to mention the rape of Marisol Valdez—but we couldn't allow ourselves to pursue vengeance at the cost of saving Levi. Besides, if we could show Joaquin Escobar that we were able to teleport in and out of his house without batting the proverbial eyelash, then he'd know he really wasn't safe. With any luck, maybe he'd reevaluate his plans for world domination and crawl back into whatever hole he came out of.

"He'll get his," I said. "Believe me. But first things first."

She nodded. "You're right, of course. I just can't stop thinking about my cousin Miguel. He deserves some justice."

"He'll get it," Connor promised. "Just maybe not today. For now, though, we have to concentrate on where we're going, and what we're going to do when we get there. Angela and I know our destination, because Lucinda let us look into her mind to see it. If we all take hands, then I think our combined knowledge of the house should be enough to bring you along with us, Luz."

"I hope so," she said, smiling a little, although I could tell that smile was pretty shaky around the edges. Well, I couldn't give her too much grief for that. I knew exactly how she felt.

"The journey takes less than a second, even at that distance," Connor continued. "So we all need to be ready the second we leave this room. Best-case scenario, Levi's there, Escobar doesn't have enough time to react, and we get Levi and pop back here. One and done."

"That sounds very neat and clean," Luz remarked. "Unfortunately, my experience tells me that best-case scenarios rarely exist in the real world."

She definitely had that right. I said, "Then we go to Plan B. If Escobar is in the room, then we try to take his powers away. Luz, you'll mostly be providing extra strength for that spell, since you've never performed it. If we hit him fast and hit him hard, he won't have any time to react."

"Again, best-case scenario," Connor said. "Or

at least, that's the best outcome we can hope for if it turns out Escobar is there. If we have to fight him...." He let the words trail off, but from the way his lips pressed together, I could tell he wasn't too thrilled about having to face that particular possibility.

Neither was I. Yes, we'd faced down Connor's brother, who before Joaquin Escobar was the strongest warlock I'd ever encountered, but the situation wasn't remotely the same. At the very least, I'd never had to worry about Damon Wilcox having the ability to render my own powers useless.

But that was a remote possibility. There was no record of a null ever neutralizing a *prima*. Luz had said so. Which meant we had more than a fighting chance.

"Then there's the third possibility," Connor said. "That the room is empty when we get there. If that's the case, we'll have to decide whether it's worth the risk to start searching the house for Levi."

"Of course it's worth the risk," I retorted. "What would be the point of us all going there if we just turn around and come back here the second our plans don't pan out the way we thought?"

"The point would be giving us time to regroup, figure out what we're going to do next."

Luz shook her head. "I agree with Angela. There's no guarantee that Escobar won't be able to detect our presence, won't be able to figure out how we came to be in his house. We'd be giving up the element of surprise if we simply left. It's better for us to look for him, if it comes to that."

A sigh. Connor didn't look too thrilled at the idea, but since it was two to one, it seemed as if he was willing to give in on that point. "All right," he said. "But only if the house isn't overrun with other witches and warlocks. There's a limit to how much we're able to do. Just because Angela and I have managed to tap into some new powers doesn't mean we're suddenly invincible."

"I know," I said. "Believe me, I'm not eager to get into a brawl with a bunch of Santiagos. And there's also Marisol to keep in mind—from the way Lucinda talked, it sounded as if she's pretty out of it, but there's no guarantee she won't come to Escobar's defense. And she is a *prima,* which means her powers match ours."

"She would still be outnumbered three to one if she did try to attack us," Luz pointed out. "But I understand. We can't get over-confident."

"If Levi's not in his room and we go to look for him, and there are a bunch of Santiagos hanging around, we'll be out of there *tout suite,*" I said. "I'm not crazy. We'll just have to play it by ear, and be ready to bug out if we have to.

Connor, do you want to come back here, or to the Jerome house?"

"We might as well come here," he replied. "If we're successful and have Levi with us, it'll be simpler to drop Luz here at home and then continue to Jerome after that."

"Right." For a moment, I worried about whether Connor and I would be able to teleport both of them. It would be a strain, but I thought we should be able to manage it, especially with Luz's powers bolstering our own." I paused, and looked from Connor to Luz. For a change, she wasn't wearing one of her signature sheath dresses, but instead a pair of well-fitting slim jeans, flats, and a sleeveless blouse in the hot pink shade she seemed to favor. At least I wouldn't have to worry about her trying to face down Joaquin Escobar in a pair of kitten heels. "Are we ready?"

"Define 'ready,'" Connor said, but he smiled as he spoke, which meant he was just trying to tease me a little.

"Ready as we'll ever be," Luz added. "Let's do this."

I pulled in a breath, then reached out my hands. Connor took my right hand in his left, while I wrapped the fingers of my left hand in Luz's right. She took Connor's free hand, and the circle was closed.

Already I could feel the energy humming

between us, as though our *prima* and *primus* powers remembered when they had been joined a few minutes earlier, and wanted to do so again. Good. We needed them to cooperate.

Shutting my eyes, I visualized the room Lucinda had shown us, with the high arched windows and wooden floors, the small glimpse of the bathroom with its cheerful yellow and blue tile. A little shiver went through me as I realized we would soon be standing there. "Do you see it?" I murmured to Connor.

"Yes," he said.

"Then let's go."

15

Angela

THE WORLD SHIFTED BENEATH MY FEET. Once again that sensation of warmth enveloped me, only this time it was even stronger, because Luz's energy had mixed with Connor's and mine, giving us what felt like a sudden burst of adrenaline.

Or maybe that was simply my own nervous energy.

As soon as I sensed solid ground beneath me again, I opened my eyes. We stood in the room Lucinda had described to us, but it was definitely empty. A slight mussing of the quilt told me someone had once lain on the queen-size bed. Otherwise, though, there was no sign that anyone had ever been here.

Luz stepped forward and laid her hand on the quilt. "I can feel his magic here, although muted. I think Levi was in this room at one point, even if he's not here now."

Yes, Luz had always been good at detecting magic and those who wielded it, if not quite as gifted as her mother. I supposed I should be glad that she was able to pick up even this trace of Levi's presence. At least we knew we were in the right place.

"Is he still in the house?" Connor asked, his voice barely above a murmur.

She paused, one hand stretched out toward the door. "I think so. I can definitely feel three witches or warlocks in the house, and…." Her words trailed off there as she frowned.

Every muscle in my body seemed to tense. "What is it?"

"The fourth…I can't tell. There's something, but it's dark, indistinct. Possibly that is Joaquin Escobar, his null powers blocking me from being able to detect anything specific."

That made sense. At the same time, I had to let out a relieved little breath, even though I couldn't really allow myself to relax. The mere fact that we stood here now meant Escobar's null energy wasn't able to cancel out our *prima* powers. Otherwise, we would never have been able to teleport into the house.

At the same time, though, I was cursing that we hadn't thought to ask Lucinda about the rest of the place. I knew from Caitlin that the living room was quite formal, and apparently had real Picassos and other priceless works of art hanging there, but that level of detail wasn't enough to make for a safe destination when it came to tele-porting.

As I looked over at Connor, I could tell he was thinking much the same thing, since his brows were pulled together, and he was staring at the door that opened onto the hall as though a fire-breathing dragon waited on the other side. Then his shoulders lifted, and he said, "We'll have to do this the old-fashioned way. Still, there's no reason why we can't try to confuse them a little."

For a second, I wondered what in the world he was talking about. But then his dark hair light-ened, went to a mid-brown before transforming all the way to Levi's flaxen blond. At the same time, his hazel eyes shifted to clear blue, and his features altered subtly, becoming the face of the being who had lived among us for the past year and a half. Very little about his body had to change, because Connor and Levi were almost the same height, and the same kind of rangy, well-muscled build.

"Well, that is handy," Luz remarked. "I knew that was your talent, Connor, but this is the first time I've had a chance to observe it. Very convincing."

"And disconcerting," I added. "Luckily, he doesn't have to use it very much. But seeing another 'Levi' walk in might throw off Escobar—and whoever he has with him—long enough that we can grab the real Levi and get the hell out of there."

"Assuming he doesn't already know we're here," Connor said. "But then, if that were the case, you'd think he'd already be beating down the door. We'd better get going before he figures it out."

I nodded, and tried to ignore the rapid beating of my heart. It hadn't been too frightening standing in this room, because no one had attacked us, and we'd made it here safe and sound. But now we'd have to venture out in search of Levi—and probably Joaquin Escobar—and suddenly the danger we'd put ourselves in felt far too real. Still, we were here, and we couldn't back out now, no matter how much the thought of going downstairs and searching for Levi scared the living hell out of me.

Connor put his hand on the doorknob and turned it, then opened the door. Outside was a hallway with several doors that opened off it. A long, expensive-looking Persian runner covered the floor, and on the walls between the doors hung equally expensive-looking art.

No one was around, although I thought I could hear the faint murmur of voices drifting up the stairs. Definitely two men's voices, and another voice, female and fairly young-sounding.

Connor gestured for Luz and me to step into the hallway. He pointed toward the staircase, although really, there wasn't anywhere else we could have headed. At the same time, he made a movement that seemed to trace the shape of a big bubble, and I nodded. We'd been able to generate one of those protective fields back at Luz's house, and it made sense to do the same thing now.

Because Connor was already using some of his power to maintain Levi's image, I reached within myself to tap into my own energy and have it join with Luz's. I visualized the field of protection we'd cast, its faint shimmer, its unbelievable strength.

And there it was, surrounding Luz and Connor and me, a shield that should keep us safe from anything Joaquin Escobar could throw at us.

With that protection in place, we quietly inched down the stairs. One of them creaked, and I winced. However, I didn't hear any break in the conversation, which seemed to be coming from the living room. Maybe they were talking loudly enough that they wouldn't be able to detect something as minor as a creaking step.

As we made our way to the bottom of the staircase, the voices became louder. I recognized Levi's, and another man's, cold and clipped, with a definite accent. Not Mexican, though. But then, I knew that Joaquin Escobar came from El Salvador.

"…you need to see reason, Levi," Escobar was saying. "Your loyalty to the McAllisters—perhaps some would find it admirable. I merely think it short-sighted. You can accomplish much more, be a far greater force in the world, if you stay here with us, with Miss Ludlow."

Miss Ludlow? I shot a puzzled glance at Connor, who only responded by lifting his shoulders. But then, what else could he do? It wasn't as though we could stop and have a conversation on the bottom step. We had to continue now that we were set upon this course of action, even though every instinct was telling me to grab Connor and Luz by the hand and teleport right out of there.

"I tried to tell him that," came a young woman's voice, petulant, annoyed…and also very young. Not much more than a teenager, from what I could tell. "But he doesn't want to listen to me. That's why I thought we should all talk to him."

"Those people, they are in your past," Escobar said. "Forget them. Your place is here with us. You need to forget them, because if you don't—"

He let the words hang there, but the threat within them was obvious enough. If he went along with whatever it was that Joaquin Escobar —and this Ludlow girl, although I couldn't quite figure out how she fit into all this—wanted, then maybe the McAllisters would be left alone. If not....

A shiver went over me. The presence of a Ludlow witch seemed to indicate that the other California witch clan had thrown in its lot with the Santiagos. If that turned out to be the case, then we really would be in a world of hurt. They outnumbered the Arizona witch clans, and probably out-powered us, too.

Luz leaned forward and whispered in my ear, "We need to go in now, while they're talking."

I swallowed and sent Connor a questioning look. His jaw hardened, and then he nodded. It was strange to see expressions and movements I was used to in my husband echoed in Levi's features, but of course that was still Connor under there, no matter what he might look like on the surface.

Another step, and he was standing on the tiled floor of the foyer. It was an impressive-looking space, with its two-story ceiling and gilt-framed paintings and vases of live orchids set on pedestals around the room. However, I didn't have time for much more than a brief glimpse, because then

Connor strode forward, and I had to hurry to keep up with him, making sure that he stayed within the protective bubble I'd cast. Behind me, I heard Luz's soft footfalls and knew she was taking the same precaution.

And then we were passing through the arched doorway that led into the living room. I had a sudden quick impression of four people sitting in there—Levi in an armchair, his blue eyes lighting up in surprise as he saw us, a black-haired Hispanic man in his forties who must be Joaquin Escobar, a girl of around twenty or so, with perfectly curled, long light brown hair, and another young woman maybe a few years older, Hispanic, with something hazy and confused about her big dark eyes, a confusion that only seemed to grow as she looked from my disguised husband to Levi and back again.

As did the girl with the pretty brown hair. She frowned, then said, "What's going on? I thought *he* was Levi!" And she pointed at him where he sat in his chair.

Escobar began to stand up, but Connor didn't hesitate. "Levi!"

He catapulted himself out of the wing chair where he'd been sitting and ran toward us. I knew he must have seen the flicker of the bubble that encased our little group, must have known that was his only chance.

"Oh, I don't think so," Escobar said, raising a hand.

It was like getting doused with a bucket of ice cold water. I gasped, and realized that the bubble was gone, that somehow the dark warlock had managed to dispel it. And yet...I could still feel the power coiled within me, knew that he hadn't managed to touch the core of my *prima* energy. He had only destroyed the physical manifestation of that talent.

Smiling slightly, he raised his other hand. "Levi."

The poor man stopped dead in mid-stride. His jaw clenched, and I could see him struggling against the invisible force that kept him from moving any closer to us. However, he didn't seem able to budge.

Well, I'd already known that Joaquin Escobar played dirty. Time for me to do the same.

Without even stopping to think, I raised both my hands and flung a pair of fireballs in his direction. One flew over his head and hit the curtains that framed the window behind him. They promptly caught fire, causing the young woman with the bemused expression to cry out, "Oh, no!" and run toward them. What she intended to do, I wasn't sure, but the important thing was that I had distracted her.

The other fireball should have struck Escobar

right in the chest. At the last second, though, he threw up both his hands, as if creating his own protective barrier. The fireball impacted against his palms, but didn't seem to do any actual damage.

However, he'd had to transfer his concentration to saving himself, thus freeing Levi to continue on his mad dash toward us. He slipped between Connor and me, gasping, "Wish...I could help."

I wished he could, too. Unfortunately, Escobar's null powers seemed to work on him just fine. But he was with us now, which meant we could get the hell out of here. "Connor," I whispered urgently.

He nodded.

At the same time, the Ludlow witch had begun to advance on us, eyes lit with fury. "You can't take him. He's mine!"

"Yes," said the other young woman, turning away from the flaming curtains. She raised a hand. "He needs to stay."

And Joaquin Escobar lifted his hands as well, then pushed outward with them. It was as if someone had picked up a brick wall and flung it at us. I gasped as the weight of it hit me, the breath choking in my throat, and Connor staggered back a pace before he managed to steady himself. Behind me, I heard Luz whisper, "No," followed by an ominous thump.

I allowed myself a quick look back. She'd fallen to the floor, looked as if she'd passed out, her slim body crumpled, arms slumped to either side. Shit. *Shit.*

"You see?" Joaquin said to Connor, sounding almost conversational. "I, too, have a pair of *primas* with me. Well, one is only a *prima*-in-waiting, but she is still powerful enough. Far more powerful than that one." His contemptuous gaze flicked toward Luz, who still lay sprawled on the Persian rug.

Get up, I thought. *Luz, please, get up.* I knew I wasn't strong enough to pick her up, especially while fending off Escobar's attacks.

"Maybe," Connor said. He'd let the "Levi" illusion lapse, probably because he'd realized that he didn't need it anymore, and also because he needed every spare ounce of energy to maintain his own defenses. "By the way, your house is on fire."

For just the briefest second, Escobar's gaze flickered away from us, toward the curtains, which were now almost fully engulfed and about to spread toward the chair that was positioned next to the window. During that second, Levi bent and gathered Luz in his arms, clearly realizing that I was in no position to do so, and that he might as well make use of his muscles even if his magic was still nullified.

I reached one hand toward Connor. He gripped it and then extended his free hand to Levi. No stranger to teleporting under duress, Levi laced his fingers through Connor's.

Even as the acrid scent of smoke began to reach my nostrils, the room faded around us. This time, the journey didn't feel quite as instantaneous, probably because only Connor and I were powering the spell, what with Luz knocked out and Levi not immediately able to join in.

But then the de la Paz *prima*'s living room took shape around us, and I let out a sigh of relief. Levi went to the sofa and laid Luz down, then pressed his fingers against her throat. Frowning, he bent and leaned his head against her chest, stayed there far longer than he should have needed to. After all, Escobar's magical blow had only knocked her out…hadn't it?

A terrible, roiling fear began to churn in my midsection. It wasn't possible….

I stood rooted in place as Connor, his face a mask of worry, went over to Luz and did the same thing that Levi had, only he also lifted her wrist so he could test for her pulse there as well. Still wearing that strained, taut expression, he very gently laid her hand on her chest.

"No!" I burst out. "We have to do something —call the de la Paz healer—"

Connor came over to me and took me in his

arms. I wanted to fight back, tell him that I didn't need to be held, that instead of trying to comfort me, he should be calling Alba, the Phoenix area's healer. Somehow, though, I knew there was no point to any of that.

Levi spoke then, his voice calm but sorrowful. "She's gone, Angela. No healer could fix what Escobar has done to her."

Hot tears poured down my cheeks. "It's all my fault—I should have stopped her, should have realized that she didn't have the same protections Connor and I did—"

"No," Connor broke in. His hand moved over my hair, stroking it, doing his best to calm me down. "She was insistent, Angela. This was as much her idea as it was ours. You saw how determined she was. She wanted to get vengeance for her cousin. Leaving her behind would have been an insult. Besides, we needed her strength to get us there…or at least, we thought we did."

As much as I wanted to rail against him, to tell him those were specious arguments at best, I knew he was right. Connor had been the cautious one; it was Luz and I who wanted to go on this mission, and not wait to do it. That realization didn't make me feel any better, though.

Beneath the sorrow, a dark, smoldering anger burned somewhere at the center of my being. Oh, we'd make Joaquin Escobar pay for this. I didn't know how, and I didn't know when, but sooner or later, that bastard was going to get the fate he so richly deserved.

In the meantime....

I leaned my head against Connor's shoulder and said, "We have to call Zoe."

16

Zoe Sandoval-McAllister

ZOE SHIFTED SLIGHTLY ON THE LEATHER recliner Evan had bought for her not too long after Michael was born, trying to find a more comfortable position. Usually she could relax into the chair and start dozing off immediately—and God only knew, she needed her sleep, when the baby still didn't stay down all night, despite being almost eight months old. This afternoon, however, she was restless, on edge, although she couldn't really say why. Yes, there were those problems with that warlock in Southern California, but Luz seemed to have all that handled, and besides, nothing had really happened for the past few weeks....

The energy lanced into her, white-hot, so bright she gasped aloud and clutched the recliner's arms. Her fingers scrabbled for the remote on the table next to her so she could get the chair back into a more upright position. As she sat up and the pain receded, realization hit her.

No.

No, it wasn't possible. Luz had told her what it would feel like when the *prima* powers came to her, but this couldn't be happening. Not now. The two of them had talked only a week ago, of the baby, of how there didn't seem to be anything to worry about, that Escobar appeared to be licking his wounds after losing his only son. Luz hadn't said anything about being sick. Besides, she was only fifty-two years old, far too young to die. She should have been *prima* for at least another thirty years, probably more.

Was it a car accident?

As Zoe began to push herself out of the recliner, her phone, which she'd left on the coffee table, started to buzz. With shaking fingers, she reached for it, dimly recognized that the number on the display was Angela McAllister's.

"A-Angela?"

"You felt it." The words weren't phrased as a question, but a flat statement.

"Yes." Zoe gulped some air into her lungs, prayed that it would be enough to give her the strength to ask what the hell was going on. "B-but how? I don't understand."

"We need to talk, Zoe. Can you come over to Luz's house?"

Luz's house. Dimly, Zoe realized that house would be hers now.

She didn't want it. She didn't want any of it. This was her house, the beautiful home she and Evan had made together, brand-new and sparkling, the place where they'd brought Michael home from the hospital. She didn't want to live in the rambling hacienda that had once been Maya's. It had always felt like something out of a different world, although a good deal of expense and care had been lavished on it to make sure everything within was kept up to date.

"I just got Michael down for his afternoon nap—"

"Do you have someone who can watch him?"

Of course she did. A de la Paz cousin was only a phone call away, and Teresa, one of the relatives who had been Michael's most stalwart babysitters, could be here in less than five minutes. Yes, Zoe knew she could have Evan watch the baby, but she needed him with her. Right now, her hands and her knees were shaking so badly, she didn't trust herself to drive a car. No, Teresa would have to watch Michael.

"Y-yes," she replied. "I just need to make a

call. Evan and I should be able to make it over there in about twenty minutes, depending on how long we have to wait for the babysitter."

"We'll see you then." A pause, and then Angela added, "I'm so, so sorry, Zoe." This was followed by a little gasp of air, as though the McAllister *prima* had taken a breath to try to push back her tears, and then the call ended.

Just that little gasping breath was enough to start the tears burning in Zoe's eyes. However, she knew she needed to sound calm when she called Teresa. The word would get out soon enough, but right now, she wanted to hear from Angela exactly what had happened before she was forced to tell the de la Paz clan that they had a new *prima.*

She pushed the phone icon next to Teresa's name on her contacts list, then shut her eyes and told herself she needed to stay calm, needed to act as if this request wasn't unusual in any way.

Luckily, Teresa picked up before her phone could even ring three times. She was a retired teacher, her own two children grown but without children of their own yet, and so she was home a good deal of the time. At once Zoe trotted out the story that she'd made up, that she just realized Evan had gotten the wrong size diapers the last time he went to Target, and that they needed to run out and get some of the right kind before Michael needed changing again.

"I'd just send Evan," Zoe said, trying to sound fond and exasperated at the same time, "but since he got the wrong diapers the last time, I thought it was probably better that I went with him. We really shouldn't be gone too long."

"Take as long as you need," Teresa told her. "I'll be right over."

"Thank you," Zoe replied, relief coursing through her. Yes, there were other relatives she could have called if Teresa wasn't available, but they would have taken even longer to get here. "I just put him down for his nap about fifteen minutes ago, so he'll probably sleep the whole time you're here."

"Well, if not, I know what to do. Anyway, I just need to get my purse, and I'm out the door. I'll see you soon."

Zoe thanked her again, then ended the call. She knew Evan was out in the garage, changing the oil in his Barracuda. Luckily, they had a second vehicle, an Audi SUV they'd purchased as soon as they knew Michael was on the way. The oil change would have to wait.

She stopped briefly at the door to Michael's room to peek in at him, but he was fast asleep, long dark eyelashes pressed firmly against his chubby cheeks. Right then, she could only be overwhelmingly glad that he wasn't a girl, because that way he would never have to worry being *prima* one day.

The house was built into the side of a hill, and so the garage was on a lower level than the main portion of the structure. Zoe hurried down the stairs, heart pounding, wondering what she was going to say to Evan, worrying that she would burst into tears before even two words left her mouth. After opening the door that led into the three-car garage, she saw him in the farthest bay. Or rather, she saw his legs sticking out from under the Barracuda, since it was up on ramps for the oil change.

"Evan," she called out.

He didn't emerge. "What?"

Oh, if only he didn't sound so annoyed. She couldn't even blame him, because she was interrupting him in the middle of a messy job. It wasn't his fault that he didn't know their entire world had just been up-ended.

"It's—it's bad, Evan. A-angela McAllister just called me. L-luz—" She had to break off there, because despite her best efforts, her voice had begun to shake, and the tears that had been pooling in her eyes all this time now started to slide down her cheeks in earnest.

He didn't answer, but immediately pushed himself out from under the car and rose to his feet. Clearly, whatever he saw in her face was enough to tell him this was terrible news, because he came over to her and then stopped, looking down at his oily hands in frustration because he knew he didn't dare take her in his arms. "What about Luz, sweetheart?"

"She's—she's gone. I'm the *prima* now."

"Oh, my God." His hands tightened into fists. "What happened?"

"I don't know. Angela told me to come over to Luz's house. I don't even know why she's down here in de la Paz territory. But we need to go. Teresa is on her way over to watch Michael."

Evan nodded, then reached up to brush away some of Zoe's tears. "Okay. Let me go get cleaned up and change—and you need to blot your eyes before Teresa gets here. I assume she doesn't know?"

"N-no." Zoe made herself take a breath, then another. That seemed to help dry up the flood of tears. "I thought it was better to find out what happened before we started spreading the news."

Another nod, and he bent down and kissed her cheek. "This is terrible, Zoe, but we'll get through it. Okay?"

"Okay."

Just the sound of his voice was reassuring, as was the way he stayed close behind her as he followed her up the stairs. They went to the master bedroom, where she did her best to repair the damage to her eye makeup, while he hurriedly stripped out of his smudged T-shirt and jeans, washed up, and climbed into a fresh set of clothes. Nothing fancy, because it was obvious that he didn't want to arouse Teresa's suspicions by getting dressed up when he could usually be found in jeans and a tee about 360 days a year.

They had just finished their prep when Zoe's phone buzzed. She looked down to see a message from Teresa.

I'm outside. I didn't want to ring the bell because it might wake the baby.

Thank God Teresa was so conscientious. Zoe all but ran to open the front door, and flashed a grateful smile when she saw her cousin standing outside, with her ubiquitous Vera Bradley quilted floral bag stuffed full of knitting draped over one arm.

"Come on in," she said. "Michael's still asleep, but there's a bottle in the fridge if he wakes up and is hungry. This shouldn't take more than an hour."

"If it does, that's fine," Teresa replied. Her dark eyes narrowed slightly. "Are you all right, Zoe?"

"Oh, I'm fine," Zoe said hastily. She hated to lie, but she just couldn't get into explanations right now. "One of my potions sort of blew up on me earlier, and I'm still trying to get the itch out of my eyes."

Teresa appeared to relax after hearing that clarification. "Well, I'm sure it will clear up soon enough."

Evan came to the foyer, car keys in one hand. "Hi, Teresa. Thanks so much for doing this."

"It's really no problem. Go ahead and run your errand, and don't worry about Michael and me."

He flashed a smile, the one that still made Zoe's knees go a little weak. "Well, still…thanks." His gaze shifted. "Ready, Zoe?"

"Sure am."

They went back down to the garage, and Evan climbed into the Audi's driver seat while Zoe got in on the other side and fastened her seatbelt. While he didn't exactly peel out of the driveway, he did take off at a good deal faster than their development's posted speed limit of twenty-five miles per hour.

Since he knew the way as well as she did, he didn't say much, only pointed the SUV in the direction of Luz's Scottsdale home. Zoe clung to her purse, some part of her hoping that this had all been a terrible joke, that she'd get to her destination to find that her aunt was just fine.

But there was the *prima* energy coiled within

her, bright and terrible. It wouldn't have come to her if the Luz was still alive. That wasn't how all this worked.

A sob bubbled up in her throat, and she choked it back. If she really was the new *prima* of the de la Paz clan, then she needed to keep it together, to learn how to stay strong no matter what happened. The mere thought of all the people who now depended on her made her stomach clench in terror, but she shut her eyes and told herself it would be okay. This transition had happened hundreds of times in the past and would happen again in the future. She had Evan with her. With him at her side, she figured she could survive anything.

Maybe.

Luz's house was only about ten minutes away, but the trip felt as though it was taking forever. Eventually, though, they pulled up into the driveway of the big Spanish-style house, then got out and let themselves in through the gate that led into the courtyard. As they did so, however, Zoe couldn't help frowning. Angela had said to meet here, but there weren't any other vehicles in the driveway or parked on the street. It seemed doubtful that they would be in the garage.

She knew she was distracting herself because she didn't want to think about what Angela might say. Still, it was strange that there weren't any cars around except the Audi she and Evan had driven here.

He pushed the doorbell, and almost before the chimes had stopped ringing, the door opened. Connor Wilcox stood there, his expression somber. "We're in the living room."

That was it. No hellos or any other kind of pleasantries. Maybe he'd decided the situation didn't really warrant those sorts of empty words.

Evan reached over and took her hand, and the two of them followed the Wilcox *primus* into the living room. Zoe caught sight of Angela, looking pale and frightened, and standing a few feet away from her was Levi. What in the world was he doing here?

But that concern fell away, because then she saw Luz lying on the sofa, her hands folded on her chest, her eyes shut. It looked like she was only sleeping.

Zoe wished that were true. God, did she wish it. But she knew that her aunt wasn't asleep, that she'd already passed beyond the veil into the next world. Blinking back tears—and reminding herself once again that she was the *prima* now, and that she had to stay in control—she said, "What happened?"

Angela's lips pressed together, and she sent a

stricken glance toward her husband. Connor said, "Maybe you should sit down."

She didn't want to sit down. But Zoe knew it would be even more awkward to stand here and demand explanations, so she went over to one of the worn leather chairs that matched the sofa and took a seat. Evan followed, although he didn't sit, only stood next to her. She swallowed, wished her throat wasn't so dry. "*What happened?*"

"It was Joaquin Escobar," Angela replied. "He'd kidnapped Levi. We went to get him back. Only…." Her words trailed off there, as if she knew it was horribly clear what was supposed to follow that "only."

"Angela and Luz and I found a way to combine our powers," Connor said, his voice calm, reasonable, as if he wasn't talking about matters that had just changed all their worlds. "We thought it would be enough. We just didn't realize how strong Escobar was. He sent some kind of shockwave against us. I don't know why Angela and I survived, but I think it has something to do with our *prima/primus* bond. It helped to protect us, while Luz didn't have that kind of a buffer."

None of this was making any sense. Zoe looked from Connor to Angela, then quickly over at Levi before returning her attention to the Wilcox *primus*. Although she'd heard through the grapevine that Levi had finally found someone, and certainly wasn't pining after her, it still felt strange to be in the same room with him after all this time, like running into that guy you kinda/sorta dated a million years ago and never really broke up with, just drifted apart from.

"Why didn't I hear about any of this?" she asked. "Why didn't Luz tell me someone had kidnapped Levi?"

"I don't know," Connor said. "A lot of this happened pretty quickly. The three of us decided that we'd have a better chance of success if we worked together. At first, it seemed as if things were going to be all right. But then Escobar hit us with that…whatever it was."

"I'm so sorry," Angela said. Her green eyes glimmered like brilliant emeralds; it seemed that Zoe wasn't the only one having a hard time holding back her tears. "We knew we were taking a chance, but we didn't realize Luz would be so vulnerable. And—and we knew we couldn't let Escobar have Levi. The risk was too great."

"She's right," Levi said, speaking for the first time. He'd been standing near the bookcase on the far wall but came forward now, his fair hair catching a stray beam of sunlight as it slipped past the heavy curtains. "Actually, it was worse than even Connor and Angela and Luz knew, because Escobar was offering me as bait to the Ludlows."

"The Ludlows?" Zoe repeated. She'd heard that name before—or at least she thought she had—but right now her brain felt so muddled that she was lucky she could even remember her own name.

"They're the witch clan in northern California," Levi told her. "It seems that Escobar was trying to forge an alliance. The Ludlows' *prima*-in-waiting thought I'd make a better consort than the men she'd had presented to her, and Joaquin Escobar was all too willing to make her wish a reality."

Since Zoe had conjured Levi as her own perfect consort—before she realized that her soul mate had been here all along, was the very man assigned to clean up the mess she'd made when she brought Levi to this world—she thought she could sympathize with this unknown *prima*-in-waiting, if only a tiny bit. Who wouldn't rather have someone who looked like a god—and had godlike powers—instead of some spindling second cousin?

She looked over at her cousin Luz's still face. There was no sign of trauma or injury, no sign that she'd died violently. That was something, Zoe supposed, but after hearing what had happened, her sorrow was rapidly turning to anger. Who the hell did this Escobar asshole think he was? The clans had always gotten along because they'd kept

to themselves and respected each other's boundaries. And now this dark warlock was trying to
create alliances, make himself that much more
powerful?

"Then I suppose it's a good thing that you got
away," she said. "Was the cost worth it?"

No one spoke. Angela bit her lip and seemed
able to look everywhere but at Zoe. Connor
frowned.

It was Levi who finally said, "We can never
calculate a person's worth in such a way. Angela
and Connor said that Luz knew the risks, was
willing to take them. She was a very brave
woman. I can tell you that it's a good thing Escobar's plan was foiled. Not only because I did not
relish becoming the consort of someone I did not
love, but because the Ludlows are also a powerful
clan. If they had been able to unite with the
Santiagos and Joaquin Escobar, then things
would have become very difficult for the Arizona
clans. Now, though…." His words trailed off
there, as if he wasn't quite sure what would
happen next.

It wouldn't bring Luz back, but Zoe thought if
her aunt's death had prevented the dark warlock
from continuing with his plans for world domination, then that was something. Because it was
clear that the man needed to be stopped.

"Now…what?" she prompted, hoping either

Connor or Angela would pick up where Levi had left off.

It was Angela who answered, although her words did little to reassure Zoe.

"We don't know," she said. "We just don't know."

17

Angela

IT WAS SORT OF STRANGE TO SEE MY COUSIN Evan take charge after that. He'd been mostly quiet as we tried to explain to Zoe what had happened during our ill-fated foray into Santiago territory, but as soon as it was clear that we didn't have a lot of answers left to give, he thanked us for the explanations, then guided his wife into the kitchen so he could pour her some iced tea.

After that, the phone calls began. The de la Paz clan was a big one, but they clearly had some kind of phone tree set up to spread the news, just as we McAllisters did, if not on such a grand scale. In between two of those calls, I murmured to Evan that we needed to get Levi home, but we'd be in touch, and that in the meantime, he and everyone else in the clan needed to stay on guard.

Evan didn't bother to ask any questions. He knew there wasn't much we could do to change things.

Or…could we? Even as Connor and Levi took my hands and we sent ourselves back to my familiar kitchen in Jerome, I began to wonder if there was some way we could still fix this. After all, Danica had traveled back in time to save her husband Robert's life. This wouldn't be nearly as large a jump, only a few hours, not more than a hundred years.

The kitchen materialized around us, sunlight slanting through the windows, the little pot of rosemary sitting on the sill looking serene, as if nothing terrible had just happened.

"What about Danica?" I asked abruptly as soon as I knew we were safe at home.

Both Levi and Connor shared a single puzzled glance before Connor asked, "What about her?"

"Can't she use her power to travel back and stop what just happened? We could fix this whole mess."

My husband looked distinctly uncomfortable. He reached with one hand to scratch the back of his head, a gesture I recognized as one he tended to deploy when he knew he needed to give me an answer but wasn't quite sure how to do it.

Before he could speak, however, Levi came to his rescue. "That wouldn't work, Angela. Danica was only able to send herself back across all those decades. She's not a *prima*—she doesn't have the ability to have other people travel through time with her."

"But she brought Robert here to the future—"

"Because Jeremiah Wilcox lent her his power," Connor reminded me. His tone was gentle, however, and he came over and threaded his fingers through mine, as though he could tell I needed the reassurance of his touch right then. "There was no way she could have done such a thing on her own."

I'd conveniently forgotten about that part of the story, probably because I was hoping so desperately that Danica might be the one to save the day. "But if we joined our power with hers—"

"I still don't think that would work," Connor said. "Remember, Jeremiah sent Danica and Robert to the future on a one-way trip, no more. We were able to combine our powers with Luz's because she was also a *prima*. Danica's just an ordinary witch. Well," he amended hastily, "not completely ordinary, since she has a very unusual talent, but still…."

All right, maybe that particular straw wasn't worth grasping, but I had more to reach for. I turned toward Levi, who'd been watching

Connor's and my exchange with a sober expression on his face, even though he clearly didn't want to interrupt. "Then what about Hayley?" I asked. "Her power could boost Danica's, and then she'd be strong enough to go back and get Luz out of there."

"You would put Hayley in reach of Joaquin Escobar, when you know that he covets her power for the clan he's suborned?" Before I could answer, try to defend myself, he went on, "That still wouldn't work. I have no doubt that if Hayley joined her power to Danica's, she could give Danica the ability to send herself much farther back, perhaps even give her the ability to work her time-travel magic on someone other than herself. But it would not provide her with the sort of strength needed to withstand Joaquin Escobar's null powers. As soon as she came in range of him, she would be helpless."

Damn it. I hadn't thought of that. It seemed no matter what we did, that damned warlock had us outfoxed, blocked in at every turn.

"So there's really nothing we can do?" I asked, my voice nearly cracking on the last syllable. I hated myself for that sign of weakness, even though I knew I had every reason to be on the verge of tears once more. It would have been easy to blame my lack of control on pregnancy hormones, but I knew it was simply our current situation threatening to overwhelm me.

"There's always something," Levi replied. To my surprise, he smiled. "We just haven't thought of what it is yet."

Maybe he had a point. I just hated to accept the reality of Luz's death, to think she'd died only a foot away from me, and I hadn't been able to do a damn thing about it.

"I think we all should rest," he went on. "I need to go see Hayley, let her know that I'm safe."

"And you need to stay that way," Connor said. "Don't leave Jerome for anything. If you need something from down in Cottonwood, we'll have someone bring it up for you. We don't dare risk Escobar attempting to steal you again."

"No, of course." Still wearing a lopsided smile, Levi added, "To be honest, after the events of the past few days, I'm perfectly happy to remain here in Jerome for the foreseeable future."

With that, he nodded at the two of us, then let himself out the door that led down into the backyard. From there I assumed he would take the path that ran alongside the house and met the sidewalk out front.

After he was gone, I looked up at Connor. The horrible knot of misery that had taken up residence somewhere inside my chest hadn't gone away. If anything, it had only grown. "I don't—I don't know what to do, Connor."

His fingers tightened around mine. "Let's go sit down. Do you want some water?"

I started to shake my head, then stopped when I realized I actually was horrendously thirsty. "That's probably a good idea."

We filled up a couple of glasses from the dispenser in the refrigerator door and headed out to the living room. Why we'd gone there, rather than the family room, which opened off the kitchen and was much cozier, I couldn't say for sure. However, we tended to conduct most of our "official" business in this space, and I supposed it made sense for us to sit there and try to hash out what in the world we were going to do next.

"We'll need to talk to the elders," Connor said after we'd seated ourselves and I'd swallowed a few mouthfuls of water.

"Do you really think they're going to come up with anything?" I couldn't quite keep the bitterness out of my voice; after all, it seemed like lately mostly what they'd done was shoot down my ideas, or at least attempt to.

"I don't know," he admitted. "But they need to be informed about what happened. If nothing else, it's a courtesy. Remember, Alex is Tricia's son-in-law. She needs to know that his mother just passed away."

God, that was right. Sometimes it got so tricky, trying to remember all the connections that now existed between our clans. Alex would be devastated, and Caitlin wouldn't be in much better shape. I knew that she and Luz had grown close, what with Caitlin's own mother being hundreds of miles away here in Jerome, while Caitlin was learning how to run a household down in Tucson.

"Of course." I made myself drink some more water, mostly because I thought it might help to prevent me from dissolving into tears right then and there. Stress, and sorrow…and probably a good helping of rampaging hormones on top of everything else. I put one hand against my stomach, although I hadn't really begun to show yet. "Connor, what do you think all this is doing to the baby?"

Immediately, he leaned over and kissed my cheek. "I don't think you need to worry about that. You've been using your magic, same as you did when you were pregnant with the twins."

"But that blow Escobar hit us with—"

"Do you feel any different?" Now I could hear the sharper edge of worry in my husband's voice, although his expression remained calm. "Any pain, any bleeding?"

Since I hadn't been to the bathroom recently, I couldn't answer that last question with any certainty. However, I hadn't felt even a twinge, except for getting the wind knocked out of me right after Escobar's attack. "No," I replied. "I think I'm all right. But…how long can we keep taking these chances?"

His mouth tightened, and I noted how he didn't want to look at me, kept his gaze fixed on the view of the street outside the living room window. "Well, we're not doing anything like that again. Yes, Levi is safe, but the cost of that rescue was way too high."

"And if we do nothing?" I asked. "What if Escobar brings the fight to us? He's got to be pretty pissed off about us snatching Levi."

"With any luck, we just burned that asshole's house down. Maybe he has more important things to worry about right now."

That would have been nice—although I couldn't help experiencing a pang of regret at the thought of all those priceless paintings going up in smoke—but I guessed that putting out a fire was child's play for Joaquin Escobar. And he'd also had Marisol and the Ludlow witch to help him. "Probably, but I doubt the house is one of them. It's more likely that he's having to explain to the Ludlows why their spoiled brat of a daughter didn't get the consort she wanted for Christmas."

At my scornful words, Connor couldn't help

smiling slightly. "How do you know she's a spoiled brat?"

"Oh, please. Anyone with hair like that is a spoiled brat. Who else has time for that sort of thing?"

"Maybe getting it to curl like that is her talent."

"In which case I doubt she would have been chosen as her clan's *prima*-in-waiting," I said crisply, although I had a feeling that Connor was teasing me a little, trying his best to lighten the mood.

"You're probably right." He hesitated, then went on, "Do you want me to text Tricia? We really shouldn't put off that meeting for too long."

As much as I wanted to say no, I knew he was right. The elders needed to be informed. Maybe if we all put our heads together, we could come up with some kind of a plan. To be truthful, though, I was really hoping they'd be the ones to figure out what to do next. I was so tired and discouraged and overwhelmed, right then I wasn't sure if I could get a single synapse to fire.

"Yes, text her," I said wearily.

He didn't reply, only got the phone out of his pocket, a frown pulling at his brows the whole time. I knew he was worried about me, but I couldn't come up with the words to tell him that I was all right. Maybe I wasn't. Oh, physically I was okay, but as for the rest? I wanted to go to the window seat in our bedroom upstairs and bawl like a baby.

Then I thought of Zoe, who'd just lost an aunt and had the responsibility for her entire clan dumped on her. The de la Pazes didn't have elders like we did, although I knew their clan had a network of older members who functioned in much the same manner, even if their setup wasn't as formal. Even so, in many ways, Zoe was on her own now, barely twenty-three, and with an eight-month-old baby to look after. I could still remember how out of my depth I'd felt when the twins came. I couldn't imagine facing motherhood for the first time while basically being in a state of war.

"They'll be over in a few minutes," Connor said as he set his phone down on the coffee table. "I figured you probably didn't want to go over to Trish's house."

Good call. Right then my legs felt like rubber, so even walking a block would have been a chore. Luckily, the house was clean enough for company —at least the public parts of it, like the living room and the guest bath just down the hall.

"Not really," I told him. "I'm really not looking forward to this. You know Boyd is going to rip us a new one for even daring to go to Escobar's house."

"Well, Boyd isn't the *prima*," Connor said reasonably. "Or the *primus.* He's entitled to his opinion, but that doesn't mean we have to listen to it. And I can see you beating yourself up, so I'm going to tell you again—this was as much Luz's idea as it was ours. It wasn't like she was forced into it. Of course I feel terrible, because Luz was an amazing woman, and she didn't deserve what Escobar did to her. But don't you dare try to tell yourself her death was your fault, because it wasn't. There's only one person to blame, and that person isn't you."

I leaned my head on his shoulder, treasuring that stolen moment of intimacy, needing to feel his strength. Connor always had been my rock. With him there to hold me up, I knew—well, I didn't know if it was going to be okay, but I did know that we'd somehow manage to get through this.

The doorbell rang, and he gently slid out and away from me, then got up and went to answer the door. Outside, as expected, were Tricia, Boyd, and Allegra. Tears glittered in Tricia's blue eyes.

Oh, no.

"Caitlin just called me as we were walking over," she said as she came inside. "How could this have happened?"

"Luz was a very brave woman," Connor said. Once the other two elders were also standing in the foyer, he closed the front door. "Come into the living room. We need to talk."

"I should say so." Boyd almost always looked irritated about something, but right then, with his heavy eyebrows knitted together and his thin-lipped mouth pressed tight, he appeared on the verge of an apoplectic fit. "What the hell were you thinking?"

For some perverse reason, his anger made a little of my sorrow recede. Maybe it was only that fighting with Boyd might help to make me forget how much it hurt to know that Luz was gone. "We were thinking of rescuing Levi," I shot back. "None of us planned for this to happen. We thought we would be safe."

Allegra stepped forward, silver bangles clinking together as she raised both her hands. "Please. There is no point in fighting about this, not when the damage has already been done. We all know that Angela and Connor would only act for the good of the clan."

Boyd looked almost startled, as if he hadn't really thought Allegra would intercede. That made two of us; usually she was the elder who hung back, who didn't speak until the other two had already spoken. But maybe she'd realized that Tricia was in no shape to be arguing with Boyd, so she'd stepped in.

"Unless you thought it was a good idea to

leave Levi in Joaquin Escobar's hands, that is," Connor remarked, and Boyd's scowl deepened to a ferocious level.

"I never said it was good idea," he retorted. Jamming his hands in his jeans pocket, he continued, "I only said that, valuable as Levi is to this clan, he isn't as valuable as you two. What happened to Luz only proved my point. What if that had been you?"

Almost against my will, my hand moved toward my stomach. Boyd was locked eye to eye with Connor, and Tricia was still holding back tears, so I didn't think either of them noticed. But Allegra saw my gesture, and tilted her head to one side as she gave me a considering look. Since I couldn't take back the gesture, I scratched the side of my belly, praying she would only think I'd had an itch. I doubted the subterfuge worked, though. Allegra Moss might cultivate the image of a distracted hippie-dippy witch, but there was a shrewd mind under all the jewelry and gypsy skirts and crazy graying hair.

"It wasn't us," Connor said. His voice was calm, but I could hear the tension in it. More than once he'd told me that he'd practically had to sit on his hands to prevent himself from socking Boyd in the jaw, and I really couldn't blame him. Boyd tended to have that effect on people. "But just because it wasn't, doesn't make Luz's loss any less difficult."

"But the transition went all right?" Tricia asked. Her eyes still looked far too bright, but her voice was steady enough.

"Yes," I replied. Since everyone else was standing, it felt strange for me to remain seated on the couch. I stood up and straightened my shirt, and prayed that Allegra wouldn't feel the need to start inspecting my midsection. "Zoe is now the *prima* of the de la Paz clan. She's a tough girl. She'll be able to handle it."

"Good thing she's married to a McAllister," Boyd said. "Evan's a steady kid. Even so…."

"Even so, Zoe is new to all this, and she has a baby," I said. "Which means I'm not sure how much help she's going to be able to give us."

Allegra's watery blue eyes blinked behind the wire-framed glasses she wore. "How much help do we need? After all, you did get Levi back."

"Yes," Connor said. "But I doubt Escobar's going to take that lying down. Also, I'm not sure if he knows that Luz is dead. I thought—I think we all thought—that she'd only been knocked out. It wasn't until we got her back to her house that we realized the worst had happened."

"Even if he didn't know right away, he probably knows now." I spoke with certainty, although I wasn't sure why. From what I'd been able to tell,

Joaquin Escobar didn't seem to be a mind reader, but he sure had an uncanny ability to know what was going on in both the McAllister and the de la Paz clans. "Which means he knows that the de la Pazes are now headed by an extremely inexperienced *prima*. That can't be good."

Tricia pushed back a lock of flaming red hair, tucking it behind her ear. "No, it's not. But unfortunately, I'm not sure how much we can do about it. We already have asked everyone in the clan here to be careful—to not stay out of Jerome too late, to try not to go outside the town alone. I'm sure the de la Pazes are doing the same…and the Wilcoxes, of course," she added, glancing over at Connor. "But how much good will it do? They were still able to get Levi."

"Because they set a deliberate trap for him," I said. Briefly, I explained how we had encountered the Ludlow *prima*-in-waiting at Joaquin Escobar's house, and how Levi had told us they'd intended him for her consort. "I don't think any of us are that valuable to them. At least now we're wise to their game."

"Well, that's just wonderful news," Boyd grumbled. "So now we have to worry about the Ludlows, too?"

I glanced over at Connor, and he shrugged very slightly. "We don't know for sure. They could have cut their losses and backed out, or they could be working with Escobar to figure out another way to steal Levi. Problem is, we know next to nothing about their clan, except that there are a lot of them. Whether any of them have the kind of magical skills to pull something like that off —who knows?"

"One thing I could tell," Connor put in. "The Ludlow *prima*-in-waiting—she was very clearly there of her own volition, and working with Escobar. I didn't see any sign of mind control with her, whereas it was pretty obvious that Marisol, the Santiago *prima,* was foggy and out of it. She's there because Escobar is keeping a firm grip on her head."

A silence fell, during which the elders all seemed to share a quick look, although nothing constructive seemed to come of it. I had to wonder then why Escobar was able to control Marisol so easily, when Connor and I seemed, if not impervious to his various powers, then at least strong enough that they didn't have much effect on us. Was it because of the bond that we shared, or was it only that he'd grabbed Marisol right after the *prima* powers came to her, before she'd had any chance to learn how to use them?

I wasn't sure if we'd ever get the answer to that question.

"They may be an unknown quantity, but it's pretty clear the Ludlows are no friends of any of the Arizona witch clans," Tricia said. "Otherwise, they would have come to us and told us about Joaquin Escobar's plans. We'll just have to treat them as another hostile clan, even if we're still not sure whether they're going to continue actively working with Escobar and the Santiagos."

"Well, I doubt any of us were planning any trips to the Bay Area, so it should be pretty easy to avoid them," Connor remarked.

"Unless they bring the fight here," I said. "That Ludlow *prima*-in-waiting—she looked pretty pissed off. She might be able to talk her own *prima* or her clan elders or her parents or whoever is calling the shots into continuing to go after Levi."

Connor shook his head. "Well, then, unless we're planning to lock him up in a lead-lined bunker or something, I don't know how we can keep Levi completely safe."

"We conjured that protective field like Alex's," I said. "Why don't we try casting that same spell so it encases his whole apartment? He'd be stuck inside, but he would be safe."

"I'm not sure how well that would work," Tricia pointed out. As Alex's mother-in-law, she probably had a better idea than most how his particular gift functioned. "The field emanates outward from the spell-caster, and it moves with him, too. If you and Connor cast the spell together, then it'll stay with you, move with you. Levi would have to be the one to do it if it's going to work at all."

"Well, he should be able to," I told her. "He's already shown that he can do almost anything, magic-wise, so it shouldn't be too much of a problem. Again, he'd have to stay in his flat, because even in Jerome, someone walking down the street encased in a big shimmery bubble is going to draw too much attention, but better house arrest than getting kidnapped all over again."

"We'll go talk to him about it," Boyd said, in tones that brooked no argument. "You and Connor have done enough today."

I wanted to tell Boyd that I was the *prima* and I could do as I damn well pleased…but I realized what I wanted to do was stay home and pretend this day had never happened. If he wanted to take Allegra and Tricia with him and tell Levi he was basically stuck at home until all this blew over, then he was welcome to the task. "All right," I replied, causing my husband to look at me with lifted brows, as though wondering why I hadn't tried to argue the point. "You talk to Levi, and Connor and I will stay here. Tomorrow…well, I guess we'll worry about tomorrow when it comes."

"A very good idea," Allegra said. "You've had a very trying time, and you need to take care of herself." For just the briefest second, her gaze slid toward my midsection, but, thank the Goddess, she didn't say anything more than that.

And while I knew that maybe I should be talking to Zoe, letting her know that the McAllister clan would be here for her, no matter what, I just didn't have the energy. Evan was with her, probably telling her the same thing. Right then, she needed to be with her family. I'd be more than happy to give her any assistance I could, but Allegra was right about one thing. I needed to be more mindful of the tiny life I carried within me. If that meant I needed to put my feet up, have Connor bring me a lemonade, and push all my worries aside for a few minutes or an hour, so be it.

Past experience had taught me that those worries—and the people causing them—weren't going anywhere.

18

Caitlin Trujillo

THIS WHOLE THING HAD TO BE A NIGHTMARE. Her brain just couldn't accept the reality of what Alex, pale under his dark skin, jaw set in an attempt to hold back his tears, had just told her—that his mother was dead, and at Joaquin Escobar's hands. There was more, about Levi's kidnapping and eventual rescue, but Caitlin knew she'd have to wait to absorb all those details. What mattered was that Luz was gone, and that Zoe was now in charge of the de la Paz clan. Zoe, who might have grown up a bit over the past few years, and yet seemed to be forever etched in Caitlin's mind the way she'd first seen her—with a streak of pink in her long dark hair, wearing Doc Martens, and a T-shirt from Hot Topic, and a pair of the world's skinniest jeans.

How could any of this be happening?

They'd driven over to Luz's house as soon as they got the call from Evan, Alex silent and grim-faced, clutching the steering wheel so tightly that Caitlin could clearly see his knuckles standing out white against his brown skin. When they'd gotten there, they spotted the Mercedes that belonged to David, Alex's father, parked in the driveway, next to an ambulance.

Seeing the ambulance brought the whole thing home to Caitlin in a way that no overheard phone conversation could. Its presence startled her for a moment, since she didn't think the clan would have brought in outside medical help for something like this. Then she realized that the de la Pazes probably had EMTs among them, just like they had doctors and lawyers and insurance adjusters and anything else that helped the family blend in with regular civilian society.

Because there was no room in the driveway, they parked on the street and went up the front walk, Alex gripping Caitlin's hand the whole time. She wished she could give him some words of comfort, some wisdom to help guide him through this, but she didn't know what the hell she was supposed to say. You weren't supposed to lose your mother when you were in your late twenties.

A wave of guilt went over her then, that they'd delayed having kids until Caitlin felt she could manage the interruption in her writing career. She should have just sucked it up and given Luz at least one grandchild. It was an irrational thought, she knew, because Alex's older brother Diego and his wife Letty had a daughter already, and another child on the way. They must be driving up to Scottsdale, too, but since they lived on a vineyard somewhere out near Bisbee, it was going to take them even longer to get here.

Alex didn't bother to knock on the front door, but let himself in. A murmur of voices came from the living room, and so the two of them headed that way, went in to discover Zoe and Evan talking quietly to Alex's father, who looked as if he'd just aged ten years, his strong, even features etched with sorrow. Standing off to one side next to a gurney was a man around thirty, movie-star handsome like Alex, wearing an EMT's uniform. Caitlin wanted to kick herself for not remembering the EMT's name, but really, there were so many de la Pazes, it was almost impossible to keep them all straight, especially the members of the family who lived here in the Phoenix area rather than down in Tucson where she and Alex had made their home.

At once the conversation died away. David opened his arms, and Alex went into them, an

Alex Caitlin had never seen before, lost and frightened, tears glittering in his dark eyes. Oh, he'd been upset when his grandmother Maya passed away, but it was a very different thing to lose your own mother. She didn't even want to think about that, to think about what her life would be like if she lost Tricia so soon.

Evan touched Zoe's arm, as if to excuse himself, then came over to Caitlin. "Did you call your mother?"

"Yes, as we were driving over." It felt hard to get the words out, to push them past the thickness in her throat. "She'll let the elders know, and I suppose the news will start to spread. I just—I just can't—" She had to stop herself there, partly because the de la Paz EMT standing by the gurney shifted slightly, and she was able to catch a glimpse of Luz lying on the sofa, a knitted throw covering her up to her chin.

Her cousin seemed to have noticed the source of her distraction, because Evan's gaze flickered in that direction before he returned his attention to her. "I know. This whole thing is a nightmare."

"How's Zoe?" Caitlin murmured, watching as the new *prima* walked over to David and Alex. Their brief, fierce embrace over, father and son were now talking in low tones.

"About as well as can be expected." Evan paused and pushed at the lock of dark red hair that always managed to fall over his forehead. Caitlin remembered all too well how some of their more distant cousins used to go all goo-goo-eyed whenever he did that. "She'll hold up because she has to, but just between you and me, this Escobar thing has me scared shitless. How could he manage to kill a *prima?*"

"*Primas* are mortal, just like everyone else," Caitlin said sadly, right before she realized that probably wasn't a very diplomatic thing to tell someone whose wife had just become *prima.* "What did Angela and Connor say?"

"Not a lot. They told us that they'd come up with a way to combine their powers, and so they can use types of magic they really hadn't been able to access before. They thought that was probably how they'd managed to survive, even as Escobar's attack killed Luz."

That was something Caitlin didn't know much about, but then, she'd been kind of out of the loop down in Tucson. And, looking at everything that was going on, she thought that was a good thing. Bad enough to get called in to investigate that creepy apartment, where she'd had that terrible vision of Levi being hauled away down the stairs. Yes, it sounded as if he'd been rescued in the end, but still....

Her phone buzzed right then, vibrating away in her purse. Caitlin was inclined to ignore it—

she thought it might be rude to answer a call or a text while Alex and David and Zoe were so obviously grieving—but on the other hand, if it was her mother calling back, Caitlin would feel terrible about missing the call.

"I should probably get that," she said apologetically. "It might be my mother."

"It's fine," Evan replied. He offered her a half-sympathetic, half-encouraging smile before going back over to the little group so he could put his arm around Zoe, hold her close.

Caitlin pulled her phone out of her purse, saw that it was a text she'd missed, not a phone call. She didn't recognize the number, although she thought it might be a California area code.

California? She went to the messaging app and pulled up the text.

I need to talk to you. You and your boyfriend were kind to me once.

Boyfriend?

Caitlin had never really had a boyfriend, until she met Alex. Even then, she couldn't exactly classify their quickly intensifying relationship, which had happened over the span of a few days while they searched for Roslyn and Danica, as a mere girlfriend/boyfriend sort of thing.

After glancing over at Alex, who was still huddled with his family members, having some kind of hushed convo, she typed, *Who is this?*

Olivia. Olivia Gutierrez. My brother was Matías Escobar.

Holy shit. Once again Caitlin looked toward Alex and the rest of his family. Now the EMT had joined the discussion; he made a brief, sad gesture toward the sofa where Luz's body lay, and she realized they were probably discussing where to take the body. Did the de la Pazes also own a funeral home? They must, to make these sorts of situations a little easier to manage.

How did you get this number?

I found it in Lucinda's room, in a little book she had tucked away in a drawer.

Caitlin could only be relieved that apparently Joaquin hadn't searched that room, had left it alone after Lucinda was rescued. *Where are you?*

I'm here in Phoenix. I ran. I need to talk to you.

Phoenix was a very big place. Caitlin replied, *Where in Phoenix?*

In the Motel 6 in north Mesa. I knew the de la Pazes were here in the Phoenix area, but I didn't know where exactly.

They're all over, Caitlin thought, *from Scottsdale down to Tucson and even farther than that.* But she didn't want to complicate matters. The important thing was that Olivia was here now.

I'll try to be there as soon as I can, she typed back. *Can you give me an address?*

It's 336 W. Hampton Ave. I'm in Room 221.

Got it. That's about twenty minutes away, so just hang tight.

I'll try.

Caitlin shoved her phone back in her purse, then swallowed. How the hell was she going to manage this? Alex needed to know about Olivia, although the last thing she wanted to do was drag him away from his family at such a terrible time. But it sounded as though Matías' sister possessed some kind of information she wanted to share, or why would she be reaching out rather than continuing to run as far as she could?

Deep breaths, she told herself, then went over and touched Alex on the elbow. "Alex, there's something I need to talk to you about."

He turned toward her, dark brows lowering. "Now?"

"Yes. It's really important."

For a second he hesitated, but then he said, "All right," and moved away from his father so he could follow Caitlin over to the bookcases on the far side of the room. Because it was Alex, he didn't look exactly angry over the interruption, but rather confused. He knew she wouldn't have broken into a conversation like that if she didn't have a very good reason.

Making sure to keep her voice soft so it couldn't be overheard, she said, "I just got a text from Olivia. You know, Matías' sister in California?"

At once comprehension dawned. "You're kidding."

"No, I'm not." She got her phone out of her purse so she could show Alex the message thread. "I don't know what the hell she's doing here in Phoenix, but it's pretty clear that she's scared. We need to go get her."

"I—" Alex looked over at his father, who had now gone to the sofa so he could lay his hand on Luz's forehead. Even from this distance, the glitter of tears on his cheeks was obvious. "This is a hell of a time for us to be taking off, Caitlin."

"Don't you think I know that? But we can't just leave Olivia in some motel. It's not safe."

Alex's jaw clenched, but then he let out a breath and slowly nodded. "You're right. I'll figure something out."

He headed back over to his father and laid a hand on his arm, speaking quietly enough that Caitlin couldn't hear what they were saying. David looked startled for a moment, but then he reached out and touched Alex's shoulder briefly. Alex bent and laid a kiss on his mother's forehead, and Caitlin had to choke back her own tears as she watched. She shouldn't be dragging him away. Not now. Not like this.

Unfortunately, they didn't have much choice.

He came back over to her and took her hand in his. "Let's see that address."

She showed it to him again. "I'm really sorry about this—"

"It's all right. Like you said, Olivia wouldn't be here and wanting to talk to us if it wasn't important."

They went outside and got in their car, and Alex pointed them toward the 101 Loop heading south. As they drove, Caitlin retrieved her phone and typed, *We're on the road. Not too much longer.*

This time, Olivia didn't respond right away, and Caitlin could feel a thin trickle of worry work its shivery way down her back. What if Joaquin Escobar had somehow managed to catch up with his runaway daughter in the past few minutes? There was no way in the world Caitlin and Alex would be able to take him on and defeat him.

But then her phone pinged, and a new message came through. *Okay. I'm waiting.*

The traffic was starting to get cloggy with the onset of the afternoon rush hour, and Caitlin had to force herself not to jiggle her foot or tap her fingers on the armrest to alleviate some of her impatience. Doing so would only distract Alex, and it wouldn't get them to Mesa any sooner.

Eventually, though, they pulled into the parking lot of a modest-looking motel at the north end of the town. Only a few cars were parked there, including an older-model Honda with California plates. Caitlin didn't know why, but she felt almost certain that one must be Olivia's, even though one of the other vehicles was also from California. It was a big flashy black Escalade, though, not something that matched the modest one-story home in Temecula where Olivia lived...or at least where she had lived a few years ago.

Alex pulled up next to the Honda, and they both got out. Luckily, the room number Olivia had given them was almost directly in front of the spot where they'd parked, so they didn't have too far to go. Even before Alex lifted his hand to knock, the door opened, and a pair of frightened dark eyes peered out at them.

"Come in," she urged them, and they hurried inside. As soon as they'd cleared the door, Olivia shut it and engaged both the locks, even though they all knew that door locks were no barrier to even an ordinary witch or warlock, and certainly no problem for someone like Joaquin Escobar.

The room didn't look as though she'd planned to stay there for very long. A small weekender-style bag sat on one of the two double beds, but otherwise, there was no sign that anyone was even staying in the place.

"Go ahead and sit," Olivia said, moving

toward the bed so she could get the bag out of the way.

Caitlin and Alex sat down gingerly on the edge of the bed. Olivia seemed full of nervous energy, taking the bag to the closet so she could set it on the luggage stand there, coming back and peering out past the drapes before she finally also took a seat.

As she watched the other woman move around the room, Caitlin recalled how Olivia had had a young boy when she and Alex had come to visit her all those years ago, trying to get more information about Matías Escobar. That child would be around kindergarten age now, but obviously still far too young to be left alone. Maybe the father was watching him?

"Are you all right, Olivia?" Alex asked, bringing up the question that had been floating around in Caitlin's mind.

Olivia rubbed her hands on the knees of her faded jeans. Somehow, she looked thinner than the last time they'd seen her, pale and drawn, her high cheekbones standing out in sharp relief, her black hair straggling and limp on her shoulders. Before, she had been blooming and happy, content in her life with her civilian husband, even if she didn't have any magical powers to speak of, was a *nunca,* which meant she'd never developed magical gifts the way all witches and warlocks were supposed to. "I'm alive, and I'm here," she said. "I don't know about 'all right.'"

Caitlin didn't want to sound pushy, but on the other hand, she needed to know what Olivia was doing here in Phoenix. "Can you tell us what happened?"

"I—" Olivia swallowed and pushed a strand of hair behind one ear, then sent a nervous glance toward the window, as if she somehow feared any attacks would come to her that way. "Matías told me that our father was in Southern California, but he also said I didn't need to worry, that Joaquin didn't care about me." A bitter chuckle, and she added, "Why would he? I was of no use to him. But then I learned of all the terrible things he had done, how he had killed Simón and Beatriz, had taken Marisol for his own and killed her husband as well. Still, I didn't know what I could do. I had no real powers. I supposed I hoped that he would ignore me, would pretend that I didn't exist. I didn't fit into his plans, after all."

"There really wasn't anything you could have done," Caitlin said gently. She knew too well that feeling of thinking that there must have been some way she could have intervened, could have prevented someone from getting hurt. Problem was, those sorts of notions tended to be wishful thinking.

"I know," Olivia said. She pushed her long,

wavy hair back over her shoulders. It looked like it needed a wash and a brush, but Caitlin figured the other woman could be forgiven those small details, considering the circumstances. "But then —then Matías was killed. Joaquin called me to the house. I thought he wanted me there so I could mourn my brother. I did mourn him," she added quickly, her tone almost defiant, as though she wanted to see whether Alex or Caitlin would challenge her for mourning someone who really was a despicable human being. Since they both remained silent, Olivia continued, "I mourned him because he was my brother, nothing more. After the funeral, I thought Joaquin would send me back to Temecula. I needed to get back to my husband and son. But Joaquin had other plans."

She paused there, her eyes filling with tears. Caitlin hated to push the other woman, but she was acutely aware of the way she was keeping Alex from his family, how the precious minutes kept ticking by. Maybe the ambulance had already left the house, taking Luz's body to the funeral home.

"What were those plans?" Caitlin asked softly.

"William—my husband—he never knew about me being a witch. I told him I was an orphan, which was half true, or maybe three-quarters, since it wasn't as though Joaquin was around to be any kind of a father to me. Anyway, while William knew about Matías, I'd only said that we were estranged and hadn't spoken for a long time, that he would never be a part of our lives." Now a tear finally began to trail its way down her cheek; she reached up and wiped it away, but absent-mindedly, as if she'd done that very same thing many times before. Giving a rusty chuckle, she said, "It's not that strange a story. Family can be a nightmare."

For Olivia, it definitely seemed that way. Caitlin couldn't say such a thing about her own clan, because she'd always felt welcomed and loved, even back when she was doing her best to hide her talents as a seer from everyone. But she supposed she would have felt very different if her father and brother had been walking nightmares like Joaquin and Matías Escobar.

She settled for giving a sympathetic nod, while Alex rubbed his chin, clearly worried about what was going to come next. Or maybe he was only thinking about his own family, about how he should be with them now.

"I had car trouble. I suppose I should have realized it was a convenient coincidence, but at the time I didn't think much about it. My car has a lot of miles on it, and I don't always maintain it the way I should. Joaquin offered to have someone in the clan look at the car, but in the meantime he said he'd drive me home, since he knew I didn't want to be away from my son Robert any longer than I had to. It was an awkward drive—I didn't know what to say to Joaquin. I mean, I knew he was my father, but we had no connection. I didn't even remember him. And of course I didn't dare say anything to him about what he'd done to the Santiagos. I might be his biological daughter, but I knew that didn't allow me to speak my mind."

"How old were you when you came to California?" Alex asked, and Olivia shrugged.

"Not even a year. It's the only place I've ever known." Another tear rolled down her cheek, and she wiped it away with yet another of those oddly automatic gestures. "Joaquin walked me inside the house. Will was there, watching Robert. He seemed a little surprised to see Joaquin, but when he learned he was my father, he relaxed a bit. He shouldn't have, though. Because as soon as the introductions were over, Joaquin told him that I came from a long line of witches and warlocks, even though I didn't have any real powers of my own. Then he smiled and pointed at Robert, and said there was a good chance our son would grow up with witch talents despite all that."

Caitlin listened, wide-eyed. She knew that Joaquin Escobar was evil, but she couldn't quite figure out why he would go out of his way to hurt his daughter's family. "What happened?" she asked.

"Will asked me if it was true, and I said yes. I

told him I was sorry for misleading him, but because I didn't have any real talents, had never developed them, that I didn't think it was so important." She stopped there so she could pull in a hiccuping little breath. Now tears flowed from both eyes, although she seemed to be ignoring them for the moment...or possibly no longer had the energy to wipe them away. "He was...angry. Told me our whole relationship was a lie. And then he told me he wanted me to leave."

That seemed awfully harsh, but Caitlin didn't know anything about Olivia's husband, since she'd never met him. She supposed he could have felt horribly betrayed by the secrets she'd kept from him, even if those secrets hadn't done any real harm. "Did you?"

Olivia's fingers dug into the bedspread. "Yes. I didn't have much choice. From the way Joaquin was standing there and watching the whole thing, smiling to himself, I guessed he'd planned this from the beginning...and I had a suspicion that those were his words in my husband's mouth, that he was manipulating him even as I stood there. Joaquin hated the idea of me being married a civilian, of living a civilian life. I didn't want to get into a huge fight in front of my son, because I knew it wouldn't do any good. I figured I'd leave, then try to come back and talk to William later, when Joaquin wasn't around. I packed a few things, and we went back to Pasadena."

"I'm so sorry," Caitlin said. The words were beyond inadequate, but she wasn't sure what else to do. From the way Olivia held herself, rigid and not quite looking at either her or Alex, it seemed pretty clear that she wouldn't welcome a hug.

Another one of those brittle lifts of Olivia's thin shoulders. "At least Robert and Will were safe. It was probably better for me to be away from them. I didn't speak to my father on the drive back—what would be the point? He'd gotten exactly what he wanted. In fact, I realized that even more when we got to the house and he said he was glad I'd be staying with them, that Marisol needed help around the house. I understood then why Joaquin wanted me there. He wanted me to be his servant, since I didn't serve any other useful purpose. For the past few weeks, I've been running errands for him and Marisol, making their dinners, not much more than a slave."

"But you ran," Alex said gently.

Her lips pressed together, and she nodded. "I had to. I knew something was going on when the Ludlows started visiting, along with that brat of a *prima*-in-waiting of theirs. And when they kidnapped Levi McAllister, I knew they would never stop."

"We got him back, though," Caitlin said, guessing that Olivia couldn't have known about Levi's rescue, since she must have been driving from California to Phoenix when all that occurred.

However, the other woman didn't seem at all relieved by that revelation. In fact, her eyes widened in fear, and her fingers dug into the cheap bedspread once more. "You think that's the end of it? Joaquin will come after him—he has to, because otherwise he can't count on the Ludlows' support. And the Ludlows will have their own witches and warlocks come here as well, because whatever their little princess wants, she gets. I know Joaquin doesn't think much of the McAllisters, or the de la Pazes. He's confident that he can beat all of you."

Sounded like someone was a little too full of himself. Caitlin looked over at Alex, whose jaw was set, mouth tight. This was all the last thing he needed to be hearing, especially when he'd only just learned of his mother's death. "Don't forget about the Wilcoxes. It's not like they're going to stand by and let some madman come after the other two Arizona clans. They're part of this fight, too."

"It doesn't matter," Olivia replied, her expression hopeless, almost tragic. "I don't think you have any idea how big the Ludlow clan actually is

—or the Santiagos. Put together, there are far more of them than there are McAllisters, Wilcoxes, and de la Pazes combined."

"This is still crazy," Alex protested. "I know your father is kind of nuts, but even he has to realize that some all-out witch war is going to draw the attention of the civilian authorities. You can't exactly sweep that kind of thing under the rug."

"He isn't worried about it." Olivia glanced from Alex to Caitlin, her haunted dark eyes pleading with them to understand. "Someone like Joaquin—he thinks he can manage every situation. Even if this thing blows up to a point where outsiders might notice, so what? He can control civilian minds just as easily as he can the minds of witches and warlocks."

Right. Caitlin had forgotten about that very important point. A wave of despair went over her. What on earth could any of them do against an opponent like Joaquin Escobar, someone who could control your mind at the same time he was destroying your ability to use your magical gifts?

As much as she hated to even entertain the thought, maybe Levi wasn't worth it. Maybe it was better to sacrifice one person than to drag all three of the Arizona clans into the fight to protect him.

No, she knew Angela and Connor would

never agree to that sort of thing, not when Luz had been sacrificed to save Levi in the first place. Besides, giving in to Escobar wasn't really an option. If they caved on this one matter, then he'd know they would give in on many others. Their days of freedom would be over.

"Dragging civilians into this might work to our advantage," Alex said. "I mean, if Escobar's busy controlling civilian minds to keep this whole thing on the down-low, maybe he won't have much energy left over for the rest of us. There's got to be a limit to his powers, right?"

Olivia tilted her head to one side, apparently considering his question. "If there is, I haven't seen it. I'm not sure how he does it, but as far as I can tell, every member of the Santiago clan is working with him and happy to have him in charge. I'm not going to lie—I know there was always a faction who weren't happy about having Simón running things, who thought Beatriz should step aside, since she wasn't a fully functioning *prima*. But those people were a minority. I guess it's possible that my father doesn't have to use his mind-control skills on that group, because his goals are in line with theirs. There were far, far more who wouldn't agree with what's going on, though, and they're just as compliant as the others. So I guess that's the long way of saying that if he does have a limit to those powers, I haven't seen it yet."

This was getting better and better. Caitlin wondered if Joaquin Escobar was also controlling the Ludlows, although it didn't really sound that way. It was more like what Olivia had just described about the Santiagos who didn't much care for Simón's leadership—the Ludlows' goals were in line with Escobar's, so it made sense for them to work together.

"So what do we do now?" she asked.

Olivia shrugged again. "I don't know. I just wanted to tell you what I'd heard, what I know. My father isn't going to give up, and neither are the Ludlows. They want to expand their power, and an alliance will do that."

"Well," Caitlin said, "one thing I do know is that we need to get you out of here. You're certainly not safe in a motel room by yourself. We'll take you back with us, figure out a place for you to stay."

"That's not necessary—"

"Oh, yeah, it is," Alex broke in. "We're not going to leave you here. Once your father gets over Levi being stolen back, he's going to figure out that you're gone—and because he has the resources of the Santiagos and the Ludlows at his fingertips, I'm pretty sure he's going to figure out fairly quickly *where* you've gone. The best thing to do is make sure you're surrounded by other witches and warlocks. I guess we'll have to leave it up to Zoe, since she's the new *prima*."

Olivia frowned at that comment, delivered so matter-of-factly, although Caitlin could guess how much effort it had cost Alex to speak so naturally about the transfer of power that had just occurred. "I thought your mother was the *prima* of the de la Pazes."

"She was, until your father killed her."

At once Olivia's hand went to her mouth, and her olive skin paled visibly. "Oh, my God, Alex. I am so sorry. I didn't know—I was driving—"

"It's okay," he said, his tone probably sharper than he'd intended. "It's not your fault. But now we need to get you out of here, and we need to let Zoe and Connor and Angela know that your father is going to be bringing the battle to us." His dark eyes glittered with barely suppressed fury. "We just have to make sure we're ready, no matter what."

19

Angela

M‌Y RESTFUL AFTERNOON DIDN'T LAST FOR very long. True, I did doze for about a half hour, more out of sheer overload than anything else. My body knew that it needed a reset, even as I fretted over what the hell we were supposed to do next.

Because I'd brought my phone with me upstairs to the bedroom—against Connor's wishes; he told me to leave the damn thing behind so I could get some real rest—I heard it the second it started buzzing. I rolled over and picked it up, checked the screen. Inwardly, I'd hoped it was Trish, calling to provide a status update on the elders' meeting with Levi. I doubted he'd give them too much trouble about staying in his apart-ment, because he knew better than anyone else how much at risk he was. But still, it would have been good to know how he reacted.

But it wasn't Trish calling. It was Zoe.

I picked up the phone, glad that Connor had stayed downstairs to allow me to sleep. He'd said he was going to try FaceTiming with Emily and Ian again. I hoped he'd been able to get through. My last text from Margot had indicated that they were maybe going to take the kids into town for ice cream.

It all sounded so normal, so fun. I remembered when the only thing I had to worry about was whether Ian's shoes would last him for more than a month or two. Now five and a half, he was growing like a weed.

Pushing those thoughts away, I put the phone to my ear. "Hi, Zoe. How are you doing?"

"As well as can be expected, I guess." Her voice wavered a bit on the last word, but when she continued, she sounded firm enough, back in control. "Word's gone out among the clan, and my cousin Stephen just took Luz to the funeral home. We're hoping we can have the funeral in three days, but we'll just have to wait and see."

"Wait and see for what?" I asked, although I thought I knew the answer. With Joaquin Escobar still on the rampage, it was hard to make plans that were too far off in the future.

Her answer confirmed my suspicions. "See if

things are going to be quiet enough. That's why I called. Alex and Caitlin slipped off to do something while I was talking to David and Evan. It turns out they'd met up with Olivia Gutierrez."

The name wasn't familiar. "Who's that?"

"Joaquin Escobar's daughter. The *nunca*."

To be honest, I'd almost forgotten she existed. Because she didn't have any true magical powers, she'd been on the periphery of things. But what the hell was she doing in Phoenix, of all places? "What did she want?"

"To provide information. I guess her father basically yanked her out of the life she'd been living and made her his servant. She took off this morning, I guess, running here because it was the only refuge she could think of." Zoe paused, then added, "And also to let us know that her father isn't going to give up just because we got Levi back. He and the Ludlows are apparently pretty serious about making sure their *prima*-in-waiting gets the consort she picked out. I suppose Olivia could be exaggerating, but Caitlin made it sound as though we should be expecting World War 3 or something."

It would be nice if this was all an exaggeration, but I didn't think so. And if Joaquin Escobar decided that an all-out witch war was the only way to get Levi back and keep his Ludlow allies happy, I wasn't sure what would stop him.

Certainly not Connor and me alone. We'd barely survived the last encounter. I couldn't ask Zoe to step into that kind of situation, not when I had no way of knowing she wouldn't suffer the same fate as her aunt.

"Well, it was a risk we were willing to take," I told her. "I wasn't kidding myself into thinking that Escobar would take all this lying down. We'll figure something out, though. In the meantime, just stay on your guard, as you have been doing. If anyone sees or hears anything suspicious, no matter how small it might be, make sure you let me know about it."

"I will." Zoe actually sounded almost relieved, as if she was glad that I'd stepped in and was taking charge.

Which I would continue to do—with Connor at my side, of course. I couldn't expect Zoe to assume much of a leadership role right now. She needed to mourn her aunt, and she would also need some time to become familiar with the *prima* power within her. That last thing I wanted to do was drag her into a council of war or something. At some point, I would have to include her in our decision-making, because her clan was just as involved in all this as mine was, but if I could put that moment off even for a day or so, I thought she'd be in a much better position to help out.

A person could only take so many shocks at once.

"What are you going to do about Olivia?" I asked. To be honest, I was hoping Zoe would say she'd already found a place for her somewhere among the de la Pazes; we'd already taken in Lucinda, and even though Olivia clearly wasn't on her father's side in all this, I thought it might be better to keep the two women safely separated, at least until all this was over.

"She's going to stay with my cousin Susanna down in Tempe. They're about the same age, and since Susanna isn't married and has a house with a spare bedroom, it seemed like the easiest solution for now. Evan and I have the room, but…." Zoe trailed off then, and gave a sigh that was audible even through my phone's speaker. "I guess I'm going to have to think about moving soon."

"I think you can put that off until we get this Escobar situation straightened out," I told her, hating more than ever the stupid tradition among witch clans that the new *prima* always had to move into the former *prima*'s home. It provided some continuity for the clan, but at what cost? "I mean yes, eventually you'll need to be in the *prima*'s house, but no one's going to expect you to pick up and move before you're ready."

"I don't know if I'll ever be ready." She hesitated, then said, "How did you ever manage? It just feels like everything is rushing at me all at once."

"I had my clan's elders to help me, and my friends," I replied. "Just like you have Evan and Alex and Caitlin and your parents, and anyone else you need to lean on. Don't be afraid to ask for help. It's not a sign of weakness—the opposite, actually."

Zoe managed a weak chuckle. "I'll try to remember that. Anyway, I need to go. Evan just let me know that Michael woke up and is hungry. But…."

"But what?"

"Do you know what you're going to do, Angela? *Really* know?"

Now it was my turn to sigh. "Not yet. But I will."

We ended the call and I pushed myself off the bed, then reached down to pick up my discarded flats and slide them back on my feet. All seemed quiet enough downstairs, so either Connor hadn't been able to FaceTime with the twins after all, or he'd already spoken with them.

As it turned out, he was sitting in the family room off the kitchen, rapidly texting with someone. I raised an eyebrow at him as I approached, and he mouthed the word "Marie." Well, that made sense. If anyone in the Wilcox clan possessed the knowledge we needed to fight

Joaquin Escobar, it was probably Connor's cousin Marie. Technically my stepmother, too, although I still found it difficult to think of her that way. It wasn't so much her prickly nature—which, I had to admit, had smoothed out a lot over time, thanks to her marriage to my father after so many years of believing she'd always be alone—but more that I hadn't even known Andre Begonie was my father until I was an adult. He hadn't raised me, so why would I look at Marie as a stepmother? She just happened to be the person my father was married to.

I went to the kitchen and retrieved the glasses of water Connor and I had left sitting on the counter there, then returned to the family room and sat down on the big overstuffed armchair that was my favorite seat—when I could actually sit in it, that is. The twins loved it, too, and so there was almost always a squabble as to who would get it when it came time for TV watching.

Thinking of those mundane family activities made me ache inside. I wanted this over with. I wanted to go back to the life Connor and I had had with our children before Joaquin Escobar intervened. Probably an outsider would have laughed at the thought of a family of witches and warlocks being "mundane," but it was true. Yes, Connor and I possessed some very unusual powers, but we still went grocery shopping and drove the kids to preschool and took time out to go to the movies in Sedona. We drove up Mingus Mountain in the winter so we could build snowmen—that was the only place near Jerome where the snow fell thickly enough to make that activity at all practical—and escaped to Flagstaff in the summer to enjoy our house in the cool pines. On the surface, it was a quiet enough existence, but I loved it with every ounce of my being.

And I wanted it back.

At last Connor ended his convo with Marie and laid his phone down on the sofa cushion next to him. "I thought you were going to take a nap."

"I did—for about twenty minutes. But then Zoe called me."

"Everything okay?"

"There haven't been any new catastrophes, if that's what you mean." I couldn't help grimacing slightly at the thought of everything that had happened over the last twenty-four hours. The only good to come out of the whole situation was that Connor and I had taken control of some new powers, but for what good? Luz was gone, and it seemed that Joaquin Escobar was still gunning for us.

I told Connor about Olivia Gutierrez's escape from Southern California, and how she had gone to the de la Pazes for help. "She's safe, which is something," I went on. "But she's really convinced that her father is never going to give up. Levi is the condition for the Ludlows' cooperation, and so Escobar is going to keep trying until he succeeds. He doesn't care about collateral damage, or exposure to civilian authorities. Nothing seems to be much of a deterrent. We can try to face him as best we can. But I'm worried, Connor. I'm worried that even all of us put together isn't going to be enough."

He rubbed his hand over his chin. "The Ludlows are really going along with all this?"

"It sure sounds that way. They want Levi for their *prima*-in-waiting. Having someone with his powers would be an incredible advantage, at least on the surface. The thing is, I don't think they have any idea how pure-hearted Levi is. He doesn't do things for personal gain, or to increase his own powers. I don't see how they think they can just change his personality like that."

"They don't have to," Connor said grimly. "Or rather, they can have Joaquin Escobar mind-control him into doing whatever they want."

"Does that sort of thing even work on Levi?"

"I don't think any of us had the time to ask. But since Escobar's null powers clearly had an effect on him, I think it's safe to guess that his mind-control talents must also work, although maybe not as effectively as they would on most people."

"So…." I leaned over and picked up my water glass so I could drink; for some reason, my mouth was suddenly dry. Tension, probably. Too bad the source of my stress didn't have any intention of giving up so I could relax. "I guess we'll have to explore our options. What were you texting with Marie about?"

"When we first found out what Joaquin Escobar was, I asked her to go back through the Wilcox family archives and see if there were any records of anyone with null powers. She had a lot of crap to sift through, but she said she did find something from the early 1920s. It wasn't that anyone specifically called out this cousin's powers as 'null,' but more that it sounded as if people's talents didn't work around her. However, that was all Marie was able to locate. If that Wilcox witch was actually a null, she didn't seem to use her powers to hurt anyone, and they certainly didn't interfere with…." Connor paused there, and looked like he was doing some quick mental arithmetic. "I think it was Jonah Wilcox who was *primus* at that point. Anyway, there didn't seem to be any interruption of his 'rule,' so to speak, and it also doesn't sound as if the talent has appeared in the Wilcox clan since then."

"Which only reinforces what Luz first told us, that it's a very rare gift. Our records aren't that organized, but I'm pretty sure either Boyd or

Allegra would have mentioned it if there had ever been anyone like that among the McAllisters." I set my glass back down on the coffee table, then tucked a piece of hair behind one ear. "Anyway, none of that really helps us with our current problem. As strong as our clans are, I don't think they're strong enough to face down this threat if Escobar really gets serious."

Connor picked up his phone and placed it on the coffee table, then patted the seat next to him. While I loved my big squishy armchair, I loved him a lot more. Right then, I could use the comfort of his presence next to me. So I got up from where I'd been sitting and plunked myself down next to him, was gratified to feel his arm move around my waist so he could pull me in close.

"What's your plan, then?" he asked. "Do you think we should ask for outside help?"

"It's the only thing I can think of," I replied. "I just don't know who. I can't imagine that the clans in Oregon or Nevada would be too happy to find out about this alliance between the Ludlows and the Santiagos, but I barely know the names of those clans. I wouldn't know who to reach out to."

Fingers playing with a lock of my hair, Connor said, "No, the Wilcoxes have never had a connection with any of those clans, either. And geographically speaking, it would be hard to form an alliance of our own with the witches and warlocks in Oregon. Nevada, maybe, but…I really think our best bet is the Castillos."

Of course. They were the clan that held sway in New Mexico—all of it, which was somewhat unusual. Most of the time, a witch clan didn't cover that much territory. Then again, New Mexico wasn't exactly what you could call a heavily populated state.

More importantly, the Wilcoxes had a connection to the Castillos going way back. I didn't know all the details of the story, but apparently the Wilcox healer had done a favor for the Castillo *prima* when the Wilcoxes were traveling to their new home in the Arizona Territories, and the two clans had remained somewhat friendly ever since. There was certainly more history to draw on with them.

"Do you think they'll be receptive?"

"All we can do is ask. Isabel Castillo—she's the *prima*—was open enough to allowing Lucas and Margot to travel to Santa Fe for their honeymoon, so at least we have some recent contact with the clan. And I find it hard to believe that Isabel would take kindly to having a usurper like Joaquin Escobar parked next door…if the worst happens."

I didn't want to imagine what that "worst" would be…the dark warlock somehow steamrollering his way through Arizona, subjugating the clans here just like he'd suborned the Santiagos. In that world, there wouldn't be any room for Connor and me—or Zoe and Evan. Would Escobar allow our children to live? I somehow doubted it. He'd make sure to wipe out any possible heirs to the Wilcox, McAllister, or de la Paz clans.

A shiver went over me, and Connor pulled me closer to him, let me absorb some of his warmth. I needed it right then, needed his touch to remind me that the two of us had once prevailed in circumstances almost as difficult as these. I was so close to losing hope.

"The worst isn't going to happen," he murmured, bending down so he could brush a kiss against the top of my head. "If Isabel Castillo doesn't think the threat is great enough, we'll reach out to the Nevada and Oregon clans."

"But first we need to talk to her." I shifted slightly so I could look up at him, look into those crystalline gray-green eyes. Although he appeared troubled, he certainly didn't look like someone who was frightened for his very existence. "Do you have her number?"

"Yes. I found it in Damon's papers when we were closing up the house to sell it. I've only talked to her once, though, to get permission for Margot and Lucas to travel to Castillo territory."

"What was she like?"

Connor gave me a rueful smile. "It was a very short conversation, Angela. She sounded older, and she had a really faint accent, even though I know her family has been in Santa Fe for generations. And she also sounded like the sort of person who doesn't take crap from anyone, but I could say that about pretty much any *prima* I've met."

I made a face. "Not funny."

"I wasn't trying to be funny. All I'm saying is that I didn't get nearly enough of a read from her to attempt to guess how she's going to react to all this. The only thing we can do is try."

"Do you have her number with you?"

"Yeah, I entered it in my contacts list. I figured it was better to have it on hand, just in case." He moved away from me a little so he could reach in his jeans pocket and extract his phone. After unlocking it, he went to his contacts screen and scrolled down briefly. "Here it is." Pausing with his finger next to the little green phone icon, he added, "Do you want to do the honors, or should I?"

"You do it," I said. I'd never been big on cold-calling people, probably because I hadn't had much interaction with anyone outside my clan until I went to high school. "You're the one who's already talked to her, remember?"

"Right." He pushed the button and held the

phone to his ear. For a second I wondered why he didn't put it on speaker. But then I realized that a lot of people might find that kind of behavior rude, if he did it without asking for permission. The last thing we wanted was to piss off this Isabel Castillo before we even got started.

"Hello?" Connor said. "Is this Isabel Castillo?" A pause, and he went on, "This is Connor Wilcox. I—right. Yes. That would have been a couple of years ago now. There's something that we—that is, my wife Angela, *prima* of the McAllisters, and I— need to talk to you about. It's important." Another long pause, and he said, "I can under- stand why you'd want a face-to-face on this, but —" He stopped there, as if she'd cut him off. "All right. We can be there quickly. No, no, we don't need to drive. Twenty minutes? Okay. Twenty-five Gonzales Road? Got it. Thank you."

He put down the phone, while I stared at him, appalled. "She's expecting us there in twenty minutes? Have you looked at me lately?"

Puzzled, he tilted his head to one side and gave me a quick once-over. "You look fine to me. Beautiful, really."

When a guy says something like that to you, it's really hard to get too mad. However, his devoted admiration wouldn't change the fact that my hair was flat in the back from lying on it during my quick nap, or that I didn't have on a speck of makeup except for some mascara. "I've got to fix myself up," I said, rising from the sofa. "And you'd better do some primping, too, Mr. Man. I doubt that a T-shirt and jeans are going to do it for the *prima* of the Castillos."

His mouth twitched, but he had the good sense not to argue. Instead, he followed me up the stairs to our bedroom, where we both hurriedly changed—me into an elbow-sleeve top in dark green and a flowy peasant skirt that contained that same shade of some green in its print, along with hues of turquoise and teal. Connor had exactly one pair of what he called "thin pants"—in other words, dress slacks as opposed to jeans—in his wardrobe, but he dutifully climbed into those and a pale gray shirt. While he was trying to find the only pair of dress shoes he owned, buried somewhere in the back of the closet, I popped into the bathroom and did my best to tidy my hair, then brushed on some lip gloss and a bit of taupe eyeshadow. Some turquoise earrings and the gorgeous necklace in multiple shades of turquoise that Connor had given me for Christmas a few years back, and I was about as presentable as I was going to be.

"You look amazing," he said as I exited the bathroom. "Maybe we should hang out in Santa Fe for a little while after we meet with Isabel.

Aren't they supposed to have some pretty great restaurants there?"

I wanted to tell him that we didn't have time for that sort of distraction, but really, when you factored in the whole teleportation thing, it didn't matter so much where we were, as long as we were reachable by cell phone. "I think I heard that somewhere," I said cautiously, knowing deep down that we wouldn't linger in Santa Fe, not with the situation in Jerome so fraught. Then I recalled the restrictions of our teleportation ability and frowned. "How are we even supposed to get where we're going? We've never been there before."

"No problem." Connor held up his phone, showing me what looked like a fairly impressive stretch of stucco wall, with tall old trees and a glimpse of some adobe buildings behind it. "Isabel gave me the address, so all I had to do was use Google Street View to find the house. Or at least the entrance to the house, which is good enough."

I came closer and peered down at the image on the screen. Yes, there was enough detail that we should be able to travel to that spot without too much trouble. It still wasn't ideal, just because we'd be materializing right on the sidewalk, instead of safely tucked away inside the house where no one could see us, but it was the only way we could get where we were going. With any luck, we'd arrive as no one was passing by. Hard for me to say, since I didn't know much about Santa Fe, how busy it was, whether there was much foot traffic.

Well, I supposed we were about to find out.

"Ready?" Connor asked me. He put his phone in his pocket, then held out his hands.

"Ready," I said, grasping his fingers. In my mind, I saw again that low stucco wall, the large sycamore and cottonwood and aspens trees which lined the street.

And we jumped.

20

Margot Wilcox

SHE COULD HEAR THE SHRIEKS OF ANGELA'S twins, along with the more subdued giggles of her own daughter, Mia, coming from the backyard. Margot sat on the deck and sipped some iced tea, keeping half an eye on the trio. She wanted to make sure they didn't get into the kind of trouble that might necessitate a hasty trip to see Ellen, the Wilcox clan's healer, but she also wanted the children to have the chance to play on their own without an adult hovering over them. Back when Margot was a little girl, her mother had let her roam wild all over Jerome, but times were different then. Still, kids needed some autonomy.

She glanced at the display on her phone. Four-thirty. Lucas had run out to the store to get buns for their planned burger cookout tonight. Normally, that wasn't the sort of food they served in their household, but Margot was doing her best to make their time here enjoyable for the twins, to make it seem as if they were only on some kind of extended vacation. So far, none of the children seemed to have noticed anything was wrong, but she and Lucas had had several private discussions about how long this whole charade could be maintained. It was one thing to come and stay for a few days—the twins had done that once or twice before when Angela and Connor desperately needed some alone time—but as the days began to stretch on and on, Margot wondered how long they could keep this up. Sooner or later, Ian and Emily would start to ask questions.

They were beautiful children, with their dark hair and green eyes, just like their parents. Ian was a little taller than Emily, and a good bit taller than Mia, who idolized him and would follow him everywhere like a puppy dog if allowed. Already a few people had started to speculate as to whether that would be a match one day, talk that made Margot want to shake her head. They were just little children, for God's sake. They had a huge chunk of time ahead of them before they needed to start making those sorts of decisions.

Once again she glanced at her phone. Stupid, really, since it had only been a few minutes since the last time she checked, but she knew Lucas should have been home by now. The grocery store was less than ten minutes away, and even if he'd gotten distracted by chips and candy bars and cookies and all the junk she tried to keep out of the house but which he was sure would make the twins' stay more fun, his shopping trip shouldn't be taking this long.

Relax, she told herself. *He might have stopped for gas, or bumped into someone he knows and started chatting. That would be Lucas all over again.*

It was true; her husband did have a knack for running into friends and relatives every time he left the house. Some might say it was coincidence, but Margot knew it was probably just his gift for luck manifesting itself.

She knew she was too on edge. It was hard not to be, what with Connor and Angela so worried about the situation with Joaquin Escobar that they'd been forced to send their own children away from Jerome. Margot had had several talks on the subject with Marie, the clan's seer, but Marie had been able to offer much in the way of helpful insights. She hadn't seen anything involving Escobar, had in fact said that her vision had felt clouded lately, as if something was blocking her. At first Margot thought possibly the dark warlock had a way of reaching across the miles and blocking other people's visions of him, but she'd heard that Caitlin had had a vision of Levi's kidnapping, a kidnapping that had involved Escobar himself, so that explanation didn't feel quite right. Then again, he could have managed to block Margot but not Caitlin…magic wasn't what you could call an exact science.

Either way, Margot would have felt a lot better about the situation if Marie had been able to offer some information about what he was currently up to. Connor had FaceTimed with the children earlier, but he'd seemed preoccupied and didn't say much beyond the usual pleasantries. That alone was enough to worry her, because Connor wasn't the type to hold back important information, especially from the person he and Angela had quietly designated as the children's guardian if anything should happen to them before the twins came of age.

Margot pushed the phone away from her and stood up. The ice cubes had been melting into her tea for the past half hour, and it needed some freshening. A quick glance told her that the children had abandoned the fort they'd been working on and had retreated to the play area, where Ian was now pushing Mia on a swing and Emily was sitting beside her on another swing and doing her best to keep up.

They're fine, she told herself. *Don't hover.*

She went inside, blinking a little at the contrast from the bright sunshine outside with the darker interior of the house. A few toys lay scattered on the family room floor, and she stepped over them on her way to the kitchen, making a mental note to tell the kids to pick them up when they came back inside. A little clutter was all right, but she really didn't need either Lucas or herself tripping over the damn things when they weren't paying attention.

As she poured some more iced tea into her glass, she heard the automatic garage door open and relaxed slightly. All that worrying, just because her husband was running twenty minutes late. It was foolish, because she knew nothing really bad could happen to Lucas; his gift of luck would always protect him.

She went to put the pitcher of iced tea back in the refrigerator. As she closed the door—and heard the door that led from the kitchen into the garage open—she remarked, "I hope you didn't forget the cheese. You know Mia won't eat a burger if it doesn't have cheese on it."

"I'll make a note of that," said an unfamiliar voice.

Standing just inside the door was a dark-haired Hispanic man of middle height, probably in his late forties. She'd never seen him before, but as Margot watched several unfamiliar witches and warlocks filter in behind him, she knew who he must be, impossible as it seemed.

Joaquin Escobar.

Instinct took over. She didn't respond, only turned on her heel and fled for the deck, where she paused long enough to scream, "Mia! Ian! Emily! Run!" And although she had no idea how long it would last, not with Escobar's null powers enough to destroy any of her own magical gifts, she cast a spell of illusion on the children, cloaking their forms in the shapes of squirrels, making them far more difficult to see.

Those squirrels immediately scampered away from the play equipment and disappeared into the pine forest which backed up to the property. The adults in their world might have done their best to shelter those children from the harsher realities of the witch community, but Ian and Emily knew enough that if an adult told them to run, they would...and Mia would follow along with whatever they did.

They'll be fine in the woods, she told herself, pushing aside worries of bears and stray dogs and any other dangers that might lurk in those woods. *They're children under those disguises...very smart children.* Mia had been taught to memorize both Marie's phone number and the number of the clan's healer, just in case. They'd run to a neighbor's house and ask to use the phone. The illusion was only a temporary one, intended to shield them from Escobar's eyes until they had disappeared into the forest.

He came onto the deck, his lackeys still surrounding him. Margot noted that they didn't appear to all be Hispanic, so some of them clearly weren't Santiagos. Was there another witch clan mixed up in all this? The situation had been changing so quickly, she didn't know for sure what was happening anymore.

Only that the darkest warlock in recent history had somehow found his way to her house, and she had no idea what to do next.

With one hand, he waved toward the forest. "Find those children," he commanded, and two warlocks and one of the witches left the little group and hurried across the backyard, heading straight into the forest. Then Escobar turned toward Margot. To her surprise, he was almost smiling, a corner of his mouth lifted in an ironic curl. "I suppose you think you are very clever."

She crossed her arms, chin held high. Whatever happened, she wasn't about to let him see how frightened she was. Tone casual, she replied, "No, not really."

"What if I told you that I thought you were? Turning those children into squirrels—or at least the semblance of them—was rather inspired, especially done on the fly, as they say. I assume your talent is only one of illusion, and not actual trans-formation?"

"Why don't you let me turn you into a toad, and we'll find out?"

At that response, he chuckled slightly. Margot supposed he could afford to be amused; he had her completely outnumbered, and outgunned as well. Her gift with illusions was very strong, but it couldn't begin to compete with the powers this man commanded. "No, I think we will skip that for now," he said.

As he spoke, a satisfied expression settled on his swarthy features, and Margot turned slightly to see what he had pleased him so much. To her horror, she saw the two warlocks and the witch emerging from the woods, each of them gripping one of the children's arms. Ian was struggling with his captor, whereas Mia only looked bewildered. And Emily—her little mouth was set, as if she was already mentally rehearsing what she would do to the man who gripped her so firmly…once she was old enough to exert her powers, of course.

"You let them go," Margot bit out. "They're children. They have nothing to do with any of this."

"Oh, I am afraid I don't agree with you there," Escobar said. "This is all about clan versus clan, after all, and so the children are just as much a part of it as anything else." The falsely pleasant expression he wore shifted, and a cold mask clamped down on his features. "All I want is a trade. I have three of yours. I will give them back in exchange for what should be mine—my fool of a daughter Olivia, the young woman named Lucinda Santiago, and the man you call Levi McAllister."

Margot had had no idea that Escobar's only remaining child had somehow defected. On the surface, it seemed like a fair trade...but would Connor and Angela agree to it? They'd gone to some lengths to make sure Levi was safe. That was before the lives of their children were at stake, however.

"I—I don't have the authority to make that bargain," she said, forcing the words out past her dry throat. How she hated this feeling of helplessness, of knowing there wasn't a single thing she could do to fix this situation. Her entire life, she'd done her best to feel as though she was in control. Now, however....

"Oh, I know you don't," Escobar replied. "You are only a glorified babysitter. But you can speak to Angela and Connor, make them see reason. They should care little for what happens to Olivia and Lucinda, since they are not kin to them. Even this Levi, who has been adopted into the McAllister clan—I doubt they will think he is worth more than their own children. But I suppose we shall see. You will contact your *prima* and *primus,* tell them that they will need to make a trade if they want to see their children alive again."

Margot swallowed. Right then she could only be glad that she hadn't eaten recently, or she worried she might be sick to her stomach. She was also glad that Lucas was safely away; he couldn't have done anything to help, but he might have tried to confront Joaquin Escobar, with disastrous results. "How will they contact you?"

A thin smile. "Oh, they know where to find me."

"I'll need my phone. It's on the kitchen counter."

Still wearing that mocking smile, Escobar gestured toward the French doors that opened on the kitchen. Margot went inside, all too aware of the weight of his gaze on her, the cold-eyed scrutiny of his followers, the fear and worry on the faces of the children. She cursed herself for being so helpless, even while she knew deep down that there was nothing she could have done to stop this.

Swallowing, she picked up the phone and began to write a text.

21

Angela

WE REAPPEARED ON A QUIET, TREE-LINED street, right next to the thick adobe wall I'd seen on Google Street View. From what I could see, there didn't seem to be much traffic here, whether by car or on foot. Yes, I heard the faint, hushed murmur of cars off in the distance, but where we stood, we might as well have been the only people around.

Not for very long, though. A few yards away, a heavy gate of age-darkened wood swung outward, and a dark-haired man who looked as if he might be somewhere in his late thirties or early forties peered out at us. "You are Angela and Connor Wilcox?"

We nodded. I didn't bother to correct the

stranger, to tell him that I was going by a hyphenate these days. Judging by the no-nonsense set of his mouth, I guessed such a pronouncement wouldn't go over very well.

"This way," he said, gesturing for us to come inside the gate.

Connor glanced down at me, brows lifting slightly, and I shrugged. This was what we had come here for. There was something somewhat ominous about both the high walls that surrounded the property before us and the utter quiet of the street where we stood, but we really didn't have much choice.

I moved first, Connor following a pace behind me. As I passed through the gate, I could see that the grounds of the property were even more extensive than I'd thought, and must take up almost an entire city block. Huge cottonwoods, their leaves a bright, fresh green, towered over-head. The grass still looked somewhat patchy, but I remembered that Santa Fe was a good deal colder than Jerome, and could get snow even later than Flagstaff some years.

Ahead was an enormous house built in the old hacienda style, with thick adobe walls from which jutted exposed beams. A porch made of the same age-darkened wood as the gate dominated the front of the building, and on that porch were flowers beginning to bloom in pots—snapdragons and pansies and bright blue lobelia. Off to one side I spotted a smaller house, not much more than a cottage. A casita, I guessed.

"She's waiting for you in the living room," the man said as he led us up the steps to the front porch. "I am Juan Castillo, by the way—Isabel's oldest son."

"It's very nice to meet you," I said politely, while Connor murmured something along those same lines.

"But the circumstances are not so nice, are they? Even here in Santa Fe we've heard something of the problems in California."

Maybe that was a good sign. If Isabel Castillo already knew about all the mayhem Joaquin Escobar had been up to, then I wouldn't have to waste valuable time explaining the situation. On the other hand, if the Castillos knew what was going on, why hadn't they reached out to help us?

I nodded, unsure as to how I should respond. Actually, I was glad I hadn't, because in the next moment, Juan had guided us into a large room with lofty ceilings, more exposed beams, and an enormous wrought iron chandelier hanging down in the center of the space. Although all the windows were open, somehow it still felt dark and oppressive in there, possibly because of the heavy antique furniture, or the thick tapestry drapes that framed each of those windows.

Sitting in a large carved chair placed directly in front of the enormous stone hearth was a woman. Her dark hair was swept up into a complicated knot at the back of her head, and she wore a dead-simple long-sleeved black sheath dress with a huge silver and coral cross hanging in the center of her chest. As we approached, she rose from the chair and extended a hand.

I retained just enough presence of mind to take it, although some part of me wanted to curtsey, so queenly was her attitude. Connor did the same after me; she gave him a quick glance up and down, then smiled slightly, although I couldn't begin to guess whether she'd done so because she found him pleasing, or because his hastily put together "good" outfit made him look so ill at ease.

"Welcome, Angela, Connor," the woman said. "I am Isabel Castillo—although I'm sure you've already guessed that. Although I know why you are here, I thought it might be a good idea to hear it from your mouths."

From the way Connor's eyes narrowed slightly, I could tell he didn't much care for these sorts of games. However, he knew the stakes here as well as I did. He wasn't about to do or say anything that might jeopardize our mission. "Joaquin Escobar, a dark warlock from El Salvador, has taken over the Santiago clan, and now he's doing his best to forge an alliance with the Ludlows in northern California. Both those clans are large and powerful. Together—especially led by someone like Escobar—they could be a very real threat to everyone, not just the Arizona clans."

"Ah," Isabel said. "I assume you've tried to make peace with this man?"

"We don't much like his terms," I told her. "Apparently the *prima*-in-waiting of the Ludlows wants one of our clan members for her consort, even though he's already in a relationship with someone else. There's no way we're going to hand over one of our own just so some Ludlow witch can get the boy toy of her choice."

Isabel's mouth quirked. She wore a dark brick-colored lipstick, although it didn't seem as if she had any other makeup on, except mascara. Then again, she didn't need it. In her features, I could see the proud, clean bones of the conquistadors who must have been her distant ancestors. She was still very beautiful, the kind of beauty that only seemed to become more refined with age, even though I guessed she must be at least in her late fifties, but more likely her early sixties, judging by her son's apparent age. "You speak very plainly, Angela. And while I can understand that this man Escobar has caused trouble for you and your clan, I am not quite sure what you expect from us. He has not approached us in any way, hasn't come anywhere near our territory. If he had, I would know."

"No, he's been a little busy making our lives hell," Connor said, his tone wry. "But if he gets his way, manages to do to the McAllisters and the de la Pazes and the Wilcoxes what he's already done to the Santiagos, then he's going to be camped right on your doorstep. I'm not sure you're going to like that very much."

"Most likely not." Isabel stepped away from us, moved to one of the windows so she could gaze out into her expansive garden. What she was looking for, I wasn't quite sure. Maybe she just wanted to reassure herself that all was still calm in her corner of the world. "What he has done goes against all that we witches are taught. We are supposed to be content in our clans, in the territory that our families call home. To take that which belongs to another, to seize lands which aren't yours—it is a terrible thing. But we are also taught that wars among witch-kind are a terrible thing as well, and something to be avoided."

"Believe me, we would have preferred to avoid all this," I said. "Unfortunately, it ended up in our laps whether we wanted it or not. Now all we can do is figure out how to survive. We believe the same things you do, Isabel. But those beliefs aren't what's going to save us. It's having enough people on our side that Joaquin Escobar won't have a chance. That's the only way we're going to survive this."

For a moment, the Castillo *prima* didn't speak. She watched me carefully, then tilted her head to one side. "How far along are you?"

"What?" How could she have known I was pregnant? It had only been in the last week or so that my jeans had begun to get tight, that I'd realized I was going to have to start shopping for maternity clothes in the near future. And the flowing skirt I currently wore certainly hid any of the small telltales I'd begun to notice.

"I told you—I see many things. I can feel when there are interlopers in my territory, and I am able to sense certain things about people. It is one of my gifts, although not the only one."

Every once in a while I really wished that I'd been born into a completely normal family. No witches, no magic, no weird powers I had to deal with. This was one of those times…not that I could do much about it. "A little over three months," I confessed.

She nodded, that same small smile playing around her lips. "I can see why you would be especially fierce in your desire to protect your clan. You want your child to be born into a safer world than the one you inhabit now."

"Yes, exactly," I said. Her words encouraged me, because it seemed clear enough that she understood my situation. "I assume you would wish the same for your own children."

"My children—all five of them—are grown, and quite able to take care of themselves," Isabel responded. "But yes, of course I would not wish to see any harm come to them. So you can understand why I might be reluctant to drag them into a war that has nothing to do with us."

"Nothing to do with you...yet," Connor said, his tone grim. "There's no guarantee that Joaquin Escobar won't come for the Castillos once he's done with us. Working together, we have a chance to stop him. Who will come to your aid after he's swallowed up all the Arizona witch clans, and you're left to fight him alone?"

Again a small silence fell. I could tell Isabel was considering Connor's words, because her mouth tightened again, and she crossed her arms. An enormous diamond winked on the ring finger of her left hand as she did so, and I wondered about her consort. So far we hadn't seen any sign of him, but that didn't mean much. Traditionally, a *prima*'s consort didn't get involved with the day-to-day management of a clan unless he was asked to. And from what I could tell of this proud, imperious woman, she didn't seem the type to ask for assistance very often.

My phone pinged. At once I reached into my purse, digging for it, even as I said, "I'm sorry, but

I'll need to check this. With everything that's been going on—"

"I understand," Isabel cut in. "Go ahead and see what it is about, if only to set your mind at ease."

I pulled the phone from my purse, took a glance at the message on my home screen. My whole body went cold, as if someone had just flicked on the room's air conditioning at full blast.

"What is it?" Connor asked at once, clearly seeing how upset I was.

"It's—it's Margot," I told him, holding out the phone so he could read the message on the screen. "He has the children—he has our twins, Connor! Our children, and Mia, too!"

"My God." He rubbed a hand over his face, as if by passing his hand over his eyes, he could change the reality of what he'd just read. Then his gaze moved to Isabel Castillo, his expression turning hard. "You see who we're dealing with here? This man doesn't care about rules, about honor, about anything! Anyone who'd stoop to using children as a bargaining chip—"

"What is this bargain he is proposing?" she asked.

"It's crazy. You don't bargain with terrorists."

"Of course not," she responded, still cool, still completely unruffled. "But I would still like to know what he demands from you."

"His daughter Olivia, who ran away to take refuge with the de la Paz clan," I said. "Lucinda Santiago, the daughter of the late *prima*…she's been staying with us in Jerome. And the man I told you about earlier—Levi McAllister, the one the Ludlow *prima*-in-waiting wants for her consort."

"Three for three," Isabel mused. "What do you plan to do?"

"I suppose a lot of that depends on you, Mrs. Castillo," Connor said. His eyes were so hard, they might have been chips of green ice. I could tell he wanted to get the hell out of there, back to Arizona so he could talk to Margot, so he could try to do something. Every second wasted in conversation was another second that that monster had our babies.

Tears stung my eyes, and I did my best to blink them away. Terror and panic were beginning to well up in me as the reality of the situation sank in. Joaquin Escobar, with my two children and Lucas and Margot's little girl in his possession. I already knew there was absolutely nothing he wouldn't do to achieve his ambitions, and that thought frightened me more than anything else, made my stomach churn with the sour acid of fear.

Isabel Castillo's cool, proud features were almost sympathetic. Her dark gaze lingered on me for a moment, so long that an entirely different kind of unease began to creep over me. At last she spoke. "No, I think now it very much depends on Angela."

"On me?" I asked. What the hell was she driving at?

"I have...a feeling. Nothing more than that, but my feelings have never steered me wrong. I will give you the support of my clan...if you give me the child you are carrying."

"*What?*" Connor and I both burst out simultaneously. I was so upset that I couldn't find the words to respond right away, outrage and shock warring for dominance in my mind, but my husband definitely didn't have that problem.

"That's a hell of a thing to ask," he said fiercely. "This isn't a fairy tale, and you're not some modern Rumplestiltskin. We don't give up babies in exchange for favors."

This outburst didn't seem to ruffle Isabel at all. She stood there watching the both of us, arms still crossed. "I am not asking for your baby. I want the woman she will grow to be. You will be able to raise her, to enjoy her childhood. But on her twenty-first birthday, she is to be sent to me."

"For what?" I asked. This all sounded unbelievably strange. Isabel couldn't think that the child I carried would be the next McAllister *prima,* did she? For one thing, even though she clearly believed I was going to have a girl, I didn't know the sex of the baby. But asking the child to be sent when she turned twenty-one—the same year a *prima*-in-waiting was supposed to find her consort—seemed a bit too much of a coincidence.

"For my grandson," Isabel replied imperturbably. "The only son of my youngest daughter, who is our *prima*-in waiting. He is five years old. I want her for him."

This was crazy. Absolutely insane. I sent a pleading glance over at Connor, who looked like he was ready to commit murder. Most of the time, I would say he didn't share much of a resemblance with his late brother, but when he got really angry, something of Damon Wilcox did seem to surface in his features.

"That's the most ridiculous thing I've ever heard. This isn't the Middle Ages—we're not going engage our daughter to your grandson while she's still *in utero!*"

"We don't even know that she's going to be the next *prima*—" I began, but Isabel held up a hand.

"I did not say she is going to be the next *prima*. I know that the daughter you have now—Emily?—will be your heir. But this one…she will have her own purpose, her own destiny. And it lies here."

Connor stared down at me, mouth hard. His

voice echoed in my head, seemingly coming from nowhere. *Can you believe she's asking this?*

Just another shock, although I didn't know why I should be so surprised he was able to speak directly into my mind like that. Over the past few days, we'd both begun to explore powers we'd never possessed before. And I had to admit it was handy to be able to talk without Isabel being able to hear what we had to say. Still, I had to wonder where it would all end. I pushed that worry aside and thought at Connor, *I don't want to believe it. But she's serious.*

We can't give up our child.

I know that. Or at least, I thought I did. Right then, I was so panicked and worried about Ian and Emily, I didn't know what to think.

"It's really very simple," Isabel said. "Joaquin Escobar has your children. If you promise to send the daughter you carry to me when she reaches her twenty-first year, I will pledge the support of the Castillos. We will help you to prevail against this dark warlock and ensure that he can harm no others. I am a mother. I do not ask this lightly, for of course the bond between a mother and child doesn't end when that child reaches adulthood. But I have seen that your daughter belongs here with us. Really, is it so very different from her falling in love, say, with a warlock of the de la Pazes, and going to live someplace several hours away from the place where she grew up? It is not as though I am asking you to send her to the ends of the earth."

"No," I said. "But you are asking us to commit her to a relationship she'll have no choice in. Like Connor said, this isn't the Middle Ages. Arranged marriages aren't really in fashion anymore."

"Oh, they are still in some cultures. What I'm asking is not so very far beyond the pale." Her shoulders lifted, slender beneath the perfectly fitted dress she wore. "That is for you and Connor to decide, however. If matters are as dire as you say they are, then I'm afraid you don't have many options. Your daughter will be the child of a *prima*. She will understand why you had to do this." Isabel smiled then, but in an almost rueful way. "Rafael is a very young child, but I know he will grow to be a handsome man. He will always have a prominent position in the Castillo clan, for one day his mother will be *prima* after me. I don't think that what I am offering will present all that much of a hardship to your daughter."

Easy for Isabel to say. If the man who had brought us here to see her was any indication, then sure, the Castillos weren't exactly lacking in the genetic department. But there was so much more to a marriage, to a relationship, than having a good-looking partner. What if it turned out that

Connor's and my daughter and this Rafael hated each other?

I didn't think I could ever forgive myself for that.

But then, how could I forgive myself if I turned my back on this offer of help, and Joaquin Escobar ended up taking control of my clan? What if something terrible happened to the twins, or Mia? I would know that I'd had the chance to save them, and had walked away because of worries about something that might never happen.

You're seriously thinking about this.

I have to think about it Connor, I told him, even my internal voice sounding as though it was on the verge of tears. *We're running out of options. We already know that we're outmatched and outnumbered.*

And what happens if you make this promise and it turns out the Castillos can't help us after all? They're a big and powerful clan, but they're just ordinary witches and warlocks, same as the rest of us. I doubt there's anyone among them who can withstand Escobar's null power.

Connor had a point. But surely there was something to be said for strength in numbers. If the Castillos worked together with the Arizona clans, there would be enough of us to overwhelm the Santiagos and the Ludlows. As for Escobar—

well, we'd already established that his dark gifts didn't work on us, not completely. Maybe we could get Isabel to bond with us the way Luz had. True, that hadn't turned out very well, but I could tell that Isabel was far more powerful than Luz. Also, she'd been *prima* for decades, had a wealth of experience and knowledge to support her. It was entirely possible that Luz would have been like that one day…if she'd been given the chance to grow into her talents and her position.

I can't make this decision on my own, I told him. *We have to be in agreement on this. But the future of both our clans rests on what we choose to do—and the future of the de la Paz family as well. And…and he has our children, Connor. We thought we were keeping them safe by sending them away, and all we did was make them an easy target.*

Hey, he responded, *we did think they were safe. They should have been safe. If nothing else, Lucas' talent should have helped to protect them.*

Well, obviously it didn't.

Yeah, I kind of know that now. The mental equivalent of a sigh, and he went on, *I hate to say it—hate to even think it—but you're right. I don't think we have any choice but to accept Isabel's offer.* A long pause, and he added, *And hope that one day our daughter will forgive us.*

How could I respond to that? This baby

wouldn't even be along for another six months, and already we were thinking about how much she'd probably end up hating us for selling her off like this. She couldn't know how desperate we'd been, how few options we had.

"All right," I said, my voice hard. "We agree to your terms—if your assistance allows us to defeat Joaquin Escobar. If he's not dead at the end of this, then no deal."

Isabel smiled. "You have a ruthless streak in you, Angela. I appreciate that. And I agree to your terms. It would not be fair to hold you to our little arrangement if you did not get the outcome you desired. So we can consider the deal sealed, for now at any rate."

"Great," Connor said, although he didn't look thrilled at all. "What should we do first?"

"This mode of travel you used to get here—"

"Teleporting?" I asked, and she nodded.

"Yes, this teleporting. Can you only send yourselves back and forth in such a way, or can you take someone else with you?"

"We brought Levi back from Joaquin Escobar's house, so yes, we can do that," I replied. "But that was Connor and me working together. I don't know whether each of us can manage another person or not."

"Well, let us try," Isabel said. "I have two people in mind to send with you now—they are both very skilled at defensive magic, so they should be able to help with any attacks by regular witches and warlocks, whether or not they're Santiagos or Ludlows."

"But they won't be able to do much against Escobar," Connor said.

Isabel didn't look overly concerned by his comment. "No, of course not. That task will fall to us, as the leaders of our clans. What of the *prima* of the de la Paz family?"

Connor and I exchanged a glance. That wound was a raw one. To my relief, he spoke first.

"Escobar murdered the former *prima* of the de la Paz clan. Zoe, her successor, has been in charge for barely a day. I'm not saying that she won't be able to help, but I honestly don't know how much she can really manage."

"Unfortunate," Isabel said, although her tone was so bland, I couldn't really tell if she thought it was unfortunate or not. "Well, for now it is probably better if we don't count on her for much assistance. Even so, I think the three of us working together should be able to defeat this dark warlock. The two of you share what seems to be boundless power, even if you're not always certain as to how to use it."

I thought that we'd need to figure it out, and soon, if we wanted to see our children alive. Once again I had to push away the panic that welled up in me. Freaking out wasn't going to do anyone any good. "Who do you want to send with us?" I asked.

"My middle son, Alberto, and Rosella, a very talented witch. They'll be able to help shore up your defenses in Jerome—for if that is where Levi is staying, I think that is where the next attack will come."

"Then we'd better get back—" I began, panic all too clear in my tone, and Isabel shook her head.

"I don't think you have to worry too much, at least not about Escobar himself. No doubt he is already long on the road, taking his captives with him. He will want to defend them from his home ground and make sure they don't leave his sight. Any attacks on Jerome will come from the witches and warlocks working for him."

"They're going to be in for a nasty surprise, then," Connor said, looking grimly satisfied at the thought of any Santiagos or Ludlows getting some blowback. "When Escobar isn't around to tamp down his powers, Levi can be pretty impressive. And his girlfriend Hayley is no slouch, either."

"Her gift is that she can magnify another witch or warlock's power," I explained.

"Ah. That is useful." Isabel seemed to consider for a moment. "You should still take Alberto and Rosella with you. In the meantime, I will send word to everyone in my clan who has talents that could be useful. They will follow by more conventional means, since there is no one among them who can travel instantly in the way you do. But they will be there soon enough. I assume you want them divided somewhat evenly amongst the three clans?"

"Yes," Connor said. "Or actually, maybe more of them down in the Phoenix area with the de la Pazes, since they seem to get targeted first. I know we need to be protecting Levi, but if a bunch of strange witches and warlocks suddenly show up in Jerome, people are going to start asking questions. That's the tough thing about living in such a small town." Frowning, he added, "What about Escobar?"

"We will deal with him, have no doubt of that." Isabel gave us what she probably intended as a reassuring smile, but its frosty appearance didn't do much to bolster my courage. "Once you're back in Jerome, reach out to him. I assume you have some way of making contact?"

"Yes—Luz gave me a number for the Santiago house in Pasadena." It seemed strange to consider contacting Joaquin Escobar through the very mundane means of a phone call, but I didn't have any other way of reaching him. Maybe it was possible for me to beam a thought right into his head, but no way did I want to get that close to that sick mind of his.

"What do you expect us to say to him?"

"Make it seem as if you want to talk terms. Of course you don't, but the point is to make him think you're willing to cooperate. It will buy us enough time to get our reinforcements in place. Then we will take the battle to him."

And get the twins and Mia back, I thought. *Goddess, they must be so frightened. Blessed Brigid, look after them and keep them safe.*

"I assume that means you want us to come back for you at that point," Connor said.

"Yes. Once we know your people are protected from attack, you can come here and get me, take me with you to this house in California that Joaquin Escobar has taken for his own." A strange expression passed over her patrician features, one that seemed to be a mixture of curiosity and amusement. "I must admit, I am rather looking forward to experiencing that mode of transportation."

Someone knocked softly on the doorframe to the living room, and we all turned. Standing there was Juan with another man a few years younger, someone who shared such a resemblance with him —the same thick black hair, the same long, aristocratic nose—that I guessed this must be his brother

Alberto. The woman who stood with him was probably around his age, her dark hair pulled back into a low ponytail. Unlike Isabel, she looked downright casual, in jeans and an embroidered Indian-style top, turquoise earrings a contrast to her olive skin.

How Isabel had managed to summon them without us even noticing, I had no idea. Had Juan been eavesdropping outside the whole time, and made the calls once he heard Alberto's and Rosella's names mentioned?

Either that, or Isabel had the ability to reach out with her mind and make her wishes known. I thought I liked the first possibility a little better.

"Angela, Connor, this is Rosella and Alberto. They'll be traveling with you," the Castillo *prima* said.

"Hi," I said, with Connor echoing the word and sounding almost as awkward as I felt. "We're going to be teleporting. I know that sounds strange, but—"

"It's all right," Rosella broke in. "We know what we need to do."

She came over to me, even as Alberto approached Connor. No doubt she thought it would be slightly less awkward for us to transport someone of our own sex. As I began to reach out and grasp Rosella's hand, however, my phone started buzzing in my purse.

"I need to take that," I said apologetically. "Hang on a sec."

"No problem," Rosella replied, stepping back a bit to give me some room.

The number on the display was Levi's. I hurriedly lifted the phone to my ear. "Levi? What is it?"

I wasn't sure I'd ever heard him sound so worried. "Where are you? All hell is breaking loose over here."

Oh, no. "On our way."

I ended the call and shoved the phone back in my purse. "Sounds like we might be going into a combat zone. Are you ready?"

Rosella nodded, and, a few paces away, Alberto did the same. I locked my fingers around those of the Castillo witch, closed my eyes, and jumped.

22

Levi

WHILE HE HADN'T BEEN THRILLED AT THE thought of being confined to his apartment indefinitely, Levi thought there were far worse fates he could have suffered. At least he had Hayley here with him. At the moment, her head was pillowed on his lap, his feet up on the coffee table, as they discussed the various options available to them on Netflix. Such an ordinary little scene. It was hard to believe that he'd been held captive by Joaquin Escobar only a few short hours ago.

Levi wanted to put those memories behind him. While he was glad to be safely away, and doubly glad to be here now with Hayley, he couldn't forget the very high price they'd paid so that he could return to his life. The de la Paz clan had lost their *prima,* and now no one was quite sure what was going to happen next.

"What about *iZombie?*" Hayley asked. "I never got a chance to see that."

"You're interested in zombies?" Levi inquired, faintly surprised. He hadn't thought Hayley was the type to watch shows with that kind of blood and gore.

Her big blue eyes blinked up at him. "Well, the lead character is a zombie, but she doesn't go around killing people. Or at least, that's what I've heard. It's definitely not like *The Walking Dead.* If you don't like it, we can find something else."

"Sure," he said, knowing that he would have agreed to watch just about anything with her. The important thing was being here, having her lie on the couch with her head on his lap, the sweet herbal scent of her shampoo drifting up from the blonde tresses that flowed over his thighs.

She was already holding the remote, so all she had to do was shift slightly so she could point it at the television. As she began to work her way through the Netflix menu, however, footsteps pounded up the stairs, and the next moment, someone was banging at the door.

"Levi!"

It was Lucinda's voice. Levi knew she was alone today, because Brandon had to go back into work.

"Great timing," Hayley grumbled, but she obligingly pushed herself out of the way so Levi could rise from the couch and answer the door.

His senses were already on high alert, though, because he knew Lucinda wouldn't pound on the door like that unless she had a very good reason. He flung it open, saw her standing there, chest heaving as though she'd just run up both flights of stairs. Actually, he assumed that was precisely what she'd done.

"They—they just got out of their van and started breaking windows," she gasped.

"Who?" That sort of destruction sounded like the work of local hooligans, although he hadn't thought anyone would be foolish enough to do something like that to any of the store owners here in Jerome. Most people down the hill in Cottonwood and Clarkdale had no idea that the little tourist town was half populated by witches and warlocks, but they knew enough to understand it wasn't a good idea to risk invoking the wrath of the people who lived and worked there.

"They're witch-kind," she replied. "I didn't recognize any of them, though. Must be Ludlows, because if Joaquin had sent Santiagos here, I would have known who they were."

So the war had begun, although he thought starting off with a series of broken windows didn't have quite the same impact as shooting a cannon.

Actually, he guessed that such low-level mayhem was merely a ploy to draw him out. The question was, would he allow them to do such a thing? He was supposed to stay safely inside and avoid presenting himself as a target.

Even as he mulled that notion, he knew he would have to go out. He couldn't hide here in his apartment and expect those with lesser magical skills than he to manage the defense of the town. Hopefully—sooner rather than later—Angela and Connor would get wind of what was going on, and come down to assist him. In the meantime, he had Hayley. He could only hope that the two of them would be enough to drive back the invaders.

"Hayley," he said. It was all he said, but it was enough. She'd already sat up and slipped her shoes back on as soon as she heard what Lucinda was saying, and now she came over to meet them at the door.

"I'm ready," she told him.

He had to admit that she looked ready. Her chin was firm, and the fire blazing in her azure eyes told him she was all too willing to take the fight to these witches and warlocks who'd brought mayhem to their peaceful little town.

"Where?" he asked.

"Down the hill, at the gallery just below the Flatiron."

It made sense that the invading witches and warlocks would start there. If they caused enough destruction, they'd block the highway before it split into two one-way streets, with the Flatiron building serving as the break point. That would make it difficult for anyone to come up the hill to provide assistance.

He took Hayley by the hand. She knew what he intended to do and nodded, joining her power with his. Levi wished he had enough strength to bring Lucinda with him as well, but her minor talent with weather-working really wouldn't help all that much here.

"Summon everyone you can," he told her, and she blinked at him, right before he placed the image of the Flatiron in his mind and sent Hayley and himself there.

When they materialized on the sidewalk in front of the triangular building, they were greeted by the sound of destruction, only this time it hadn't come from one of the storefronts, but from a car heading downhill as it crashed into the one in front of it. Levi immediately saw why the fender-bender had occurred: The driver in the lead had stomped on his brakes to avoid careening into the line of witches and warlocks who stood blocking the road—all dressed in casual street clothes, as though they'd stopped in on their way to go shopping at Costco—and the car to his rear had smashed right into him.

Hayley still clung to his hand, her power coiled, ready to assist him. While Levi knew he could employ some of the same tactics he'd used against the demons Escobar had sent to attack the town, he knew they would most likely kill the people who confronted them now, rather than simply drive them off. While some would have said this was war, and the Ludlow witches and warlocks enemy combatants, he wasn't sure he wanted to go quite that far. In the back of his mind, he hoped they would be able to come to a resolution at some point, and any future peace-making would surely be made that much more difficult if he managed to kill several members of the Ludlow clan. What he really needed was to get them off the street.

Of course.

The wind came howling down off the mountain, stronger than any winter gale Jerome had ever seen before, strong enough that even Levi had a difficult time standing upright, although he'd made sure it wouldn't reach full strength until it had passed him and Hayley. She clung to his hand with both of hers, long blonde hair flying around her head like ribbons of tortured gold.

There were seven Ludlow witches and warlocks, enough to easily block the narrow street.

As soon as the wind hit them, however, they went over like bowling pins, rolling and tumbling down the steep incline. A few hundred yards from where Levi stood, Highway 89A took a jog to the east, and that was where they all collected, washed up against the fence of the vacation rental property there like so much flotsam and jetsam.

"You don't really think that's going to keep them away, do you?" Hayley asked.

Her question was a valid one; even as Levi watched, the Ludlow witches and warlocks began to climb to their feet and struggle their way back up the hill.

"No," he said. "I only wanted to buy a little time." Glancing around, he saw that a crowd of tourists had begun to gather, expressions more curious than frightened. Quite possibly they thought this was all a show put on for their bene-fit, like the street shootouts he'd read about down in the former mining town of Tombstone.

More important, though, was the arrival of the elders. Boyd wore a pair of overalls and had a hammer hanging from the loop on his pants leg, which meant he'd probably been in the middle of one of his numerous "projects" when he got word of the invaders. Right behind him were Tricia and Allegra, both of whom looked pale and frightened.

"How many?" Boyd asked.

"Seven," Levi replied. "So far I haven't had a chance to see what kind of powers they control, although they've already managed to do a lot of damage."

"I can see that," Tricia said, looking at the shattered storefronts, her mouth tight with anger.

"Where are Connor and Angela?" Hayley asked, looking past the elders as if expecting to see the *primus* and *prima* show up at any moment.

"I don't know," Boyd replied. "We stopped by their house on the way down here, as soon as we got word that something was happening, but no one answered."

That was not good. While it was certainly within their rights to come and go as they pleased, Levi thought that the clan leaders could not have chosen a worse time to disappear.

What was also not good was the rapidly closing distance between him and the advancing Ludlow witches and warlocks. Even from yards and yards away, he could see the scowls they wore. Apparently, they didn't much appreciate being knocked over like a group of ninepins.

Allegra glanced at the watching civilians, her sparse brows furrowed with worry. "We should not be doing this in front of an audience," she said.

Hayley frowned as well, but more out of irritation than worry. "Well, if you have a way to snap your fingers and get rid of all of them, go for it. Otherwise, I think we have more important things to worry about."

"Oh, my magic doesn't work like that—" Allegra began, but Boyd cut her off.

"We'll worry about the consequences later," he said. "They got past our wards without setting any of them off, which means they're strong. We're strong, too, but not the kind of strong that can knock out a group of invading witches and warlocks."

"That's all right," Levi replied, although inwardly he wasn't sure whether it would in fact be all right. "The important thing now is to pool all our strength to prevent them from getting any closer."

He held out his free hand to Boyd, who took it. Seeming to understand what Levi was planning, Tricia stepped forward and twined her fingers with Boyd's. Then Allegra came to close the circuit.

Yes, they were strong. Levi could feel the energy sparking amongst them, amplified by Hayley's remarkable gift. He took that energy, imagining an invisible wall, a barrier that no enemy witch or warlock could ever penetrate.

It shot up before them, not quite invisible, but nearly so, a faint shimmer in the air that one could really only see if it was looked at sideways.

The wall stretched from one side of the highway to the other, touching the storefronts to either side.

Just in time, too, because the Ludlows had picked up their pace, despite the steepness of the hill they were climbing. Almost as one, they collided with the barrier and were jolted backward, sparks flying from the contact.

Once again they were knocked off their feet, falling to the pavement with multiple thuds that made Levi want to wince. They had to be picking up a nice collection of bumps and bruises.

"You can't keep us out forever," one of them said as he stood up, face tight with pain. He was a man who looked to be in his early or middle forties, with sandy brown hair and light eyes. In his khaki pants, plaid button-down shirt, and dock shoes, he looked more like he was dressed for a backyard barbecue or perhaps a boating party than a warlock bent on the destruction of an enemy clan.

Then again, the whole point was to blend in. Unfortunately, no one was blending in very much at the moment. Levi wasn't sure what they would do about that. While he could blank a person's memories of a single unfortunate incident, there had to be at least fifty people looking on right now, with more arriving as word got out that something very strange was happening at the intersection of Main Street and Hull Avenue.

"Possibly not forever," Levi replied. "But long enough. There are only seven of you, after all, versus an entire town."

"I don't see that many," the Ludlow warlock sneered.

Well, true, but even as they completed this exchange, more McAllister witches came hurrying down, pushing their way through the watching crowd as best they could. Levi saw Angela's cousin Kirby, and his boyfriend Jordan, and then Rachel and her husband Tobias.

At the sight of Tobias, Levi couldn't help letting out a small sigh of relief. Not so much that he thought the other man would be useful in this confrontation, but more because his studio was located down near the old high school, and if he'd been working there, he would have been separated from Rachel, caught behind the Ludlow witches.

And there was Lucinda as well, trailing along behind Rachel. Levi knew she wouldn't have stayed away, but he hoped she would know enough to keep out of the fight. Her gifts weren't strong enough to make any kind of a difference here.

One of the Ludlow witches stepped forward to stand next to the warlock in the plaid shirt. She seemed to be around the same age as the warlock, and also wouldn't have attracted notice at the local grocery store, in her jeans and loose knit top and flat shoes. He bent and murmured something to her, and she moved forward again, this time going right up to the barrier Levi had erected. Slowly, she raised one hand, palm facing outward, as if she intended to press it against that nearly invisible wall.

But she didn't touch it. No, she stopped less than half an inch away, so close that Levi could see small sparks come and go within the barrier, longing to reach out and give her a good zap.

"Well?" said the warlock as the other members of the Ludlow contingent looked on.

The witch smiled in a manner that Levi didn't much like. "It won't be a problem," she replied.

Then she laid her hand flat against the magical wall. Sparks shot out from beneath her palm, but she merely gritted her teeth and continued to press against it. As Levi and the rest of the McAllister witches and warlocks looked on in horror, small gleaming cracks began to appear in the barrier, spreading outward faster and faster, until the whole thing shattered and disappeared into nothingness.

"Get back!" Levi cried out. His gaze caught that of Tobias, who was a big, burly man, someone who would be very useful in herding the crowd of civilians out of harm's way. "Tobias, get them out of here!"

The tall warlock nodded and began pushing people back, driving them up the hill and away from the Ludlow group, including the two people involved in the fender-bender, who'd been so wrapped up in their argument over whose fault the accident was that they didn't even seem to have noticed what was going on. Some of the other McAllisters, including Rachel, got the idea —probably realizing that their gifts with growing plants or brewing potions wouldn't be of much use here—and also helped to drive the civilians out of the combat zone.

Their absence provided a little more breathing space. Not that Levi was given the chance to catch his breath, because one of the other Ludlow witches approached and flung a fireball at him and the elders.

"Down!" Levi, still holding on to Hayley's wrist, dragged her down to the sidewalk with him. She looked at him with terrified blue eyes, but she did as she was instructed.

So did Tricia and Allegra...but not Boyd.

He stood straight and tall, eyes filled with rage. Faster than Levi would have thought possible, given the elder warlock's age, Boyd pulled the hammer from its loop on his overalls and flung it at the Ludlow witch.

The hammer flew through the air and connected with the side of her head with a sickening crunch. She crumpled to the ground, fair hair spilling around her as she lay limp on the pavement.

"You son of a bitch!" the lead warlock snarled. He raised a hand, then twisted it to one side in a strangely sinister movement.

Boyd let out a gasp. His eyes opened in shock, and he clawed at his throat, as though no air was getting through to his lungs. Then he, too, slumped and fell onto the hard surface of the street, and didn't move.

Levi felt him go, felt his spirit leave his body. Why, he wasn't sure. Was it because they had been linked together only a few moments earlier? Even as a wave of sorrow washed over him, he knew he couldn't pause to ponder what precisely had happened, because another of the warlocks came forward, lightning spiking out of his fingertips.

It didn't reach the little group that lay huddled on the ground, however. From out of the clear blue sky, raindrops began to descend, falling on the warlock who'd summoned the lightning. The water pooled around his feet, and, before he could react or step away, the bolts shot from his fingers into that water, then charged back into him. He let out a shriek and fell, writhing as smoke billowed from his clothing.

Startled, Levi looked back over his shoulder to see Lucinda crouching behind him. She shrugged and said, "It's a minor gift, but sometimes it can be useful."

"That's for sure."

No time for further words after that exchange, because the remaining Ludlow witches and warlocks were advancing again, their faces contorted with rage. So much for avoiding bloodshed. Yes, everything the McAllisters had done was purely in self-defense, but Levi doubted that Joaquin Escobar—or the Ludlow *prima* and her consort—would care much for that minor detail.

If that was how they wanted it, then fine.

A wall of flame roared into being, blocking the Ludlows from coming any closer. Levi got to his feet, pulling Hayley with him. Tricia and Allegra rose as well, clinging to one another and staring at Boyd's lifeless form as if they weren't quite sure what to do next.

Levi could understand their shock. Yes, they were clan elders, and possessed of extraordinary gifts, but all the same, their lives had been fairly sheltered. Even the death of Tricia's niece had happened off stage, so to speak. The McAllister elder hadn't been there to witness the brutality of Roslyn's death. Now, though...now there was no escaping from the destruction the Ludlows had brought to their clan.

The wall of fire seemed to have halted them, but only temporarily. He took advantage of that brief respite to pull his phone from the pocket of his jeans and hurriedly connect a call to Angela's cell phone. She must be very far away, or else she and Connor would certainly have arrived by now to see what was going on. Not that distance mattered much anymore, not with the way she and her husband had managed to learn how to teleport.

Her voice came from the speaker. "Levi?"

"Where are you? All hell is breaking loose over here." That, he thought, wasn't too much of an exaggeration.

Only three words, but they reassured him more than any others could have. "On our way."

Hayley's hand gripped his arm. "*Levi.*"

The wall of flame disappeared, doused by a downpour that made Lucinda's little rain shower seem like nothing. Worse, once the fire was gone, Levi could see that the five remaining Ludlow witches and warlocks had been joined by another group of seven.

But even as their lead warlock began to smile and advance, a group of four people materialized in front of him, blocking his progress. Two of them were Connor and Angela, far more dressed up than Levi usually saw them. The other two were a witch and a warlock he'd never seen before, the man perhaps in his late thirties, the witch probably close to the same age, both of them dark-haired and dark-eyed, clearly of Spanish extraction.

Angela and Connor grasped hands and faced the intruders. The *prima*'s chin was up, her eyes nearly spitting green fire.

"I'll thank you to get the hell out of our town."

23

Angela

EVEN THOUGH LEVI HAD SAID ALL HELL WAS breaking loose, I hadn't exactly expected to reappear in the middle of a war zone. One glance revealed broken windows, a couple of cars locked together in what must have been a hell of a fender bender.

And…oh, shit. *Shit.*

There was Boyd, lying face down in the middle of the street in front of the Flatiron. Boyd would never allow himself to be seen in such an undignified position. Unless….

Unless he was dead.

I had to push that horrible realization aside for now, because I saw that at least a dozen Ludlow witches and warlocks stood in the street before us. Although I'd been holding Rosella's hand as we traveled, she let go immediately and stood straight and tall to my right, just as Alberto did the same on the other side of Connor.

Without thinking, I reached out to him, twined my husband's fingers in mine. A rage unlike any I'd ever experienced before filled me then. How dare they? How *dare* they come here to my town and bring their evil with them? This was my home, the home of my family. My cousin— one of the clan's elders—lay dead in the street because of these bastards.

"I'll thank you to get the hell out of our town," I said, my tone carrying across the space between us, clear and cold.

Connor's fingers tightened on mine, but he remained silent, letting me take the lead for now. If this scene had been playing out somewhere in Flagstaff, we would have reversed roles, since that was his town.

But Jerome was mine.

"Easy enough," said the lead Ludlow warlock, who looked like someone's dad on his way to a parent-teacher conference, not a minion of one of the blackest warlocks the world had ever seen. "Mr. Escobar is willing to talk terms."

Oh, I'd bet he was, since the bastard was currently holding my children captive, along with

Margot and Lucas' daughter. He thought he had all the power in the world.

"And what are those terms?" I asked, forcing the words out past my clenched jaw.

"Your clan becomes part of his clan. All your Arizona clans will merge with his, and he will lead everyone from the Pacific coast to the New Mexico border."

I let out a derisive chuckle. "Oh, is that all?"

"That should be enough...to start, anyway."

No doubt. I had no intention of giving in to Escobar's demands, but even if I'd paused to entertain the notion, I would have realized soon enough that, once we'd surrendered, he would have found more and more ways to encroach on our freedoms, our lives. He certainly couldn't be trusted to hold up his end of a bargain.

I wondered if the Ludlows had stopped to consider that particular downside to working with such an evil man, or whether they thought he wouldn't turn on him. If that was the case, then they were fools.

Planting my hands on my hips, I said, "I think we'll take a pass."

The warlock shook his head, his expression falsely pitying. "You don't know who you're dealing with."

"Oh, no," I replied. "I know exactly who I'm dealing with. That's why you can tell Joaquin

Escobar to take his shitty terms and shove them up his ass."

A scowl passed over the man's unremarkable features. He began to lift a hand, but whatever he'd intended to do, it didn't have quite the effect he'd been expecting. At once both Alberto and Rosella spat out a series of syllables in Spanish. I didn't understand the words, but I saw their effect right away. The pavement beneath the warlock's feet—and beneath the feet of the rest of the Ludlow crew—began to ripple and undulate, as if the asphalt of the road had come alive. The lead warlock lost his balance and fell to his knees, as did the majority of his followers. Even those who'd managed to stay on their feet were stumbling around, arms flailing as they tried to remain upright, looking like people trying to cross a rope suspension bridge and not succeeding very well.

That was the only opening we needed. Casting a wall of flame, as I knew Levi was able to do, might cause too much damage. The same with flinging lightning bolts at our opponents. We needed to get rid of them, render them powerless.

I glanced at Connor. "Give them the Matías treatment?"

He grinned, a ferocious baring of his teeth that again made him look a little too uncomfortably like his older brother. "Well, they don't seem to have a problem following someone who can take their powers away whenever they're around him. Let's see how they like it when the condition is permanent."

As the ground continued to rumble—and as Levi bent to gather up Boyd's lifeless body and remove him from any further harm—Connor and I stepped forward a pace, stopping before we got to the part of the street that Rosella and Alberto had made dance. We raised our hands, facing the Ludlow witches and warlocks.

"If you can't use your powers for good," I said, "then you don't deserve to have them at all."

The *prima* gift surged up through me, connecting with Connor's, shooting forth in a blaze of energy that felt a hundred times stronger than the power we'd summoned to burn the magic out of Matías Escobar and the Aguirre cousins. I didn't know why it was so much stronger now. Maybe it was simply that Connor and I had been working together so often lately, had been flexing our magical muscles so much that our gifts had grown correspondingly more powerful. The power flowed outward, connecting with the Ludlow witches and warlocks one by one.

They felt it, too. I watched as their expressions turned to ones of dismay, of utter horror. The lead warlock stared me, his face so white, I didn't know whether he was about to faint.

"You—you took it away," he gasped, even as

Rosella and Alberto lowered their hands and the pavement settled down, albeit with hundreds more cracks, both large and small, than it had had a few minutes earlier. "How can you do that?"

"You mean Escobar didn't warn you?" I asked. "We did the same thing to his son, after all. He might have at least let you know the risk you were taking."

One of the witches came to stand next to the warlock. She was pretty, with long red hair that reminded me of my cousin Caitlin. Her eyes were haunted, her hand shaking as she laid it on the warlock's arm. "Is it—is it permanent?"

She was probably thinking of how Joaquin Escobar's null power had a limited range, and once you were outside it, you were fine. "I'm not sure," I said, even though I knew damn well it was permanent...unless we tried reversing the spell. I supposed such a thing was possible, since the demons summoned by Matías' half-sister had brought his gifts back. Still, I didn't see any reason to give this witch any hope by mentioning that particular fact. The rage burned within me, reminding me that these people's leader had kidnapped my children. "For now, I think you'd better get back to where you came from."

"But—"

Connor let go of my hand and stepped

forward. "You drove here, right? I mean, you're not all a bunch of teleporters, are you?"

The warlock shook his head.

"Great. Then get back in your minivans or whatever, and get the hell out of Dodge. Let your fearless leader know what happens to people he sends to invade our territory."

"That's—that's it?" the red-haired witch asked, looking both relieved and terrified.

"Yes, that's it," I replied before adding, "After all, you're not a threat anymore, are you?"

The warlock standing next to her flushed with impotent fury, but the witch only said sadly, "No, I guess not."

Connor and I stood there and watched as they gathered up their fallen companions and began to shuffle back down the hill. There was a public parking lot just past where the road jogged, and I assumed that was where they'd parked. After the morose little contingent disappeared from sight, I turned back toward the sidewalk, where Levi was waiting, Boyd's body clutched in his arms. Hayley stood next to him, her face white, and beside her were Tricia and Allegra, also pale.

Feeling very tired, I said, "Let's take Boyd home. And I don't know quite how to manage it, but we need to get as many tourists out of this town as possible. The situation is just too unstable right now."

"Allegra and I will handle that," Tricia said. Her mascara was a smudged black mess, and her eyes still looked red, but at least she appeared in command of herself. "We'll get some traffic cones and some barricades out here, tell people the road has become unstable and that they'll need to go up and over the hill into Prescott to get out. It's not that implausible—all of Cleopatra Hill is shored up and jury-rigged, thanks to the abandoned mines beneath it. We'll make it work."

"Thanks, Tricia," I said, feeling immeasurably relieved she'd taken on that responsibility. Yes, you could say that was part of the job, since she was an elder, but still, we were all a bit shaky. I looked over at Levi. "Can you manage to carry Boyd all the way to his house?"

"Of course," he replied. "It's the least I can do for him."

I offered him a tremulous smile before turning to Rosella and Alberto. "Thank you so much for your assistance here. I'm pretty sure we'll be safe for a while, but do you mind staying in this spot for now, just in case?"

"Of course not," Alberto said. "This is what Isabel sent us here to do. You take care of your fallen warrior."

Fallen warrior. I glanced again at Levi with his grim burden, and then at Connor, who looked like he was ready to fight off any future interlopers with his bare hands. Hot tears stung my eyes, and I swallowed. I didn't have time for tears right now. We had to go take Boyd's wife the terrible news, and then…

…well, and then we'd have to go and face our real adversary. No time for phone calls, as Isabel Castillo had suggested. This needed to end.

I felt as though someone had spent the past hour beating me with blunt objects, but I knew none of us had any time to rest. After going to see Boyd's wife Meredith and bringing her husband's body home, Connor and I went to our own house. Allegra stayed with Meredith, to offer her what comfort she could—she'd known Boyd far longer than Tricia or I had—and Tricia went off to see about blockading the town as best she could. A precaution that might not be needed, since we were about to take Escobar's fight to his own front door, but I felt safer knowing there wouldn't be any innocent bystanders around to get sucked into another magical battle, should the dark warlock send another wave of attackers against us.

Once we were home, Connor and I changed out of the good clothes we'd worn to visit Isabel, and got back into much more practical jeans and boots. I put on a black top, out of respect for

Boyd. A tiny gesture, one he wouldn't even see, but I felt I had to do something to show my gratitude for the way he'd stood up to the Ludlow witches and warlocks.

After that, it was back to Isabel's house, although this time we sent ourselves directly to her front porch rather than bothering with appearing outside the gates to the compound. I'd barely lifted my hand to knock on the oversized front door when it opened, and she gazed out at us. A swift glance took in my black shirt and pale face, and she nodded.

"You have bested your attackers, and yet the confrontation was not without its losses," she said as she let us inside.

"No," Connor said. "We lost one of the McAllister clan elders. The Ludlow witches and warlocks Escobar sent against us are running back to California with their tails between their legs, but this has to end here. No more deaths. No more destruction. We have to hit him now, and hard."

"One more death," I put in, my voice cold and hard, not even sounding like myself. "Joaquin Escobar's."

Isabel Castillo nodded. "Yes, I think it is time. You appear armed for battle"—she gave us a quick look up and down—"and so I will do the same. Give me a few moments. There is a pitcher of lemon water and some glasses on the coffee table in the living room."

And she moved away from us, up the curved staircase that led to the second floor. Incongruously, I realized I was thirsty, so I went ahead and walked into the living room and poured some water into two of the glasses that waited there. I handed one to Connor, and he raised an eyebrow.

"It's kind of creepy, don't you think?" he asked with a lift of his chin upstairs.

"Creepy how?" I swallowed some of the lemon water, glad of its cool tang.

"Creepy how she seemed to know we were coming, had this water waiting for us. Like she's a seer, but not a seer like Caitlin, who only has visions occasionally. It's almost as if Isabel knows everything that's going to happen."

"Well, I don't know about *everything*," I said. My free hand touched my stomach, just for a moment. "Yes, she knew I was pregnant, and she seemed to think she'd seen a future where our daughter came to live here in Santa Fe, but if she was really omniscient, then she'd already know how all this was going to turn out."

"All right, maybe not everything," Connor allowed. "But a lot."

"That's probably why she's *prima* of such a powerful clan." I shrugged, trying to appear unconcerned. "I'm sure if she actually did know whether we were going to succeed against Escobar, she would have told us."

"Yes, I would have," came Isabel's voice from the doorway. I gave a guilty start, and she continued as she walked toward us, "I see a good deal. I do not see everything, for that would make me uncomfortably like God, would it not? At any rate, I had a feeling you would need Rosella and Alberto especially, and that was true, wasn't it?"

"Very true," Connor replied. "I'm not sure we could have managed without them. That's why they're still in Jerome—Angela and I thought it better if they stayed and provided some cover while we were gone."

"It's not a problem, is it?" I asked.

Another one of those cold smiles that never seemed to reach her eyes. Even though she'd changed her sheath dress for a pair of black slacks and a wine-colored button-up shirt, she still had that aspect of a queen granting an audience. "No, of course it isn't a problem. I sent them to help with the defense of your town, and it seems that they are continuing to do that very thing. I have no worries that you will not send them back once they have served their purpose."

Well, I wasn't going to argue, although the way she spoke of Alberto, who was her own son, did disconcert me somewhat. You'd think she'd be a little more concerned about what happened to him…but then, if she could see bits and pieces of the future, she probably knew there was nothing for her to worry about.

"So…what's our plan?" Connor asked. "We don't have a lot of time to waste. Yes, those Ludlows are going to have to limp back to California on their own power, but you know they must have already called Escobar to let him know what happened in Jerome."

"True," Isabel said. "Still, I would not be too concerned for your children. Not yet, anyway. They are the only real bargaining chip he has, especially now that he knows you can mount an effective defense. It's more likely that he will attack elsewhere, in either Wilcox or de la Paz territory."

"Do you think he'd go after Zoe?" I asked, worried for the newly fledged *prima*. She might not have been defenseless, but she also couldn't command the sorts of powers that Connor and I working together did.

"No," Isabel said at once. "I had a flash of her, in a house not unlike this one. She had many witches and warlocks around her, including one who commands defensive spells."

"That must be Jack," I said, realizing that Zoe must have sent for everyone in her clan that she thought could protect her. Was it enough? It would have to be. "Jack Sandoval, Zoe's cousin.

That's his gift. So I think we can relax about her…I hope."

"But my clan is basically undefended." Connor grimaced. "I knew we should have checked in with Marie before we came here."

"Marie knows what she's doing," I said, hoping my words would help to reassure him that the Wilcoxes weren't as easy a target as he thought they were. "And Margot is there, and Lucas and so many others. They know to be on their guard."

Connor's shoulders lifted, but I saw the way his hands clenched into fists at his sides, straining against what he probably saw as circumstances rendering him impotent when it came to defending his clan. "I'll have to hope so. Anyway, we know the layout of the Santiago house well enough now, so we should be able to teleport in there without too much trouble. Last time, though, Escobar had both Marisol—the Santiago *prima*—and the Ludlows' *prima*-in-waiting with him. Together, they were too powerful for us." He paused then, face going still and sorrowful as he recalled the way we'd lost Luz.

"A tragedy," Isabel said. "But I am far stronger than the de la Paz *prima* was. Let us reach out to one another with our powers now, to see what we are working with."

Even though I knew it was necessary to perform such a test, I hesitated for a moment. It was one thing to join with Luz, whom I'd at least known fairly well after working together for the past few years. But to let my energy mingle with that of this cold-voiced woman who didn't seem to be ruffled by anything? My instincts cried against it, but I made myself extend a hand to her.

She reached over and took it, and Connor wrapped his fingers around mine on the other side. At once I flared with so much energy, I felt as though a nuclear reactor had come alive inside me. I stared down at the hand that held Isabel's, halfway expecting to see it glowing from within. It looked the same though, the same faintly tanned skin, the antique diamond Connor had bought for me glittering on my ring finger.

"Wow," he said, and let go, breaking the contact.

I let go of Isabel's hand as well, and she nodded. "Yes, that seems as though it will work, even if he is working with the *prima* and the *prima*-in-waiting. The Santiago witch is still newly come to her powers, correct?"

"She is," I replied. "And Escobar's been controlling her with his mind the whole time, so she's not exactly as on top of things as she could be. And I honestly don't know if the Ludlow *prima*-in-waiting is even there anymore. You'd think her clan and her parents wouldn't want her anywhere near the Santiago house after our last attack."

"You would think that," Isabel said. "But who knows what might be going through their minds? We will have to prepare ourselves for the possibility that she might still be with Joaquin Escobar. But she is young and does not have access to all her powers yet, so she should not be much of a threat."

I hoped so. However, I warned myself not to get too confident, no matter how strong the three of us working together might be. Going up against Damon Wilcox back in the day had been frightening enough.

This…this was terrifying, because I knew exactly what the stakes were.

"So," Connor said, "the upstairs bedroom, or the living room? If we go straight to the living room, there's a chance we'll end up right on top of Escobar. But if we appear in the bedroom, it's pretty likely that we'll have to spend more time searching the house for him."

"The living room," both Isabel and I said simultaneously. Under other circumstances, I might have laughed, but I didn't find anything funny about the situation. I paused, and Isabel went on, "We want as much of an element of surprise as possible. Of course, he must be expecting you to come back and try another attack, especially now that he has your children. But I don't think he yet knows that you are working with the Castillo clan—Rosella and Alberto didn't identify themselves in any way, did they?"

"No," I replied. "There wasn't much time for introductions. If anything, the Ludlow witches probably thought Rosella and Alberto were de la Pazes."

"Good," Isabel said. "Then I think Joaquin Escobar will be surprised to see me." She held out her hands. The diamond she wore on her left ring finger glittered balefully in the light coming through the tall windows, like a watchful eye.

I took a breath, then clasped her hand in mine. Connor held my other hand, and reached for Isabel's fingers. The circle was complete, and the room faded around us.

As it disappeared, I prayed that we weren't making a huge mistake.

24

Angela

THIS TRIP SEEMED TO MOVE EVEN MORE quickly than the previous times we'd teleported. It could have been that having Isabel's powers connected to ours gave us an extra jolt, like applying nitrous to a race car's engine. Whatever the reason, I barely had time to take in a breath, let alone release it, before the three of us appeared in the living room of what had once been Simón and Beatriz Santiago's house.

It was empty.

We all took a quick glance around, but I could tell no one was here. One of the windows was open, and the filmy curtains on either side of it moved languidly in the mild May breeze. From the street outside, I heard the sound of a car moving past, but otherwise, all was still. Well, outside anyway. Inside, I was all jangling nerves, my blood fairly singing with adrenaline.

Connor moved to the entrance and looked into the foyer, then down the hall. "Nothing here, either."

Isabel and I came up behind him. As he'd said, all seemed to be empty. Then again, this was a big house. Escobar could be anywhere.

"Check upstairs?" I asked, and Isabel shook her head.

"No, he's not up there. Someplace outside…out back."

Both Connor and I arched an eyebrow at her, and she smiled.

"As I told you earlier, I don't see everything, but I still see a good deal. It seems there's some kind of building out there, one with many windows."

"The greenhouse," I said, and Connor looked at me in surprise. "Caitlin told me about it once. She said that Lucinda had mentioned it, that her father's hobby was raising orchids."

"Got it," Connor replied. "Then we'd better go check it out."

As we headed toward the back of the house, I wondered what had happened to those orchids. Had anyone been taking care of them these past few weeks, or had Joaquin Escobar allowed them to wither and die, their fragile lives unimportant to him, just as the lives of everyone who wasn't an ally weren't important?

The hallway opened up into what was clearly the TV room—it was furnished with several large overstuffed couches in caramel-colored chenille, and a vast flat-screen television hung on one wall over the fireplace. Under other circumstances, I would have thought it a welcoming space, but now I could only look at the French doors that opened out onto a terrace and know that once we stepped through them, there was a very good chance we might never come this way again.

Isabel reached out and took my hand. "Courage, Angela," she said. "I haven't seen the end of this thing, but I know your strength. We will prevail."

I wished I could be that confident. Since I knew anything I said would be inadequate, I merely nodded in acknowledgment and took hold of Connor's hand as well. He opened one of the doors, and we stepped out onto the terrace.

It was large, with tastefully arranged iron furniture and blooming flowers in oversized urns. Although it was late afternoon, the air was warm, caressing as a kiss. Three steps led down to an expansive lawn, and off to one side was a handsome glass structure, clearly the greenhouse.

However, I didn't get much of a chance to get

anything more than a glimpse, because my heart seemed to stop at an all-too-familiar sound.

Ian and Emily, laughing.

Yes, there they were on the lawn, throwing a large blue ball back and forth, playing keep-away with Mia. A horrible mixture of relief and fear rushed through me, seeing them like that, because although they seemed to be well enough for the moment, I understood the danger they were in. Their backs were to us, and so I guessed they didn't even realize we were there. But standing close by, watching as they played, was Joaquin Escobar, and the pretty young woman I knew had to be Marisol Valdez. A pair of sunglasses concealed her eyes, so I couldn't tell if she wore the same blank expression I'd noted the last time I saw her.

Escobar looked up and saw us standing there on the top step of the terrace. A slow smile spread across his lips…not a smile of welcome, but one of triumph.

"I thought you would come," he said.

"You didn't think we'd let you keep our children, did you?" I asked.

A shrug. He wore a loose-fitting white linen shirt and tan linen pants, and looked as though he should be sipping margaritas at a beachside cantina somewhere. "No, of course not. I was waiting for you. Now we can finish what I started the last time you tried to bring the fight to me."

"Oh, we'll finish it, all right," Connor said. "Right here, right now."

"In front of the children?" Escobar asked, eyes widening in an expression of feigned innocence. Since his eyes were so deep-set, this didn't have quite the effect he'd probably intended, because to me he looked more sinister than ever.

Mia and Ian and Emily had continued to throw the ball to one another as Escobar and Connor and I spoke, but now Emily held the ball tight to her little chest and turned so she could see us.

"Mommy!" she cried out, then took a step forward.

That was all she could manage, however, because it seemed as if she had just walked into an invisible barrier of some sort. She dropped the ball and put out her hands. They smashed up flat against the wall that had been erected to keep her from going any further, for all the world making her look as if she was imitating a mime's "trapped inside a box" routine.

"You let her go!" I cried, even as her face screwed up and she began to cry.

At once Marisol moved forward and took her in her arms, attempting to soothe her. Emily would have none of it, however, and began struggling and writhing to get away. Ian saw this and ran to her, pulling on Marisol's arm so she would release his sister.

And Mia stood and watched, and began to cry as well, probably because she didn't know what else to do.

The sudden commotion made Escobar's mouth twist in distaste. "Enough," he said, snapping his fingers. At once the sound of the children crying blanked out. It wasn't that they had stopped—I could still see their mouths moving, but whatever sounds they were making had been eliminated somehow.

As much as I hated Joaquin Escobar, I had to admit that was a handy little trick.

"No," Isabel said. She'd been quiet this whole time, but now she leveled the dark warlock with a flat stare as she stood shoulder to shoulder with me. "It is the rest of us who have had enough. You will let those children go."

"And who are you?" he inquired, giving her a half-contemptuous glance. He must have been able to sense something of her *prima* energy, but maybe he thought she would be as easy to beat as Luz Trujillo.

Isabel's chin lifted, and her dark eyes flashed fire. "I am Isabel María Constanza de Léon Castillo, the *prima* of the Castillo clan. And I say it is enough." She made an abrupt slicing motion with the hand that wasn't holding mine, and suddenly we not only heard the children crying again, but saw that Ian had managed to pry Emily away from Marisol, who was probably startled that a five-year-old could possess such strength. He then grabbed Mia by the arm and bolted toward us.

"Get in the house, Ian," Connor said, and even though Ian usually tended to argue with every instruction he was given, this time he bolted up the stairs and past us, Emily and Mia in tow.

I didn't exactly let out a sigh of relief, but knowing the children were out of Escobar's immediate grasp did make me feel a bit better. He, on the other hand, scowled furiously and stuck a hand out toward Marisol. She took it, and I could almost feel the connection they made, feel it like ozone building before a thunderstorm.

"You should not have done that," Escobar gritted, moving toward us.

Looking supremely unconcerned, Isabel said. "On the contrary. It was the only thing I could have done. You should have known better, Joaquin Escobar, than to drag children into a fight which doesn't concern them."

His mouth tightened, but it appeared he wasn't going to waste time by making a retort, because in the next moment, he'd struck out with one of those horrendous unseen shockwaves, the same thing that had knocked the wind out of me and dealt poor Luz a fatal blow.

The results were slightly different this time. I wasn't sure whether it was because Connor and I knew something of what to expect, or because Isabel was so much more powerful, but the blow came toward us and then bounced off, almost as if we'd cast one of Alex's protective bubbles. I honestly didn't remember doing such a thing, and yet I knew we had survived the attack without taking any kind of hurt at all.

The startled expression that passed over Escobar's face was so comical, I almost wanted to laugh. *Weren't expecting that, were you, asshole?* I thought. *Let's try something else.*

Again, it wasn't so much that I had a conscious thought of doing so, but more as if my mind and body knew what they needed to do, drawing the power from somewhere deep within. It sent Escobar's shockwave back at him, hitting the warlock and his companion with such force that they both went tumbling to the ground.

Marisol let out a shocked cry, her hand going to her belly as she painfully pushed herself back upright. Oh, hell—in the heat of the moment, I'd completely forgotten that she was pregnant. With Escobar's child, true, which meant I might be doing her a favor by having her miscarry.

No. I couldn't let myself think that way, no

matter how much I might hate Joaquin Escobar. If we all survived this, and she decided to end the pregnancy, that was her decision, but I sure as hell wasn't going to make it for her.

Eyes locked on her, I called out, "Marisol, this isn't your fight. I know you can't understand that right now, not with this man controlling your mind. Fight it. Don't let him use your power."

She blinked at me, a flash of comprehension, of horror, showing in her dark eyes before the familiar blankness closed down again.

"Nice try," Escobar said with a curl of his lip. "But she is mine. She doesn't have the strength to break free. Just as you don't have the strength to defeat me."

Without warning, the marble step beneath our feet began to crumble. I stumbled and could feel myself starting to fall—but then Connor's strong fingers tightened on mine, holding me up.

Isabel, however, was not so lucky. Her hand slipped from my grasp, and she tumbled onto the lawn. But, just as quickly as she'd fallen, she was back on her feet, brushing at the knees of her dark slacks. Her expression was more one of irritation than alarm, and she planted her hands on her hips and stared back at Joaquin Escobar, lip curled in derision.

"Is that the best you can do?"

"Hardly," he said. The ozone smell intensified,

and lightning crackled around him, taking shape as it coalesced into a blue-white ball almost too bright to look at. He flung the ball at the Castillo *prima,* who held up her hands just in time to block it.

Or rather, she kept it from colliding with her head, but it still crashed into her, blackening her hands and forearms. She let out a cry of pain, even as Connor and I hurried toward her, wrapping our arms around her waist because we feared we would only hurt her further if we took her by her hands.

"Can you manage?" I asked in an undertone, noting how drawn with pain her face now was, how white her usually olive complexion had turned.

"Yes," she said, voice tight. "But you must know, Angela, that my daughter Genoveva knows of our bargain. If anything happens to me, she will still hold you to it."

"Don't—" I began. I'd meant to say, *Don't talk that way,* but I wasn't given the chance, because Escobar had flung another ball of lightning at us.

This time, Connor and I reacted together, immediately conjuring a supercharged version of the same barrier we'd used earlier, Isabel's power blending with ours. The ball lightning crashed into it and scattered white-hot energy sideways, but it didn't touch us. Still, I could tell how much power had been contained in that attack, how even the three of us working together might not be able to shield ourselves indefinitely.

Isabel staggered, clearly having felt the drain on her resources far more than we did. Over her drooping head, Connor and I exchanged a frightened glance. How many more of those assaults could we withstand?

As many as we need to, I told myself fiercely. *This ends here.*

And we gathered up our own energy, only this time in a bolt we could send directly against Escobar. Even though we hadn't consciously made such an agreement, my husband and I both knew that we needed to avoid attacking Marisol if at all possible. She was an innocent, and certainly didn't deserve to share her captor's fate.

The lightning bolt flew across the backyard and connected. Or rather, it seemed to hit the dark warlock, only instead of knocking him down, it flowed around him, encasing him in a coffin of shimmering light before disappearing altogether.

His lip lifted in a sneer. "Is that the best you can do?"

Another shockwave hit us, coming so fast that our defenses hadn't yet recovered from the last barrage. I staggered and bit my lip so hard I could taste blood, metallic on my tongue. My arm tightened on Isabel's waist; on her other side, Connor held her up as well. She made no sound except a sharp, hissing intake of breath, but I somehow knew that the impact had taken its toll on her, that it had only served to worsen the injuries she'd already sustained.

Then, improbably, she smiled. Her voice echoed in my head.

Take my power. Take all of it, and use it against him.

I can't—

You will, and you must. You are the prima *of the McAllisters. Your bond is with the* primus *of the Wilcoxes. Only the two of you can take my gift and make it into the weapon you need in this moment.*

Tears leaked from my eyes, dripping down my cheeks. I'd thought Isabel cold and haughty, and yet I wasn't sure I would have been able to make the same sacrifice.

My life has been a good one, Angela. There is no sorrow in this. We do what we must to protect the ones we love. Only...do not forget your promise to me. Swear that you will send the child to my clan.

I swear, I told her. *I will. No matter what.*

Then take it.

An enormous flare of yellow light, like the sun coming up over the horizon. And yet I was able to stare into that blazing light, let its heat and its power and its warmth move through me, join with my own *prima* power, twine with Connor's *primus* energy, creating something so far beyond any of us, it was almost like looking into the face of the Goddess...or of God.

In that moment, names didn't matter.

The only thing that mattered was striking down the man who was the very antithesis of that light, a black hole of negative energy, the null who had caused all of this. Connor and I held up Isabel's limp form and channeled that power, sent forth a blaze of energy that crossed the distance between us in less time than the space of one heartbeat.

The glowing ball of light hit Joaquin Escobar and flared out even more brightly, consuming him the way a gasoline-fueled fire might consume summer-dry wood, jumping from limb to limb in less time than it took me to pull in a breath. He writhed where he stood, body shuddering as the fire took the dark life from him. One high-pitched cry that felt as though it would be seared into my eardrums forever, and then he was gone, nothing left except a pile of black dust. The wind picked up that dust, swirling it around and around like a miniature tornado. And in the blink of an eye, the dust was gone, nothing left, no hint of the man who had stood there a moment before, or of all the terrible things he had done.

Only Marisol lying on the grass, great heaving sobs shaking her slender form. Connor and I gently laid Isabel's body on the ground, then hurried to the Santiago *prima* and knelt beside her.

"Marisol?" I asked.

"Where—" She blinked at her surroundings as if she'd never seen them before. Slowly, some of the haze left her dark eyes, although she still seemed more confused than anything. "Is this my Aunt Beatriz's house?"

"Yes," I said gently, then glanced away from her to meet Connor's worried gaze. "Do you remember anything at all?"

"No," she replied, reaching up to wipe away the tears that stained her cheeks. "I don't even know why I'm crying. I just know that I feel horribly sad for some reason."

My heart ached for her—for her, and for Isabel, and Boyd, and Luz, for everyone we'd lost. Soon we'd have to tell her what had happened, that her aunt and uncle and husband were gone, that she was now the *prima* of her clan, even as she carried the child of the man who had tried to usurp its power.

There would be a time for all that. Now, though, I only wanted to go inside and find my children. Take them by the hands, take them home, far away from this terrible place.

"Let's go and sit down," I told Marisol. "And then…we'll do our best to explain what's happened."

Lucinda Santiago

SHE SET THE PHONE DOWN ON THE COFFEE table, all too aware of the way Brandon sat a foot away from her on the sofa, pretending to scroll through the offerings on Netflix but really doing his best not to watch her. When the call had come through, he'd asked whether he should go into his bedroom so she could have some privacy. She'd demurred, mostly because she'd halfway known what the call would be about as soon as she saw the number on the caller I.D., and she'd wanted him to stay with her, hadn't wanted to deal with this by herself.

Voice flat, she said, "Marisol wants me to come back to Pasadena. She sounded…almost like herself again, but tired."

Still not really looking in her direction, Brandon replied, "Well, I can understand why she'd be tired—and why she would want you to go back to California. She's been through hell. It makes sense that she'd want you by her."

He sounded reasonable…too reasonable. And Lucinda knew that what he was saying made sense, because she'd entertained thoughts along those same lines. Marisol had lost her husband, was now *prima* of the Santiagos years or even decades sooner than she'd thought she would be. Lucinda's parents were dead, and since Marisol was her maternal aunt's oldest daughter, they were some of the closest relatives either of them had left. Why on earth would she stay here in Jerome instead of returning to her home, to a place where she could help rebuild the clan Joaquin Escobar had tried to tear apart?

Why, indeed.

Lucinda watched Brandon out of the corner of her eye. His expression was studiously neutral, so she couldn't begin to guess what might be going through his head. And what had she been expecting, really? For him to go down on one knee and declare his undying love for her, tell her that she had to stay here with him? That was just crazy. She wouldn't deny that she had feelings for him—and she hoped those feelings were reciprocated—but they really didn't have all that much to go on. Some stolen kisses, a few precious evenings where she'd come here to his apartment and snuggled with him as they watched TV? The relationship hadn't gone any further than that because she wasn't sure if she was ready. Not after what Matías had done to her. Besides, everything had been so crazy, she'd known it wasn't the right time to try to take their relationship to the next level. Why plan for a future when you didn't know for sure if you would even have one?

When she didn't immediately reply, Brandon shifted on the sofa so he was facing toward her. "Do you want to go?"

"I—" Suddenly Lucinda's throat was dry. She reached for the glass of water she'd left sitting on the coffee table and took a long drink. In her mind, she saw the cool shadows along Oak Creek, heard the soft chatter of water over stones. That day she'd spent with Brandon, she'd thought she could be happy here, hadn't wanted anything to do with the life she'd left behind in Southern California. Now, though, with the heaviness of family responsibility weighing on her, she didn't know what she wanted. "I'm not sure. I mean, I know everyone is expecting me to. It would be the right thing to do."

"More than staying here with me?"

There. He'd said it. And thank God for that, because it meant she wouldn't have to wrestle with herself over whether she should force herself to bring up the subject. Voice small, she said, "I suppose that depends on you. Whether—whether you'd want me to stay."

At once he set down the remote and moved closer to her, pulled her toward him so he could wrap his arms around her. "Of course I want you to stay. But I also understand why your family needs you in California. So…why don't I come with you to Pasadena?"

She stared at him, into his earnest storm-blue eyes. He meant it. He really did. She could tell, because otherwise he wouldn't be able to meet her gaze so directly.

Somehow she found her voice. "You mean that?"

"Of course I do, or I wouldn't have said it."

"But—" She faltered and gave a quick glance around the room, at the large window and the spectacular view of the Verde Valley beyond it. "You'd really leave Jerome? What about your sister?"

He gave her a wry smile. "She has Levi. I think she'll be able to survive my absence. And we'd only be one state over. The lines are getting blurred between the clans—I don't think territories mean as much as they used to. There wouldn't be a problem with coming back and visiting here when we wanted to, would there?"

"No." Her eyes blurred with tears—happy tears—and she blinked. "No, there wouldn't be a problem. How could there be, since Marisol would still be Joaquin Escobar's slave if it weren't for your *prima* and her consort?"

"Well, you never know." His arms tightened around her, and she pulled in a breath, glad to feel the strength in his embrace, the reassuring solid warmth of him.

"And your job?" she asked, now fairly convinced he really meant what he'd said but still wanting to make sure. "That job is your life."

He shook his head at once. "No, it's a job. A job I really enjoy, but it's not my life. I want to make my life with you. Besides," he added, a grin lifting his lips, "Southern California is the center of car culture. That's where it all started. With my credit on *Dream Machines*, I know I can get a job in one of the top custom shops there, no problem."

Happiness washed through her at his words, but she couldn't help teasing him a bit. "Oh, now I get it. You just want to come with me so you'll have a chance at the big time."

Expression deadpan, he said, "Yes, that's exactly it."

Before she could reply, he bent and kissed her, kissed her so thoroughly that all her doubts and worries seemed utterly foolish. Oh, she loved him, loved the way he tasted, loved the way he could be passionate without trying to dominate her, how he seemed to admire her, respect her opinions. She'd never experienced that kind of consideration before, not with her father, and certainly not with Matías Escobar.

After the kiss ended, she said, "We won't be living in my parents' house—that goes to Marisol as the *prima*. But she said we could take her house instead, if we wanted to."

"What, I'm going to be denied the mansion with all the Picassos?"

Obviously, someone had been talking. Even though she knew he was joking, she answered him seriously enough. "No Picassos. But you know, I always liked Marisol's house better. It's friendlier. It's a Craftsman-style bungalow in a historic neighborhood called Orange Heights. I think you'll like the house—it even has a bit of a Jerome vibe to it."

The teasing grin he wore sobered, and he took his hands in hers. "If you're there with me, I know I'll love it…just like I love you."

Oh, God, he'd said it. Maybe he hadn't gone down on one knee, but he'd still told her he loved her. Which meant she had to utter those words as well, the ones she'd been holding close to her heart because she hadn't known whether it was the right time to say them.

Well, it was definitely the right time now.

"I love you, too, Brandon McAllister."

He took her in his arms again, and she kissed him, kissed him to let him know how much she cared, how much she wanted him in her life.

They'd go back to California, and they'd try to make things better.

Angela

THE CORNER OF THE COTTONWOOD cemetery where the McAllisters were always laid to rest had a new headstone, although there were so many floral arrangements surrounding it, you could barely see the simple marble monument, engraved only with the dates of Boyd's birth and death, and "Beloved Father and Husband" inscribed beneath those. No doubt if Boyd had been there, he would have shaken his head at what he would have considered the waste those expensive floral arrangements represented. For the rest of the clan, though, it was the least we could do to pay our respects.

Boyd's wife Meredith was pale-faced but calm. She'd made her peace with his death before we ever set foot in the cemetery, and his two sons were likewise stoic, their faces almost expressionless. It was only when you looked closely that you could see the strain in their eyes, the taut set to their jaws. This composure might be costing them, but I wasn't going to take them to task for that. They had too much of their father in them to break down and weep in front of others, even family.

I noted how Lucinda Santiago and Hayley's brother Brandon stood off to one side, their hands clasped together. Just the day before, they'd told me of their plans to go to California, to help Marisol get their clan back on its feet and start the road to recovery, now that Joaquin Escobar and his controlling influence were gone. While I was a little saddened that they wouldn't be staying in Jerome, I knew it was the right thing for them to do. And I was even happier that they'd somehow managed to find one another in the midst of all this chaos, to send another signal to the universe that love would always find a way.

The simple graveside service over, we all headed back to our respective vehicles so we could return to Jerome and attend the reception for Boyd in Spook Hall. Again, he probably would have shaken his head over such a gathering, and all the food and drink we "wasted" there, but we all needed closure, needed a way to thank him for the long years he'd spent as one of the clan's elders, making sure we were kept safe from harm.

Connor helped me up the steps into the hall, his hand sure on my elbow. Maybe it had been foolish for me to put on my only pair of heels for the funeral and the reception, but again, I wanted to show Boyd the proper respect. Anyway, it wouldn't be too long before my feet and my waist-line started to swell for real. I might as well try to look like a lady while I still could.

Everyone was here. I guessed the hall must be over capacity, although I thought any members of the volunteer fire department in attendance would look the other way at such a minor transgression. Allegra looking red-eyed—she'd been an elder nearly as long as Boyd and had spent most of her life working with him—Tricia weary but serene. I could tell she was relieved that Caitlin and Alex had driven up from Tucson for the reception, and I was, too, if for no other reason than I wanted to see as many of my clan members as possible, wanted to reassure myself that we were all safe now, that we no longer had anything to fear.

And there were Margot and Lucas, Margot's eyes shadowed with grief, even as she smiled to see Mia run over to Ian and Emily, whereupon Ian snagged a cookie off one of the trays on the banquet tables and magnanimously handed it over to her. As far as I could tell, none of the children seemed to have experienced any negative effects from their brief time as Joaquin Escobar's hostages. Ellen, the Wilcox healer, had looked them all over and pronounced them to be whole and healthy, and so about all I could do was hope the incident would soon be nothing more than a distant memory.

Margot came up to us then, Lucas a pace or two behind her. She surprised me by giving me a fierce hug before stepping back and looking her usual composed self again. "I really do think they're going to be okay."

"More than okay, if the stack of pancakes Mia ate this morning is any indication," Lucas added with a smile.

I couldn't help but smile back at him. Lucas had that effect on people. I wasn't even angry that he hadn't been there to protect the children. Marie had explained to me that she thought his absence had only been another manifestation of his peculiar gift for luck, which of course looked after him rather than anyone else. "His gift kept him away," she'd told me over the phone. "It was the only way to ensure that he would be safe. That's how it generally works with Lucas—he doesn't consciously decide to do these things. But his talent makes sure he always experiences the best possible outcome."

Would that unique talent have continued to

function in Escobar's presence? I doubted it, which meant that was probably another reason it kept him away.

"Sounds like someone's headed for a sugar crash," Connor remarked with a grin.

Considering that Mia had just stuffed another chocolate chip cookie into her mouth, I thought he might be right. But since I wasn't the one who'd be wrestling with her to go to sleep that night, I decided I wouldn't worry about it.

Margot, who usually was a very observant parent, didn't seem to notice at all. Her gaze was fixed on Levi, who stood on the other side of the hall with Hayley next to him. They were chatting with Brandon and Lucinda; all seemed amicable enough, but I got the impression that Hayley wasn't too happy about her brother's move to California. I couldn't blame her, and yet I also knew it was the best thing he could do.

"I've been thinking about Levi," Margot said.

"Oh?" I asked.

"I think he would make a wonderful elder."

Startled, I looked at her more closely, but I could tell she was completely serious. "But...he's not a true McAllister."

Her shoulders lifted. In her simple black dress, with her dark hair pulled into a low knot at the back of her neck, she gave off more than ever the impression of a retired ballerina. "In terms of blood, maybe not. But he's done more to safe-guard this clan than most people who were born right down the hill at Verde Valley Medical Center. He's going to be a McAllister by marriage in the very near future, unless my eyes deceive me. Can you think of a better alternate?"

She had me there. In the four days since Boyd had died and Joaquin Escobar had been defeated, we'd had a lot going on. Even so, Connor and I had found time to discuss the issue of choosing someone to replace Boyd. An elder didn't have to be elderly; he or she just had to be a very powerful warlock or witch. In this case, we needed a warlock, because the McAllisters always had two witches and one warlock function as their elders, but the pickings had been fairly slim. We discussed Henry, my Great-Aunt Ruby's older son, but he was getting up in years, and we would have preferred someone younger. There was Marcus, Jenny and Roslyn's father, but we weren't sure he was a strong enough worker of magic.

Why neither one of us had thought of Levi, I didn't know.

I glanced back at Connor, who stood behind my right shoulder, nursing a glass of punch. "What do you think?" I asked.

"I think it's a great idea," he replied. "Margot's right. Levi's commitment to this clan matters a lot more than his origins. And I know he'd be honored to be asked."

"Okay," I said. Frankly, I wanted the matter settled more than anything else, and I knew I could trust Levi implicitly. Where he had come from wasn't important. What mattered was that he happened to be both very powerful and very honorable, a combination you didn't see often enough. "We'll talk to him tomorrow, after"—I flapped a hand at the assembled McAllisters —"well, after all this is over."

Margot smiled. "You're making the right decision, Angela." She turned to Lucas, saying, "We'd better collect Mia. It looks as though Ian is encouraging her to eat every cookie on that plate."

A wave of guilt went over me, because I probably hadn't been paying as much attention to what the twins were doing as I should have. However, even as I glanced in their direction, I saw Rachel approach Ian and bend down to speak to him, even as she deftly snatched the cookie out of his hand and set it down on a napkin.

As they say, it takes a village. Or in our case, a haunted mountain town full of witches and warlocks.

～

The reception lingered into the early evening, but

at last it was over, all of us scattering to our various homes and apartments and cottages. Ian and Emily were sleepy and wobbly, full of sandwiches and cookies and too much punch. Connor carried Emily up the hill, her dark head pillowed on his shoulder, while I held Ian by the hand and helped him along as best I could. Despite protestations of wanting to stay up just a little longer —"it's not even eight o'clock, Mommy!" — they both conked out almost the moment their heads hit their pillows.

Right then, I could relate. There might have been a few other times in my life when I'd felt this tired, but I couldn't remember when they were. It was hard to believe that only several days earlier, we'd been transporting ourselves from place to place in the blink of an eye, had stripped the powers from a dozen witches and warlocks, had somehow managed to defeat the greatest threat the witch world had yet seen. Connor and I hadn't spoken much of the energy we'd wielded, of the way we seemed to become much more than just a *prima* and a *primus*. I thought that both of us wanted to put it aside, to go back to what we once had been. In ancient times, men had hung up their swords when they returned from war, wearied by all they had seen and done, and that was what I wanted to do now. Put those swords away, and hope we would never have need of them again.

Connor took me by the hand and led me out to the front porch, where the wooden glider we'd set there the year before beckoned. He placed a glass of water with lemon in my hand, and guided me to sit down on the gently rocking bench.

"I thought you could do with a little decompression time," he said. "And also, I wanted you to see that."

He pointed eastward, where a full moon was just beginning to come up over the Mogollon Plateau. A few thin, high clouds ringed the huge yellow disc, giving it the appearance of a crown.

"It's beautiful," I said.

He'd remained standing, and stood there and smiled down at me. "So are you."

"With butter smeared in my hair from that roll Emily didn't finish, and my lip gloss long gone."

"Especially because of that." Still smiling, he sat down next to me. We rocked in silence for a moment, and then he said, "It's going to be okay, Angela."

"Is it?"

Of course I was relieved that Joaquin Escobar was dead, that the Santiago clan seemed to be knitting itself together—and that the Ludlows had slunk off in disgrace once they realized the alliance they'd hoped for was now shattered forever. It also hadn't hurt for them to understand that we now had an agreement with the Castillos.

The Castillos. Connor and I had brought Isabel's body back to Santa Fe at the same time we returned Rosella and Alberto to their home, only a few hours after our confrontation with Joaquin Escobar. How she had known we would be coming, I didn't know, but Isabel's daughter Genoveva had been waiting there in the huge hacienda for us.

Or maybe I did understand how she knew she must be there. Genoveva had to have felt the *prima* energy flow into her, once Connor and I were done using it. She'd known we were working with her mother, had known of the pact we'd made with her.

She'd watched, lovely features still and drawn, as Connor laid Isabel down on the living room sofa. Then she'd turned to us and said, "I haven't forgotten. You will send the girl to us on her twenty-first birthday."

"I'm very sorry—" I began, but she held up her hand, an imperious echo of her mother's same gesture.

"'Sorry' will not change what has happened. Only remember the promise you made to my mother, and send the girl when the time comes."

I'd opened my mouth to speak again, but

Connor seemed to know it was better not to attempt to continue the conversation. He'd nodded, and taken me by the hand and whisked me away home before I could say anything else.

Now, though—all I could think of was the child I carried, and the way I'd signed away her future in exchange for the Castillos' help. I knew that Connor and I most likely couldn't have prevailed against Joaquin Escobar without Isabel's energy to strengthen us, and yet....

"It will be all right," Connor said. He laid his hand on mine, his presence warm and comforting in the mild late spring night. "We'll explain to her everything that happened. She'll understand. And maybe...just maybe she'll look on this future of hers as an adventure."

An adventure. I watched the rising moon, saw how it shifted from gold to white as it climbed ever higher in the sky. One day my daughter would watch that same moon rise, and see it through her own eyes. She would have to make her own way in the world, make peace with the destiny that waited for her, just as I had.

And for now...for now I was with the man I loved more than anything else in the world, and the people of my clan were safe.

I couldn't ask for anything more than that.

The End

~

Darktide concludes the Witches of Cleopatra Hill series. A spin-off series, the Witches of Canyon Road, will launch in March 2018. Turn the page for a sneak peek at the first book in the series, *Hidden Gifts!*

SNEAK PEEK: HIDDEN GIFTS,
PROLOGUE

Santa Fe, New Mexico, twenty years from now....

GENOVEVA CASTILLO SET HER PHONE DOWN on the bulky carved desk that dominated the study, a small smile touching her mouth, like a cat that had just swallowed a particularly tasty canary. "She is on her way."

In that moment, watching the quiet triumph on Genoveva's face, Rafael Castillo thought he'd never hated his mother as much as he did right then. However, he knew better than to betray anything of what he felt; Genoveva was the *prima,* or head witch of their clan, and her magical gifts only enhanced an already powerful gift of observation. The two of them had shared an uneasy détente for more than fifteen years now, ever since he was old enough to truly begun to understand what the horrible bargain she had made truly entailed for him. No chance to choose the woman of his heart, no opportunity to make his life his own, and all because his grandmother had made a deal with the *prima* of the McAllister clan in Arizona to provide some desperately needed magical help when they needed it most. Rafe couldn't even blame Angela McAllister all that much; she'd been stuck between a rock and a hard place, fighting a dark warlock whose powers had seemed invincible. This terrible arrangement hadn't even been her idea, but had sprung from some fancy of his grandmother's.

Voice as level as he could make it, he said, "I can't believe you're actually going through with this."

Genoveva's smile faded. She turned away from him and went to the window of her study, twitching the heavy tapestry drapes aside so she could gaze out at the grounds of the property. This late in October, most of the leaves had fallen from the sycamores, but the cottonwoods were gamely hanging on, bright gold against the sullen sky. "Why shouldn't you believe it? We've been planning this for the past twenty-one years. You've had plenty of time to get used to the reality of Miranda coming here."

That was a load of crap. Rafe knew he would never get used to the idea of an arranged marriage, of having someone he'd never met foisted on him. And Genoveva actually thought he was supposed to be happy about all this? "Keep telling yourself what you want to believe, Mother."

Her lips thinned. Back in happier times, he'd thought of her as "mom." But as the distance between them grew, he'd slipped into using the much more formal epithet. Rafe could tell that Genoveva didn't like it, because she wanted to pretend that everything was fine between them, that they were a model family and an example for the rest of the clan.

There was a joke. His older sisters Louisa and Malena had managed to make their escape already, Malena to Corrales, Louisa to Tesuque, the village just north of Santa Fe. They had lives and families of their own, and could safely distance themselves from their mother. Cat, his little sister, hadn't been so lucky, even though more than once Rafe had encouraged her to date on the down-low, to maybe try seeing civilians in her quest for the man of her dreams. But as free-spirited as his younger sister could be in some ways, she didn't have quite the strength to break away from their domineering mother. He couldn't really blame her; he knew the only reason he had as much independence as he'd been able to enjoy in his adult life was that his future had already been sewn up neatly—at least, in Genoveva's eyes.

"There is no need to sulk," she said, her voice cold. "You would think we were marrying you to a gargoyle."

Miranda McAllister was anything but a gargoyle. Rafe knew that for a fact, because he'd seen the pictures Angela McAllister, her mother, had sent Genoveva. And that wasn't the point. What difference did it make how beautiful Miranda was if he didn't get any say in the matter? As his jaw clenched and he tried to think of the best way to reply, his mother continued.

"It is not as if I had any say, either," she said. "The *prima*-in-waiting must go with the consort that God decrees for her."

"False equivalencies," he shot back. "No one arranged that bond. It just happened. And at least you knew Dad."

"Not well," she replied, although her tone wasn't quite as confident as it had been a moment earlier, as if she knew she was on shaky ground here. True, Rafe's father Eduardo had grown up in Belen, south of Albuquerque, and so hadn't spent a lot of time with the Santa Fe branch of their witch clan, but even so, he had met Genoveva a handful of times before they shared the fateful kiss that bound them together forever.

"But he wasn't a goddamn stranger."

"Language, Rafael." Genoveva turned her back on the window and faced him, arms crossed. "You have had plenty of time to reconcile yourself to this marriage. Stop acting like a child and accept your responsibility to your clan."

"Responsibility" and "clan" were two words Rafe would be happy never to hear again. "And what if I don't?"

This time true anger, rather than mere irritation, flashed in his mother's dark eyes. Her elegant, patrician features hard with displeasure, she said, "You would go against the will of your grandmother, her vision that this was the match fate had decreed for you?"

"Her words to you," Rafe shot back. "It would have been nice if she could have specifically mentioned why it was so important that I marry Miranda McAllister. Vague mentions of possible futures don't really do it for me."

"Events were moving quickly. I did not have much time to speak to her before she went with the McAllister *prima* and her Wilcox consort to confront the dark warlock in California." Genoveva drew herself up; she was not a short woman, but she still had to work to look directly into her son's eyes. "But your grandmother's sight was never wrong, Rafael. She might not have had time to tell me the particulars, but I would never question her judgment."

"Well, that's convenient," Rafe remarked. He was tired of this, tired of the whole thing. The clock on the wall told him he had only a few hours of freedom left. No, the wedding wouldn't take place the second Miranda McAllister stepped off the train, but as soon as she set foot in Santa Fe, he would be as bound to her as if he'd already put a ring on her finger. He ran a hand through his hair, then said, "Text me when she gets to the house."

"Rafael—"

He had no desire to stay and have his mother browbeat him any further. Without responding, he turned and left the study, and slammed the door behind him. A childish gesture, he knew, but the only thing he could think of to show how angry he was without actually becoming violent.

In a few hours, his life would be taken away forever.

And there wasn't a damn thing he could do about it.

Defender

Bad Blood

Deep Magic

Darktide

Books 1-3 and Books 4-6 of this series are also available in two separate omnibus editions at special boxed set prices.

THE DJINN WARS*

(Paranormal Romance)

Chosen

Taken

Fallen

Broken

Forsaken

Forbidden

Awoken

Illuminated

The first three books of this series are also available in an omnibus edition at a special low price!

THE WATCHERS TRILOGY*

(Paranormal Romance)

Falling Dark

Dead of Night

Rising Dawn

THE SEDONA FILES*

(Paranormal Romance)

Bad Vibrations

Desert Hearts

Angel Fire

Star Crossed

Falling Angels

Enemy Mine

The first three books of this series are also available in
an omnibus edition at a special low price!

TALES OF THE LATTER KINGDOMS*

(Fantasy Romance)

All Fall Down

Dragon Rose

Binding Spell

Ashes of Roses

One Thousand Nights

Threads of Gold

The Wolf of Harrow Hall

Moon Dance

The Song of the Thrush

Books 1-3 and Books 4-6 of this series are also available in two separate omnibus editions at special boxed set prices.

THE GAIAN CONSORTIUM SERIES*

(Science Fiction Romance)

Blood Will Tell

Breath of Life

The Gaia Gambit

The Mandala Maneuver

The Titan Trap

The Zhore Deception

* Indicates a completed series

ABOUT THE AUTHOR

Christine Pope has been writing stories ever since she commandeered her family's Smith-Corona typewriter back in the sixth grade. Her work includes paranormal romance, fantasy romance, and science fiction/space opera romance. She fell under the Land of Enchantment's spell while researching her Djinn Wars series and now makes her home in Santa Fe, New Mexico.

Christine Pope on the Web:

www.christinepope.com